Games

Head
Games

MARY B.
MORRISON

KENSINGTON PUBLISHING CORP.
www.kensingtonbooks.com

DAFINA BOOKS are published by

Kensington Publishing Corp.
119 West 40th Street
New York, NY 10018

ISBN-13: 978-1-4967-1085-7
ISBN-10: 1-4967-1085-1
First Kensington Hardcover Edition: September 2018
First Kensington Trade Edition: April 2019
First Kensington Mass Market Edition: January 2020

ISBN-13: 978-1-4967-1086-4 (ebook)
ISBN-10: 1-4967-1086-X (ebook)

10 9 8 7 6 5 4 3 2 1

Printed in the United States of America

To my family
Jesse Byrd Jr. and Emaan Byrd
Heidi Abbass
Wayne Morrison
Andrea Morrison
Derrick Morrison
Regina Morrison
Margie Rickerson
Debra Noel
Edward Brian Allen
LaTasha Allen
In Loving Memory, Elizabeth Morrison

One unanimous decision will change their lives . . . forever.

PROLOGUE

The Crewe

June 30

"**B**lack women are easy, homies. Especially . . . the married ones." Trymm—pronounced "trim"— the most influential of the crewe, valet-parked his black Mercedes GLS at The Cheesecake Bistro. "Where y'all at?"

Females stood in clusters outside waiting to dine at the bistro that had some of the best dishes and drinks. Some held flat, square pagers. A few guys sprinkled throughout the crowd stared back and forth at Trymm's car, then at Trymm.

"Right behind ya, my brother." Blitz drove up in his midnight-blue BMW Alpina B7, responding to the group on their conference call. "I'm telling y'all, black professional women are easier." Handing the attendant his key, Blitz joined Trymm on the grimy sidewalk.

Standing on St. Charles Avenue, they watched two streetcars travel in opposite directions on the neutral ground paved with more dirt than patches of dried grass, more brown than green. Nawlins was a city that care forgot. True for local government and tourists in search of their wildest experience, but the crewe took pride in what they called home.

"Nope, under twenty-five. They're the easiest." Dallas backed his platinum Lexus LX into a space up front, secured his gun in his side pocket, set the car alarm, and kept the keyless remote.

"Nah, D. The overweight ones. They give it up real quick." Kohl opened the door to his bronze Bentley Bentayga, retrieved his ticket from the guy wearing a red vest.

Valet parking at the bistro was for customers only. Kohl handed the guy his usual $100 tip, to keep his mouth shut.

En route to their destination, the crewe walked side by side. A group of four women smiled back and forth among the guys. One woman complimented, "Nice cars, fellas."

A simple acknowledgment from Trymm as he held his wedding ring high, wiggling his finger. "Thanks, love," and the guys continued their stroll.

"Hold up. Where're y'all headed? Y'all not coming in here?" the woman inquired.

No one replied. Q and A with a female none of them were interested in was a waste of time.

"Women, women, and more women, my brothers." Blitz rubbed his hands.

"And all of 'em passing out free pussy." Trymm led the way across St. Mary Street.

A large oval sign, with THE TROLLEY STOP CAFÉ painted in bold green letters, was plastered under the flat roof, right above the door. OPEN 24/7 was displayed in caps on a white banner that stretched column-to-column, ten feet in front of the wooden green-painted wheelchair ramp. The red neon OPEN sign in the window was always lit. The twenty-two-year-old establishment, designed like a real city car—faded maroon framed windows gave the appearance diners were eating on the trolley—could easily be mistaken for being half a century old.

A staple in the community, the restaurant commanded a hefty crowd all day during Essence Festival weekend. Too many badass females to count, the line snaked around the island centered in the parking lot, extending to the sidewalk. The all-too-familiar two-hours-plus wait wasn't for the crewe.

"Excuse us." Trymm opened the door.

The humidity welcomed the morning sunshine as four of New Orleans's finest eligible bachelors entered the standing-room-only café. At a glance, it was clear that beautiful, scantily dressed women outnumbered the men three to one.

"Glad you texted me, bro. Thanks for holding down the fort for us." Trymm patted his eldest brother, Walter, on the back as Walter and his three friends stood. Trymm, Kohl, Blitz, and Dallas settled onto four of the six barstools at the counter.

Walter placed his hand on Trymm's shoulder. "No problem. You know I got you."

A gentleman in a crimson buttoned-down shirt had three top buttons undone. A gold cross lay flat on his furry patch of gray chest hairs. His matching colored shorts were meticulously creased. Standing erect, he confronted Walter. "Man, no disrespect, but we been waiting to be seated for over an hour." He conspicuously clutched his Bible over his heart.

"None taken, but y'all gon' hafta wait a little longer. Ya heard me." Walter, a six-three, 250-pound former professional wrestler, wasn't asking.

Trymm, Kohl, Blitz, and Dallas pushed their stools toward the counter. Stood facing the man. Dallas eased his hand into his pocket, gripped the handle of his gun. The crewe knew the dirty South could get filthy without notice. Dallas was always strapped.

"Bay-bay, y'all sure looking extra fine today! Sit."
Dana, the crewe's usual waitress, wiped away the food
particles on the forest-green top, slapped menus in front
of the fellas. "I got y'all in a sec, Trymm." Mixing orange
juice and champagne into a plastic container, Dana
stacked four red acrylic tumblers on her tray, then headed
toward the main dining room.

The Trolley Stop Café had three areas—the bar was to
the left upon entry; the street car section was to the right,
up three stairs and another right; the interior was to the
right up three steps, then left. Each square table was the
same lacquer-coated cherrywood. Forty tables, 166 seats.
Not one chair was empty.

Walter redirected his attention to Trymm. "I'll swing
by and help Penny set up, but don't be chillin' all morning with these cats." Walter scanned the eyes of Trymm's
friends. "Chasing pussy will leave you eating in the dark,
gentlemen." Walter positioned his wrist in front of
Trymm's face, pushed the start button on his stopwatch.
"You've got two hours tops. See you at noon. Sharp. Not
twelve-o-one."

Trymm clenched his teeth, braced himself. Being the
youngest among ten children had benefits, and draw-
backs. No need to respond. Walter wasn't asking, nor was
he joking.

A wrestling competitor in high school and college,
Walter, at the age of forty-five, had muscles solid as boul-
ders. He bench-pressed three times his weight every
morning before sunrise. "I have to make tracks to open
my restaurant, and Penny can't manage this incoming
Essence Fest crowd by herself. Shit gon' be busier tomorrow, so don't even bring your black ass ova here." He
punched Trymm on the arm. Trymm leaned into Kohl,
then sat up straight. "And don't forget to give me your
twenty-five hundred for Mom and Dad's fiftieth anniversary party next month."

Trymm dug into his pants, peeled off twenty-five C-notes, slapped them in his brother's hand.

Walter stuffed the cash in his wallet. "Keep flashing. One of these fools gon' bust you upside the head and empty all your pockets. Your ass gon' get got too, Blitz. Let that Rolex rest. Y'all too old to say none of you have a wife. Trymm, what you holding out for? Disrespecting the family's last name and shit. Francine ain't going nowhere. Get the ring or I'ma get it for you. You're proposing at Mom and Dad's event. An hour and fifty-eight, Trymm." Walter followed his buddies out the door.

Trymm sat on the edge of his seat, planted one foot on the floor, the other on the bridge below, tightened his lips, looked at his crewe.

Blitz stared back at him. The watch was a family heirloom (from his grandfather) gifted to him by his father when he'd graduated from college. "What? You sour, nigga? At least you have a tribe of siblings. Wish big Walt was my brother for real. Being an only child is the worst. I still get blamed for shit I didn't do."

Sixteen years separated Trymm from Walter. Trymm was blessed to stand six inches taller than the brother who was like his second father. Disciplinarian was the role Walter assumed when they were kids. Mom, a housewife, and with their dad working sunrise to sunset each day of the week to make sure all of his kids had degrees and owned a business, Walter stepped up to help their mom, and he didn't hesitate to beat an ass or two when he felt it was necessary.

"Squash the monologue, Blitz. Man, I've been tripping all morning off of how weak black women are. They hawking us right now. Bet we could fuck a dozen each. That, and the fact that we're all about to hit dat big three-o this year. When we gon' slow our roll?"

People heading to and from the restrooms walked sideways, squeezing their way between the back of the barstools and the customers lined along the wall. One more row of twelve diners and no one would have enough space to move.

Unfolding the *Times-Picayune* newspaper Walter had left behind, Trymm Dupree adjusted the crotch of his gray, white, and black camouflage cargo shorts, giving his seven flaccid inches space to stretch out.

He stroked his freshly shaved head, where three-carat-diamond studs lit up both of Trymm's ears. Blackberry skin coated with coconut oil glistened on his flawlessly smooth face, thick lips, toned biceps, long athletic legs, all the way down to his pedicured feet, which rested in black leather open-toed sandals. Trymm scanned the front page of the metro section, slid the remainder one counter space over to Kohl.

"We should do some unforgettable shit!" Kohl peeled off the sport pages. "Let's take a thirty-day trip, dip to the DR, Jamaica, Puerto Rico, St. Martin, the Bahamas. Wherever it's hot, the chicks are freaks, and they won't hesitate to suck all of our dicks for the price"—nodding upward, he gave the crewe a tight smile that barely showed his teeth—"of a po'boy."

Blitz slapped Kohl on the nape of his neck. "The dime a dozen are in Brazil, nigga."

"Well, Rio de Janeiro, Ipanema, then," Kohl snapped back. "You ain't Walter. I'll take you down. You know what I meant."

Standing at six-two, tipping the scale at 270 pounds, Kohl was an only child. Unlike the rest of his crewe, Kohl's midsection was flabby and wide. From his hairline to his ankles, a stray bullet wouldn't hit him in the ass. Kohl's toasted-almond skin had red undertones from his Indian heritage. His jet-black hair was braided into a foot-long ponytail. Letting it down drew too much attention. Adopted son of a preacher man and a stay-at-home mom, Kohl wasn't permitted to pierce or tattoo any parts of his temple. His gold polo, with a fleur-de-lis logo, black slacks, and lace-up, hard-sole shoes were the most casual he'd dress.

"Fuck all that flight hopping, so it won't get back to Rev. and the First Lady. When I was stationed in Afghanistan, Dubai was my one-stop shop for all the pussy I wanted." Dallas smiled, lifted his left brow. "I had women from all the places you mentioned"—he pointed at Kohl, then touched each finger as he continued—"and add Africa, Asia, Australia, Russia. They were all within a few blocks' radius, and that's not half the list. And, hear me out, paying for pussy over there is legit."

Dallas didn't have an incentive to return to the United States while he was enlisted in the military, so he vacationed abroad. With two half-brothers by his father, Hawk, they might as well all have been dead, Dallas's combat buddies became his overseas family. The crewe was as close as he'd come to having brothers stateside. During deployment he'd gone eighteen months without seeing a woman he didn't have to kill.

Their section was packed. Squeezing had turned into pushing and shoving. A few verbal confrontations erupted. The newest owner, son of the original founder, yelled, "I need everyone to clear this aisle. *Now.* If you do not have a space to stand against the wall, if you're not going to the restroom, wait outside." Maroon dude with the cross secured his position in front of the window. None of the crewe inched their seats closer to the counter.

Kohl, as usual, had to prove he knew a lil more about the subject at hand. "And they let you have babes waiting in your bed when you check into your hotel room."

"Touché." Dallas didn't want to get into a pissing match with Kohl over the trivial when Dallas had more firsthand experiences than he could count. "It's hypocritical. Kinda like how your folks know you own that strip club and hookah lounge, but they take your tithes under the table."

The smallest of the crewe, five-ten, 180 pounds, 80 percent of Dallas's left side of his body, from his chin down, was covered in tattoos. There was nothing to fight for after his mother drowned in their house during Katrina. The military trained him to kill the enemy. Problem now was determining who the real enemy was. Being raised in a Baptist church didn't save his soul. Dallas harbored animosity for God. Posttraumatic stress disorder was God's fault.

Blitz joined in. "All pussy taste different, but when I'm ready to bust a nut, smashing is the same. I don't care where's she's from, long as she ain't dumb. I'm gon' get mine, if that bitch doesn't get hers, that's on her." He snagged the front part of the paper leaving the classifieds for Dallas.

"Y'all see all the fine sistahs jam-packed up in here?" Kohl pointed out. "I'm not driving to the West Bank for a 'bj,' and that's five minutes away, ya heard me."

The ratio was now five females—high heels, hair flawless, makeup impeccable—to every guy as departing guests changed seats with new customers. Laughter and chatter drowned out the background music as men made new acquaintances with jovial women.

Trymm smirked at Kohl. "Second that, homey, but you keep leaving out your baby mama. The mere fact that she hasn't gotten a penny of child support outta your ass in ten—"

Kohl sang aloud, " 'If she only had a brain—' "

"Or took it to the head," Dallas tagged on.

Blitz remained silent. Stole away to his private fantasy of Kohl's alleged baby's mama. Ramona was a sexy motherfucker.

"My married sides crawl to me on their belly like reptiles." Trymm had an hour and a half remaining. He glanced across the room.

Dana rushed from a table of four guys to a group of twelve women, scribbled orders, then disappeared into the kitchen. Dana was light-skinned; short, tapered blond hair framed her full face. Her wide hips and round ass shifted side-to-side as she reappeared, balancing four plates on a tray.

Kohl frowned. "Nigga, they have to. What they supposed to tell their husband? 'Move over. Big-dick Willy coming through.'"

Blitz and Dallas laughed, nodding in agreement.

The boy, a fifth grader, was possibly Kohl's son. At nineteen, Kohl wasn't ready to become a father. Ten years later, nothing had changed.

Trymm twisted his lips to the side. "Don't hate, homies."

"Whateva. It's the Fourth of July weekend, which means it's a Black Mizz America pageant for the next three. . . ." Blitz paused, eyeing an Amazon chocolate woman heading toward them. "Contestant number one, come through."

Silence among the crewe ensued. Chatter from guests lined along the wall behind them, determined to grab the next available seats at the bar, conspicuously lowered.

The crewe's stares beamed like infrared lasers at the white halter dress that clung to the woman's voluptuous breasts, highlighting her perky nipples. As she passed, the guys' heads turned in unison, fixating on her curvaceous hips that seductively swayed like a gentle breeze kissing everything in its path. Her naked back blessed them with a gold lace thong peeping from underneath the white scoop that stopped right above her bodacious booty.

Trymm rotated his platinum band, showcasing the diamonds, wet his lips as he admired the wedding set the woman wore; then he gently grasped her hand. "Excuse me, goddess, you mind blessing me with your name?"

The crewe sat on the edge of their seats as the woman's gaze lowered toward Trymm's lap.

As she bat her lashes, her cheeks rose higher, and higher. "Kandy. Capital *k,* small *y.*"

Slowly releasing her soft, slender fingers, Trymm returned the smile. "Stay beautiful, Mrs. Kandy."

Trailing the split wedged between her cheeks, Dallas's dick began to swell.

The conversation was mute until Blitz cleared his throat. "She came here for this." He slid his hand down his abs to his partial erection.

An even six feet, weighing 210 pounds, Blitz had a shadow-thin mustache and a neat, upside-down, triangular patch of hair, which was centered directly beneath the dimple in his naturally red bottom lip. The facial hair made him appear distinguished. His crystal-gray eyes pierced in an arrogant, confident way. When he was unsure of himself, he was the only one that knew it.

"You're disillusioned, homey." Trymm pulled up his left sleeve, flexed, then rubbed the horseshoe brand on his bicep. "You'd betta crunch that wallet if you want to eat," he sang, "Kan-dy."

Blitz lamented, "Every man isn't cheap like you and Kohl, my brother."

Trymm directed his response to the crewe. "I can charm a woman out of her pussy before she takes off her panties. They buy me shit. I bet all of y'all, one, Kandy with a *y* isn't her real name, and two, she wants to feel my Clydesdale slide on her clit and pound the bottom of that pussy till she's raw."

Dallas and Kohl nodded.

Blitz flicked his tongue. "Women don't require all that banging. Brothers like you"—he pointed at Kohl, then Trymm—"don't do shit for women. Dropping a few hundred or a designer bag on a chance to do the unforgettable, to come inside of that, man, that's chump change."

Blitz's cell rang. He declined the familiar bill collector's call.

More diners exited into the parking lot, which was as filled with new faces. The guy in maroon stared at the crewe with discontent. Dallas noticed him. Long as dude didn't make a move in the crewe's direction, he'd live to see another day. Dallas placed his palms on the countertop, stared up at the purple, green, and gold Mardi Gras beads hanging high upon the wall among bottles filled with whiskey, tequila, rum, and vodka, then resumed reading the paper.

"Correction, homey. You mean the unimaginable. That's one-of-a-kind pussy right there. She's got her own money. She's not thirsty." Trymm smirked at Blitz. "You ain't gon' get with that for a few hundred dollars." Trymm held up his pinky. "I'm just sayin'."

Kohl held up the menu to Blitz, then pointed. "You speak out of sheer ignorance, my bruh. Why buy the cow when I can milk her with grits, eggs, bacon, toast, coffee, and orange juice, and have change left ova from a twenty to treat her girlfriend, and tip. Do the math. Oh, that's right, I forgot. That's your accountant's job."

"You've never worked a day in your life, Blitz." Dallas looked up from the newspaper, snatched the menu from Kohl.

"I object!" Blitz slapped the menu out of Dallas's hand. It slid behind the counter. "I've never worked a day in my life for anybody *else*. Must I remind you Negroes, my degree is in psychology? My mother is an oceanographer, and my father is a politician. I live off of my investments."

Dallas exhaled. "With the exception of Trymm and his tribe of nine, none of us have siblings. The two my sperm donor had after leaving my mom, y'all know how I feel about them. Blitz, your problem is you don't respect money. Run into the wrong bitch, you gon' end up broke."

Stroking his chin, Blitz nodded upward. "And what the fuck you call Dupree Seafood? Trymm riding on his daddy's legacy."

"What the fuck?" Trymm's brows drew closer. He knew his parents wanted to live to see all of their children have kids, and he was the only one single with no kid. But Trymm wasn't ready for a wife or a baby. "Don't forget I played professional basket—"

Kohl interjected, "D, why you always starting nonsense? Your mama left you straight with that fat-ass insurance policy. Worse than disrespecting Blitz's cash flow, why you won't collect your retirement and disability checks from Uncle Sam? You earned that."

Dallas didn't respond. He rubbed his face really hard, rubbed his head, then stared at Kohl.

Blitz commented to the crewe as Mrs. Kandy retraced her steps behind their barstools. "I don't mind breaking off females—" He winked at Kandy.

She smiled at Trymm, winked at Trymm's dick as she kept walking, never acknowledging Blitz.

The crewe had no words as they each lusted, not for a chance to court the woman in white, but for an opportunity to feel what she felt like, outside and in.

"Y'all good?" Dana asked. "Trymm, I saw that. Don't start no shit up in here today with these married women. Take yo' ass 'cross the street where y'all park, or one betta, to Dupree's. I heard Walter. You got about an hour twenty to get your ass outta here."

Trymm caressed Dana's hand. "Line up our usual. I'm hungry."

"Don't talk yourself outta this tip, Dana." Blitz waved a $100 bill.

"Chump change, right, homey?" Trymm snatched the money, gave it to Dana.

Blitz watched as in one continuous motion Dana stuffed the cash in her bra.

"Thanks, Trymm. I got y'all in a sec." Dana mixed more mimosas.

"Yes!" resounded from the game room behind the double swinging doors. Inside the small game room, which was a few feet away from the bar, were two slot machines. A man parted the doors, dancing his way to the counter. "Pay me, baby!"

Wasn't as though there was a $1 million bonus. But if he'd won $1,000, that could potentially cover all of his bills for a month.

Trymm eyed his crewe. "I just came up with an outrageous challenge for y'all."

Blitz directed his attention to Dana. "I got a feeling whateva dat nigga fixina say is worth a setup. Make it a Hen."

Dana reached underneath the counter, retrieved an unopened bottle, plopped four empty red acrylic cups by Trymm, four more filled with ice, and the Hennessy. He poured equal portions until the bottle was empty, then dropped one cube in each cup, enough to chill, but not to dilute the alcohol content.

Dallas stared at Dana and wondered why she always gave Trymm preferential treatment. Wasn't like Trymm requested the setup.

"Give me your ticket, baby." Dana took the piece of paper from the overjoyed guy. "Wait for me by the kitchen."

Kohl tapped his waterproof GPS watch. "Dude, we can't get faded this early. You gotta clock in, and I have to open up my spot."

Dallas asked Kohl, "You been up since what? Six?"

Kohl shook his head. "Five-thirty."

"Give yourself the rest of the morning off, nigga. Drink. Your hookah-lounge-slash-strip-club ain't going nowhere. *Fuck.* It's not as though you served in the military. I did." Dallas took a huge gulp.

Kohl stood, stepped behind Blitz's stool, and saluted Dallas. "You still having them triggers? Flashing on women and stuff? Your problem is you've got too much time on your hands. When the last time you choked a chick?" Kohl flinched at Dallas, then quickly sat in his seat on the opposite side of Blitz.

"Aw, hell no." Being the fairest of them all, Blitz was not accidentally taking one on the chin. Blitz scouted back, granting Dallas direct access to Kohl's face.

Trymm's eyes grew large. He swallowed a mouthful of liquor.

"Not up in here! Sit y'all's asses down!" Dana yelled from across the room as she handed the guy who'd given her his ticket, fifteen $100 bills.

Glad to avoid having Dallas get out of his seat and whoop Kohl's ass, Trymm followed with, "She's right. Squash all that. How about, starting today, we fuck as many whores as we can?"

"Why they got to be whores?" Kohl inquired, sipping on his Hennessy.

"Okay." Dallas stared at Kohl. "Bitches. Like you."

Dana placed Trymm's plate in front of him. Dallas ripped his newspaper in half.

"Don't hate. You ain't never gon' be me, homey." Avoiding eye contact with Dallas, Trymm smiled at Dana. "Thanks, baby girl. Breakfast looks almost as delicious as you."

Dana wiggled her bare left ring finger before serving the others.

Dallas glanced across the room at all the pretty women, wishing one day he could have a relationship where he didn't scare a woman off. Maybe the thick one in denim shorts. Or the other one at the next table wearing a short dress. He could almost see everything she had to offer a man between her thighs. His dick became hard. His heart was good. It was his head that was fucked up.

Blitz's cell phone rang. He declined the "No Caller ID" call. Consumed a portion of his drink. "Fuck them, then what?"

"Man, that's enough." Kohl glanced around the restaurant. "Yas lawd. I'm down. I'll start lining 'em up, and banging the juicy ones in the restroom right now."

Blitz narrowed his eyelids at Kohl. "Yo', ruthless, collar-wearing, Scorpio ass would."

Dallas laughed. "Ain't nothing wrong with calling the Lord's name. I do it every day."

Blitz wasn't talking about a priest collar. He was referring to Kohl's polo.

"Listen, we bet on tunk, dominos, every damn Saints game. Let's make the challenge the biggest gamble we've ever made." Blitz looked to his right at Dallas, then left at Kohl and Trymm. "Two hundred and fifty thousand dollars. Each."

"For pussy?" Kohl questioned. "You done lost all your damn marbles." He placed the rim of his glass on top of his bottom lip, then flipped the plastic cup upside down.

Trymm leaned on the green laminated counter, looked two seats down to Blitz. Kohl tilted backward.

"Chump change, homey. I'm in. Winner takes all." Trymm held up his glass.

"Dat's what's up." Blitz scanned the faces of Dallas and Kohl. "I know y'all not scared. This is our last rendezvous of this decade. We are all turning thirty this year," Blitz said, laughing.

"'Laissez les bons temps rouler,'" Dallas replied. "Fuck it. I can write a check today." If Dallas lost the bet, with all the money he'd saved not frivolously spending on females, he'd still have a net worth of over seven figures.

Shaking his head, Kohl thought about the money he'd stashed to open a second location for Kash In & Out. Winning would mean not having to use any of his funds.

"It's not that I'm not in. It's too simple. I mean. How we gon' keep count? What about, in addition to banging the most chicks, you have to actually make them fall in love with you?"

"Y'all might as well cut me a check now," Trymm boasted, then told Dana, "Let us have another bottle."

Dana refilled each glass, placed the empty bottle next to Trymm, then left.

"And," Dallas interjected, "you have to dump her ass publicly in front of a whole lot of people."

Trymm added, "Or on social media. That's the ticket."

"Cool. But how are we to prove the love connection 'cause y'all niggas lie?" Blitz added, "Let's scrap that part. Toss in video footage and photos, and both have to be posted on social media."

The fellas eyed one another with excitement and certainty that they each would win.

Dallas insisted, "That shit that disappears in a snap doesn't count, either. Let's post pics or videos. We don't have to do both."

Kohl frowned at Dallas. "It has to disappear in a short time. I ain't tryna get sued. I have too much to lose."

Trymm raised his plastic cup. "Double points for live social videos that exceed an hour. Drink up. I'm not trying to get knocked upside my head today. I'm making time to secure my cashier's check, but one of y'all have to swing by Dupree's and get it."

Blitz quickly volunteered. "Tomorrow, July first, is the official start date. We end on July thirtieth."

"And I gets my mil soon as the bank opens the following business day." Trymm, self-assured he'd outdo the crewe, waved at Mrs. Kandy, who was walking toward the exit.

"She's a piece of work and waste of time. My bank is down the street." Dallas stuffed the last piece of his hot sausage patty in his mouth, then swallowed. "I'll cashier up my quarter of a mil soon as we're done."

"Me too," Kohl added.

"Y'all reconvene at my bank at two o'clock. Trymm, if you're good on time, I can meet you at your bank now." Blitz had to have control and full access to the million. Even if he didn't win, with the right short-term investment of the crewe's money, Blitz could skim enough off the top to pay off his debt.

"I'll get it to you, nigga. What's the rush?" Trymm stared past Kohl, focused on Blitz. "When y'all lose, I don't want to hear, 'No, I had too much to drink.'"

"I second that. We're settin' this up with a four-signature authority." Kohl wanted to close all the loopholes. "Wait, Trymm. Let's go over all the deets again, and oh, oh, Trymm, you've smashed too many vaginas, bruh. Exes don't count."

"*My* exes don't count." Trymm had never smashed any of the crewe's girlfriends, but qualifying for the grand prize might change all that.

Blitz grinned at Trymm. "So I can fuck fine-ass Atlantis? She's not married, but I heard she's engaged."

"Sure. Long as you can handle the ass whuppin' I'ma put on you, homey." Trymm didn't know the one he'd let get away was back in town. And she was engaged? If Blitz was telling the truth, Trymm couldn't let Atlantis walk down the aisle and into the arms of another man.

Kandy approached Trymm. Opened his hand. Wrote her number in his palm with a red marker, then walked away without saying a word.

Trymm adjusted his crotch. "Twelve-oh-one I'ma be all up in that. Ya heard me."

Anxious to secure the funds before any of the crewe backed out, Blitz dropped $200 on the counter. "Let's do this."

Everyone stood in unison.

"Wait," Blitz said, picking up his cup. "A toast. Let the head games begin."

"You a fool, boy." Trymm held his glass the highest. "I like that shit, though."

Kohl nodded. "Me too."

Dallas downed the last of his Hennessy, then saluted the others. "Laissez-faire, my brothers. Laissez-faire."

CHAPTER 1

Trymm

Day 1

"A yacht?" BobbyRay questioned.

"You heard me, homey. I didn't stutter. Huge. Three levels. None of that forty-six-foot shit, either. The kind you rolled out for me when I was ballin' professionally. I need a trick that can accommodate a hundred naked babes. Comfortably," I demanded.

"A hundred? Females? With no clothes on? How many dudes?" he inquired.

BobbyRay had jokes not worthy of laughter.

"One. Me." I was solid on that. "Hold on. Let me catch this convo."

With fifteen minutes to opening my restaurant, I had to make a quick stop. Prayed Walter was at his location, not mine. Texted my sis Penny: **Be there in 15–20 tops!**

Putting BobbyRay on mute, I parked curbside, honked my horn, lowered the tinted window of my GLS.

Blitz turned off his garden hose, approached the passenger side, reached toward his back pocket, handed me an envelope. "Here's your deposit receipt and proof of the balance. Everything is all set up. In thirty days you can kiss your cash good-bye."

"And right this second you can kiss *my* ass. You know how crazy Walter is, and I had to come ova here. You shoulda dropped this off to me yesterday, homey." I ripped the seal, peeped inside. "This kinda light. Where the rest of the deets?"

This wasn't my first time opening an account. I needed every piece of paper they signed, along with the full account number, and online monitoring access.

"Nigga, don't get new over a bet you're going to lose. Oh, text me a copy of your driver's license. My banker, Ralph, needs it for the file."

"Fuck that. I'll drop by the bank at my earliest to make sure everything is in order. I'll give it to him then."

Nigga seemed a little hesitant as he said, "That works."

"For sho." I had to get back to organizing my shit.

"I got a few female intellects lined up while you . . . at work." He looked at his Rolex wristwatch. "What time you get off, my brother?"

I wasn't down with women who were all suited up, with balls bigger than mine. CEOs. COOs. He could fuck all of them soldier-marching, briefcase-carrying, sleeping-alone-at-night, uptight broads. Blitz's last name got panties to drop, but not that lil dick he had since we were in middle-school gym class.

"I've got to go, homey."

"Oh, guess who I ran into."

"Text it to me."

He blurted, "Atlantis."

For a split second I was stuck. "What the fuck? My ex?" Regrouping, I realized he was trying to throw me off my game. "Nigga, you outta your league. But if you think you can hit it, then 'Swing, batter. Batter, swing.'"

Atlantis would never sleep with any of my boys. If

there was one ex-girlfriend I wished I hadn't fucked over, it was Atlantis. She still had my heart.

Blitz turned, resumed watering his front lawn.

Speeding off, I unmuted BobbyRay. "I'm back."

"You a fool, Trymm. Give me the pantyless details."

Fuck Blitz, one-at-a-time, pussy-eating, ain't-never-had-a-threesome ass. Hope his ass gets lockjaw.

"Hun*ded,* man," I reemphasized to keep BobbyRay focused on the pertinent.

My boyz weren't ready for me. Shooting hoops with my brothers and sisters since I was two, starting every game when I was in high school, I'd stayed up many nights strategizing how to stack the *W*'s to get into the league. Landed overseas four years straight out of college, never made it to the NBA, but I enjoyed damn near every foreign pussy presented to me. Missed that wild life.

"How long you need it for?" BobbyRay asked.

I was going to be so far ahead out the gate, the crewe might as well concede and give me the mil now. Initially, when I called my homey, I thought a Saturday cruise was cool, but it was Friday and I had to muscle up at the family biz this weekend.

"If you can crank it up for midnight and get the word out by mouth, no flyers or social shit, let me do tonight, tomorrow, and Sunday." Couldn't chance the fellas getting wind of my plan before I set sail.

"Cool. Sounds like I should be on board," he said, then laughed.

A boatload of females was more than I could handle if all they did was lick my dick three times each, shared a few rounds of my seeds, and posed in front of my hidden camera. I could dump all those bitches online at the same damn time. Glad we'd ditched the "I love you" confessions, but I might make the ladies confess to piss the fellas off.

BobbyRay was my frat. The purple and gold bled purple and gold.

"Ruff! This is a straight sexfest, homey. I'ma need video footage from midnight to three a.m. You might have to take something to hang. I sure am. Concentrate on married women who want to have unadulterated fun immediately after the concert is over.

"Fuck Vegas," I added. "Vegas ain't got nothing on this here dirty South. 'What happens, didn't' shit is about to pop the fuck off. Ya heard me. I need Chance the Rapper blasting, free-flowing booze, and lots of food. Bitches get irritated when they hungry."

Blitz had better not stick his dick in Atlantis. She'd better not let him. Atlantis still had feelings for me. I could get back with her, and every woman I dated, if I wanted to.

"Count me all the way in, but I can't promise that many pussies will be balled and chained by law. I got you on the music, but scrap Chance. There's a lot of sex groups in town from DC, Cali, New York, from all over. Females will cruise for the fun of it. I'll connect with the organized ones first. They know how to keep locations under wraps for real."

That was what I was talkin' 'bout. "Damages?" Friend or not, I always confirmed my out-of-pocket commitment up front. My dad taught all of us that.

"I'll discount you to forty dollars a head times three, plus food and alcohol. A flat twenty g's for all three days," BobbyRay insisted.

"Thirty grand flat, homey, and let me put that beauty on reserve for the next three Saturdays, too." Just in case one of the crewe had a better plan I didn't know about and I needed a second wind to cross the finish line.

I pulled into the garage of my condo building in the French Quarter, off Bourbon Street. Sat in my SUV, then added, "Forty tops, add the three Sundays of this month. That's a total of nine sails."

"You ahead of yourself, Trymm. I'd love to take your money, but ain't no more big festivals in July, and who's going to do a midnight sail on a Sunday after the holiday weekend? Let me do you a solid on the twenty g's, we get past Essence, and take it one weekend at a time. I'll have everything else in place, just in case."

That was why I fucked with BobbyRay. "Cool." Retrieving my credit card, the one with weight on it. Not that plastic bendable, BobbyRay was right.

Homey said, "I'ma need—"

I cut him off with, "5452 . . . Before you bill me, e-mail me a contract so I can verify we on the same page. Wait. Remember to use my government for the charge. François Dupree. Peace."

CHAPTER 2

Trymm

Day 1

Ending the call with BobbyRay, I jogged six blocks to the family restaurant, which I co-owned and managed with my sister Penélope. Everybody called her Penny for short. My mother loved the kind of names where people couldn't tell our race. Last night had gone into the morning. I stood up Kandy, with a capital *k*. Had plans to make her number one on my hit list, but I didn't get off till damn near sunrise. Wasn't getting a refund from BobbyRay, so I sure nuff wasn't missing the boat tonight.

Sent a quick text: **Hey, sweet goddess, had to work late. Let me make it up to you. Swing by Dupree's at 8 p.m.**

Tagging on the address for Kandy, I went to the back door of Dupree's to enter. Our upstairs tenant came down the stairway. "Hey, Alex. What's up?" I said, pounding his fist with mine.

"Thinking about popping the question, man. Nervous," he said with a flat smile. "You know I look up to you. Any advice?"

Alex was Scottish. Tried hard to be like a brotha. "Don't be nervous. Be sure," I told him, entering the restaurant.

"Hey, sis. Thanks for holding it down for me. I'm going to need you on standby every day for the next thirty days. Working on the unbelievable! Fifty grand in your hand if you got me." More like needed her to find my replacement.

During special events, to maximize our bottom line, we opened at 7:00 a.m. Come Monday, we'd be back on the daily of 10:00 a.m. until midnight, or until business slowed down.

"Ba-bay, you are not going to have my husband pissed at me. I barely see him as it is. You're the one in a relationship acting as though you're single. You should cover for me so I can ride my man's dick every once in a while," Penny complained. "Don't think I didn't hear you. I want my fifty-grand promissory note up front." Reaching toward the counter, she slapped a napkin to my chest. "Write it on here or text it to me."

A fine female sat at the bar alone. Immediately I noticed her wedding set.

"Cool. Help me out. Call DJ and see if he can be here by eleven tonight." Damn, forgot about Kandy just that quick. "Make it eight o'clock. Please." Donald Jr. would do anything for Penny. Nothing for me.

"Donald Jr.? Come here *before* he closes his location? Ba-bay. You pushin' it. You lucky I love you. Regardless, I got you. But I want my money, Trymm. My daughter can use the extra change. If DJ can't fill in, she'll help out," Penny said. "I've got to check on things in the kitchen. Don't be rude. Help the staff service the customers."

Penny was thirty-four, five years older than me. Her eighteen-year-old (whom our mother raised the first six years) was starting college next month. My sister claimed

her husband was the only man she'd had sex with. *Ever.*
They'd married right after high school. Women lied all
the time, and although I had no proof, I did not believe
my sister had never let another man dip his stick.

A text confirmation, **CU@8p,** registered from Kandy.

The Mrs. at the bar—her dude was either rolling in
dough or broke as hell, still paying on that rock damn
near bigger than Gibraltar on her finger.

Leaning on the bar, I stared in her eyes, then asked,
"What can I get you?"

My sister yelled from the kitchen, "One day Francine
gon' kick your ass! Stop holding out. Marry that girl and
give Mom a grandbaby!"

Dana at the Trolley Stop, Penny, they heard every damn
thing. Francine knew I was not a one-pussy man. No matter how many chicks I banged or times I got caught,
Francine wasn't going anywhere. Besides, we were on my
off-again break. I'd make sure it stayed that way the entire
month.

The woman at the bar stared back. I loved the confident ones. Shy girls lowered their heads. Spoke low. Always wanted a man to make the first move in and out of
the bedroom. Fuck that! The attitude-for-no-reason ones
were worse than the shy females. Thought they were en-
titled to being treated well, even when they acted like
shit. Fuck them, too! Whenever a lady was uncomfortable, she avoided eye contact by staring to the left, right,
or down when speaking. Everywhere except in my eyes.

This one didn't blink when she spoke. "Heard the
Hand Grenades here are so big I'll need both hands to
hold it. Is it true?"

I took a step backward. Immediately her eyes did a
quick scroll down to my dick, then froze.

Propping her elbow on the bar, she spoke to my geni-
tal. "Looks like it'll explode the second I suck on it. Give
it to me."

Wow. In most cases I didn't want the pussy if it was easy, but her timing was impeccable, and the way she kept staring had me intrigued. "We don't serve the Grenade but our Atomic Bomb, you gotta be real grown to get that down your throat. Can you handle it?" I widened my stance.

She nodded. "That'll work."

Hadn't noticed Penny was behind me until sis said, "You're moving slow. I'll make her an Atomic Bomb."

"No, thanks," the customer countered. "He's going to give it to me," she said, focusing below my waist.

Date. Dick. Dump. Fall in love. Proof. Had to find a way to get my first notch. A flow of customers walked through the door. *Damn, my condoms are in my car.* I couldn't leave. A few more guests came in. Penny and the staff had them covered. Occasionally I took randoms down the street to my villa. No time for that. If I did ole girl out back, in the lot, how was I going to prove I hit it?

"What's your name?" I asked, filling the huge black official basketball-sized container with frozen mixed grain alcohol, tequila, rum, gin, and orange liqueur.

"Does it matter?" she questioned, taking the drink. "They say the best thing for a hangover is what got you there in the first place. I just want to enjoy one more giant *cock*tail, then be on my way." The tip of her tongue circled the circumference from the bottom up to the straw.

I'd never seen her in here. "Where are you from?"

"From is past tense. I have no address. Travel the world. I live wherever I am. Never overstay my welcome," she said, then dragged the icy liquid into her throat. "My flight leaves in a few hours. I need something to sober me up."

Sounds like she was in town with one of those sex groups BobbyRay mentioned. I knew sexually deprived married women were thirsty, but damn. For sho, she knew how to get wet and leave without drying off.

"Would you like a tour? I could show you my"—slowly I scanned down to my dick, then toward the back—"office."

A few more guests entered, then left. With lots of sex clubs, places to shop, eat, and grab drinks to go in the French Quarters, peepers were common on Bourbon Street.

Sliding the straw in her mouth, she nodded once.

"Sis," I called out, "hold it down for a few minutes. I need to take a private call in *my* office."

Penny was in the back. The workers were on top of things. I gave ole married gurl a slight nod, then led the way.

Locking the door, I unbuckled my belt. Ole gurl unzipped my shit. I reached for her pussy. She blocked my hand. One, two, three, she yanked down my pants and boxer briefs at the same time, shoved me back on my desktop, dropped to her knees, and started sucking me off.

Resting on my elbows, I made sure we were in full view of the camera inside the charcoal dome on the ceiling. My naked ass was atop the desk with a cold paperweight wedged between the crack. I couldn't move. Could only see her head, neck, and shoulders. Her esophagus felt supercalifragilisticexpialidocious. All I heard was slurping as my nuts cradled in her firm hand. I wasn't sure if I wanted her to speed up so I could get back to work or slow down for me to appreciate where I was.

"Give me this cum, you filthy bastard. I love hot cum in my mouth. *Skeet.* I promise you I won't waste a drop. Your beef is the thickest I've eaten."

Six brothers. All of my dad's boys had the family blessing and curse of being hung like thoroughbreds. She bounced and bobbed. Let her mouth ride my dick. The inside of her cheeks felt pussy soft, the suction was vacuum strong. Her hand pumped up and down.

"Fuck," I grunted. Smothering my word, I tucked in

my lips. Wanted to say, *"Yes, bitch, yes."* Didn't want to interrupt her flow. Desperately wanted to come. Didn't want the feeling to end.

"Trymm, get out here!" Penny slapped once on the door.

"O-kay!" I shouted. Closing my eyes, I prayed my sister would go away.

"You'd better not let Walter catch you. He's on his way." My sister almost screwed up the moment.

Shit! She, whatever her name was, kept on sucking and stroking like a star.

Dupree New Orleans Seafood restaurants had been in business since 1964. We owned five locations. I was the youngest and the only one of our parents' children that wasn't married. This was why I couldn't commit. Too many options.

My parents wanted me to, but I'd never make Francine an honorable woman. That responsibility was hers. Bought her a ring five years ago, but never felt right about giving it to her. This thirty-day challenge was the perfect opportunity to get the . . . ruff! . . . outta my system before falling in love again. Atlantis got away, but Kandy might be the one if I can convince her to . . .

"Aw, shit. I'm about to come," I grunted, picturing Kandy with a *k* on her knees before me.

"What you waiting for?" she asked. "I told you I have a flight to catch. Come or I'm done."

I felt my shit squirting in her throat. She swallowed until my shaft stopped pulsating. Suctioned out the seeds lingering in my tube. My shit drooped like melting taffy. No way I could do this all night long. Needed some serious enhancements to recoup.

I couldn't wait to see this footage.

She pulled down her dress, stood. Before I'd requested to see her pussy, she insisted, "I know the way out," then left.

The crewe messed up taking that "fall in love" part out, I thought, imagining if I had my brains blown out on a regular by a stranger, I'd be the one with my heads fucked up. Relocking my door, I pulled up my pants, tucked in my shirt, sat behind the desk, rewound the footage on our laptop.

Wow, she had mad skills. Francine needed to see this so she could learn how to treat my dick right.

I watched her hand slide up and down my wood. All of my andouille sausage was down her throat. Loved the way she bounced in those heels.

This female was a close second to my favorite performer in Atlanta, "the Showstopper." Now that stripper was double-jointed talented, on that Cirque du Soleil grind. Could teach those lazy broads at Magic City how to set themselves on fiyah.

"Whoa!" I admired myself coming again. Rewind. Stared. Her clit was phat. Rewind. Rattled my brain. Zooming in on her squatting. I paused to get a close up on what I'd imagined to be that one-of-a-kind pussy.

"Sexy muthafucka," I whispered, then mouthed, "Wow!"

My eyes felt as though they'd pop outta the sockets. "What the fuck?"

That isn't a clit! That chick has a . . . dick?!

Slamming the laptop shut, I thumped my forehead several times, stood in front of the desk. *This was a first.*

"That shit did not just happen." *He'd bet not eva stroll his ugly trifling ass up in here again, or I am dragging that dude out by the balls.*

I didn't have a problem with LGBTQ rights. We grew up around all kind of folk. Hell, I was Big Freedia's biggest fan. Deceptive muthafuckers . . . that was the type of shit that could get him killed.

Opening the laptop, I resumed the video. He was commando. He started jacking off while getting me off. Squatting, I looked at the front of my desk. Wet cum stains were on the oak, and my Persian rug.

No way I can show my homies this shit!

Atlantis. Saw her earlier. #realsexy might have to get with that, Blitz texted

I hit DELETE for everything recorded in the restaurant starting at midnight up until now. I had to erase the footage before Penny or anyone else in my family saw it.

I replied, **She'll never give you my pussy, homey.**

Opening the door, to get a package of cleaning wipes, *wham!* My face snapped to the right. I touched my jaw.

Wham! My face and neck snapped left. I stumbled, regained my balance.

"You fucking on the job now." Walter's eyes were filled with disgust.

I couldn't tell him about the bet or swear I had no idea I was going to get my dick sucked. Standing close to Walter, I made it harder for him to swing on me again.

"Is that why you won't marry Francine? You using her and won't marry that girl. I told your ass Penny can't handle this Essence crowd by herself and no way in hell is DJ leaving my location to put in extra hours here so you can chase chicks."

I was only gone for twenty minutes and Penny had betrayed me. There was no escaping my big brother. Retreating into the office was not a good idea.

"I'm not ready, bro, you know that. I can't marry her just to say I have a wife. I appreciate the way Francine takes care of me. I'm not 'in love' with her, and I'm not going to spend the rest of my life with her. She'll never become a Dupree."

Walter stared into my eyes. I braced myself for a tackle, or a punch to my gut. "Then stop using her. That girl has been faithful to you since y'alls freshman year at LSU. It's time for you to do the respectable. Let her go. Or buy her a ring."

I shook my head. "No can do, big brother. I got the ring, but I'm not giving it to her. I can't do it."

"Then you will marry her. I'm not asking."

If I were going to be forced to permanently commit, might as well put her ass on the clock. I hit up Francine with a text, **Get ova here right now. Need you to work my shifts all weekends.**

She replied, **omw, babe!**

CHAPTER 3

Francine

Day 1

"Francine. You have got to be kidding me." Rene was like a sister.

I hated disappointing her. We'd met on LSU's campus at a Greek show during our junior year. I was there supporting Trymm. Rene was solo enjoying the entertainment.

En route to Dupree's, I exited Interstate 10 at Tchoupitoulas. "I know. I feel bad, too. I promise I'll pay you back. How much was my ticket?" I asked, driving across Poydras Street. Traffic was stop and go, cars were separated by pedestrians traveling toward Harrah's Casino to my right and the Windsor Court on the left adjacent to what was once the W Hotel. After acquisition and an almost $30 million renovation, Le Meridien was our newest competitor. Being a hotel manager of a five-star chain, I knew the forty-five dollars for third-party valet service which did not offer a validation discount to diners caused their hotel to lose money.

A text registered from Trymm, **You coming or what?**

Quickly glancing at my keyboard, I typed, **omw,** before creeping upon Canal Street.

Wasn't as though he'd given me sufficient notification that he needed me to fill in for him tonight, tomorrow, and Sunday. In forty minutes I'd showered, gotten dressed, swept my hair into its usual ponytail (that I was literally sitting on), beat my face, and I was less than twenty minutes away. Give or take five.

"The price isn't the problem. You know I planned our girls' night out six months ago. Bought four front-row, center, tickets with VIP backstage access for tomorrow's concert and this is the thanks I get? Why can't you make it and you'd better not let Trymm's name come out of your damn mouth because y'all still on break." Rene's huffing projected through my car's Bluetooth like static.

Couldn't say if she were in my shoes, she'd do the same. Rene was happily married to her high-school sweetheart. I, too, could find balance in my relationship if Trymm weren't unpredictable. But just like with Rene's husband, my man came first.

She didn't understand how badly I wanted to be a Dupree, and Trymm was the last one who'd marry. A long family tradition, Duprees did not divorce. I'd never be a single mom, and I'd planned on giving my father- and mother-in-law a baby right away. But not accidentally, the way Penny had done. Trymm would never forgive me if he felt trapped.

The love, time, energy, I'd invested in Trymm for almost ten years, I was not going to risk throwing away for one night at the Mercedes Benz Superdome partying with my girlfriends.

"I appreciate and love you," I said, making a left off of Decatur.

"Too bad you don't appreciate and love yourself. You're

beautiful, young, sexy, intelligent, and if you don't wake
up, one day you're going to look in the mirror and see a
bitter, single old woman with no babies, who wasted the
best years of her life on a man that she granted permission to use her up anytime he wanted. You haven't cut
your hair since you met him because he won't let you. *He*
won't let you!" she shouted, then added, "It's your damn
hair, Francine! Trim your edges. Apply for the general-
manager position you deserve." Rene exhaled her frustrations onto me.

Marrying Trymm would be my promotion.

You know what. Forget it! Trymm texted. **I can't de-
pend on your selfish ass for anything.**

Rene was right. I was always there for him. The same
as she was for her husband. I replied, **Looking for a park.**

"Rene, I promise I'll repay you. Forgive me. I'll explain Monday, when I see you at work."

Might take me longer this time to get back in her good
graces, but I was her supervisor, she wasn't mine. I'd
hired her as my assistant manager and taught her everything I do. I wasn't jealous of Rene, but I'd be lying if I
said I didn't want what she had. A husband. Two children.
Out of respect I'd given her a day to find my replacement.

"He's never going to marry you," Rene said, then
ended our call.

She was wrong. Over my dead body would I let François
marry another woman. Parking at a paid lot off of Bourbon
Street, I headed to Dupree's. Marching on the uneven
brick roads, coated with dirt, gutters were lined with plastic fishbowls, green plastic grenades, black atomic bombs,
and Styrofoam containers, some with leftover food.

"Excuse me," I said, zigzagging between mostly happy,
and a few intoxicated, females. Thank God, Trymm hadn't
left. I spotted him behind the bar. I gave my man a lingering hug.

"Thanks for helping out. You know I love you for this." Trymm stepped back, pecked my cheek.

Our on-and-off relationship was one I'd become accustomed to, but I desperately wanted us to stay on. The longest break he'd given me was two months. Remaining faithful to Trymm wasn't hard. Where was I going to find a dick that big, unless I had married one of his brothers? I'd heard Penny mention all of her brothers had a gigantic one.

"Love you, too," I said. "I guess we're back on track."

"I was never off track," he said. "When you learn to do what I tell you to do, when I ask the first time, and stop making me repeat myself, I can take this off." He wiggled his ring finger. "And put on a real wedding band."

I hugged him, pressing my breasts against his stomach for comfort. "Baby, I'm trying."

"Try harder. I told you I need you to close for me the next three weekends. Be on time. If you do a good job, I might propose."

That would be great. All I ever wanted was to be his wife and birth his babies. I was determined to do an outstanding job. Checked my cell. I may have to work the remaining Saturdays and Sundays of this month. Best not to mention that right this moment, else he'd put me on break again. I'd figure out something. Might have to beg Rene to take my shifts.

I was his wife in every way, except on paper. "Since I have to come back tomorrow, I'll spend the night at your place after I get off?"

Four, five, or six in the morning, whatever time Penny closed Dupree's, going to my house in the East would take fifteen minutes, but I'd be too tired to drive. Kept a change of clothes in my trunk, since Trymm didn't like me leaving my personal belongings at his condo. I missed my man. Desperately wanted to sleep with him in my arms, even if we haven't had sex in thirty-five days.

"Kohl needs me to help him out at Kash. No telling what time the club is going to shut down. Since I'ma be out your way, go to your house. I'll come there." Trymm glanced up at the red light inside the charcoal dome, then pivoted toward me. "If Walter comes by asking for my whereabouts, tell him I'll be right back. I had to make a cash drop. Be sure to clear the drawer right away if he walks in."

Like a good soldier, I marched with my orders. Entering the kitchen, I put a spoon of white rice in a bowl, added a scoop of seafood gumbo. Penny's signature roux saturated my taste buds. *Scrumptious.* Placing the empty bowl in the sink, I checked the stock on shrimp, blue crabs, andouille sausage, Patton's hot sausage, catfish, greens, corn bread mix, pickled watermelon, spices, and nonedible supplies. I updated an order that was already in the computer for what we'd need to handle Sunday's crowd.

Penny walked in. "Girl, thanks for covering for my brother. How he gon' go to the concert with Blitz when we have a line out the door? Check the liquor at the bar for me and put in an order for what we need. I'm going to help close out some of these tabs. When you're done, work on seating guests."

Penny must've gotten Blitz mixed up with Kohl, and the club confused with the concert. She always got things twisted when it came to my guy. That was why I'd stopped listening to her dog Trymm.

Turning to head to the host stand, I bumped into Walter.

"What the hell you doing here? Where's Trymm?" he demanded, scanning every corner.

I stared at the floor.

"I don't have time to keep up with Trymm," Penny said, swiping a credit card.

Facing Walter, I lied, "He went to make a cash drop."

Oh, shit! The drawer opened. It was stuffed with cash. Penny closed it.

Walter stared into my eyes. "Leave, Francine."

Opening my mouth in protest, Walter sternly said, "I'm not Trymm, and I'm not asking."

"Thanks, gurl. Bye." Penny swiped another card.

I overheard Walter say to Penny, "We know why he stays with her. She's too nice."

On my way out, I paused. A beautiful chocolate lady, wearing a red halter, fitted jumpsuit, sat at the bar. She exuded confidence. I wondered if it was the sparkling wedding set on her finger or if she was always that way.

"Excuse me," she said, looking at Penny. "When you get a moment, I'd love to have an old-fashioned."

I noticed Walter replacing the almost overflowing drawer with one that I should've popped in, which had five 20s, ten 10s, ten 5s, twenty singles, two rolls of quarters, a roll of nickels, and one of pennies.

Soon as I got outside the door, I typed, **Walter came in. He put me out.**

Regardless of how Walter knew, or if it were happenstance, Trymm would blame me. I heard his voice in my head, *"You dumb bitch! I'm not coming to your place!"*

Felt like a fool for canceling on Rene and my girlfriends. Erasing the text to Trymm, I called Rene.

"I hope you reconsidered about tomorrow, 'cause I'm not selling your ticket," she answered.

"Can you meet me for a drink at The Ritz?" I asked.

Heard her say, "Baby, I'll be back. Going to meet Francine for a drink at The Ritz"; then she confirmed, "I'm on my way. Margaritas? Or Hurricanes?"

Margaritas signified a happy get-together. I responded, "Hurricanes."

No need to get my car, the hotel was a few blocks away. So was Trymm's apartment. What sense did it make for me to have a key I seldom used? I'd barely come off of a break with Trymm, and now he had reason to shut me out again for God only knew how long.

Maybe Rene could tell me what I was doing wrong and how to get Trymm to put a ring on my finger without her judging me.

CHAPTER 4

Trymm

Day 3

"Cozy crib," Kandy complimented after entering my villa. Tossing her oversized canary-yellow purse on the sofa, she strutted through my French doors, stepping onto the balcony. "Wow. This courtyard, with the water fountain, is making me wet. All the times I've paraded through the Quarter, I never would've guessed all of these amenities existed inside these cement walls."

My complex wasn't unique in that regard. A privacy barrier was standard for most residential properties north of Canal and east of Rampart. Besides being less than a half mile from my restaurant, not having to worry about females that I'd smashed showing up unannounced made my $700,000, two-bedroom, two-bath investment worth it.

Joining Kandy outside, I stood behind her. "Damn, your husband is one lucky man. No way I'd let you outta my sight." I had to touch her ass. Let my johnson do the honors. Her arms were silky smooth. "Coconut oil?"

"That, and a little shea butter," she answered.

I exhaled, wondering how the rest of her felt. I swept

her hair aside, French-kissed the nape of her neck, let my lips rest there as I slowly inhaled.

A whiff of strawberries, mixed with vanilla maybe, made my dick crawl up her spine. The warm summer breeze blended my next breath with the scent of wild magnolias dangling on tree branches that hovered over benches below.

Speaking like Athena, the goddess of wisdom, Kandy let me know. "I stay because my husband worships me. Almost impossible to find a man that respects himself, let alone his woman." She turned around. Gazed into my eyes.

I felt the alleged respect pumping blood through her veins. *Get the fuck outta here.* She was lying. A woman who had a husband that put her on a pedestal wouldn't freely give his pussy to a man she barely knew. Kandy wasn't even a challenge. She was more of a mystery. My standing her up didn't keep her from showing up tonight. Perhaps her wedding ring was as illegitimate as mine.

There was a part of me that wanted to take my time. Caress her nakedness. Hold her in my arms. Then there was the dawg in me, dying to lean her over the rail, hike up her purple sundress, snatch her hair, and fuck the shit out of her. Then right before I'd come, I'd pull out and spew white seeds all over those luscious gold heels she was wearing.

I'd never lusted for Francine. She was on first base 'cause she was consistent. All the things she'd done for me in college—date one, Francine cooked and invited me to dinner at her aunt's home in Baton Rouge. Week two, she cleaned my dorm room, top to bottom. Week three, according to her, I was the first man she'd performed fellatio on. What was there not to like about having a woman that did it all because she was crazy about me?

"We don't have to pretend, Trymm? Right?" Kandy unzipped my pants. "You invited me and I came for your big dick." She lowered her strapless dress to her navel. "Put it in whatever hole you'd like."

Damn! Her natural tits with those huge nipples . . . "Um, um, um." *What the hell?* I watched the purple lace descend to her feet, scanned the courtyard below, grabbed her hand, and escorted Mrs. Kandy indoors. Confirming that her nipples tasted like chocolate, I needed the video, didn't want to risk my neighbors posting my ass on social.

"Leave the doors open," she insisted.

Running my fingers through her thick, shoulder-length strands, it was fluffy and—thank God—track free. Slowly I lowered the waistband of my pants over my erection. She smiled at my dick and I swore my one eye winked back at her.

"Let me help you," she insisted as she peeled my cotton shirt from my body.

Kandy picked up an armless chair from my dining table, turned it around, knelt on the cushion. Bracing herself, she glanced over her shoulder, then moaned, "Kiss my sweet pussy."

The moment I'd anticipated arrived. Saliva flowed, I swallowed. I didn't have time for foreplay. In a few hours I'd have to board the yacht, set sail on my third voyage. While she started masturbating, I said, "Don't move," then placed my cell on the shelf and started secretly recording a video.

Spreading her juicy buns wide, I placed my nose against her asshole, inhaled. *Damn, everything on this woman is fresh.* I stuck my tongue in her vagina. Man, her name was fitting. I sucked her clit, then teased her asshole again. Cream coated my finger when I slid it in and out of her pussy.

"I'm getting bored. Let's switch," she said, standing.

Well, that made two of us. I was attempting to accommodate that bitch. Positioning her back to the video, I questioned, "You want me to get on the chair and tilt my behind in the air?"

I did as she'd instructed. No matter what she'd do, she couldn't take my manhood, and I'd already confirmed she was indeed a woman.

Returning the favor, Kandy tea-bagged my nuts, French-kissed every inch of my buttocks. "Goddess, I love you." Wanted to know if I needed that confession would I get it.

"I love you, too, Trymm. Right?"

I chuckled at her attempt to play me. I was cool with not going all the way. What we'd done definitely counted as a date, sex, and an unnecessary confession.

Wasn't often I'd come across a real woman that knew how to toss salad and didn't mind doing it. Standing, I asked, "How long you in town for? I have to help out at the family restaurant in a few, but I really want to see you again."

"Have a seat," she said in a low seductive tone, before pushing me down.

Straddling my thighs, she wiggled her butt on my knees. Kandy held my shaft down, aligned her pussy, then slowly danced until the head was in. "So, is this what you men do?"

I placed my hands on her hips. She removed them. "Do what? I don't understand."

"You and I are married. Obviously, your wife doesn't know about this spot. For all I know, my husband may have a hideaway where he takes his bitches, too. How can I find out for sure?"

What the fuck? I needed her to shut up and concentrate on me. The way she took her time was nice. Her body simulated a wave motion.

Slap! "Answer me," she demanded.

I grabbed her wrist. She gently touched the side of my face.

"Damn! I confess. I'm not married. I wear the ring be-cause I hate explaining to random-ass females why I don't want to be in a relationship with them. I don't want to justify my intentions with them when all I want is . . . a woman like you."

"I see," she said. "Less headaches. That's why I'm en-joying your amazing dick. Tired of faking orgasms with my husband."

Admiring her hourglass frame, I twirled her nipples. All I wanted to do now was enjoy watching Kandy get off. I pulled her upper body to me.

Now that I knew she was like most women I'd met, who weren't being dicked down properly by their man, I said, "If we were together, you could ride this all day, every day."

Her legs shivered uncontrollably. A sound deep inside her belly rumbled. She roared like a wild animal in the jungle mating for the first time. Her breasts, arms, stom-ach, and back became moist.

Catlike, she stood, picked up her purse, tiptoed into my bedroom. I followed her. Stopped as she entered my bathroom. I heard the door lock. Returning to the living room, I retrieved her dress from the balcony, ended the video.

Sitting on the edge of my bed, I opened my social page, started to post. Rethought that move. Created a fake page, clicked upload, watched our video. Had to shake my head. I could make some dollars off of that shit. See how much her husband worships her if he witness this.

The shower flowed seemingly forever. Kandy un-locked the bathroom door. I stood ready to feast my eyes one last time on the body of a brainless goddess.

Kandy was fully dressed in a red sundress. Scanning down to her feet, the heels matched. Trailing her to my front, I picked up her purple dress, handed it to her along with her golden heels. Didn't regret exposing her.

She opened the front door, looked up at me. "Keep it as a gift. Trymm? Right? I know my way out."

Downing two male enhancement tablets, I needed Kandy to hold on to that "what's his name?" attitude. She'd made it easy for me to leave her on my fake page and log out of my new account. See how long it takes for her to never forget me.

A text message registered from Francine, **Sorry about the Walter situation. I miss you, babe.**

Yeah. Right. She could get the fuck outta my life too.

CHAPTER 5

Francine

Day 3

"Aren't you happy you didn't miss the concert of a life-time?" The question was rhetorical. Rene couldn't stop raving about Common, but Mariah Carey gave my girl-friend life.

Rene strolled beside me along the Riverwalk, singing all the lyrics to "We Belong Together," when all I was trying to do was deny I needed to replay "Shake It Off" in my mind. The pit of my stomach churned. My gut felt like spoiled whipped butter. How much longer would I endure this heartache. I stopped, gazed at the full moon. Watched boats docked at the pier on the muddy Missis-sippi.

"You're right. I'm glad I didn't miss our girls' night out yesterday." But in a way I had. Every song performed, I couldn't stop thinking, worrying, wondering, *Where is Trymm? Who is he with? When will this break end? The next one begin?*

R. Kelly's music blasted in the distance. Rene stood beside me. "Check out all the people gathered by that yacht." She started dancing. "My husband and I did a midnight cruise as part of our honeymoon package." Rene smiled as though she had an X-rated flashback. "Maybe someone is hosting an Essence after-party. Let's go be nosy."

It was an hour before midnight. The last headliner was probably on stage at the Mercedes-Benz Superdome. "An after-party doesn't make sense this early. I'm good. All I see is a bunch of women. Where they gon' sail to in the dark?" I asked, then answered, "To the West Bank?" That was less than a ten-minute drive from where we stood.

"Darling, where females gather, men follow. The best parties always let women in first." Staring into my eyes, she questioned, "Aw, honey. Why do you stay with Trymm when clearly he doesn't care about you?"

Rene was sincerely an upbeat person who couldn't relate to my pain. I confessed, "The thought of letting him go creates a level of anxiety that makes me feel"—I paused, feeling vulnerable—"like I'm going to go out of my mind. Or, worse, die." There, I'd admitted it to someone for the first time.

If my family and coworkers knew my truth, they'd call me stupid. I'm not. I'm highly intelligent when it came to my job. And I had a plan. Once Trymm and I married, knowing his family didn't believe in divorce, the real Francine was showing up and out. "I can't live without him, Rene."

All I had was what President Obama had instilled in me. Hope kept me from acting out on the rage—making him a punching bag, destroying his car, bleaching his clothes, tearing up his home. I feared that would make him take longer to propose or, worse, he'd break up with me for good and some other woman would enjoy the married life I deserved.

"'Can't'? Or don't want to? No man is worth wasting a decade of your life on," she said.

I knew that. But try convincing my heart.

"You're scared of what? Doing better? Meeting a man that will respect you?" Holding my hands, she continued to speak. "Francine, I have never seen you truly happy with him since I've met you." She touched the top notch of my braid. Her fingers meandered to the tip that was below my hips. I felt her untangling the end.

I panicked. "Stop! Don't do that to me!" Snatching my ponytail from her, I draped it over my shoulder, held on to it as though it were my lifeline to Trymm.

"That's what I'm talking about. You can't even let your own hair down without Trymm's permission. Women spend thousands of dollars for good Indian hair. God blessed you with it and you keep it coiled up just like your real feelings." Rene cupped my face in her palms.

I bit the inside of my lips hard as my eyes watered, then broke her bond. I knew she cared, but I didn't. She had her husband. I deserved mine. "Please don't touch me."

Rene stepped back. "Pretty lil light skin, five foot ten, slim, curvy, sexy, had all those fine-ass men last night competing to buy you a drink. Begging you to take their number. And one by one, you rejected them all. For what? A man that makes you miserable."

I nodded at her. No matter what Rene said, we knew last names in New Orleans, Louisiana, had meaning. One could say Hankton, Carter, Bartholomew, Morial, or Allen and automatically an association with an entire family was made. Dupree was prestigious.

"I love you, Francine. I saw a post the other day stating 'Black Women Are Weak.' That post could've very well . . . had your picture on it. You are the weakest woman I know."

Bad relationships could turn good. Sometimes so-called perfect marriages became nightmares. Tired of listening to her give me her opinion, I said, "Thanks for judging me, my friend. Hopefully one day I won't have to return the favor."

I wasn't weak. I was determined.

CHAPTER 6

Trymm

Day 3

Fucking around with Kandy's ass almost made me late for my own yacht party.

Arriving three minutes before eleven, I zigzagged through my pack of soon-to-be carnivores, pumping my fist to Chris Brown's "Privacy." BobbyRay unhooked the red velvet rope, let me board, then refastened it.

He whispered, "This sex group is international. Most of them like females, too. The organizer heard about the other clubs. She came to me and requested an exclusive. The only way she'd agree to the terms was in exchange for a twenty-thousand-dollar donation. I took care of it. But you owe me. Cool?"

I told him, "They're here now. Next time run that shit by me before, not after. Give me ten minutes to get ready for my internationals."

Heard a voice say, "Hey, Trymm, baby. Remember me?"

She could've been from anywhere in the world. I'd find out who she was soon enough. Not bothering to turn around, I headed belowdecks to my bedroom. Learned the hard way, had to ensure there were no repeats on anything foul. First thing I did was move the ice containers to the corner. Didn't want any of the ladies getting extra creative by turning my circular king-sized mattress into an ice bath. Had enough of those as an athlete. No liquor in or near my throne. Refills required getting up and not throwing up on me. I made sure there was plenty of appetizers on the upper deck, far away from me. Refused to have anyone stuffing my face . . . with food.

Kandy crossed my mind. Wondered how she was trending on social. I wanted to see her again. Ask her to leave her husband. Should be able to double up on my count if I could pull off convincing one of my married pieces to file for divorce.

As I made my way back to BobbyRay, the muddy Mississippi was cleaner than the two hundred wedded females that set sail with me the last forty-eight hours. I was sure I had another beating coming from Walter, but winning the mil was my priority.

'Bout to stack another hundred. Make that a *hunded*, just like basketball days, and add on an 'and one' for Mrs. Kandy. No one would ever know about dude that sucked me off.

"Hey, Trymm." A sexy Southern belle, the first to greet me, smiled, waving her fingers and swaying her ass in the wind as she stepped off the ramp onto the yacht.

"I'ma need you to enter your name and sign this waiver right here," BobbyRay told her as he held my iPad. "Use your finger. Remove your hat and sunglasses."

Laughing, she did as he'd requested. BobbyRay tagged her upper left shoulder with a sticker that revealed her number, *#1*. She struck a pose. He snapped her photo with the same device, then moved on to the next guest. I'd left my cell in the glove compartment of my GLS. Didn't need it. BobbyRay had surveillance setup from every angle on the yacht.

"Welcome . . ." Before I could finish my sentence, Southern Belle put on her shades, unwrapped her dress, let it fall to those gladiator spiked heels. The brim of her wide sun hat flopped over her forehead as though the sun was beaming at high noon. Women waiting to come aboard started undressing in line.

Southern Belle encouraged a male enhancement rise outta me that couldn't be denied. I'd lost track of how many pills I'd taken since Friday. Had to slow down. Tomorrow. Get back to work at my restaurant.

I slid my hand from the nape of her neck to her front hairline as she grabbed the rim of her hat before it hit the floor. Wanted to feel her silky strands tickle my balls. Had to admit, I was a dog well before I'd pledged purple and gold.

My boy counted off the number of women boarding. "Thirty-one, thirty-two."

Southern Belle licked my dick, then said, "I'm on deck for whatever you want, I just hafta be first."

That bitch was a lotta bit too late. Thanks to Old Granddad, my grandfather, and a street ho he called Desire, who did it all for a few dollars, I'd lost my innocence at the age of eleven.

Southern Belle's lashes blinked once. "Where and how do you want me?" she asked, holding on to my shaft.

BobbyRay was halfway through to my maximum count. A twerking contest with all naked babes jumped off right in my face.

"Suck it three times, take as much as you can handle, then say, 'I love you, Trymm.'"

Dumb bitch tried to do it. Barely got past my frenulum before gagging. Mutual exchange was no robbery. She got what she wanted. I got what she'd come for. Whoever her stupid husband was he should cut his losses and pawn the bling on her finger. Her beauty faded in the shadow of other conquests. Southern Belle could take a swamp tour, fall overboard, get swallowed by an alligator, I didn't give a fuck. She was number 202 and officially under my belt.

"Ninety-nine, one hundred," my homey BobbyRay said aloud. "Time to set sail, Captain!"

BobbyRay gave forty-four a flute filled with bubbly, then placed a glass of cold champagne in Southern Belle's hand to wash away what I perceived as a bad attitude, as I gawked at forty-four dumbfounded. Quickly, forty-four turned her back to me.

Lawd, have mercy! I was about to put everyone off the yacht. Elbowing BobbyRay, I whispered in my homey's ear, "Who the fuck is fordy-fo, yo'?" *Dat ass, though.*

Turning from the female flow to give me his undivided, BobbyRay said, "Guess she's just out to have fun like the rest."

Spotted the ring from the distance. "Who's her ball and chain? You know?" I had to find out. Not really. She was here, and that nigga could stay wherever the fuck he was, ya heard me.

"Not sure. I imagine she's in town for the festival like most. How you want me to handle her?"

I couldn't dog her like the rest. Couldn't let her see my trickin' game. "Save her for a real date."

"One better," my homey said. "Do what you came to do. I'll set her up alone in my suite, let her relax, and whenever you're ready for that one-on-one, she'll be all yours."

Too late to get her number and put her off the yacht. "Don't fuck her," I said. "She's mine. Something about her is special."

My boy smiled. Nodded. "You can trust me. They're all yours, bruh. I'm just eating leftovers."

Started moving closer to fordy-fo to intro myself. Asked, "What's your name, suga?"

Damn, her smile makes me melt. Feel like a kid. Hadn't

experienced butterflies since I dated my first love and high-school sweetheart.

Untying her scarf, she said, "It's me. Heard about your party. Thought I'd come. See you haven't changed."

Oh, wow! I removed her sunglasses, stared into her big brown eyes. Her nose was smaller, lips crazy bigger, slender hips were rounded. Taking her by the hand, I spun her in a 360. She had what must've been quadruple boobs. "Atlantis Broussard?"

Slowly she nodded.

My heart raced. I held on to her left hand. "You married yet?"

AB. That was what I used to call her. She was flat everywhere when we were in the twelfth grade. She'd rounded out nicely. Now the only thing flat on her was her stomach. Spinning her around again, I bit my bottom lip. Blitz, that nigga was right. Atlantis looked incredible.

"Engaged," she answered, seeming all happy and shit.

Blitz had talked her up. Or had that nigga sent her here? No way he could've found out about my secret sails. Nor could he cozy up to this right here. Hell, I might have to use my old-school charm on AB.

Atlantis continued with, "To him."

No fucking way my competition was about to ball-and-chain my favorite female. Staring deep into her eyes, I spoke what I felt in my heart. "Don't marry that nigga. Let me change that."

Atlantis knew I was a freak but I prayed she hadn't seen Southern Belle give me those three licks and that she wasn't about to walk down that aisle with my competitor. That homey was a straight nerd. Atlantis was here. That meant she was searching for something. Looking for me. I'd hoped.

Hearing Atlantis say, "François Trymm Dupree, I still love you" made my dick hard as a fucking rock.

Waving her palm face-up, she added, "But this is why we could never be."

The mission could not be aborted. I placed Atlantis's hand in BobbyRay's, then told him, "Take excellent care of my future wife."

As I headed belowdecks, Clydesdale was the true super-stud. Women gasped watching him crawl past my belly button. Stood in line to touch my dick to see if it was real. Examined it like they had credentials.

A porn-type chick set the bar by announcing, "If you can't make the whole dick fit, you gotta suck, suck, pass!"

The relay was nonstop until we docked. Long as they kissed, licked, or rode (successfully or not), I was the victor.

Witnessing the number of sexually deprived women drinking and partying in their birthday suits was astronomical. Two muthafuckin' thumbs-up to all the homies that left their hot, juicy, pulsating pussy on pause just so they could bang another bitch.

Trymm got your wife, bruh. Once I spank her with this colossal, she might leave you, homey. And don't come crying or bitchin' to me, bitch. Just remember where you busted your last nut, nigga.

CHAPTER 7

Trymm

Day 9

Needless to say, I never made it to number 301, after Atlantis stayed isolated by BobbyRay. A text from Kandy registered, **Back in town. Wanna meet up?**

Kandy? Right? was my response. Although I'd removed the video of her this morning, there was no way in hell she hadn't seen or, at a minimum, heard about a tape going viral of a woman French-kissing a man's asshole.

Locking the door to the office, I booted up my iPad. My homey had downloaded all the footage from my three voyages last weekend. I'd created four social pages with a white horse profile pic and named them all Clydesdale2930.

Kandy's dude was more than likely a spitting personality of me living that "Mind of a Man" life Usher sang about, which meant I'd probably done him a favor exposing his wife. Who gave a fuck if he saw it? If I knew him, I'd direct message that nigga on the strength.

None of the crewe specified our face had to be shown. I edited out my frame from the neck up, and blurred the females boarding in background. All that was left was Southern Belle's face and Clydesdale hanging out of her mouth. Soon as I posted ole gurl, the one who had to lead the group, I looped her video.

I pressed ENTER. Posted three more times, DM the link to my homies. Instantly my cell blew up and after answering one call, I was in the mix of a conference with Kohl, Dallas, and Blitz.

Francine messaged me, **See you later?**

"I'm on speaker? Y'all best not be at the Trolley Stop," I said, shutting down my iPad.

Dallas replied, "Ain't nobody called you 'cause Walter supposedly had you on that short leash. Otherwise, you woulda been posting all day, every. What the hell you sent us?"

Blitz chimed in, "Yeah, bring your ass over to Jax now so we see what else you got."

"We outside," Kohl added.

"On my way," I said, putting my computer in the drawer.

On second thought I took it with me, but I wasn't showing my hand. Best to put Francine on pause until the challenge was over. I texted Atlantis, **When can you steal away?**

Found out that Atlantis had let her fiancé move in with her. That told me he was a bullshit nigga that couldn't rub his coins together. Had to balance getting back to bangin' and courting my one-and-only true love. More like persuading her to call off her lame-ass engagement.

Wiping down the bar, I was sure to intimidate my homies if I told them my count. "Sis, cover for me. I need a lunch break. Be back in an hour," I told Penny.

"Thanks to you, Walter is watching our every move. Don't mess up because it's the weekend, Trymm. You been doing great all week. Even Walter said so. And don't forget we're closing all locations early for the family meeting at Mom's to finalize the details for the anniversary party."

Hmm. Hope at the party, in front of the fam, Walter doesn't bring up my proposing to Francine. He needed to let that go. "Cool." Probably an executive decision by you-know-who, to discuss the deets of what was obviously no longer under wraps but I had to ask, "What happened to it being a surprise?" Before I got a response, six new customers walked in. Penny rolled her eyes at me, greeted them.

What did that mean? Glancing over my shoulder, I hesitated to walk away, stared at Penny, then exited. She could handle it. I wasn't looking forward to seeing the rest of my siblings later. Did a light jog eight blocks to Jax Brewery on the river.

Blitz greeted me, "Nigga, you cold-blooded, my brother."

"Thanks for the reconnect," I told Blitz. "AB is back in my starting lineup."

Blitz nodded as Dallas said, "Trymm's ass always been the most scandalous. I got something for y'all tomorrow."

"Y'all are clueless. I have to make tracks to confession after all I've done," I said, sitting at the outdoor table with the fellas.

They all laughed as I placed my iPad in front of me.

"C'mon, dude. 'Clydesdale'?" Kohl replied.

"Don't forget the '2930,'" Dallas commented.

"You know a nigga that's bigga, homies?" I asked proudly. "Y'all betta shut up and catch up." I stroked my chin, tapped my tablet. "If I told you my official smashdown that's right here, you'd think I was lying."

"I'm from Missouri," Blitz said. "You gotta show me."

The waitress asked me, "What would you like to drink?"

The crewe each had five beer shots lined up on wooden planks. "I'm good. Can't stay long."

Dallas drained a shot down his throat. "Bring him what I have," he insisted. "Man, this challenge opened my eyes to how small this city is. After the festival's randoms scattered, all that's left are chicks I've ran through already."

I smiled. "New faces require new places, D. What's up with you, Kohl?"

Smiling back, he said, "Ain't never a shortage of big gurls in the South. I feed 'em, then fuck 'em, and if they let me fuck 'em first, they're screwed."

"Gimme some," Dallas said, slapping Kohl's hand.

A text registered from Atlantis: **I'm available now. We need to talk about last Sunday.**

"What about you, Blitz?" Dallas inquired what I had been thinking.

He answered, "Ain't none of y'all threw out a number. You can fuck bitches in your dream, and never catch up to me. Bet."

On that note I replied to Atlantis, **Headed to a family meeting. Will hit you when I'm done.**

Glancing at the crewe, I let 'em know, "Lunch. Noon. Saturday. Right here. Outside patio, so we can check in for real, ya heard me."

The waitress brought my flight. I tossed them back one after the other. Burped. Stood. "Oh, and save the date. My parents' fiftieth anniversary party is July thirty-first, and I expect each of you to show some respect."

The crewe stared at one another. Blitz shrugged, then said, "That's the day we have to vet and determine the winner? I can't make that promise. You might wanna push the date back, my brother, 'cause if you a no-show. No dough."

"Blitz, that ain't right," Kohl said.

"No, Trymm ain't right," Dallas countered. "I can tell you now. The thought of being one pussy short of winning, I'm going to fuck until midnight, then I'm sleeping until noon, then I want my money. I'm not going to be there."

"Yeah, I'll send my love and gift," Kohl added.

"Fuck all y'all losers. If I never bang another chick, I already got this." Picking up my iPad, I left.

Seemed like those niggas were up to no muthafuckin' good.

CHAPTER 8

Trymm

Day 9

Returning to the restaurant, Penny had already locked up and was gone. I doubled-checked to make sure everything was secured, then headed to my parents' house.

Ten cars were lined up in their circular driveway in Carrollton. That was one too many. *What is Francine's ride doing here?* I parked at the very end of the crescent entry, put my computer in the glove box, then trotted up the paved stretch.

The lawn was a healthy dark green. The huge oak tree, over a hundred years old, was one I'd played under growing up. I wasn't a fan of any residence on a plantation, but my dad wanted to own a mansion his ancestors were not allowed to step foot in.

"Hi, Mom." I kissed her cheek. Hugged my father. "Hi, Dad."

Everyone was gathered at the formal dinner table. Immediately I noticed there were two empty seats instead of one, both opposite Walter. I'd seen her car, but where was she? I sat by Donald Jr., who was a year older than me.

According to my parents, he was supposed to be their last Dupree.

Copping a squat, I was ready to dig into the red beans and rice, jambalaya, mac'n'cheese, fried chicken, and collard greens. Two doberge cakes decorated opposite ends the mahogany Victorian. This was the point where Mom would have us hold hands, and Dad would bless the table.

Everyone was unusually quiet with their eyes fixated on me.

Wham! A fist jabbed my face. My blood splashed on DJ. I grabbed my mouth, stared at Walter.

"What the hell you do that for?!" I said, but no one else spoke a word.

DJ wiped his face, placed his napkin, which had my blood on it, across his lap. Francine entered, sat next to Walter. *Fuck this!* I stood.

"Sit you ass down," Walter demanded.

I didn't say shit. Did as he'd told me. My lips were tight. I wiped my face with my napkin. Better Walter knock me upside my head than for my dad to lay me out. Whatever the fuck was going on, I wanted it out and over.

No one spoke until our father said, "François."

Immediately I responded, "Yes, sir."

"You know how hard I've worked to build the Dupree legacy for my kids, grands, great-grands, and all the rest that are to come, including yours with Francine."

"Yes, sir," I answered, cutting my eyes in the opposite direction toward Francine.

She shook her head, but I swore she'd best not be carrying my child.

"I don't think you do. What's all this talk around town about you disrespecting boatloads of naked women?" he asked.

There was no justification for the game. I never considered how my actions might adversely impact my family. Gazing at Mom's famous crawfish pasta, I apologized to my mother, sisters, brothers, and my dad. "It won't happen again." Curious how they'd found out, I stared at Francine, then at Penny. Francine could be a stalker at times. Penny was the only one with the code to my safe. My sister shook her head. Francine didn't do shit.

"'Clydesdale2930,' huh?" Whenever our dad lowered his voice, he was furious. "You know what's next."

"Yes, sir." What I had coming was worse than any ass whuppin' I'd ever had.

Whenever any of us tarnished the family's name (in any kind of way), we all voted on whether or not the person at fault would remain a shareholder of Dupree Seafood Restaurants. DJ had bought his wife a $100,000 BMW in the company's name, and with company money, without getting prior permission. Penny had paid for her daughter's, and her daughter's friends', tour of Europe, but didn't re-imburse the family's account. Walter had a baby out of wedlock and he bought his side chick and kid a house. This was my first misappropriation. The withdrawal of funds I'd made was from our restaurant's line of credit, which I was depositing back in about three weeks with interest.

The family had unanimously voted to allow DJ, Penny, and Walter to maintain ownership. As a first-time offender, I believed I deserved the same consideration.

Dad voted, "The level of disrespect I saw to that young lady licking you was beyond my imagination. Probably some stuff you picked up overseas while playing profes-sional basketball. Since it's your first offense, I say, 'in.'"

She was no lady, in my opinion. If she were, she wouldn't have been on her knees voluntarily sucking my dick. She was a cheating, married whore.

Mom voted, "What you did is a disgrace to all women and our ancestors. Unequivocally, you're 'out,'" she said.

Youngest to eldest began to vote. After everyone had

spoken, the count was five out. Five in. Walter had the final say. A tie was the same as a hung jury and I'd remain an owner. Once forgiven, no one could bring up the same situation. I couldn't be mad at any of my family members. Nor were we allowed to hang our head in shame. Dad didn't play that.

I lowered my eyes, stared at the pasta.

If Walter voted me out, I'd have to work off every dime doing janitorial duty at all the restaurants, or I'd need to win the "date, dick, and dump" challenge for real to repay my debt to the family. If I lost, the crewe wouldn't care. I'd have to contact my agent to see if he could get me back into a foreign league and leave the country.

If Walter voted me in, I still had to win because if Mom found out about the bet, she was the only person with veto power. Didn't want to be the first.

"Walter, it's time for you to vote, so we can eat," Mom said.

Penélope stared at me with tears in her eyes. "I love you, François."

Bet that promissory note I'd signed was in her safe. She couldn't vote against me and not risk exposing her involvement. I loved her more.

"Penny," Mother demanded. "Quiet."

"Yes, ma'am," Penny answered as tears streamed down her cheeks.

Walter placed a black box on my empty plate. "I'm going to let you decide if you're in or out. Diminish the shame you've brought on our family's name. Propose to and immediately marry Francine. And you're in."

I glanced around, fearing our pastor would appear from the back, the way Francine had, if I agreed. "'Immediately'?"

"You heard me. File for your license Monday, the seventy-two-hour wait period will be met by Thursday, pick up your certificate, and Saturday y'all will marry here. It's all arranged," he said.

Dad asked, "What's it going to be, son?"

I wanted to snatch Francine by her braided ponytail and choke that bitch with it.

For the first time since I'd met her, I hated her ass.

CHAPTER 9

Francine

Day 11

Wiggling the fingers on my left hand, I told Rene, "You're looking at the new, soon-to-be Mrs. François Dupree." The corners of my lips spread as far as I could stretch them. My face started hurting. Holding my smile, I didn't care if my cheeks went numb.

Finally I could prove all the naysayers wrong. Trymm had done a bad thing. I realized that. But he hadn't raped anyone or gotten somebody pregnant. Walter acted as though his illegitimate daughter didn't have a different mother.

Closing her office door, Rene said, "You're kidding me, right? After what he posted on social media a week ago, you're going to marry that . . . that scumbag."

Standing face-to-face, I told her, "Love is blind, and your husband isn't perfect. Name one guy in this city that we know who hasn't cheated on his woman. You don't talk about your husband's affairs, but he does his dirt, too."

"Bitch, don't you ever let anything come out of your

mouth about my husband or my kids. Fuck this job and our friendship, I will beat your ass royally."

Stepping back, I'd never seen her that upset. I wasn't afraid of Rene. What I'd said was true. But at least her husband respected her. "Dang, sorry." I slid a stack of magazines across her maple desk, then placed my thigh on the edge, and planted my stiletto on the floor.

"Damn right you sorry." She sat behind her organized papers. Without looking at me, she said, "I apologize. I didn't mean that. But Trymm is up to something. You'd better pray it's not illegal. Give me the deets on how he proposed."

What difference did that make? She wasn't happy I was engaged. If I shared that my man hadn't formally proposed, she'd feel justified in putting down my fiancé. I knew I could get another man, but he'd probably cheat on me, too, and there was no guarantee he'd be good in bed or financially stable.

The reason I'd told Rene first was: "I want you to be my matron of honor. The wedding is Saturday."

She released the documents in her hand. They floated to the floor. "What the hell, Francine? Saturday?"

"This Saturday," I confirmed.

Rene leaned back in her leather chair, folded her arms, swiveled. "As your friend, I won't do that to or for you. Trymm is a womanizer. You're stuck on that gigantic dick, that millions of women, and now men, all over the world have seen."

Not that many. "Trymm said it wasn't him in that video."

"Lawdy, Jesus. Are all of the liars and sexual abusers taking denial pills? You can't seriously believe it wasn't him. I'ma pray for you for real. You think if a video of your vagina went viral, he'd stay with you?"

I stood, placed my hands on her desk, got closer to her. "You're taking this too damn far, Rene! No one accused

Trymm of a criminal act. I did not meet François yesterday. He's played professional ball all around the world.
Met all types of women. Marriage is for better or worse."
I bet if I was miserable and single, Rene would be my
friend. Now that Trymm put a ring on my finger, she was
hating. "Don't forget who gave you this job. I've always
been there for you."

There was nothing I could do to undo the video.
Trymm said it wasn't him. I knew it was, but I was marrying more than the man. The entire Dupree family had
accepted me. I didn't trap Trymm with a baby. We had
one abortion that no one knew about. I never gave him an
ultimatum to make me his wife or left him when he
needed a break.

I held up my hand, admired my three-carat engagement ring, which Walter let me pick out. "Mrs. François
Dupree."

"You, my friend, are stooping to a new low. Don't
come running to me when he beats your ass."

Was that supposed to scare me? Or was that what she
wanted him to do to me to prove she was right? "François
has never laid hands on me, and you know it. Why would
you say such a horrible thing?"

I gazed at the framed picture on the wall. Rene, her
husband, and children's smiles were bright.

Click. Click. Click. Click. Pinky to pointing, Rene repeatedly tapped eight nails against the desktop. "You
don't get it. He doesn't have to physically abuse you.
Mentally, you are brainwashed. That's worse. He controls
you, Francine."

No, he did not. I stayed with my man by choice. I
loved him. Was tired of justifying my love. If I were ever
to leave Trymm, which I wouldn't, it would be my decision, not Rene's. Was her husband better because he covered his shit with dirt like a dog?

"None of the Dupree men divorce their wives. That's what Walter said," I explained. "Marital security is what I want."

"Oh, I see. Walter said so. Well, there's a first time for everything. This is a good time to give you this," she said, handing me a printout. "This is my two weeks' resignation and . . ."

"Rene, no. I apologize. I didn't mean to offend you," I pleaded, staring at the paper. Pacing the word SAINTS on the area rug, I told her, "You don't have to agree with my decision. I just want you to be happy for me." I put the page from the bottom on top.

"How can I, when you're not happy with yourself? I'm tired of your drama."

I read in disbelief. "General manager?" I re-read it. "They offered you the position over all the hotels in our region?"

She'd go from a one-hundred-square-foot space with no window to an office at corporate big enough for a conference table. Maybe a corner office with a view.

Rene stood for the first time since she'd sat down. "They . . . didn't *give* it to me. I know my worth. That and, I learned from the best. I earned a job you should've had."

"Congratulations." I meant that. Soon Rene would become my boss. "I have one question."

"I'm listening." Her feet were on the first capital *s*. Mine on the last.

Standing face-to-face, I asked, "Who makes you happier? Your husband? Or your kids?"

Quietly I exited her office before she answered. Trymm may not love me unconditionally, but I knew our kids would.

CHAPTER 10

Trymm

Day 13

Not my ring. Never going to be my wife. Who in the fuck does that arranged-marriage bullshit in America? Not blacks, for sho.

Walter acted as though Mom and Dad had a terminal disease and both were going to die waiting on me to take a wife then get her pregnant.

Placing my phone on speaker, I called Atlantis.

She answered with the sweetest "Hello."

"Hey, AB. This is Trymm." I wiped off the bar.

Hurricanes, Atomic Bombs, Fishbowls, Crash and Burns, none of that was stuck to the counter the way it was two weeks ago. This was one slow, quiet hump day. I turned the eight stools at an angle facing in the same direction, toward the door.

"I do have caller ID. And I see some things really don't change," she said. "I don't have time for your boyish mentality, Trymm. Bye."

"Wait. Don't hang up. I really need to see you," I begged. "You are the only one who gets me."

Penny came from the stock room. "Need anything before I leave?"

Hit MUTE, told my sis, "Go ride your husband's dick. Wanna see you bouncing off the walls full of energy in the morning."

My sister wiggled her butt. I smiled, watched her dance out the door.

Atlantis had no idea all I'd gone through. I needed to be with someone who loved me *for me*. She always took care of me. Not in the motherly way like Francine. Needed that, too. Atlantis knew how to make me feel like a man.

"Your dick went viral on social media all down some woman's throat and you need to see me? After leaving me in hemmed up with BobbyRay while you were fucking all those females on the yacht! That's a new low, man. Explain that shit!" Atlantis became quiet.

I was hoping she'd cry. That would let me know she was hurting and I could console her. If she cursed me out, that was okay, too. Anger meant she wanted my undivided attention. What I didn't want her to do was start talking to me like she was a dude and I was her bitch. That would signify she really didn't give a fuck about me anymore.

I turned chairs upside down at six tables, placed them legs up, seat down on top. Swept the floor, wall-to-wall. Business was slow. I didn't feel we needed to remain open another two hours.

The worst thing was to give a woman time to think. "They paid me to host that cruise. I was their guest. They weren't mine. It was like one of those wine classes where people paint. I was . . . a model. They were into each other. Don't act like you're innocent. For real, though. That wasn't me online. My boys were playing a joke. Blitz was probably the ring leader. You know how they

are. Honestly, I'm more pissed than you could ever be."
Crossed my fingers. A similar lie had worked on Francine.

"Y'all about to turn thirty and acting like none of you
graduated college. Y'all need to grow the hell up."

I didn't want to grow up. Not if it meant having access
to one pussy for the rest of my life. "I agree, baby. I was
hoping I could see my best friend after I close at midnight. Café Du Monde? Like we used to hang back in the
day? Make us a playlist with our favorite songs." I upped
my charm, hit her with my sexy, low voice. "Leave them
panties off and wear your hair down."

"I got that peach lip gloss, my *friend,*" she said.

"Not the peach. That's my girl. And I got your *friend.*
Seriously, AB. I hear you, but we need to discuss getting
back together. You are my soul mate." That was true.

A text registered from Kandy: **In town. Need to see
you, François Dupree.**

Biggest mistake was uploading Kandy French-kissing
my asshole and riding my dick. Her smart-ass mouth got
that behind posted to my pages soon as she'd left my
villa. Now I couldn't get her off my jock.

Say hello to your husband for me was my reply. A
call from Kandy showed on my screen. I declined.

No bitch could outsmart François Dupree. Her ass was
easy. That was her fault. She texted again.

Hit her with a canned response, **Busy. Can't talk.**

"I'll let you know if I can get away from my fiancé."
Atlantis's tone was melancholy.

Damn, I was only distracted for two seconds. A minute
ago she'd perked up. "I take that as a yes. Thanks, babe."
I ended the call with AB. Sent Kandy's next call to voice
mail. Flipped the remaining chairs. Now that I had a
chance to get with Atlantis, I could show Walter that my
path to the altar was on the right course.

I should've never bought Francine a piece of ice I
couldn't take back. Black men invested in jewelry we

could return, in case she said no, in case we changed our mind. Smart dudes get their diamonds from Costco, just in case they needed the cash or credit back on their card. Might bless Atlantis with my cube, if I can slide that joker's off her finger.

A cute petite sistah strutted in wearing a peach romper, large gold hoop earrings, and flat sandals covered with colorful gemstones.

"Give me a double Atomic Bomb," she said, sitting at the bar. "I'm about to get faded to the tenth power in an hour. Ya feel me?" She pumped her palms in the air. Blue-chrome coffin nails an inch long scraped her short dark hair into a wavy pattern.

Happy to see her wedding band, I placed two single cocktails in front of her. "What brings you to New Orleans?"

"Man, I live here. What you mean is what led to my sitting at a bar at . . ." She checked her watch, held the basketball-sized drinks, one in each hand, then alternated sucking down her drinks.

Damn! "You need to slow down, shorty. It's the middle of the week and we're closing in exactly one hour. Chill for a sec. Let me help this customer right quick." I sidestepped two stools over. I could tell shorty was easy. Suck it up, gurl! I was bending shorty over my desk in less than sixty minutes.

Nawlins wasn't like most cities. One could always find a place that served alcohol twenty-fo–seven. People walked the gritty streets with fishbowls filled with liquor that came with a $5 refill. If shorty passed out on the sidewalk, she'd get stepped on, over, but no one was picking her lil ass up. She'd have to sleep that shit off and pray the cockroaches, dragonflies, and rats didn't snack on dat pretty ass of hers.

"What can I get you to drink?" I asked the new guy.

Tapping on his phone, he said, "Let me have a po'boy.

Half and half, shrimp and oysters. Oysters fried hard, man."

I followed with, "You want that dressed?"

"What?" he said, looking up at me while still holding his cell.

Shorty jumped in with a quickness. "You want lettuce, tomatoes, pickles, mayo, and ketchup on your po'boy?"

He laughed at her. Licked his lips. "Yeah, I want all of that lil baller, and you, too. Whatever she wants, man, is on me."

Shorty didn't hesitate to move over a seat. Her cocktails made it first. "Seafood platter."

Dude interrupted my stroke count, but I couldn't be mad at him. Shorty was bad. I heard her say, "My husband think he did something by staying out all weekend at Essence Fest. He won't see *me* until I feel like walking through the door."

Did that mean she was MIA for damn near ten days straight? I glanced at the most recent family photo hanging on the brick wall of Mom, Dad, all of my siblings and their spouses. Then there was me, without Francine. The same picture hung in all our restaurants. Walter was probably set to have a replacement taken at the anniversary party.

"I'm in town for the next two days," dude said. "You want to get down and show me around? You'll never touch your wallet."

Sad, but true. A lot of females in the Big Easy hadn't been anywhere outside of New Orleans. True what Kohl always said, their pussy could be bartered for a lot less than a po'boy and two Atomic Bombs.

I had to rush the lingering guests along. Our policy of not putting diners out was not in effect tonight. Sticking my head across the threshold into the kitchen, I said, "I need—"

"Already gotcha, boss," my cook said.

Stepping out back by the Dumpsters, I hit up BobbyRay.

"Hey, Trymm, what's up? Boy, people still talking about your wild ass."

Like he wasn't there. "Man, I need you to fire up the triple decker, load it with babes just like the last times, but this round I want two hundred."

"You've got to be kidding," BobbyRay said, laughing. "Those women would throw your ass overboard and me right along with you."

I got quiet. Gave his ass a moment to marinate.

"Cool. Can't guarantee that many females, but I'll try."

"Set it up for July thirtieth. Sunset. Oh, and the only recordable devices allowed on deck is mine and yours. Charge it to the same card. Send the contract first."

No way any of the crewe could top five hundred. This would be my final and I wasn't posting shit until the last day. Dipping back in, I resumed multitasking while helping my two customers. Prepared to smash a home run the final weekend of the month made me relax a little.

A text and video came from my Scottish friend, Alex: **I couldn't wait, François.** Scottish had popped the big question and his quirky girlfriend accepted.

Looking at the bar in disbelief, I did a double take, shook my head.

Atlantis and Francine were seated next to one another. I approached Francine from behind. She turned around, smiled, gave me a hug. I hugged her tight, whispered in her ear, "You need to get your ass up and outta here. *Now.*"

Francine stared in my face like I was a damn ghost. I kissed Atlantis on the cheek, then escorted Francine out the door. We stood on the curb.

"You fucking her again? That's why I have to leave?" she questioned with trepidation in her eyes. "I came to tell you I got our certificate."

The ink wasn't dry and Francine was using profanity. I did not have time for this stupidity. "You know what." I shook my head. "*I* have to decide if your last name deserves to be Dupree. I don't think it's me you want. You fucking Walter?"

"Stop being silly. I'm hungry. I'm going to order a bite to eat," she said, trying to reenter the restaurant.

I grabbed her biceps. "Stop coming here without prior permission." I was serious. Had to squash her thinking that damn ring had superpowers.

"You are fucking her!" Francine shouted, loud enough for Atlantis to turn around.

But Atlantis did not look in our direction.

"This ain't your first rodeo. Won't be your last," I told her. "We're on break until the ceremony."

"But we just came off of break, Trymm. I don't want another one."

"Bitch, I'm not asking. Get the hell away from here," I said, then went inside.

Atlantis asked, "Why you treat that girl so bad?"

"She treats herself worse than I ever could." Francine was hanging on to opportunity, not love.

I gave Atlantis a kiss. "Glad you made it. Chill until I close up. You hungry? Want something to drink?"

Everybody was looking for something, including Atlantis.

CHAPTER 11

Trymm

Day 13

Hugging Atlantis over her shoulders, I wasn't sure which was hotter: the mid-July humidity invading every cell of my skin, or the yearning in my soul? No doubt I wanted to fuck Atlantis, hear her scream my name, then call out Jesus' name.

We strolled through the French Quarter, holding hands. If I had to be exclusive, this was the one-and-only woman that could make me come close. Atlantis was not getting away this time.

"Damn." I whispered toward her ear, "You look and smell good, baby." Not wanting to let this moment go, I stopped, pressed my stomach against her breasts. She laid the side of her face on my chest. Felt my dick hardening.

"We should get to Café Du Monde. I have to be home at a decent hour," she said.

Fuck that lame laid up at her spot. It was twelve-thirty and we were just getting started. In New Orleans decent varied from sunset to sunrise.

"Why do you do it?" she asked.

"What?" I was not attempting to read her mind.

"Disrespect Francine. That woman on the boat. Me—" she said.

I was cool with it until she added her name to the list. "Nah, see that's where you're wrong. You're different. I've *always* loved and been *in love* with you." That was my truth.

"You're *in love* with me? Right now?" she wanted to know.

I scratched my brow. "Yes. And yes. I love you. So much." What I was about to confess—"I want you to call off your engagement"—was real. I wasn't ready to become any woman's husband, but I sure as hell didn't want Atlantis to take herself off the market by marrying dude or fuck Blitz to get back at me for the cruise.

As I pulled out her chair at the café, the wrought iron scraped atop a thick layer of powdered sugar that coated the concrete patio.

"Come here," I said.

Atlantis leaned in my arms, glanced up at the stars.

She was that Nicki Minaj, Kim Kardashian, Amber Rose kinda fine that men lusted for. If Atlantis wanted, she could easily top those wannabe IG models. She had that long, straight, black Indian natural hair that chicks in the NOLA couldn't afford. Every strand was hers. She was blessed with a perfect smile, all of her teeth, and pretty pink lips. Both sets, I recalled.

The finest woman in the world couldn't keep a man from cheating. But I would always keep Atlantis first. That was fair.

I sniffed her hair. She had on one of those sexy white dresses I'd seen in lots of gift shop windows downtown. A saxophone covered in rhinestones, the shiny mouthpiece separated her titties, the lower keys wedged right where I wanted to lick.

"We'll have two orders of beignets and two cafés au lait," I told the waiter. I desperately desired to taste her sweetness. Tilting her chin, I opened my mouth, let my tongue dance with hers.

"You remember how we used to cut class, come here, eat, and chill?" she asked, stroking my thigh.

Staring into the light of her beautiful brown eyes, I nodded. "What do you see in him?"

"Who?"

I held her left hand, fingered her ring. *"Him?"*

"He loves me."

"Does he love you more than you love him?" If that were true for Kandy, that would explain why she was back on the prowl chasing my "d."

She nodded. "And he respects me."

If respect was a prerequisite to marriage, nine out of ten single women could forget about changing their last name. I rubbed Atlantis's hair. "He can never love you the way I do."

"From the ninth ward, third, Hollygrove, uptown, downtown, the French Quarter, back-a-town, Carrollton, the East, Eastover, Gentilly, the Garden District—"

Interrupting her, I asked, "Man, where are you taking me with this?"

"Too many females done rode your wild horse. Be honest. You have zero consideration for who you stick your dick in."

Could argue the fairness of it all. Most of the times women were the aggressors. Wasn't defending myself against her insecurities. *Give me another kiss.*

"I love you the most." That was the truth, too.

"More than my fiancé? Maybe. More than I love you?" She shook her leg the way she used to whenever she caught feelings she didn't want to release. "I can't trade places with Francine. How long she been hanging in there? Eight? Nine? Ten years?" Atlantis said, wedging our hands between her moist thighs the way she did when we were teenagers.

"Whatever you want, I'll do," I said, putting her hand on my erection.

"For old times' sake, all I need from you is a good lickin' and great penetration."

With that said I placed a twenty on the table, stood, knowing once she creamed on my shit, it'd be like old times; and before she knew it, she'd be blowin' up my cell with texts, calls, and voice mails. Memories flooded my mind. *Damn, I'm a dog.*

Holding hands, we strolled along Decatur, stopped, kissed like two kids in heat. She put her tongue in my mouth. I put mine in hers. She sucked. I slurped. Pushing, pulling, swerving, more sucking, I couldn't get enough of her sweetness. AB reminded me how passionate our kisses were.

If I were in this moment for personal gain, like with Kandy and Southern Belle, I would not—nor would I want to—kiss Atlantis in the mouth. Intimacy was reserved for the women I genuinely gave a fuck about.

I scooped Atlantis in my arms, swung her around, then carried her off to a dimly lit area by the stairway near Jax Brewery. We continued to laugh and play as though we were a happily married couple.

She snatched my neck, pulled me to her. This time she kissed me with her eyes open. Whenever she did that, it was her signal that she wanted me to take her. It was on!

I refused to waste a second. "Let's go."

"I miss this kind of love," she said. "I don't want to wait until we get to your place."

"What are you saying?" My dick and tongue got hard.

I knew damn well what she meant. Had to make certain she wasn't on that "fuck me, fuck me not" roller coaster some bitches teased with, leaving me with blue balls.

"Take me down to the riverfront and make love to me until the sun comes up," she said, removing my shirt.

Guess that need to get home dissipated.

I found a deserted location on the other side of the train tracks, where water splashed underneath a pier. The moonlight cast shadows upon our bodies.

"I want to see you completely naked," I said. Lifting the hem of her dress, I eased it over her head, gripped her ass. Pressing my lips against her neck, I started sucking softly.

Atlantis blocked my mouth. "Don't do that, Trymm. We are together, but I'm not going home with your brand on me."

"Cool." Had to respect her, but I was tryin' to let her nigga know he had competition. I put my middle finger inside her pussy. *Damn! My baby is hot-n-juicy.*

Atlantis pulled my finger out. Blocked my next insertion. "Don't put your dirty-ass finger inside of me. Your dick is cleaner," she said, unfastening my pants.

True dat. Shit I never think about. I might've banged many a whores, but I kept Clydesdale in order. Decided letting her take the lead was best.

"Pick me up," she whispered.

I did.

"Put it in," she grunted.

I did.

Atlantis braced her forearms on my shoulders, raised herself almost to a stance.

Holding her, I asked, "What's wrong?"

"Nothing. I forgot how big you are, that's all." She laughed out loud.

"Be quiet, woman." I flipped her facedown as I interlocked my fingers under her stomach; she held on to the rail. "Relax, I got you."

"You crazy, Trymm," she yelped.

"Shh, before someone hears us," I said, putting her down. My dick was rock solid. I hadn't felt this pussy since high school.

"It'll be easier for you to hit it doggie-style," Atlantis whispered, bending over, spreading her cheeks.

I was six-nine. She was five-eight. *Fuck it.* I took my best option. Stooping, I held those sexy hips, then told her, "Do your thang."

Atlantis started grinding on me. First a little. Then more. Her pussy was amazing. I stared up at the stars to keep from coming prematurely. My chocolate shaft was coated with her thick white secretions.

"Mmm," she moaned.

"Yes, baby. Take your dick. Get all of this dick," I said, making sure my feet were planted. "Leave him. I want—make that *need*—for you to call off your engagement. I love you, Atlantis."

"François," she exhaled.

"Yes, baby."

"François," she said a little louder.

"Yes, Atlantis," I answered, admiring the sweat rolling off her back.

Glancing over her shoulder at me, Atlantis moaned, "Come inside your pussy, daddy. Please." She pushed back on my dick until she couldn't take in any more. Staring into my eyes, she exhaled and said, "I'm coming home where I belong."

"Oh, shit." I felt her pussy walls rippling. My knees weakened. Foot slipped. Quickly I regrouped, strengthened my stance. Wanted to ask if she was serious. Couldn't say a word with her squirting on my knees.

"You coming?" she asked, facing the river.

Lifting her hips higher, I yelled like a bitch, "Aw, shit! Yes, baby. I'm coming!" Did not care who heard me. My toes curled in my shoes. Felt as though I'd never stop blasting seeds.

They said muscles had memory. Maybe that was why my dick never forgot how incredible her pussy was.

Had to pull out slowly, step cautiously. Atlantis started crying. This moment was amazing. My ego was in orbit.

A similar experience with any of the women on the yacht could've happened, but I wouldn't have kissed or wanted to see them again. The difference with my wanting an encore was that it was all about my feelings for the woman I came inside of.

In college I never got to know most women. My mottos were: Smash and dash. Come and done. Didn't know the majority of them by middle or last name. Couldn't remember half of their faces. Nor did I give a damn.

"Sorry, I squirted all over you," Atlantis said.

"Does he make you squirt?" I asked.

She shook her head. Truth or lie, instantly I was more in love.

"François Dupree," someone whispered.

Shit sounded eerie in the darkness of the night. I tossed Atlantis her dress, yanked up my pants. Protecting Atlantis, I stood in front of her.

Those words would've been cool if the woman my dick had come out of had said them.

Kandy started clapping. Loud and slow. "François Dupree," she repeated. Continuing to clap, she moved closer to me. "Congratulations."

Looking around, I refused to ask for what. I put on my shirt.

"You all right?" Atlantis asked, standing beside me. She fluffed her dress, fingered her hair, stared at Kandy. "Uh, who in the hell is that?"

"He knows exactly who I am, suga. And if neither of you want this sex video to get out"—she paused, smacked, then licked her lips real sexy—"I'll be in touch, François Dupree." Shaking her ass, Kandy slowly strolled along the Riverwalk in her high heels. She glanced over her shoulder. "Thought you'd like to know, my husband filed for divorce."

Atlantis started trembling. "Come back. I don't know what's going on, but you can't let what we did get out. You can't!"

A vision of Walter flashed before me. My mother. Father. Siblings. The video would up my count, but my black ass would have to move in with Atlantis and put her nigga on the couch.

"Don't just stand there," Atlantis said. "She's getting away."

Obviously, Kandy wanted me to chase her. I wanted to move, but refused. I had to outsmart Kandy with capital *k*.

"Until you do right by women," Kandy said, slowing her pace, "François, you're going straight to hell." She yelled, "You fucked up my good life!"

Atlantis did the unexpected. She ran toward Kandy.

"Baby, no," I called out. "Stop!"

"Awwwwww!" Atlantis screamed, then fell to the ground.

"Should've kept your bitch on a tighter leash," Kandy said. Holding up a Taser, she resumed her stride. Speaking out loud, Kandy added, "You might want to give me a call. You have until noon, François Dupree. Not twelve-o-one."

Looking at the ground, Atlantis was shaking like a leaf in the gust of a category-three hurricane.

Contacting Kandy was exactly what I was not going to do. But I swear, I never wanted to hear my full name come out of her mouth again.

"AB. I'm sorry baby. You okay?"

CHAPTER 12

Trymm

Day 17

I retrieved my passport, placed our marriage certificate on top of my iPad, which was inside the safe in my bedroom closet, closed the door, reset a new combination, then texted it to Penny. Didn't want to risk losing or relinquishing my iPad for any reason.

Life went on. Felt bad about what happened to Atlantis. Was unsettled not knowing the intentions of Kandy, with a capital *k*. Prayed she was done doing the fool and I wasn't next.

While my homies were tossing back brews at Jax yesterday, my black ass was standing at the altar facing Francine Dupree's happy ass. No apologies. I could never respect a spineless woman.

Walter had ruled out Jamaica, the DR, PR, Bahamas, convincing my mother to send us to Dubai. Mom's agreement—my blessing—was based on what she'd heard about how conservative Muslims in the United Arab Emirates were.

Plan B was to never let the cert become a license. In

twenty-nine more days, time would expire and the only way to make Walter's commitment legal would be for Francine and me to restart the marital process.

Fuck! More than halfway through the challenge and my count was frozen at 301. Would never add Atlantis. Hadn't contacted Kandy or heard from her since that bitch stunned my baby.

Sent a text to Atlantis: **Ole gurl is jealous of you. I took care of her ass. Gotta handle out-of-town biz for the fam. Be back in a week. Gotta see you to apologize properly.**

"Honey, we have to go before we miss our flight," Francine said joyfully. "We have to bring your parents back a thank-you gift for sponsoring our honeymoon." Picking up my bag, I said, "I'm ready," leading the way downstairs to the courtyard.

Francine put her suitcases in my trunk, then loaded mine. She couldn't stop smiling while I couldn't crack one. I did a 360-glance before getting in my GLS.

"I have to stop by the restaurant right quick," I said, waiting for her to close her door.

"Okay, honey, but remember we don't have much time. This flight is international and it says we have to arrive four hours prior to departure."

Bitch, shut the fuck up! She had it twisted if she suddenly thought I was going to be one of those henpecked muthafuckers. This was her first time going through customs. Not mine. I was used to long flights. Needed to improve my attitude if I was going to make it fourteen and a half hours from Fort Lauderdale to Dubai. Libation was going to be my salvation.

Parking in front of Dupree's Seafood, I entered the front, exited the back. Devising a new strategy to secure my position in the challenge, I trotted upstairs, then knocked three times on Alex's door.

"Hey, François." The tall, skinny Scottish man, with

red curly hair, lots of freckles, wearing black-framed glasses, cheerfully opened the door wide. "Is my music too loud?"

"Nah, it's not too loud. Listen, Alex, I need a huge favor."

I was here to negotiate leasing the one-bed, one-bath apartment from our tenant living above our restaurant and prepared to compensate him to stay at an Airbnb for the last week of the competition. That way I could escape on breaks, let a few chicks suck my dick, then return to work before Penny noticed I was missing.

"Lay it on me," he said real smooth.

"I have an old teammate coming in town for a week. He needs a place to crash until he finds a house, and I'd like him to crash at your spot."

"Thingy! Perfect timing. I'm flying to the Saints tomorrow with my lady. Virgin Islands hopping. Croix. Thomas. John. Then I'm taking her to Bora Bora. I'll be gone three weeks, man. Let me get you the spare key," he said.

This arrangement was meant to be. I was anxious to return from my honeymoon and get back into the game. I watched him open the cherrywood box on his coffee table. Smiling at me, he flipped up a white lid. A huge pink solitaire sparkled in my eyes, damn near blinding me.

This guy lived a modest lifestyle, despite the six figures he earned in his profession. The woman of his dreams was bland, dressed basic, loved life, people, fed the homeless, and I'd never seen her with any makeup, not even lipstick.

"You think she'll like this diamond for her wedding ring? I mean, is it big enough?" he asked.

"If she doesn't go berserk, ask me to marry you," I told him, nodding.

Snapping the box shut, he handed me a single key on a black-and-gold fleur-de-lis chain.

Bonk! Bonk! Bonk! My horn blew three sharp times.

My people loved them some Saints and that black-and-gold symbol. I did, too, but I doubted Louisianans understood what they were reppin'.

Celebration? Or degradation?

For me, I branded the fleur-de-lis on the left side of my back, next to my shoulder, to honor my ancestors who were branded with the symbol for trying to escape the whips, chains, and dying hours in the scorching sun picking cotton. If I was born a slave, I would've been a Nat Turner—*kill for freedom or die trying*—on some revolutionary shit. Fuck the Frenchmen that hung us from trees! And all the bullshit slave masters that brought their trifling ass to the Boot, enslaved and raped black women, then called the babies Creole, half-bred.

History. The movie *The Birth of a Nation* changed my mind-set forever.

"How much you want for the week?" I asked, clutching the fleur-de-lis in my palm, feeling as though it were my lucky charm.

Bonk! Bonk! Bonk! My horn blew.

"You know you're my American idol. Any baller friend of yours is all right. Who is it?" he questioned, smiling up at me.

His green-and-black plaid kilt, black knee-high socks, which flapped over, and white sleeveless buttoned-up shirt, which resembled a blouse, was representative of his heritage. He was an orthodontist, settled in New Orleans, not having any family or friends. Instantly we bonded. During the first of the five years he'd been in this small apartment, he'd met the nice, quirky, philanthropist girl, who played guitar and sang on stage at night in the Quarter.

Thought of the player Alex loved most, then lied, "LB."

Dude started jumping, dancing, and clicking his heels. "LB is going to stay in my place! Shitload, man!" He slapped my palm three times.

Perfect time to ask again, "How much you want?"

"Pssst." He waved his hand across his throat. "Your money is no good, but I'd love an autograph, and if it's not asking too much, two courtside tickets to see him play anywhere in the world. I don't care. I'm there." He disappeared. Reappeared. "Have him sign my basketball. I'll leave it on the bed so he doesn't forget. Shitload, man!"

"You got it. I'll get him to sign a team jersey, too. One that he's worn. I gotta go." I took one step, pivoted back to him. "Oh, keep this between us. Don't tell my sister, my dad, not even your lady. He's a real private person."

"You got it, François. You my homey."

I laughed. "Congrats on your upcoming ceremony," I said.

Bonk! Bonk! Bonk! My horn blew three sharp times.

That bitch had one more time to lean in and I was dropping her ass off at the airport.

"I love you, man," he said with one more click of his heels as a tear connected the dots on his cheek. Alex locked his door from the outside. "I gotta do a few errands before I take off in the morning."

"Cool." I trotted down the stairs, entered the restaurant through the back, crept up beside my sister. Penny was overseeing everything.

First she rolled her eyes at me, then shook her head. "Don't forget I voted you in. For once, be nice to Francine. It's her honeymoon."

If I stopped playing games, no longer dogged women out, and started being nice, women would hate me. The last thing I wanted was for women to hate me.

CHAPTER 13

Francine

Day 18

DXB.
"Baby, this is more beautiful than I imagined," I said, unable to contain my excitement. Wish Rene could see me now. Interlocking my fingers with François's, I finally had the title I'd longed for.

François slid his hand from mine. "You can't do that here. They'll arrest you."

"Arrest me? What for? You're my husband," I said, reaching for him.

He pulled away. "I'm serious. Don't touch me."

The nine-hour time difference from New Orleans, on top of the fourteen-and-a-half-hour flight from Fort Lauderdale, got us here at noon. Scanning the baggage claim area, I spotted one couple hugging. "What about them?" I knew it was okay to show affection if you were married. I'd read it somewhere online.

François mumbled, "Women. Y'all will search through a hundred muthafuckas to prove your point." Re-

trieving our luggage, he extended the handles, rolled my
bag to me. "Do not touch me."

"Whatever," I told him, rolling my eyes and my luggage. Let him tell it I'd get locked up for that.

Outside we got on a shuttle that took us to the Palm Islands. Pictures did not do it justice. Feeling the joy of
when I was a child, I stared at everything we passed.

BMW, Mercedes, Lamborghini, Rolls-Royce, Ferrari—fancy cars I hadn't seen in New Orleans were in
numbers I'd never seen, either. "This place is incredible.
Is everybody here wealthy?"

François was quiet. I wanted to hold my husband's
hand. Hated I couldn't share my affection on our honeymoon.

I unfolded a piece of paper. "We should go to all these
places." I flashed the map in his face, and he pushed it
away. "JBR is a beautiful area in Dubai with lots of
places where we can eat and shop late hours of the night.
I want to buy a hijab, an abaya, visit the mosque in Abu
Dhabi, shop at the souks in Sharjah, do a sunset dinner
cruise, go to the sand dunes, tour the World Market. Oh,
and I heard Rihanna is performing. Hopefully, we can get
tickets from the concierge. This is going to be the best
honeymoon, baby."

I was more anxious when the shuttle parked in front of
the Atlantis. I twirled between the huge gold columns,
danced under the skylight dome. Suddenly it hit me. Our
hotel shared her name.

François checked us in. I watched him remove and replace his SIM card.

"Where'd you get that? Do I need one, too?" I asked,
placing my phone on the counter.

"Absolutely not. In fact, Mrs. Dupree, you won't need
to use your cell while we're here. Give it to me. We will
both use mine," he insisted.

That was the first time he'd acknowledged me as his wife. "I'll hold on to it, just in case I receive any e-mails from my job."

Rene hadn't attended my wedding or responded to my messages. I'd give her time. I texted her a few pictures. Immediately, I received a failed response. I missed my friend.

"You can't communicate here without WiFi. Give it to me so I can set you up." François held open his hand.

"Fine. Let me see yours." This time I relinquished my device and took his.

While my husband chatted with the gentleman that had checked us in, I noticed his cell was unlocked, read his last text to Penny. I took a mental snapshot of the new code to his safe.

Snatching his cell, "I'll explain more when we get upstairs," my husband said, putting my phone in his back pocket.

When the baggage handler opened the door to our room, François entered first. I stood in the hallway waiting for him to carry me over the threshold. He and the handler left me there.

"Hello. Welcome to Dubai," the most attractive woman I'd seen since we'd touched down greeted my husband with an inviting smile.

Oh, hell no! I crept behind my man. "François, can we speak in private?"

"Take your time," the woman said, real sexy. "I'm available your entire stay."

The woman on her stomach in the middle of the bed propped herself on her elbows and rested her chin in her palm. Her red heels in the air pointed toward the ceiling. She crossed, then uncrossed, her legs repeatedly.

That woman needed to have on more than her panties and bra. And she needed to get out of our bed and out of our room.

"Sure, I'm listening," François said, leading the way to the bathroom. "I need to drain the snake."

I closed the door. He stood in front of the toilet, pulled out the dick I hadn't seen in weeks.

Folding my arms, I asked, demanding to know, "François, why is that woman here?"

"My mom made the reservation, not me. It's somewhat customary to have a . . . a—"

"I'm not stupid, François. She's a whore. Tell her to leave, before I do."

"Anything to please my wife." Shaking his dick, he tucked it away, washed his hands. "I'm warning you. You need to calm down. This is not America. These people will lock you up and deport you for being rude."

Opening the door, the baggage handler was putting our clothes in drawers.

I stared at François. He started talking to the handler.

I shouted at the woman crashing my honeymoon. "You need to leave. Now!" Inhaling, I released the loudest "Get! Out!"

The handler started repacking my bag. In less than sixty seconds, two security men entered our room and approached me. "You need to come with us."

François hunched his shoulders. He did not say a word in my defense.

In less than three hours in Dubai, I was on a plane headed to Fort Lauderdale, without my cell and without my husband. Gazing at the clouds for fifteen and a half hours, I pictured that woman seducing my husband. Tears streamed down my cheeks, one quickly chasing the other.

François warned me not to do what I'd done. I didn't believe him. I felt lost without my phone. Lonely without my man. Why hadn't I listened to my husband?

CHAPTER 14

Trymm

Day 23

Whew! I played that Dubai trip to a tee! Five days. Twenty-five babes. "Hey, son. Have a talk with your old man," my dad insisted, locking the front door. Dad turned off the front store neon signs, dimmed the interior lights, opened a fresh bottle of Jack Daniel's. Pop the top on a can of cola. "The only person you're fooling is yourself, son," he commented, filling two glasses with ice and liquor.

Wasn't expecting my old man to drop in. Glancing at the digital clock above the bar, I saw it was five minutes to seven on a Saturday morning. I had twenty minutes to spare before meeting up with Atlantis at my apartment. Her fiancé was out of town. I'd just gotten back and she was the first woman I wanted to see. I'd happily eat her pussy but my dick was in recovery. What I really wanted was to find out if she'd give me another chance.

Dad could be long-winded when determined to make a point. I texted Atlantis: **Having a heart-to-heart with my dad. I'll text you when we're done. XOXO.**

I knew women appreciated what I didn't give Francine, and that was communication. I'd do better with Atlantis, but Francine was salty about being deported, and I needed her to stay that way for eight more days.

"Fooling myself about what, Dad?" I asked. Sitting on the edge of a stool, I planted my forearm on the edge of the countertop.

Dad's timing was horrible. I knew he could tell I was anxious to be someplace else. Also, I knew he didn't give a damn.

Gingerly he said, "You're married now." He paused. "You proposed to Francine in front of the family." He leaned over his cocktail.

Was he not there? I was the middleman.

"It's time to give up the villa and buy your wife a house. Walter made you an appointment with a Realtor. Tomorrow."

What the fuck!

Dad eased a business card out of his pocket. Put it in my hand. Quinisha Ferguson.

Damn! She's hot! Needs her own show flipping properties.

"Your mother has arranged a special supper after you finish house shopping," he said, topping off our glasses. "Your mother and I want to live to see all of our children have children. You know this and you're the only one that hasn't contributed a baby to the Dupree legacy."

"Let Walter fuck Francine," I wanted to say.

I did not want Francine to have my last name, or my baby. If Francine were Atlantis, we would've been married with two or maybe three kids by now, living in a mansion, on St. Charles Avenue.

Seeing more of my dad's shadow than his face, I swallowed a sip and my nerves at the same time. "I care for Francine. I'm not *in love* with her," I confessed. "Dad, this was Walter's i—"

Dad shook his head. "Don't blame this on Walter. So why did you marry her?"

I couldn't disrespect my father. "Honestly, I didn't want you guys to disown me. I love and need my family to believe in me."

"Listen, son. The way you feel about Francine, I used to feel the same way about your mother." He drained the last drop of liquor, then cleared his throat.

A chocolate man, with no facial hair, with the exception of his brows, my dad could pass for fifty-five, although he was forty years older than me. Dad had what Southern people called *je ne sais quoi.*

Had I heard him right, though? I was confused. Thought my dad always loved and was *in love* with my mom. Refusing to dig in that gris-gris bag and stir the bones, I focused on me.

"I know Francine would do anything for me." And I meant *anything.*

That was how much Francine was in love with me. But it was no secret that I never felt the same. I loved the way Francine took care of me, put my needs ahead of hers, never cheated on me, even when I was overseas balling in the league, and every time we were on break. If she'd been a virgin when we met ten years ago, I'd swear I was her one and only.

Man-to-man, I needed my father's direction, so I confessed, "I'm in love with Atlantis," then texted Atlantis, **Let's do lunch.**

She replied, **Where? What time?**

I smiled.

"I know that," he replied, filling our glasses to the rim, this time tossing the empty bottle in the trash can behind the bar. "Let me tell you what I've told my other married sons. There's a right and wrong way to love your woman."

Keith Sweat's song came to mind.

Blitz hit me with, **Drago's. 1:00 p.m. Be there, nigga!**

Fuck! I messaged Atlantis, **Gotta reschedule. Stay posted. Things are hectic since I got back from Dubai.**

Dubai? she questioned.

From the alcohol, jetlag, and letting chicks from countless ethnicities suck my dick like a lollipop, exhaustion suddenly hit me. I was not acknowledging that.

Breakfast. Monday. Trolley Stop. Please, I told Atlantis.

"Son. Marriage is not about who you're in love with. Wise men marry once. The most intelligent, lifelong commitment a man can make to any woman is to the one he knows will always have his back and never abandon him. You fuck up one time too many with that Atlantis. Oh, I know she's a pretty lil thing. Beautiful girl. But she's the kind that will leave your black ass high and dry. Take everything you've got. And what you've got is what your mother helped me build for the family. Your marriage is bigger than you, François. That's why Duprees vote in every election. To protect our First Amendment, our assets, and our ass, son!"

His fist pounded the bar. I sat up straight.

"Duprees work for Duprees! Not the French or the white slave master's kids. We did something wise with our two hundred acres in Amite, Louisiana, that our ancestors handed down to us. We didn't sell like most black families did for a few thousand dollars. That land is Dupree land. Now that marijuana is being legalized, it's just a matter of time before the Boot gets the green light and we're ready to lease *our land.* But we will never sell it. That way the Duprees will always have our own. We have a line of credit that we do not use frivolously. Got it?"

Now I got it. I nodded. I thought about the certificate locked in my safe. My being Francine's husband still didn't feel right.

Jiggling my keys, I wasn't going to need to use Alex's place, after all. Nor was I going to make good on my promise to have his basketball signed by LB. That was cool. I'd just leave everything in Alex's apartment untouched, tell him LB had a conflict in his schedule and couldn't make it. I had to perpetuate the lie.

Dad drained his glass. "You need to do what I told your sisters and brothers when they got married. 'Conduct your extracurricular activities behind closed doors, never sleep with the person next door, and never make a deposit where you can't make a withdrawal.' Like it or not, Francine is a Dupree for life."

Penny, Walt, DJ, and all the rest had situationships that my father knew about? I got it, but I didn't want to be *that* Dupree. I wanted to be different. I wanted to marry the woman I was crazy about and be forever faithful to her.

"Thanks, Dad. I get it." I wondered if my father had a secret love or was simply imparting wisdom.

There was no way I could continue working long hours and win the challenge. Wanting to confess about the $250,000 bet, instead I asked, "Can I get a week off to get my mind straight?"

"I gotta get outta here. Take two weeks. Oh, the other thing, son. Do your dirt during the day. As long as you're home for dinner, and don't give your wife a reason to distrust you . . . happy wife. See you guys tomorrow for dinner. Get four or five bedrooms," he said, patting me on the shoulder.

"One last thing, son. Lies begat lies. Put my money back. All of it."

CHAPTER 15

Trymm

Day 23

"**N**ig-ga, where you been?" Dallas asked. "Haven't seen or heard from you since Jax. Thought one of those chicks may have tied your dick in a knot," he said, laughing.

Dallas had stepped his threads up. Extreme opposite of his norm. Collared, buttoned-down, short-sleeved cerulean shirt. Matching slacks. A simple gold-link chain and diamond studs in each ear, like mine. Dark sunglasses. The tats on his neck appeared more intriguing, less thuggish.

See how long that lasts.

"You were a straight no-show for our head count last Saturday," Kohl said.

Kohl looked the same. Son of a preacher man. Tailored to perfection, sporting hard-sole shoes. Fresh shadow haircut. His light brown skin shined from what I recognized as a good facial.

Blitz commented, "Ain't seen shit from you on social since Southern Belle. Guess old Clydesdale can't hang."

This pale-skinned Negro's nails were manicured? The after-five beard connected to his sideburns. Everybody had improved their appearance to measure up to yours truly.

Placing my iPad on the counter, I figured they could speculate, but when the check was made payable to François Dupree, my final count would be undisputable.

"Yeah, that's it, homey. Cialis hijacked my shit, had it on swole five days in a row. Now I can't get it up."

I focused on the oyster shells sizzling to open flames damn near taller than me as the four of us sat at the L-shaped end of the counter at Drago's. I had to cop a squat facing the grill with my back to all the happenings as the crewe had already claimed the three stools facing the entrance.

"All I know is each of you betta show your face at my parents' anniversary party at Gallier Hall on the thirty-first. Six o'clock sharp."

I texted Francine, **Got a surprise for you tomorrow to make up for Dubai.**

Blitz, Dallas, and Kohl stared in my direction.

"Count me in. We can set the bet Monday." Dallas was the one I expected to hold firm to not committing.

If the homies knew that I got married a week ago, that might be grounds for disqualifying me for the challenge. Just to secure my position, my dick had one more marathon; then I could retire with a count of 526. Give or take twenty.

I couldn't put her off until Monday. I texted Atlantis, **Put on your sexiest dress. Taking you to GW Fins. Be at my place at 8.**

Eight o'clock would give me time to build on the buzz I started earlier with my dad, and getting faded with the homies right now. Leave here. Go home. Shower. Sleep. Lower my blood alcohol level. Get up, retox with my gurl, then take her back to my place, fuck her real good without interruptions, then send her to that nigga sexually satisfied.

Dallas, Kohl, and Blitz were scanning the room, obviously for possibles.

"One of y'all say something. Damn!" I stopped our waiter. "Let us get four baker's dozen of them flame-broiled oysters on a half shell and a round of Hen."

"Gotcha," the waiter replied.

Kohl said, "I'ma 'bout to trump all y'all. Let's do a count. Write down your numbers."

"Hell no," I objected. "All I want eight days from now is proof. Videos, confessions, social posts. All that."

"You're holding out 'cause Walter been on your ass and you in last place," Blitz said. "You ain't got shit on that tablet."

Had bigger fish to fry than Blitz. And I had to buy a house I didn't want. But my old man was right.

"I'm cool," Kohl said, "'cause none of y'all put shit on social worth posting." He pointed at me, then devoured three oysters, then stuffed his mouth with butter-soaked French bread, washed it down with liquor.

What happened to that nigga was straight-up embarrassing. "Put some respect on it. Ruff. Ruff. Ruff." I gave three deep barks, pounded my chest. "Southern Belle. There's more where that came from. A lot more."

A female dressed in denim short shorts, a cute fedora, and a tight blouse thrust her cleavage in my face. Her hair was short, slick. Lips glossy. The crewe stared in my direction.

"I was at your yacht party. Remember me?" she asked all sexy and shit, eyeing my iPad.

This bitch talked too much. I had no idea who she was, nor did my dick. I slid my iPad away from her.

Blitz's eyes stretched wide. "Yacht, what?" he belted. "I see you, homey. That's why his ass been MIA."

All of Kohl's oyster shells were empty. He devoured two of Dallas's while gawking at ole girl.

"Thanks for coming over to say hi," I told her, wanting for her to get the fuck outta my face.

Her shiny lips parted as she swiped her wet tongue to the corner of her mouth. The tip wiggled at me. Her hand slid up my thigh. "I was hoping we could get together again without the other *ninety-nine* females that were all over your big banana boat."

"What the fuck?" Dallas said. "I ain't making that anniversary party, big baller. I don't know about y'all, but that nig-ga is way ahead of me."

Shining a flashlight in my face, she blinded me.

This bitch was unstable. Moving her hands, the one massaging my dick, the other in my face, I demanded, "You need to back up. Do I know you?"

She laughed.

Picturing the shit Kandy had done, suddenly I felt real uncomfortable. Scooting my barstool away from the bar, I stared into her eyes.

"'Do I know you?'" she sarcastically repeated.

Turning my head toward Blitz, I asked, "Let's switch seats, homey, before I raise up outta here."

Ole gurl jabbed the flashlight into my crotch. "Fuck!" Screaming like a bitch, I grabbed my nuts. Electrical currents had stunned Clydesdale. Bending over, holding my shit. I wanted to choke that bitch, but I wasn't moving my hands.

She shocked my left nipple. Losing control of my muscles, I felt myself descending toward the floor, landed on my shoulder, then rolled onto my side in the fetal position.

Ole gurl and people I didn't know pointed cell phones at me. My boys Dallas and Kohl were laughing hard. Wasn't shit amusing. My dick was numb. Blitz had his phone aimed at me.

"My sister didn't suck your dick for you to degrade her on social media. Thought your lil yacht party was just for fun. Thanks to you, my sister's husband is divorcing her! She has to raise her son and daughter by herself! Had to pull them out of their school because kids wouldn't stop teasing them! You broke up her happy home! I should stun you again!" she said, reaching toward me.

Dallas was the only one of my homies that defended me by saying, "That's enough. Trust me. He's sorry."

The woman swiftly pointed the flashlight in his direction. Dallas became quiet.

"Let's go," another woman said.

Calmly the woman dropped her flashlight into her purse. Dallas was on her in two seconds. Grabbed her by the throat. Started choking her.

Looking up at her, I was sure she wanted to say something, but couldn't speak. Her face turned red.

The woman's friend began crying, "Help!"

Dallas did not let go. "I strongly suggest you don't try this shit again. If you do, I'll shoot you." He stared at her friend. "I'll shoot your ass, too. Get the fuck outta here." Releasing the woman's throat, Dallas extended his hand to me.

What the hell was going on with women and these damn stun guns?

Dallas pulled me up.

"You don't look so good right now, brotha man," Blitz said, then hollered to the guy at the grill. "Yo! Lay four more dozen oysters on us and another round of Hen on me. It's gon' take this nigga a minute."

I scanned the counter. Looked around the restaurant for the women. "Where the fuck is my iPad, homies?" I searched the floor along the bar. Leaned over the counter to see if it had fallen into the sink with the sack of oysters. "Where the fuck is my . . ."

"It's gon' take this nigga's dick a while to recuperate."
Blitz reached under his shirt, handed me my tablet.

I snatched it. "Fuck you, Blitz. I'm still ahead of your
ass."

Blitz smiled. "Not for long, my brother. Not for long."

CHAPTER 16

Trymm

Day 24

Opening the car door for my ... wife, I reached for Francine's hand.

"Thanks, babe. I'm so excited!" she squealed. "I can't believe your parents are so generous. I'm ready to fill our new home with lots of grandbabies for them. Four. Five. Ten! If we have all boys, we can have our own basketball team. They can practice against one another. Or a girls' singing group and band. I love you so much."

Give a woman too much freedom and she'll give you hell. We'd never seriously discussed starting our own family. I could see now I was going to have to have a vasectomy, after the first one. Had to find out how my blackberry and Francine's light skin would blend on a boy. I did not want a girl.

This was our fourth and final viewing for today. Francine had to make a decision. I was not doing this again. Our Realtor parked beside my Benz.

Quinisha was Francine's complexion, taller, had a phat

ass, and her immaculately tapered haircut tempted me to
try and add her to my count, but fucking the Realtor was
probably worse than sleeping with the fine ass neighbor
entering the mansion next door.

Francine had worn a sleeveless magenta jumpsuit that
covered her collarbone. Conservative would be her style
every day she carried my last name. Hair was the way I
insisted. I did not care that she was five-ten; the tip of her
braid could drag the ground, I was not allowing her to cut
off an inch.

Quinisha led us into the foyer. "This four-thousand-
square-foot home has six bedrooms, seven bathrooms, a
four-car garage, two levels, two kitchens, a swimming
pool, Jacuzzi . . ."

One of my brothers, Bryan, his wife, and four kids
lived in an Eastover subdivision. I wasn't as close to him
as some of my other siblings, but Francine would have
family nearby if she chose this home.

"Has anyone died here?" Francine asked. "What year
was it built?"

Whatever property we made an offer on was going to
be her domain. I was not giving up my villa. Didn't want
to reside this far from the Quarter, or commute to work
when I could walk six blocks.

I trailed them, observing my . . . wife ask more questions while dictating notes in her phone. After listening to
my father yesterday, I realized that Francine was a lot like
my mother.

Francine wasn't weak, or easy, or passive, or dumb.
She was basic. Didn't need designer anything. Having
babies was more important than sucking dick or having
orgasms. Her ideas, opinions—now that I listened—most
of them were good. She was what I wanted in a wife and
a mother of my children.

Submissive.

Thought about my dad. He worked a lot, but he wasn't always puttin' in work, on his job. Certain I'd missed a few facts, I should've recorded our conversation.

"It was built two years ago. No one expired here. The family is relocating to California. You will not believe the state-of-the-art everything, from window treatments to the surveillance system, which allows you to see every room, outside up to three hundred feet away, and it comes with its own drone that spans nearly four-and-a-half miles. Every wall in every room, including the bathroom, is wired for cable, but, of course, you have other entertainment options. The roof is solar."

Francine's cell rang. "Excuse me a moment, Quinisha." Her eyes shined as she answered, "Hey, Penny! . . . Yes, François and I are touring a potential residence near where Bryan lives. . . . Okay . . . I'll pick that up. . . . Yes . . . I'll be sure to remind François. See you later. Bye."

"What did she say, babe?" Soon as the word "babe" escaped my mouth, it sounded awkward.

Tapping on her phone, she answered, "I've got it covered. Just ordered an Uber to pick up the doberge cakes and deliver them to your mom's for dinner tonight. Quinisha?"

Quinisha turned to Francine. "Yes."

"My husband and I need a moment to discuss which of the locations we'd like to make an offer on." Francine held my hand, coaxed me upstairs to the master suite. "I like this one." Francine unbuckled my pants, pulled out my dick.

A part of me cared about Francine more than I'd thought. "Make an offer of ten grand under asking."

Francine opened her mouth. Stuck my head in it. "What are you doing?" I said, in a tug-of-war to put Clydesdale up.

"C'mon. Let's have a little fun. Soon it will be ours."

In some ways this lovey-dovey shit was getting on my damn nerves. But I saw how sane Francine was when I was nice, and for now, I could deal with respecting her. But looking at her on her knees, with my dick in her mouth, made me feel she was trying to compete with Southern Belle. Yes, I wanted a 'bj.' No, I didn't want it from Francine. She was bad it.

My dick was flaccid the whole time Francine sucked it. "Get up. Let's finish handling business."

Reuniting downstairs with Quinisha, Francine seemed dejected as she said, "We want to make an offer of four hundred eighty-nine thousand and nine hundred ninety-nine dollars. Write it up. Email the contract to me. We've got to go."

Quinisha extended her hand. First to Francine, then to me. "Thanks. I'll have that to both of you within the hour. Here's another card, just in case."

I shoved mine in my pocket. I was definitely following up with Ms. Quinisha Ferguson soon after we closed this deal.

Driving to my parents' home, Francine was quiet.

"You good?" I asked, turning down the music.

Francine stared through the windshield. "Being your wife is making me realize, I don't know how to make you happy."

No shit!

"And if I can't make you happy, I can't keep you satisfied."

That was "breaking news," and my . . . wife was the reporter.

I swear I should've never married that woman. I did it for Walter. For my dad. For my family's honor. But all this shit was a fucking joke.

Bottom line . . . God-to-honest truth. I did not love Francine. The certificate was in my safe and I could make this situation and Francine, go away.

CHAPTER 17

Trymm

Day 30

Saturday night, after-sunset cruise, big finale, homey, I texted BobbyRay.

Don't leave me hangin' when you chillin' with yo' million, bruh, he replied.

Wasn't copacetic but I had to drop BobbyRay's asking price on him. And I had to break Penny off, and the reimbursement to the business line of credit. Money hadn't hit my account and I was already out $410,000.

Glad as hell this was the last day, I tossed my cell on my pillow. Swallowed two tablets to enhance my erection; showtime for Clydesdale was in two hours. Time off from the family business, I'd taken advantage of the opportunity to spoil my Atlantis, but she'd been here five days straight. Started leaving her stuff after day two. Dresses. Sandals. Thongs. Stopped wearing her engagement ring.

It was time for Atlantis to get out of my villa and go home to dude. Being with one woman was driving me insane. He could have her.

I placed the unmarked pill bottle on the headboard next to the half-full glass of water. Being with Atlantis was something I thought I wanted. This wasn't it, either. If a relationship was the thing to do, after the initial excitement, why was it so fucking mundane? Might need to give our situation some time, not do anything irrational. But she couldn't post up at my spot. Francine was hanging out with my sisters furniture shopping for her, not our, new house in Eastover.

Atlantis's hips were under the red satin sheet. Her breasts were uncovered, nipples hard. Her untamed hair was all over my pillowcase. Literally. No makeup. Naturally beautiful glow. Staring at her, I wondered, why wasn't she enough? Had to talk with Dad again.

"You got stunned. I got stunned," I joked, laughing. "That shit was stupid." But at the time nothing was funny about ole gurl damn near roasting my nuts.

"I've got to be crazy laying up with you after all that's happened to me. But I can't stop loving you," Atlantis said, then asked, "What's that you just took?"

"Have a slight headache." That was the truth. She'd worn my dick out. Had to cut her off yesterday in preparation for tonight.

"Mine hurts, too. I need one."

Before I could deny her, Atlantis popped a pill in her mouth, then washed it down with the water in my glass. *Oh, shit!* I had no idea what effect the drug had on women. Couldn't be that serious.

Atlantis stretched sideways across my bed. Showed me *her* pussy. "Let's go one more round, baby."

"Damn, you want all the dick. Slow your roll. It ain't going nowhere. This lil staycation has been nice, but I got some things to handle." I shut the bathroom door, praying she'd leave on her own.

Starting the water, I got in the shower, to cut down on

time, while she acted as though *"mi casa es su casa"* was in effect. Heard the door open.

"What's up, AB?"

"I came to wash your back. We need to talk," Atlantis said, inviting herself where she wasn't welcome.

Women, they did that annoying shit all the fucking time. I couldn't stand to look at her right now.

Atlantis began lathering my back with body wash. Her hands rotated in opposite directions. She said, "I did it."

I turned my back to the hot water, which I was no longer enjoying, faced her. "Did what?"

"You asked me to call off my engagement so we could be together. I did it. I called off my engagement. I was waiting for you to notice I hadn't been wearing my ring."

You don't drop that shit on a nigga out of the blue! I wasn't for sure . . . for sure she was who I wanted to be with. I already had one certificate that wasn't going to get filed locked in my safe. Didn't need two. That reminded me, I had to snag my iPad before I left.

Atlantis cleansed my genitals, squatted, circled her tongue around my corona.

Not that again. Why did women think we always wanted them to get on our mic? Even when I did want a "bj," a fresh set of lips was the hype. Not the same-o, same-o.

Cupping my hands underneath her armpits, I lifted her up, exited the shower, closed the door with her inside. I rubbed every part of my body with baby oil, then toweled off. She got out, did the same.

Quickly I slipped on a pair of pajamas pants. "I'll meet you for brunch in the morning. Commander's Palace. But I have a long day tomorrow and need to get some rest. Baby, you wore my thang out!"

"Trymm, I did what you asked. Don't ignore me. What are we going to do?"

I was speechless.

"Don't fuck me over again. I can't take it." Atlantis

started crying. I meant bawlin', ugly face, snotty nose and all. "I need to move in with you."

Nothing I'd say would keep her from being angry. She had a house. I wasn't laying down a welcome mat for her at my place. But I did need her to: "Stop fucking crying."

Atlantis placed her hand on her belly, sat on my bed, sniffled. "I don't know what's come over me. I don't feel well."

Her ass had to go! I needed to get dressed, and make it to the riverfront in an hour. This was the last day, man. Pretending I had to rest wasn't working. I picked up my cell. "My parents' fiftieth anniversary celebration is *tomorrow* evening at Gallier Hall. Penny needs me to help her out with some last-minute deets. I've got to go."

"Wow. Fifty years. If we get married this year, we'd be eighty years old on our fiftieth. Is it cool if I stay the night and go with you tomorrow?"

I don't know. Ask my wife.

Francine had to be at the gathering. I wasn't trying to get my ass kicked by Walter for ruining the celebration. "I'd love for you to come, but the guest list is closed and restricted to family members only."

Why in the fuck is Atlantis still on my damn bed?!

"That's cool. I love your parents." She flopped onto her back, held on to her stomach. "I'll just drop them off a gift from us."

Fuck it! I undressed, then put on slacks, shoes, and a T-shirt.

Atlantis sprang to her feet, raced to the toilet. Heaved once, twice.

I stood in the bathroom doorway. "Seriously. You've got to go."

She stared up from the toilet. "I should've known this was going to happen!" She stood. "You ain't gon' never change! All you care about is your feelings! I'm pregnant, Trymm."

Maybe male enhancements didn't agree with a woman's system but women played too many games. First, I knew she was lying. She wasn't pregnant before I told her to get out. Second, now I understood how my boy Kohl felt about Ramona trapping him. And third, it was her fault she was an easy lay and didn't insist on my using a condom.

Somebody needed to make pussy-on-a-stick. Thinking of pussy, I was about to miss my own yacht. "Can, you, get, dressed?"

Atlantis shook her head.

"Fuck it. Lock the door when you leave and don't come back." I couldn't play live-in attendant to her faking ass. Unlocking my safe, I retrieved my iPad, then left.

Hopefully, she'd be gone by the time I got back or I might have to call her fiancé and let him know where she's at.

CHAPTER 18

Trymm

Day 31

Midnight. July 30. My final #smashdown was 526, and I have proof.

Unlocking the front door to the break of dawn, I practically dragged myself over the threshold, into my bedroom.

No fucking way! I placed my iPad on my nightstand.

"Hey! Atlantis." I shook her hard. "Wake up."

A shake that hard would've made anybody jump out of bed. Slowly she opened her eyes. "Huh, what?"

"Get your ass up. You need to go home."

"What time is it?" she asked sleepily. "We're going to Commander's Palace, remember?"

I swear, I hate her so much right now! "It's five o'clock in the morning."

She stared at the sun's rays beaming through the window. "Wow. You have a lot of explaining to do. Where are my clothes?" she said, getting out of the bed in slow motion.

Glad to be of assistance, I tossed her dress and purse on the bed, placed her shoes on her feet. Collected the rest of her personals. Tossed them on the bed.

"I'ma have to take a rain check on brunch," she said, washing her face.

No shit! No sweeter words could've been spoken because my dick was tired as fuck, and I had to put together my super-reel. I had the women stand around me on the yacht. On a "one, two, three" count, all two hundred shouted, "Trymm, you were wonderful!" BobbyRay came up with that idea to avoid missing anyone.

Totally exhausted, I wouldn't dare get in bed with the combined DNA on my body. "Text me when you get in."

"I'll see myself out," Atlantis said. "We still have to talk. I can make brunch."

All I did was shake my head.

Leaving Atlantis to do the same as Mrs. Kandy, with a capital *k,* and let herself out. I hadn't heard any more from Kandy. I'd blocked her to keep her dumb wannabe trick ass from bothering me—hopefully, she convinced her husband to take her back.

I closed the bathroom door; I took a long, hot, relaxing shower, massaged my body with oil, brushed my teeth, toweled off; then I opened the door, praying Atlantis had not doubled-back to my bed.

Women had a way of lingering, and I had to make sure before I comfortably closed my eyes, I was not going to awaken to any surprises.

"Atlantis!" I called out.

No answer.

"Atlantis," I said, searching the living room. My front door was ajar. I stepped into the hallway. No one was there. Securing the lock, I searched my second bedroom and bathroom. The comforter, pillows, and towels were untouched.

I went to the kitchen; as I opened a bottle of water, I heard sirens in the distance.

As I sat on my bed, sirens blared louder.

I exhaled and rubbed my palms together, time to replay my latest footage. The reel was going to be surreal. Shit would be so long I'd have to upload it to YouTube. The smile on my face was so wide, both sets of my cheeks hurt.

As I reached for my iPad, my smile vanished. Ass relaxed. Sirens stopped outside my building.

What the fuck?!

Certain I'd left my tablet on my nightstand, frantically I ripped all the sheets off the bed. Going to my closet . . . *fuck!*

The marriage certificate was gone.

I called Atlantis. Got her voice mail. Called again. Same shit. This time I left a voice mail: "Bitch, I'ma kill your ass if you took my shit!"

Knock! Knock! Knock!

Who the fuck is banging like they were the police?

I grabbed my gun, stood to the left of the door. "Who is it?" I yelled.

"François, it's me. Francine."

What the fuck she . . . I put my gun on the coffee table, opened the door.

"I felt something wasn't right. Are you okay?" she asked, entering without permission.

Francine motioned to close the door, someone pushed back. "We need to enter your unit."

"Nah, homey. You not just intruding here. You have a warrant?" I asked.

"Sir, there's a dead body below your balcony. We—"

My French doors were ajar. Francine started screaming, *"Noooo!"*

I stood on the balcony, leaned over the rail. Yellow

caution tape, and a white chalk outline was in motion. "Oh, God, Jesus." All I saw was Atlantis's dress.

I ran down the stairs, into the courtyard, praying my mind was playing tricks.

Stared through tears . . . it was . . . Kandy with capital *k* and small *y.*

CHAPTER 19

Kohl

Day 1

If all dogs went to heaven, why shouldn't men cheat? Women couldn't be mad that God had given us a pass.

Lying in bed, I stared up at the ceiling, assessing the mechanics of the challenge.

Told myself, you need a master plan, bro. I had to treat this $1 million like an acquisition deal. It was 5:30 a.m. Time to get my butt up and go to work.

I was never in the military like my boy Dallas, but for sure, as stated in the Bible, sleep was for the weak. Powering on my laptop, I sat at my desk in my home office, listed my goals, objectives, and strategy on how to be the victorious one.

The goal was clear. To win the money. My objectives were: One, date more females than other members of my crewe. Two, dick—that meant sex—as many females as I could, without having them fall in love with me. That was my understanding, which meant I was going to be one cold "smash and text" brother. Three, to have documented proof of each dump.

I imagined my competitors' baseline was somewhere around two females a day, seventy at best for Dallas. Eighty for Blitz, that vagina-licking lover. Trymm, having played professional basketball overseas, that brother might be on three a day, threesomes, and orgies; but the amount of blood it would take to fill up his snake, and the fact that he didn't care much for putting his mouth on a clit, those two factors were going to hold down his count.

My guaranteed number was 101. Anything more was lagniappe. Creating a spreadsheet, I had four columns for their names, numbers, videos, and photos. My shit was going to be so organized it would hold up in any court.

If I convinced every stripper at my club to do me, kept it honest with them about the challenge, offered them a thousand-dollar kickback if I won, they'd do it. Their support would account for one-third of my goal.

Smashing customers, I could manage one a day. If I let her order from the menu whatever she wanted to eat, offered her free drinks and hookah, they'd at least suck me off in the back room at my club, but no way could I tell them the truth. That group would up me at least another thirty.

Church . . . I paused, scrolled a visual in my mind: Fifteen, make that sixteen if I included the assistant pastor's wife that's been propositioning me since I'd turned eighteen. Sister Eleanor Lewis was ten years my senior, and her husband was twenty years hers.

Word in the sacred circle was Assistant Pastor Eric Lewis was impotent. I'd have to keep my intent to accept her offer on the low, or my parents would ban me from stepping foot inside their tabernacle. The total prospects left was twenty-five on my random hit list. Had to expound on that later today.

Texted Trymm, **What made you come up with this idea?**

Trymm started this stunt. Blitz topped it off. Trymm's

response was insignificant. Confident I'd win, I flexed the left side of my chest. **I got this.**

Ballers are beasts, Trymm replied.

Further breaking down the equation, I set up a folder for each prospect. Numbered them, *Gurl 1, Gurl 2 . . . Gurl 101.* Slapping my hands together . . . all roads would lead me straight to the bank 'cause the second side of my "bp" was finding a technical reason to disqualify as many of my crewe's conquests as I could. Once I cashed out, I'd have enough funds to build a second Kash In & Out strip club/hookah lounge on the West Bank.

Opening my refrigerator, I shut the door, then put on all white: polo, slacks, hard-sole shoes. I got in my Bentley, headed out to make grocery. It was eight o'clock.

Females and guys stood and watched me park my bronze Bentayga. I was accustomed to the attention. Most of them had probably never seen one. I strolled inside my favorite one-stop, get-all store, Walmart Supercenter. The drive from my house in the East to Metairie was worth the savings. Didn't believe in overspending on females the way Blitz did.

Chicken legs, no ribs, no catfish, potatoes to mash or make French fries, skip the lettuce, big girls wanted real food. Grits, eggs, sliced cheese for the grits, they could eat all of that with the fried chicken legs. Plenty of ketchup. Couldn't go wrong with watermelon, ditch the cherries with pits, add grapes, and pineapples. Bread, none of that wheat or whole grain, had to buy the white sliced. Tossed a few boxes of "just add water" pancake mix. Syrup. Lots of cheap liquor for them. Nothing over five dollars a bottle. I didn't drink the headache-inducing grains. Would fill my glass with the premium only that was at my house.

Standing in line to check out with a cashier, I heard, "Kohl 'Kash' Bartholomew."

Some voices were unforgettable—although I wished I

could erase her from my mind. My ex hated me. *Oh, my God. Not today.* I bowed my head, mumbled, "God all powerful, please rescue me."

Once upon a time, back in the day, I was just Kash to her. The city was small, but I'd managed to avoid running into her for a minute. Turning around. "Damn!" It hadn't been that long—seven, maybe six months. How could she look like that?

"Lord, give me strength to say the right thing."

My boys didn't know all the ins and outs about my dealings with this woman harassing me for money for her kid. All the crewe cared about was my take on the situation.

I glanced at her body. Scanned her like she was grocery on the conveyor belt. Up. Down. Up . . . down. Up again. Her face was different, too. What in the world happened to her?

My ex was snatched tight—I meant—in all the right places.

From the front, round as those hips were in those short light blue denims, I could tell her ass was humongous. But this time in a nice, curvaceous way. Looked like a few ribs were missing from her waist. The pink cropped top, matching the open-toed high heels, was sinful. I wanted to cover her up or feature her center stage at my spot. Where in the world was she going dressed that way this time of the morning? Her cotton-candy nail polish accelerated my heartbeat. I wanted to feel them scratch my balls the way she used to. She was even rocking the Rapunzel ponytail.

Eleven years ago, when we were in the same Sunday-school class, the good Lord had blessed her with 230 pounds. She was the reason I fell in love with big gurls. They were easy and eager to please.

"Hey, Ramona Dandridge." My tone was flat to conceal my excitement. I opened my arms, praying for God to be merciful and let those perky nipples brush against my chest, and my hands feel the flesh of those smooth abs; then, if I got close enough, I was not requesting permission to squeeze that donkey.

Repositioning her son between us, she asked, "You don't see anyone else?" Before I could tell the dude hello, she lowered her gaze to him.

Pretty soon he'd be as tall as her. Hoped he didn't outgrow me at six feet two inches and one day whup my ass for the nonsense his mama put in his head.

"Hey, lil man. What's up?"

Dude eyed me the way I'd done his mama. His entire face was tight. That was cool. I didn't care.

"His name is William. William *Bartholomew*." Ramona put emphasis on the last name, knowing it should've been Dandridge.

I was given my adoptive parents' last name. At least her kid knew his mother. One day, perhaps I'd meet mine, but I still wasn't sure how Ramona got away with legally hijacking my surname for her kid.

"That's what you documented on his birth certificate, but whoever his daddy is, Billy boy needs to learn some manners. Get your son back in church. But not my parents' church."

"I go to church, punk. I got yo' boy right here." He hiked his crotch, then let go. "You the hypocrite!" I called him Billy boy in my head as he said, "You a deadbeat dad, punk."

I wasn't going to be called too many more of those by a ten-year-old. Nor was I removing my belt to whup a bastard I didn't know. But I'd gladly have sex again with his mother.

Licking my lips, I addressed Ramona. "He's out of order." Glancing at her ring finger, I felt my eyes widen. The ice was probably fake, like her. I said, "Congratulations. Who's the unlucky guy?"

She hunched her shoulders, then threw a left punch to-ward my face. Stopped inches from my mouth. I flinched. Leaned back. Pinched my nose.

Billy cracked up with laughter. He bent over, holding his stomach. Standing tall, he said, "Told you, you were a punk."

Yeah, let him try it. I'd have that boy on his knees in a headlock in a split second.

"None of your fucking business." Ramona didn't bother covering Billy's ears. "At least he's not trifling like you. If you're so sure William isn't your son"—she shouted as though there was a sale on aisle two—"take a paternity test. It's been ten years, Kohl!" She placed her right hand on her hip.

Better there than her swinging at me again.

"No need to volunteer my DNA. We only kicked it for a short while after high school. You didn't tell me until after I was accepted into UNO. It was too late then. I wasn't dropping out of college to play trap-dad to that. Besides, we both know you got around, probably still do." I'd never call a woman a bitch or a whore to her face. "I'm happy that you've finally pinned one down. Poor guy. Give him my condolences, then give him my number so I can let him know about the real you."

"He's got more flow than your punk ass with your big-tittie bar," Billy said, flashing three Benjamins.

Now I wanted to bust him in his mouth, then wash it out with soap. Sucking in the air around us, I exhaled. I was not showing my bankroll. Fools around here didn't care who they robbed.

"You're never going to grow up," Ramona said. "William is a kid."

With a limited vocabulary. "And you're never going to come up," I told her the truth. "Silicone titties, ass im-plants, manufactured abs. You bought all that with your EBT card? Still getting paid under the table doing a 'bj'?

You can do me anytime. Like mother. Like son. Empty somebody else's pockets."

Truth was, I hated that my ex was so gorgeous! If I couldn't have a piece, I wanted her to feel bad about herself. There was no need for me to shell out a penny of child support. Women lost their minds when a brother became an entrepreneur. Always wanting to take us for all the cash they hadn't earned because they couldn't keep their legs shut.

She rolled her eyes, and I wished they could transport her big booty out of my life right along with that kid of hers.

"Baby, go wait in the car," she told Billy.

He walked out of the double sliding doors, but I didn't see her hand him a key. Probably wasn't no car for him to get in. She was at the bus stop when I'd last seen her.

"You sorry-ass son of a bitch! In church every Sunday praising the Lord, dropping Satan's dollars in your parents' collection plate, but you can't take care of your son!" There went public announcement number two on aisle two. "You're going straight to hell! I'm tired of your black ass! Some niggas you can't be nice to!" Ramona got progressively louder. "I'll see you in court. But before I walk away, I'ma give you a reason to see me there, too!"

By now, all eyes and cell phones were on us. Ramona bust me in the eye with her ring, for real this time.

Covering my left side, I screamed, "Bitch! You could've put my eye out." She deserved to be called worse.

Scanning the room with my right eye, cellulars were focused on me.

My phone started blowing up. I answered, "What?"

"Please tell me that's not you," Blitz said, howling with laughter in my ear.

I hung up on him.

Ramona had declared war. I was downloading a copy

of the video, giving it to my lawyer, and having her arrested for assault. What was she upset about? Some brother was about to slit his throat and bleed out to be her husband. Hope she'd change Billy's last name so she could stop chasing my money.

Paid for my grocery, rolled my cart outside. Surveyed the parking lot.

A black convertible Bentley, gold-and-black interior, stopped in front of me. Blocked my path. The top retracted.

"Punk! I got next," Billy yelled. "You already dead! I'ma beat you to a corpse one day. Bank on that!"

Ramona spun her wheels until I disappeared into a cloud of black smoke, then sped off.

I understood Ramona's frustration. But Billy. Why in the hell did he hate me? I didn't know the kid. He wasn't mine.

Trymm had time to call. I didn't answer. I declined Dallas's call.

Blitz texted, **I got your back, my brother. I'll beat that pussy up for you.**

I was no fighter. Had taken a few knock-down punches from Dallas. But Blitz. Oh, I'd kick his pussy-licking ass if he fucked with Ramona.

CHAPTER 20

Ramona

Day 1

"Kohl is worth more to you dead than alive, girl. We should get someone to kill him," my friend Carmella joked. "You should've popped him again for me," she laughed a sharp, "Ha!"

Carmella tried to make me do the same to ease my pain but I didn't share her humor. I was livid. My son had been denied his biological father all his life.

We sat on the top bleacher at the stadium watching our kids practice. They were out of school for Independence Day weekend. The men stood in a row on the sideline behind the team. Most of the moms were seated ground level.

Videos of my punching Kohl in the face had gone viral. I watched the guys standing below nudge one another as they toggled their phones between one another. Moms began staring up at me. I was mad for letting Kohl make me angry.

"I don't hate Kohl. You know that. I hate that he won't acknowledge and share time with our son. He couldn't have a decent conversation with William, but his tongue was hanging out of his mouth like he wanted to fuck me with it right there in the supermarket."

"I bet he did," Carmella said. "They say all men aren't dogs. That's a lie. Some of them can reform. I suppose."

Not Kohl. I saw my son run to the twenty yard line, then back to the ten. To the thirty, then return to the twenty. That drill would continue until William and his teammates were at the end zone.

"Can you believe I had to put William between us for Kohl to stop lusting over my body? Then when William checked him on being a deadbeat, he dragged on my ass for having plastic surgery. That's why I closed that eye. He'd best pray I don't show up at his club to shut the other one."

Noticing my son's pace had slowed quite a bit, I yelled, "Finish strong, William!"

"Bet if you called Kohl right now and offered him some pussy, he'd come running with his dick in his hand," Carmella said. Her eyes darted back and forth from me to the field. "Kohl stupid. You should put a lien on his business for back child support. Take his Bentley, his house, his parents' church. That would get his attention."

I laughed to keep from crying as she kept talking.

"All the money he makes, he probably owes you half of a million. My son's father avoids working so he doesn't have to pay anything for any of his eight kids."

Carmella made a good point. Since Kohl thought he was getting over on me, maybe it was time I showed him I was the real boss. Take him to court and take all his shit.

William ran defense. Carmella's son was a standout on offense. I didn't care that William wasn't the best player. He was a preteen, part of a team, had made new friends, and (like the former First Lady Michelle Obama had encouraged our kids) he was exercising. I kept him busy to keep mine out of trouble that could land him in juvenile hall.

Carmella blurted, "All those dads down there staring up here at you. Look how their women keep staring up here, too!"

"Whatever, girl." I didn't care.

One woman held up her phone, pointed at the screen. She was cool with me before my makeover. Now she barely spoke. I couldn't undo what I'd done.

Carmella motivated me to lose weight when I could barely climb these bleachers. She was my one true girlfriend. We knew why the haters was giving me attention.

"Soon as I save enough money, I can't afford your doctor, but I'm going to the Dominican Republic and have all this fat"—she grabbed her stomach—"put into my flat ass, and get breast implants." Her eyes dimmed with sorrow. "Or you can introduce me to one of Harold's friends and I can get a sponsor the way he paid for all your work."

I could pay for her procedures, but if anything went wrong, I'd blame myself. "Long as Kohl is breathing, I have to keep trying to get him to do right by William."

Carmella held my hand. "Black men see their children as a burden, or they think we're trying to stick them for the paper most of them ain't got. At least Kohl has money. Take what's rightfully yours. My son's daddy expects me to provide for him and our son. That's why I don't let him see his son. Let his other baby mamas do that dumb stuff."

Wrapping my arms around my friend, I told her, "You're a great mom."

Leaning back, Carmella said, "Bay-bay, right back at cha." Softly, she repeated, "Right back at cha."

I couldn't speak for her, but I'd done things—I was embarrassed to tell anyone—to feed my child. Sucked dirty dicks in back alleyways to keep my lights on. Slept

with old-ass men that made my skin crawl to pay my
son's tuition. Had to admit, I was a master. I did whatever
I had to do to make sure William Bartholomew had a better start at life than I had, including positioning myself to
date the highest-paid basketball player in our town. Securing the ring on my finger was premeditated.

Our kids trotted in our direction. We crossed bleachers
until we were at ground level. Their coach approached
me, asking, "Can I have a word with you, Ramona? In
private."

"See you guys next week," Carmella said, then left
with her son.

"Yes, of course," I told the coach. "William, go get us
something cold to drink."

"It was brought to my attention that there's a video of
you assaulting a man," he said.

"He's not a man." I paused, then added, "And?"

"I don't condone violence in my program," the coach
explained.

"I understand. I apologize. I can elaborate if you'd
like." Promising it wouldn't happen again might be a lie.

"You know I have a zero-tolerance policy for violence," he said firmly.

Heading toward us, my son had two snowballs in his
hands and a big smile on his face.

The coach lowered his tone. "Respectfully, Ramona,
William is excused from the team, effective immediately."

"I got your favorite, Mama. Coconut and pineapple.
Hey, Coach, how'd I do?" William smiled and his eyes
were wide.

Coach patted William on the shoulder pad. "*You* did
great."

Suppressing my anger, I told William, "Let's go, son."

Humility blended with the increasing heat. I closed my
convertible top, turned on the air conditioner. Not sure

how to deliver the bad news to William, I was consumed by my own thoughts.

"You okay, Mama?" my son asked.

I lied, "I'm good." There were secrets a mother was privileged to hold, but if I wasn't honest, he'd eventually find out the truth from someone else. Or worse, on social media.

Nineteen with a baby. I wanted to go to college. Earn my degree. Become a registered nurse. The difference with Kohl was, altering his plans in order to take care of William was an option he'd opted out of. Once another life started growing inside of me, the dreams I had for myself disappeared.

I hated that I was so young and stupid! I loved Kohl. Trusted him!

Driving to our next destination, I thought about how I loved my son, but some days I tried imagining what my life would be like if I'd had an abortion. No sucking dicks or sleeping with the elderly. My son was halfway done with his snowball. Slowly I sucked the syrupy flavor to keep the juice from spilling on me.

I told William, "Turn off your cell. Put it in the glove box."

Frowning, he said, "What?"

"Do what I said. I'll give it back to you when I pick you up." That would give me time to work on my delivery of letting him know he was no longer a Panther.

Morning sickness, stretch marks, being uncomfortable my last trimester. Going through labor with my grandmother holding my hand while Kohl was a freshman doing his thing at UNO. Watching my grandmother die three months after William was born, my core support system was gone. Being homeless with a baby. Having Kohl reject William was equally as devastating as his Christian parents offering me a stipend *not* to come back to their church. The pastor, who used to serve me Communion, told me, "Respectfully, Ramona, you and your baby are no longer welcome in The House of the Lord."

William threw his snowball out the window, removed his football jersey, and pads. "I hate him! I know you're upset because of the video everybody is talking about. I saw it already, mama." Taking off his designer sunglasses, William cried. "I wish that punk was dead. That way he'd stop hurting us."

My son had that right to hate Kohl, and I couldn't take the pain away from him. Only Kohl could do that.

"Hate is as natural as love, baby. I want you to understand why you feel the way you do. You have the right to be mad. I am, too," I told him, parking in front of the university. "Just don't take your anger out on others. Be mindful."

"Can I keep my phone?" he asked.

I nodded.

"I'm going to ace everything again that they teach me this weekend, Mama," William eagerly said. He spread his arms, held me tight. "I love you, Mama. I'm going to make you proud, and when I have kids, I'm going to take care of them. I promise."

"Mama loves you always and . . . ," I paused.

Two years ago I tired of dating guys with low standards. My focus became to find my son a stepfather. Not any man. A good man. I didn't have to be in love with the guy, but he had to have three things: Respect for my son and me. Enough money to support the three of us. And he had to be a great role model for William.

My son said, "Forever."

In exchange for my engagement ring, I, Ramona Dandridge, catered to my man in and out of the bedroom. Always remained faithful. And no matter how down he got about losing a game, I lifted him up so high no other woman could reach him. That was how I got Harold to put a ring on it without having to lead him to a jeweler. As a mother I gave my last. Kohl never gave our child anything.

"Put everything I got . . . ," I paused.

"On it," he said.

William closed the car door, jogged to the building for his future lawyer preparatory class. Each session they had a different speaker—lawyer, judge, law enforcement officer, entrepreneur, etc. He had to take notes, then handwrite an essay in cursive about what he'd learned.

Soon as he was inside, I drove away, weeping. For my child.

It angered me the way Kohl acted as if we'd never had sex. He was my first. My only at that time. Those rumors about my having been with this guy and that one were lies. But even if they were true, he'd done with girls the same things he'd falsely accused me of doing.

Answering an incoming call, I dried my eyes, smiled, then cheerfully answered, "Hey, baby. I'm pulling up to Dooky Chase right now."

"Right behind ya," Harold said. I could hear the excitement in his voice.

Ending the call, I touched up my makeup. Refreshed my dark brown lipstick. My fiancé opened my door.

"You lookin' good in this car and them jeans, baby." He hugged me at the waist, pulled me in, then kissed me on the forehead. "Don't want to mess up those pretty lips yet. Where's William?" he asked, escorting me through the back entrance.

"He's in law prep. They scheduled tomorrow's sessions today due to the holiday weekend."

"Ah, okay," Harold said, then asked, "You want me to pick him up? You know it's going to take you forever to get ready for the concert tonight."

Want me, not need me to pick him up.

"I'll do it. And I'll be ready."

"But will you be ready on time?"

We sat at a square table all the way to the back, off to the side, in the corner. Harold sat with his back to the wall. I was seated next to him.

"Two gumbos and two sweet teas?" the waiter asked.

"You got it," Harold answered, confirming our usual appetizers.

Dooky Chase was our standing Friday lunch date during Harold's off-season.

"You think William would like touring the African-American museum this summer?" Harold asked.

My chin dropped. "William? What about me?"

"You know I got you, woman. How're my gurls doing?" He flicked his tongue.

Thrusting my breasts forward, I smiled, letting him touch one. "Diamond and Pearl are doing fine." Diamond was my left breast because she was less sensitive than my precious right.

I was still getting accustomed to my new body, but for the first time I enjoyed when I was naked and preferred not having on any clothes.

I fed Harold a spoonful of his gumbo. "Don't make me cry again. You know I appreciate your paying for everything," including the convertible Bentley.

A girlfriend that didn't have time for me when I was overweight texted, **You have any extra VIP backstage passes for tonight? I'll pay you.**

I replied, **I'm not for sale. My extras are for Carmella.**

I might write my friend Carmella a check large enough for her to decide if she wants to alter her body, but I didn't want her going out of the country. I had all my work done in Atlanta with Dr. Paul McCluskey. He was most concerned about my overall health. Did my Brazilian butt lift and liposuction first, then my tummy tuck and breast implants. The Silagen silicone products he recommended, helped my scars start to fade but I also exfoliated, moisturized with bio oil and Combat ointment, vitamin E, all that. In another few months my body should look as though the cuts never happened.

A man with a huge professional camera resting on his shoulder entered the rear of the restaurant. Heading in our direction, the person with him held a microphone.

"You have an interview scheduled?" I asked Harold, scooting over and creating space between us. I wasn't the type of girlfriend who'd hang on to or brag about my man's success.

"I'm not sure, but we're about to find out," he said, putting on a fake smile.

I stood off to the side when the news reporter spoke into her mic. "We've caught up to our newest star and the fifty-million-dollar man here at one of our favorite restaurants. Harold Thurston, 'welcome to New Orleans' may still be in order, since this is only your second season."

I watched Harold's eyes and his smile widened as he said, "Thanks. It's great to be a part of an exciting franchise."

"How are you adjusting to the Big Easy?" she asked.

Nodding straight up and down, he said, "Loving the fans. Can't get enough of this seafood gumbo, though. All that." He devoured an oyster. Chewed with his mouth closed, then swallowed.

"You got us to the conference finals. What was your secret to keeping the opponent from scoring?"

The way she licked her lips at my six-eight piece of dark chocolate was plain nasty. I was ready for her to wrap it up.

"Defense wins games. I'm always going to do my best to keep the other team from scoring," he said. Sitting back, he placed his silverware on a napkin.

The news reporter's eyes honed in on my man's dick print. Harold motioned for me to come to him.

"Well," she said, sounding more annoyed than surprised, "who do we have here?"

If I could snatch that mic, shove it in her mouth, and make her disappear, she'd be my second viral video of the day. Harold held up my left hand.

"I'd like to officially introduce my fiancée, who happens to be a native, to your local viewing audience. This is the lovely Ms. Ramona Dandridge, soon-to-be Mrs. Ramona Thurston."

"Lovely, are you?" she said, smirking at me. "Don't eat too much, Ramona. Thanks for your time, Harold." She went into her exit, giving her channel information, and then: "This is Lisa Dozier. . . . Back to you, Gary."

Giving her undivided attention to Harold, she told him, "Sorry for cutting it short, we have to get to another location. Here's my card. Call me. Anytime."

Once upon a time, I liked her segments. Today her next location could've been the hospital. Not waiting for her to turn away, I said, "Rude bitch."

Harold held my hand, shook his head. "Now that we're engaged, you're going to have to practice your media smile and attitude. Took me a while."

Might as well ask, "So you've seen my video online?"

"Who hasn't seen it?" he laughed. "If I were there, I would've run interference, beaten Kohl's ass, and taken the charge. Baby, don't sweat any of this. I got you. I could tell Lisa is after me. You," he said, then tapped the left side of his chest, "got my heart."

Two fresh bowls of gumbo replaced the ones on our table. I was hungry and dug right in.

I texted Kohl, **Take the test tomorrow or I'm filing a court order first thing Monday morning.**

Once his paternity was confirmed, I was taking all his shit before I got legally married.

His response, **Stay away from me. Or I'm filing a PO against you.**

I showed Harold.

"Why do you keep putting yourself through this?" Harold asked. "Now that we're getting married, he will demand the test, and will pray he's the dad. But he's not getting a damn dime of our money. If he does the fool, I'll personally take care of him. Ya heard me."

His last words made me laugh. "Where'd you learn that?"

"Teammates. Eat before you need a third bowl."

"I just want William to know that's his father."

"Ramona, look at me. Does Shaq know his biological father? LeBron? And I don't mean know of."

I gazed up at Harold with teary eyes.

"William can't move on if you don't. I'm his dad now. Let me be that man to you and a father to him."

This was a perfect time to say, "The football coach kicked William off the team this morning. Said it was the video of my hitting Kohl. I was violent."

"I'll handle it with the coach." Harold placed a $100 bill on the table. "Let's go before we miss the last act."

"I'm not that slow." I stood, scooped an oyster. Ate it. Went back into the filé. This time for a shrimp.

"Dang, you greedy. Stay. Finish eating. I'm picking up William. We'll see you at home. Bye."

I texted Kohl, **Harold is right. We don't need you.**

CHAPTER 21

Kohl

Day 1

Picking up the remote, I powered on all the flat screens throughout Kash In & Out. One side catered to hookah indulgers, but you couldn't have a club in New Orleans that didn't keep 'em coming for alcohol lovers. No cover, $3 well drinks, and $5 setups for hookah before 10:00 p.m. helped customers dig deep into their pockets for my big, beautiful entertainers.

I hit Blitz with, **Before the video. Had you seen Ramona?**

I follow her, he responded, which meant what exactly?

I typed, **Why?** Then I instructed the new woman delivering my hookah, "Spread the boxes across the bar in stacks of fours, according to flavor, labels facing front."

"Gonna be a busy weekend. You need tips?" she asked.

The double jelly roll separated by her omentum was sexy as hell. I wanted to grab her handles, pull her to me, tell her how hot she was. Her titties sat on top of that upper layer, where I could lay my head and fall asleep.

"What I need is to see you take off that shirt and dance

on my stage," I said, then answered her question, "Give me a thousand tips." That could be gone in less than a day.

To see her pop off on guys like you. Your eye open yet? Blitz texted.

Slightly swollen. No big deal. I didn't want to be with Ramona. She was the one that wanted us to be a family. That was the real reason she never let the test thing go.

His next text, **You cool with me hitting that, made me lose count of my merchandise.**

Had to restart after I let him know, **Ramona is off limits.**

He sent an emoji with the tongue sticking out, followed by, **And she's engaged, but you know how we do it.**

He was following her for real? I turned around. Delivery chick was on stage twerking. She had some nice moves. I played Juvenile's "Back That Azz Up." Standing at the edge, I tossed a rack at her. Slowed the music down with Trey Songz's "Love Faces."

She came out of her pants. Her bra and underwear were neutral-colored. Thighs like the Michelin Man, rubbed together, when she swayed. Legs were small in comparison to the rest of her body.

I loved that. "Damn, I could cuddle up to you every night," I said. "Take the rest off. Ain't nobody coming up in here."

"You want this pussy," she asked. Holding a chunk of deliciousness in each hand . . . Damn, her vagina resembled an overstuffed smoked sausage po'boy, dressed.

"Play with her for me," I said. Admiring her, I felt my dick starting to get hard.

Her thick fingers parted her paradise. Soon as I saw her huge clit, I hopped on stage. Jumped down just as fast. Locked the door, then got real close up on her, held a handful of areola. I alternated kissing and sucking her marshmallow nipples.

"I love every ounce of you," I said before arching my back to get close enough to shove my tongue in her mouth.

"This is lust at first sight." She wrapped her arms around me. "What you gonna do with all of this hotness?"

Damn, she was easier than I thought. Maybe it'd been a while since she was laid and she just wanted to get herself some.

She started undressing me. First went my polo over my head; next my pants and underwear were at my knees; my dick was being devoured like a hot link. Five minutes in, I fired a round of seeds down her throat. She didn't spill one.

As I pulled up my pants, she blocked my hand. "Uh-uh. You gon' give me some of that."

I held up my palms to her, stared at my limp noodle. "You suck the life outta him. Let me give you a rain check," I said. This time I fastened my belt. Put on my shirt.

"When, Kohl?" she asked.

A text from Trymm, **If Walter drops by your spot tonight or contacts you, cover my ass. I'm helping you out.**

No way was I assisting my competitor. I confirmed with Trymm, **Cool,** then texted Walter, **Trymm is not helping me out tonight,** knowing darn well Trymm was going to get messed up.

I told Gurl 1, "Let me get past the busy weekend. Get dressed. I have to get out of here. Next time I'm going to invite you to my house for dinner."

Gurl 1 was cashed out for my products. I escorted her to her vehicle.

"See you next week," she said.

"For sure." Locking up, I headed home. Had to be back by three o'clock to open for the afternoon crowd.

I filled up my large tub with more hot than cold water,

topped it off with bubble bath and essential oils. Opening my African black soap, I placed it in the dish. I had something for William's smart behind next time I saw them. I'd have a bar in my pocket. Turning on my TV, I put the plastic-covered remote within reach, reclined against the suds, closed my eyes.

Heard, "We've caught up to our newest star and the fifty-million-dollar man here at one of our favorite restaurants. Harold Thurston, 'welcome to New Orleans' may still be in order, since this is only your second season."

Harold was our team's ticket out of our losing streak. I had his jersey framed and on the wall at my clubs. A signature would be nice. Opening my eyes, I'd recognize Dooky's gumbo anywhere.

"Thanks. It's great to be a part of an exciting franchise," he said, all cool and stuff.

Ballers hated solicitations. So did I. I was going to invite him to my spot for an official-game after-party and extend him a welcome to my parents' church.

"How are you adjusting to the Big Easy?" our local news reporter Lisa Dozier asked.

Word around the city was she was extra thirsty. Maybe I could do her if Blitz didn't get to her first. She was more his type.

Harold said, "Loving the food. Can't get enough of this seafood gumbo." Filé juice spilled into his bowl as he ate a spoonful. Made me hungry for a bowl. My cooks made a good pot, but Dooky's had chefs. Might make a stop over there before I opened up.

He'd better scale back on wolfing down the fattening foods before he start looking like Charles Barkley's twin.

"What's your strategy to keep your opponent from scoring?"

"Defense wins games. I'm always going to do my best to keep the other team from scoring," he said, leaning back.

"Well, who do we have here?" the reporter asked.

The remote slipped from my grip, slid into the tub, floated. "What the hell was she up to?"

"I'd like to officially introduce my fiancée, who happens to be a native, to your local viewing audience. This is the lovely Ms. Ramona Dandridge, soon-to-be Mrs. Ramona Thurston."

"Don't eat too much, Ramona. Thanks for your time, Harold. . . . This is Lisa Dozier . . . Back to you, Gary."

So that was how Ramona had come up. Had to find a way to bring her down.

No man wanted to marry a whore, no matter how fine she was.

CHAPTER 22

Kohl

Day 3

"**S**hut it down. I'm exhausted. Announce the last song right now," I told my DJ. "'Planet Rock' all of them out the front door."

The intro to one of the longest ultimate "go hard or die trying" old school hits played. My entire club instantly became a huge dance floor.

I loved my city, but visitors lost their mind when they got to the only place in the country where clubs stayed open well into the sunrise. There was no last call for alcohol in the "city that care forgot."

Taking the mic, I announced, "You can get to-go cups for your drink on your way out."

Standing in the booth, I noticed one big gurl jumped on my stage with my stripper Big Nasty and broke it all . . . the . . . way . . . down. The gurl raised her minidress over her head, took it off, twirled it in the air, then yelled, "I run this motherfucker!"

I'd had my eye on her since midnight. I underestimated how wild she was. Had to hit it. She could stay.

Women rushed up the stairs on both sides; some hopped on from the front, the way I'd usually do. Next thing I saw were naked asses everywhere.

Females were stumbling, rolling, bouncing, twerking, like they were on payroll. Men were staggering, humping, throwing dollars in the air at seven in the morning. The sun had risen and I had to be at The House of the Lord in four hours.

Picturing myself in the mix of the mayhem, if I could do all of the women getting loose, three days into the challenge, I'd be halfway to my 101. I decided I was definitely going to make wild child, officially, Gurl 6. Everything was big, but she was ridiculously well-proportioned.

Pointing, I told my security, "Get her to my smash room." That was what I'd renamed my office. "Then I want you and your guys to usher everybody, dead or alive, outta here, then lock up."

"No problem, boss, but what you want to do about that?" he said, redirecting my attention to the hookah lounge.

Dicks were inside of every hole of every ho imaginable. Titties were in mouths. Females thighs were east and west. Some of them were in an upside down V, with their head buried in my sofa and their butts up.

This was the first time a regular club night had turned orgy. Nobody was permitted to screw in my place, except me.

"You know what to do," I told security. "I'll get my gurl. Put these fools along with their clothes out now"; then I ordered the DJ, "Cut the music off. They're about to get me shut down indefinitely."

Gurl 6 was responsible for starting the madness and I was about to hold her gorgeous behind accountable. Holding on to the opposite end of her dress, I demanded, "Come with me."

"Hey! After the party there's another party," she sang, following my footsteps.

I locked my door, bent her over in the middle of the floor. Pressing my hand against her lower back, I unfastened my buckle, unzipped my pants, and then I penetrated her deep.

"Oh, daddy. Fuck the shit out of me."

"Back that ass up!" *Smack!* I slapped her hard.

She pushed me onto my two-armed black leather chaise. I lost my balance, fell flat.

Power positions had reversed. "Stay your pretty long-ponytail ass right there," she commanded.

Slobbering on my knob, she cleaned up her own saliva. Holding each side of the chair, she rested the hind side of her knees on my shoulders, then dropped all of her weight in my lap.

"Oh, fuck!" My shaft snapped sideways. "Wait. Get up!" I yelled.

"What's my name?" she asked, hoisting, then lowering herself again like we were in some kind of wrestling match.

My stuff bent in the opposite direction. I wanted to cry like a baby.

"Fuck! For real. Stop!" I reached between her thighs to protect my shaft from another attack.

"Oh, this is some good dick," she said, wiggling. "You like my pussy?"

I was getting extra credit for this. "You love my dick?"

"Of course, I love it."

"What's my name?" I asked her.

"I love sex, Kash. You like the way I make you feel?" she asked, then said, "Let's change positions."

Praise God. I pushed her off of me. She rolled on her shoulder, splattered facedown on the edge of the chaise. Her knees hit the floor. Gurl 6 stared up at me.

Struggling to stand in those shoes, she said, "What the fuck you do that for? I oughta bust your ass."

Now that was how I felt about her snapping my dick, but I was no fool. "I apologize. Put your dress on," I said, handing it to her. "I have to make sure everyone is gone. I'll have security escort you to your car."

"I don't need no escort. You lucky I like your ass," she said, tugging at her hem.

Was she threatening me? "Or?"

"I'd own this bitch. Obviously, you don't know who you just fucked. I'm a Harrison, son. *Lema,*" she said, then strutted out.

Gurl 6 had to find another way to come up.

Inspecting the damages, a lot required cleaning. A few broken lamps. Wasn't as bad as I'd thought. I closed out my registers, locked the money in my safe. A smile spread across my face.

I decided to have a little more fun with Gurl 6. Down-loaded the footage. Blurring my face, I posted Gurl 6 on stage and in my smash box rolling onto the floor; then I hurried home to get ready for church.

CHAPTER 23

Kohl

Day 3

"Let the church say, 'Amen.'" Pastor-father solicited praise from his faithful congregation.

Dad stood behind the pulpit cloaked in his purple robe with three black doctoral bars on each side. Mom, addressed by the members as First Lady Paula, was on the front pew, inner aisle, in all peach. Dress. Heels. A small hat with an eye-length veil covered her forehead. I sat in in my reserved end seat, on the opposite side of the church from my mother, on the second row immediately behind the deacons.

"When the saints go marching into heaven, uh-huh!" Reverend Lloyd Bartholomew alternated stomping his feet, swung his elbows back and forth. His belled sleeves with deep cuffs flapped like wings.

"Will you be in that number? Can the work you've done speak for you?" Lowering his voice, he asked, "Or will it be a whisper?" He shouted, "God is merciful, but He's also mighty. Just like no good deed goes unnoticed, uh-huh! You will be held accountable for your sins." He pointed in a sweeping motion. "One way you express your love for God is through your tithes. You cannot out-give God. As you come to the altar, bless yourself by being a blessing to The House of the Lord."

My dad spread his arms, "Come. Give freely."

The organist began playing "Going Up Yonder," by Walter Hawkins, and my dad started humming the tune.

"Will you be there?" he asked. "Will First Lady Paula and I see you there?"

Since I'd opened the strip club, Dad stopped mention-ing me by name. He motioned for the choir to stand. The lead vocalist stepped forward and sang, "If anybody ask you . . ."

"Will you enter the pearly gates? You cannot outgive God," he repeated.

Standing in line to give, I noticed the assistant pastor's wife, Eleanor, fanning herself and checking me out. I dug into my pocket, dropped $5,000 cash into the collection plate at the altar. I'd done so well Friday and Saturday, I'd doubled my usual weekly contribution.

Winking at Mrs. Lewis, I exited to the rear of the church. My dad's sermon was next. Then the doors of the church and the assistant pastor's wife's legs would be open at the same time if she came back here.

I unlocked, then left the door to my dad's study cracked. Hid my phone between two books on the shelf, made sure the camera faced his desk. Eleanor did not disappoint. Locking the door, I started the video from my smartwatch.

We knew what she came for. Raising her dress over her ass, I pulled her panties to the side. *Damn!* Her butt was firm, smooth. Tried to slide my head in her vagina. *Wow!* She was tight. Had to work my way in.

"I've wanted you for almost twelve years," she said. "What a blessing."

"No disrespect, but I've admired you for a long time," I lied.

"I've checked you out, too, Kash." She yelped when I popped my head in deeper.

I covered her mouth. Heard, "The doors of the church are now opened. Don't live another day without giving your life to Christ."

"Lord forgive me. You know my heart," Eleanor said. "But I'm a young woman in need."

More like in heat.

Covering the assistant pastor's wife's mouth again, I pushed again. Paused. Her pussy pulsated, making my dick throb. Holding Eleanor around her waist. I leaned against her back, bent my knees, penetrated her all the way. When I started coming, I came hard. My body trembled. Knees weakened.

Water ran down her legs, soaked my pants. Our shoes. I stepped back, looked down at the puddle, then whispered, "Oh, shit. Stay right there."

"I'm drenched," she said, rubbing her vagina.

Rummaging through my dad's closet, I found the handkerchiefs he used to dry his sweat during his sermons, handed her a stack. I dried my shoes, but wasn't a thing I could do about my pants.

Someone jiggled the doorknob. We stared at each other. I placed my finger over her lips. Pushed her into my dad's private restroom. Whispered, "Stay quiet."

She started whimpering, fanning herself. I shook my head, sprayed air freshener onto the carpet. Grabbed a glass off of my dad's desk. Filled the glass with water.

"Anybody in there?" It was Sister Eleanor's husband.

He was supposed to be in the pulpit.

Told her, "I got you." Before I realized it, I'd kissed her, then said, "Lock the door, baby."

I retrieved my phone, powered off my video, swished the air, sat at my dad's desk, tipped the water in the direction of my lap, then opened the door.

"Assistant Pastor, I'm sorry. I spilled water all over my

pants. Was trying to dry them, but let my dad know I have to leave service early. How much did we collect today?"

"I appreciate your generosity, young man. I'd better check," he said. "Sorry for the interruption. I was looking for Eleanor."

"God bless you, Assistant Pastor. If I see her, I'll let her know," I said, closing and then locking the door.

I tapped on the bathroom door. "He's gone."

Eleanor unfastened my pants. "I want some more of that good lovin'," she demanded, kneeling before me, holding my shaft in her hands as though it was her Communion. This portion would not be on film, but it would be etched in my mind forever.

She was gentle. I was grateful.

Holding the back of her head, I looked up and whispered, "Forgive us."

CHAPTER 24

Kohl

Day 9

Blitz sat alone on the terrace at a table for four, talking on his phone, saw me, ended his call, then said, "What's up, Kohl?"

"It's all good." I asked, "You ordered?"

"Not yet, my brother."

I was thirsty. Right away I told the waitress, "Let us have two flights."

Sitting across from him, I was glad the rest of the crewe hadn't arrived. "How long you been following Ramona, bruh? Y'all friends? I mean off social."

The sun was blazing. I had on my red polo, khaki slacks, shoes hard enough to put a dent in his shin, if he said the wrong thing. The waitress placed our flights on the table, then left.

"With your joint, why you not on social?" he asked, then downed his first of five beer samples, a lager.

Kash In & Out was a spot where customers socialized old-school—face-to-face. Word of mouth spread like wildfire when I opened. I didn't require television or print ads.

I was at the top of every search engine. Type in strip clubs or hookah in New Orleans and I was at the top. Plus, I had a website with lots of photos on my home page.

Time was money. Social media was free, but the amount of time people wasted on it, they could've been getting paid doing something constructive. The only reason I established pages was for the challenge, and each one was being deactivated soon as I was announced the winner.

"Doing one another's exes is forbidden." Tension crept up in my neck and shoulders. I prepared to knock Blitz upside his head.

He tossed back his ale. I caught up. Followed my ale with an IPA.

"Too late for add-ons, Kohl. Keep it real. What nigga you know wouldn't hit that? I mean, six, seven months ago, hell to the no. Ramona was big as a whale. Now, shitz. I check her page three times a day." He stared at me, waited for my next move.

"You can only eat so much coochie before you throw up, my brother. Considering what you working with, you might as well strap on a fake one if you're serious about doing Ramona." I went there. He deserved it.

Blitz laughed. Swallowed number three, a porter this time.

His opting not to comment wasn't what I expected. "Ha-ha, my behind. Once upon a time Ramona and I were in love."

How did I expect him to respect my request when Blitz had never kept a woman for more than ninety days? My dick wasn't huge like Trymm's, but I had enough to keep Ramona satisfied.

"Drink and listen up, potna," he said, placing his elbow on the table. "One, according to you, Billy boy ain't your son. Two—"

I pounded the hardwood; beer splashed on my pants. I didn't care. I told him, "I don't know that for a fact!"

Blitz gave me that tight smile that barely showed his teeth. "Take the damn test then, nigga!"

"I, don't, want, to."

"Then shut your broke ass the fuck up. You don't own Ramona's pussy. Ramona can cash any check you give her."

Ramona didn't have money; she was marrying money. I finished my wheat beer. The tension in my neck moved to my temples. My darn head was throbbing. "Stay away from Ramona." I was two seconds from picking up my flight plank and busting Blitz in his light-skinned face. See whose bruise would be blacker.

"You won't take it, because Billy boy looks exactly like your ass," he taunted.

"Let it go" was all I said.

"I'm just fucking with you, my brother. I don't blame you for disowning him if Ramona stepped out like you said. . . ." Sucking up number four, he added, "You think she got her vagina rejuvenated? I heard that's the in thing for females nowadays. If I find out, I'll let you know." He tugged on his collar, held up his last, then smiled at me. "Cheers, my brother."

"Where's your watch?" I asked, changing the subject.

Ramona couldn't afford to get her hair done when I was with her, now she was marrying my idol? Something wasn't right. Harold must have not known she was a prostitute.

"On second thought . . . cheers. If you hit that in your count, get proof, post it to your social, and tag her. If I win, I'll give you back your quarter of a mil." Seeing Ramona and bad-butt Billy go back on welfare would have her chasing me.

"Bet. Text that to me, my brother."

The waitress cleared the table.

Dallas walked up, claimed the spot next to me. Blitz was across the table facing us.

First thing he asked Blitz, "Where your Rolex, dude?"

"Banging this poli-sci major this morning. Forgot to put it on," he said, feeling his wrist.

"I don't know about y'all, but this dick-and-dump shit is hard as hell," Dallas confessed. "Plus, it doesn't seem right. I think we should take out the social-posting requirement."

"Sexing the assistant pastor's wife in my dad's study during Sunday service wasn't right, but it's the highlight on my reel. I should get two points if I included her in my count."

"You going straight to hell for that one, Kohl." Dallas shook his head for a long time.

Blitz stared at me from the corners of his eyes. "That's low. Like snake-belly low. Dallas is right."

"How the hell y'all gon' judge me?" Between Gurls 1 through 27, I had to admit, "I'm having fun."

"Talking a chick into giving it up is a cinch. Throwing them outta my bed, I hate doing that shit. Plus, one of 'em . . . ," Dallas paused, bit his bottom lip, then continued, "I can't do her like that."

We ordered a round of beer samplers with Dallas.

"Don't tell me your ass met somebody you like," I said, then started laughing. "Put her on hold for the next three weeks, or you might as well sit this challenge out." I wasn't interested in smashing whoever she was, the way Blitz was bone-hard over Ramona.

"Nah, the deal is, the brother is having difficulty keeping it up." Blitz balled his fist, bent his elbow, flexed his bicep.

On occasion I'd said some messed-up stuff to D, but today I wasn't hitting him below the waist. The side effects of his medication could make him homicidal.

Dallas leaned back, squeezed his dick. "That's the least of my concerns. Round-the-clock breaking him out,

I'm willing to admit, my dick hurts and that nigga is tired."

A flashback of Gurl 6 almost breaking me in two, I understood. Smashing three times a day, I'd dropped back to hand and blow jobs. Big gurls were great at both, and a lot of them rode better than the skinny girls.

"You not getting your money back," Blitz insisted. "Dick. Date. Dump. Proof. No exceptions. Winner takes all."

Blitz tapped the table. "I'll give you a side challenge. Whoever that bitch is, the one you like, do something publicly outrageous to embarrass her ass and . . . if I win, I'll give you back your two hundred and fifty."

I smiled at Blitz. Shook my head. Told Dallas, "I'll make you the same proposition that Blitz just made."

"Whoa!" Dallas covered his mouth. "Hashtag Clydesdale2930 on social." His eyes were fixated on his screen.

"Whoa." I'd seen a horse's dick and Clydesdale2930 was in the running. I'd forgotten how outrageously big Trymm was. It was a wonder he ever got pussy. Francine's vagina must've been hollow.

I frowned. "She's seriously trying to cut off her air supply?" If she made him disappear, she deserved the million. Covering my mouth, I kept watching. Nah, she was lightweight, but she did usher a noticeable rise out of Dallas.

Trymm walked up. His count had to be really high or super-low.

Blitz greeted him with, "Nigga, you cold-blooded, my brother."

"His ass always been the most scandalous," Dallas said. "I got something for y'all tomorrow."

Trymm rubbed his iPad like it was a lantern and a genie was about to pop out and grant him three wishes any second. "If I told you my official smashdown that's right here, you'd think I was lying."

Dallas said, "Man, this challenge opened my eyes to how small this city is. Even during the festival all I met was local randoms. My face is starting to become too familiar."

Trymm gave Dallas a condescending look. "New faces require new places, D. Upgrade your locations. What's up with you, Kohl?"

Blitz frowned, focusing on Trymm.

Bobbing my head, I answered, "Ain't never a shortage of big gurls in the South. They come to me. I feed 'em, then fuck 'em, and if they let me fuck 'em first, I might not give 'em a po'boy or a daiquiri."

A text registered from Lema: **wtf, you blast me on social media, bitch!**

Her text didn't phase me as much as how did she get my number? She undressed herself. I replied with a lie. **Wasn't me.**

Lema followed with, **Lying bitch! You Money2930. My brothers gon' get you.**

I don't care about your brothers. Don't come back to my club.

"Changed my mind about fucking your ex, Ramona," Blitz said.

"Shitz, I'd do her right here. Right now," Dallas said. "Those pictures she be postin' puts me on swole."

Noticed his shaft filling in. "You follow her, too?" I asked.

"Hell yeah. She's got something like eight hundred thousand followers," Trymm said.

"That's tripled since Harold announced their engagement on television." Blitz scrolled his finger up and up and up on his phone.

"When did that happen?" Dallas inquired. "Kohl, you knew about that?"

Wanted to say, *"Still having flashbacks?"* But I was

more concerned about why all of them were following Ramona and not one of 'em mentioned her to me.

"Check this out." Blitz showed me a photo of Harold Thurston leaning against his Rolls-Royce and then a picture of the old Ramona on her knees with an old man's dick in her mouth.

I didn't care where he'd gotten it. "Text that to me, bruh. Pronto."

CHAPTER 25

Ramona

Day 11

I saw the tweets.

One read, **Broke bitch came up, now she 2 good 2 speak.**

Another mentioned, **I knew you when you were sucking dicks for a dollar.**

I'd never done any services for less than $20, but whatever I did, I did it for my son. For that, I didn't owe any of those haters an explanation or an apology. Scanning the feed while Harold drove, the comments became more insulting.

Harold don't marry that prostitute! Marry me! #imavirgin

You can blow me anytime Ramona. I'll pay you. #adollarright

Trick wearing a watch the price of a house. Purse the cost of a car.

Ramona has herpes!!!!

That was a lie. Harold parked in front of William's

Catholic school. Parents were outside waving, fanning, and holding picket signs:

NO HOOKER'S KIDS ALLOWED

PROTECT OUR KIDS FROM PROSTITUTES

WILLIAM GO HOME!

RAMONA DANDRIDGE IS A DISGRACE TO OUR SCHOOL AND TEAM

HAROLD THURSTON DO NOT MARRY RAMONA DANDRIDGE!

The ringleader capturing it all, and conducting interviews, was Lisa Dozier. I opened my door to curse out her and all of those alcoholic, stay-at-home moms on prescription drugs.

Harold grabbed my biceps. "Stay put."

He looked over his shoulder at my son. "William, don't let anybody tell you what or who your mother is and what she means to you. She struggled to take care of you. I got your mom and your back. That's all that matters."

"Yes, sir," William answered, then lowered his head. "None of this would be happening if my father hadn't disowned me."

The tone of my son's voice was the sadness Kohl had never heard, but I'd listened to it too many times. William was right. I did what I had to because Kohl refused to accept responsibility for his actions. If I saw his punk ass again, he had another fist to the face coming.

"Hold your head high. You eat what you earn. Nobody owes you anything. Not your father. Not your mother. Keep getting straight A's. I'm going to show you how to use your superpower for good."

William smiled. "Like President Obama?"

"Exactly. Let's go."

I watched my fiancé place his hand on William's shoulder, bypass the protestors that were screaming at both of them. Entering the front door of the school's main building, Harold ignored whatever Lisa Dozier had whispered in his ear. Before Harold came back through the doors they'd entered, a security guard gathered the angry parents and reporter into a huddle.

Whatever he said to them, the parents left dragging their signs. Lisa packed her microphone, got in the news van. Harold sat behind the wheel, drove us to the lakefront, and turned off the engine.

Grayish waves rippled toward the cement barrier. Kohl had brought me here a few times when we were teenagers. If I hadn't had William, I probably wouldn't be here with Harold.

Holding hands, we strolled the deserted area.

Before Katrina, the lake was packed with families enjoying picnics. People chilling and blasting music from their cars or portable speakers. Some tossed footballs. Others feasted on crawfish that was stacked high on top of newspaper.

I had to ask, "What did you tell them?"

Harold held my hand. "I'm not going anywhere. If they kept allowing people to disrespect us, we'd home-school William and they'd never receive another donation from us."

Wow. I'm not sure why I deserve this man, but thank You, Jesus, for Harold.

"Take care of all the details. When I get back from my trip, we are getting married," he said, then picked me up and spun me around.

"Yeah, we can silence all the haters," I said.

Harold passionately kissed me. Lowering me to a standing position, my fiancé tapped on his cell, placed it on speaker.

Someone answered, "Whatever you need. I've seen the posts, man."

"Forget those fools. I need you to process a court order demanding Kohl Bartholomew take a paternity test for William Bartholomew. If William is his, we'll go public with that information and file for back child support. If William isn't his, we're changing William's last name to Thurston."

I was 1,000 percent sure Kohl was the father, but hearing Harold request that order, I fell in my man's arms and cried.

CHAPTER 26

Kohl

Day 14

"This fried chicken is almost as good as Manchu's," Gurl 42 said, sucking the bone.

Harold hadn't called off the engagement to Ramona. That was disappointing. Guess he had too much plastic invested in all that plastic.

Why hadn't I thought of Manchu? I could've gotten one hundred wing pieces for $50. "I bet you can throw down in the kitchen," I said, texting Gurl 30, **Thinking about you.** I copied and pasted the same message to Gurls 31 to 39 with a big red balloon heart that would inflate when they read the message. Later I'd add their videos to my pages Money2930. I was the only crewe putting up real numbers.

Grabbing two handfuls of buttocks, I jiggled Gurl 42's cheeks. "I have to get to the club. Have a delivery coming in." I rocked her in my arms. "I would like to see you again."

She picked up her plate, dumped six leg bones into my trash. "I'm free tomorrow after I get off."

Leaving the opportunity open for a repeat, maybe in

October or whenever I'd become bored, I told her, "Sure. Let me text you," knowing darn well Friday was out of the question.

A text registered from the pastor's wife, **Can I come by your club now for an encore?**

Gurl 34 replied, **Miss you much.**

37 texted, **Had a great time.**

Gurls 32, 38, and 39 wanted to get with me soon.

The attention was great. Gurl 29 hit me, **Go fuck yourself!!!!! I hope you die!**

Damn, that's rude. Guess she'd seen her post, but I prayed she couldn't trace her steps back to me the way Lema had. I wasn't offended by anyone, including Gurl 29. Everyone had to die at some point. I'd never created any drama in my parents' tabernacle. Wasn't about to start. Best not to respond to Eleanor.

Opening the door for my guest to leave, a stranger greeted me, "Hey, Kohl. Man, what's up?"

I was quiet. Had never seen him.

"Kohl, don't be rude to the man," Gurl 42 said. "See you tomorrow."

Only if she made it to Kash In & Out. Loved how I got paid every time my clients inhaled hookah, and when they dropped dollars on my strippers, I took a cut.

"What's up, my brother?" Handing me an envelope, he said, "You've been served."

I suspected it was Gurl 6 trying to make me roll out dough for her. She should've thought about her reputation before voluntarily shaking her naked ass on my stage. Inserting my finger into the gap, I removed the letter. Court papers from Ramona demanding a paternity test.

If bad Billy was my biological, and Harold followed through with the ceremony, I could be the one collecting child support. I drove straight to the address on the document.

"I'm here to prove I'm the father. What do you want?" I asked the woman behind the desk.

She replied, "The same thing all women want. Blood."

Yeah, if she'd let me do her, she'd have to stand in line behind a number of angry women that wanted to make me bleed.

A text registered from Lema: **You know not the day nor the hour. My brothers are going to make you wish you were dead.**

Women. If she really thought her being exposed was my fault, Lema was the dumbest woman of them all.

CHAPTER 27

Kohl

Day 17

"**W**ell! Huh! I say, 'he who is without sin,' uh-huh! 'Cast the first stone.'" My father stomped his foot. "You didn't hear me? Huh! I said, 'he who is *without* sin, cast the *first* stone.'" He shuffled his feet, pumped his arms back and forth. His belled sleeves swayed like he was preparing to take flight.

Sweat rolled down the sides of Pastor Bartholomew's face as he looked out over his faithful congregation less than a hundred members strong. He swiped that perspiration away with his handkerchief. Hopefully, that wasn't one of the ones I'd used to clean up Eleanor's bodily fluids two weeks ago.

Watching the assistant pastor's wife out of my peripheral, I did my routine nod in response to my dad's message. Daintily, Eleanor raised her right pointing finger. Without turning, she motioned a discreet *"come hither"* to me, then tiptoed through the rear doors. I'd avoided her throughout the week, but Sundays were inevitable. Recalling how she'd gushed all over me in my dad's chambers, I felt my legs go wet. I got a tingling sensation in my groin.

Tempted to get up and give Mrs. Lewis what she craved, I knew that smashing her twice would be a waste of an orgasm. I replied to Gurl 37's text received three days ago, **Me too.**

"Are we justified to seek revenge when others have done us wrong, when we do not acknowledge nor ask for forgiveness when we are the culprit? Huh! Ya heard me. Turn to the person on your left, and repeat after me."

Wow. I paid zero attention up to this point. I faced a young girl, ten years of age, maybe. Females developed fast these days. With all the colorful ribbons in her hair, she could've been eight or nine. It was hard to tell, but this was my first time noticing how the innocence in her brown eyes shined bright. She must've been a visitor. Hadn't seen her here before.

The pastor said, "Forgive me if I have sinned against you, for it is my job to protect, not to hurt, you, for I am my brothers' and my sisters' keeper."

Nothing could be further from the truth right now, Dad. Regurgitating the words, being reared in The House of the Lord, I'd become immune to harboring guilt for my sins. Everything was sinful. The little girl's mouth moved, but I could not hear a word she'd spoken.

"Turn to your right and face your neighbor," my father said.

Seated on the end, I stared at the purple, red, green, and blue stained-glass window. No one was there for me to exchange words with. I took this opportunity to go see where the assistant pastor's wife was.

"I erase all animosity in my heart against anyone that I perceived have mistreated me," my father said as I exited into the rear.

Peeping in the study, I saw she was there. I said, "Get her ready for me. I have to get this urine out the way."

I let her use my dad's private restroom. I entered the
men's restroom. In the middle of releasing myself, I
heard a little voice telling me not to sex Mrs. Lewis. Returning to my seat, I noticed Assistant Pastor Eric, or as I
called him at one time, Reverend E, was not in the pulpit.

"If you need a church home, don't wait," my father
said. "Tomorrow is not promised." His "huh" was softer.
He glanced over his shoulder to the seat where his assistant always sat throughout the message. "Today isn't
promised." He looked back at his congregation. "All we
have is—"

"Woman, what the hell you doin' up in here naked!"
resounded from the back.

My dad looked over his shoulder, then quickly faced
the congregation, and continued, "All we have is—"

"Eric, get your dumb ass outta here right now!" Eleanor
shouted.

Mrs. Lewis shocked me. I kept a blank look on my
face.

Pastor Bartholomew motioned for the organist. He
pressed on the keys, playing "Just a Closer Walk with
Thee." The choir stood, sang, "'I am weak, but Thou art
strong/Jesus, keep me from all wrong.'"

"Will you come and be saved," my dad said as if he
hadn't heard a word of the Lewises' argument.

No one stood.

Gurl 37 replied, **I'm cooking supper. Come ova.**

Females in New Orleans, if they liked you, they
weren't really asking you to come eat. It was more like,
you'd betta show up. I decided not to respond to Gurl 37.
Maybe for another three days.

"Yes, my child. Hallelujah! Welcome to The House of
the Lord," the pastor said.

A text from Dallas registered, **After this challenge, I'm
visiting your church, man. I need Jesus.**

I went on Ramona's page. I'd messed up. She should've

been sitting next to me instead of the little girl with her mom. I wondered what my mother and father looked like. Why had they put me up for adoption? That was a can of worms not worth opening.

Interrupting my thoughts, the pastor asked his usual, "What's your name, child?"

This scripted segment would last another ten minutes. One of the missionaries would escort whoever was up there in the back. Hopefully, Eleanor had gotten dressed. Or maybe her husband was able to get it up and he was undressed.

"Lema Harrison."

Fumbling my cell, I looked up. *Aw, hell. Gurl 6. Showing up at my place of worship? She'd taken this social-post backlash too far.*

"Where are you from?" my dad asked.

"The lower ninth," she said, staring at me.

Pop. Smack. Pop. Smack. Pop. Gurl 6 blew a big pink bubble. *Pop.* It splattered over her lips. Sucking in the chewing gum, she said, "I didn't come to join. I came to deliver a message. You have thirteen days to leave my city. You," she said to my father. "You," she said, pointing at my mother. "And that bitch-ass nigga right there." Lema pointed at me, then walked down the aisle real slow.

She paused, stared at me. "Your time starts now, bitch."

Getting out of my seat, I followed her outside. Two guys, one on each side of the door, grabbed me under my arms. Nosy members stood behind me. I was nervous, but refused to show it.

"Look, man, I apologize." My feet did the Running Man, but they weren't on the ground. "I made a dumb mistake. I'll take the video down."

"What the fuck? You mean our lil sis is still up?" One of the guys pulled out a gun, fired a shot in the air.

"Nigga, you ready to die at church?" The other brother fired off two bullets. "Take that shit down right now!"

They released my arms and I stumbled, then stood up straight.

Gurl 6 sat on the backseat in the car with the door open with her phone up to her ear, laughing as I deactivated all my Money2930 pages. I said a silent prayer. *Lord, please get me out of this situation.* I knew better than to turn my back on these goons.

I stood there, pivoting my head from one to the other. Where was Dallas when I needed him? Blitz and Trymm wouldn't do shit if they were here. I took that back. Blitz would laugh hysterically, videotape, then put me on social. He was *that* dude.

If anybody deserved to die, it was me. Not the people in the tabernacle screaming. Sirens blared in the distance.

"Fuck thirteen days, nigga. Y'all need to rise up and get ghost tonight," one of her brothers told me.

"Yeah, don't let us catch you on the streets after midnight," the other brother said.

"Fuck, fuck with, text, or say boo to my baby sis again, I dare you. Everybody in this bitch is going down," her brother told me.

"Ya heard me," the other brother said. "They gon' die twice."

How was that possible?

Getting in a black SUV with Gurl 6, the tinted windows were ridiculously dark. The doors closed and I couldn't see either of them. I watched the mob drive off as the police parked in their spot.

I was pissed that I didn't have my piece. I could've fired in self-defense. Didn't think I needed to strap up at church. Starting today, I was going to carry like my boy Dallas on a daily. Two guns on Sundays.

My father stood beside me. "I knew one day that sinners' club would bring trouble here. Your mother and I built The House of the Lord from the ground up. This ministry is all we have. Son, don't lead the devil into my church again."

I nodded, but I had no idea how to keep the Harrisons from returning, even if I didn't come back.

My father placed the donation I'd made today, twenty-five $100 bills, in my hand, then whispered in my ear, "I'll arrange for you to start making cash deposits directly into the church's account, but don't come back here ever again."

Thought he was going to tell me my money was no good.

The day my dad ostracized Ramona resurfaced. She was poor, pregnant with a child, and in the one place that should've embraced her, my father had kicked her out.

And I had shut her out when she was nineteen and pregnant with what could be my dad's first grandchild.

CHAPTER 28

Kohl

Day 20

I'd survived quite a few of the Harrison's midnight dead-lines. *What is with the Harrison brothers and that number thirteen?* Hopefully, that was an idle threat too. I was ten days from winning, hopefully. Worrying about Ramona and Lema couldn't let them set me back.

Sitting in my office at Kash In & Out, I'd searched every combination I could think of for Ramona's new IG page. She'd deactivated her old account. Had no luck. Wasn't giving up. I could ask Blitz, Trymm, or Dallas. Bet they all knew, but I didn't want the crewe to know I was equally obsessed with stalking her online. That, and I was catching feelings for Ramona, wanted her back, es-pecially if William was mine.

Leaving the Easy wasn't happening. Had to find an ac-ceptable apology for Lema. Maybe I could offer her a por-tion of my winnings. My count was sixty and rising. The good Reverend Bartholomew's and First Lady Paula's be-trayal made me text what I'd hoped would hurt him, **Who are my biological parents?**

Wow! Found my baby.

Ramona had on a two-piece swimsuit. I let the video loop repeat. The ocean waves splashed against her booty, washed down the crack of her butt. Her ass was ridiculously nice. Salt water rolled down her cleavage.

I played the next scene. Harold swept Ramona off her feet. She laughed. He smiled. Kissed her. The next video on her page was of them on the beach stretched out face-down naked on massage tables, under the moonlight. Must've been a thousand candles surrounding them. Some man's hands slid along her lower back. A female rubbed Harold's ass.

I was pissed that Ramona looked genuinely happy without me.

Felt my jaws tightening. Put down my cell for a moment. Where was my son Billy boy while they were getting their freak on? I should report them as unfit parents.

Restocking my bar, I wondered, what would our life have been like if I'd done the right thing and married Ramona? Supported her dreams? Helped raise her son.

Checked her page again. William was on a horse. Another kid about his age rode beside him. Their smiles couldn't get any wider as the stallions trotted along the shore. My son was no cowboy. The next clip William and the same boy were Jet-Skiing. Parasailing. Then the four of them were dining on Maine lobsters that had to be five pounds each.

What did Harold see in Ramona that I hadn't?

As I read her next post, my chin dropped. *What the hell?*

When did Ramona post a copy of my DNA test results? I texted Blitz, **I know you saw that. Why you didn't say something?**

He hit me back, **Man, fuck that DNA! I'm da pappy!**

Oh, okay, I replied, refusing to give Blitz the satisfaction of knowing I was pissed off. This was not a scene in the movie *Life*, this was my life.

I felt like shit. I'd locked in her number from the court documents. Hadn't used it, but had to text Ramona: **I apologize. I'm ready to meet my son.**

A picture of Harold with his hand on my son's shoulder popped up on her page. No DM back to me.

I texted her again, **His real daddy is here. Homeboy can dip.**

No response.

I knew how to get her attention. **Got a check for all of your back child support in two weeks. How much do I owe?**

Gurl 1 entered. I dropped my cell in my pocket.

Quietly she arranged my delivery on the counter. Double stacked the boxes of hookah by flavors. Lined up hoses, tips, filters, bowls, tongs, lighters, and the remainder of my order.

After checking my inventory twice, I politely told her, "Thanks."

"Don't say shit to me, man. You real foul." Her mouth twisted sideways. Slowly she shook her head. "Not even an apology from your sorry ass? Took you seventeen days to take down your page."

And she should be grateful that it wasn't going back up in ten. Females I'd previously exposed wouldn't repeat. "You right. I apologize."

"What you thought was a fucking joke almost cost me my job. On top of that, you got my coworkers disrespecting me on a daily. My son fighting at school every day. The shit you did ain't right, Kash."

I knew I should feel bad, but she was a willing participant. The only person that made me feel worse than Gurl 6 was Ramona. I handed Gurl 1 my credit card. She swiped; I signed.

"Somebody gon' fuck! You! Up!" Gurl 1 shook her head and her ass out the door.

Digging in my pocket, I checked my phone for a reply from Ramona. Nothing.

A strange woman entered. My eyes got wide. Lips spread. She had a rack exactly like Ramona's.

"What time do you open?" she asked, real chipper.

"Depends."

"Today is my birthday," she said, all sexy. "I turn twenty-one."

Gurl, soon-to-be number 61, was legal, but a lil too young to be so plastic. Had to find out if the good Lord or a surgeon had blessed her. "Then let me buy you a drink," I offered.

"I came in to reserve a table and order bottle service for me and my friends."

"Aw'ight." Popping open a bottle of champagne, I locked the door, filled two flutes, handed her one. "How many friends coming?"

"Five, plus me." She sipped. "A lil cheap, but good. I'ma need Krug Brut."

I might have to pass on this one. Krug was $300 a bottle. My price. "Happy birthday to the most beautiful girl in the world."

Raising her glass, she said, "To me."

"Salute. To you. You want to give the pole a spin."

Her eyes and smile widened. "Tonight?"

I nodded toward the stage. "Sure. But you can give it a practice twirl now. I'll watch." I played, *Pour It Up*.

Enthusiasm coupled with her youth had her winding and grinding on the pole and crawling on the floor. I went in the back, grabbed two racks. Removing the rubber band, I made 100 singles rain on her.

"You're a natural. Come sit here." I patted my knee, waved the other stack.

"Can I practice my lap dance?" she asked.

"In a minute. What are you doing with your life?" I asked, not really caring, but I knew when females thought you were concerned about them, they were generous with the goods. Like Ramona.

"I was enrolled at UNO. Had to drop out. The tuition was too expensive."

Wait. Champagne taste, beer money, messed-up priorities. "I graduated from the University of New Orleans. I have connects. I'll see what I can do to get you back on track," I lied, handed the stack to her, then refilled our flutes.

"Really! That's crazy," she said. "A toast to you."

"Tuition is expensive. Besides, I've seen you move. I know you can do better than a toast," I said, unzipping my pants.

CHAPTER 29

Ramona

Day 23

Ignoring Kohl gave me satisfaction. Confirming he was William's biological father allowed me to stop chasing him to do right by our son. A ten—make that eleven if I counted my pregnancy—year emotional weight was lifted. I was going all the way in on his ass, through the court system.

Act an ass? Go to jail. Don't pay? Go to jail. As I moved forward, everything would be strictly business with Kohl.

William was on the nineteenth-yard line. The score was tied at fourteen in the fourth quarter, with three minutes left to go.

"Defense, William! Get ready!" I shouted, bouncing on the bleacher.

"Sack, sack, the quarterback!" Carmella yelled.

My son had gone from being excused from the team to starting. There were players that were better than William, I'd admit. Whatever Harold told the coach and the things he'd taught William worked in our favor: calisthenics, jogging, stretching, watching recorded game footage, explaining plays to our son. William deserved a chance to prove himself worthy. And I learned a valuable lesson: Kohl wasn't going to control my emotions ever again.

"Oh, my gosh! Yes! William! Run, baby!" I bounced hard on the bleacher. My cropped top dipped below my areolas.

Carmella yanked it up. "Run, William!" she yelled.

"Thanks, girl."

Carmella laughed. "No one saw your goods."

Hopefully, Carmella was right. My followers had moved on to the next trend. I did not need to give them a reason to circle back to me.

We were in our usual seats at the top. Harold was on the sideline with the other dads cheering on our son. William intercepted the ball. Harold ran on the sideline motivating William to keep moving. Our baby went straight up the middle. "That's my boy! Keep going! You got this, baby! Touchdown!"

Overheard a parent for the other team complaining, "He can't run with him. That's not fair!"

She wasn't close enough to hear me say, "Shut up, bitch. Life ain't fair."

At the start of the next play, Carmella's son was on offense. I heard a familiar voice: "That's my boy, son! You ain't his daddy."

"Aw, hell no." I stood to confirm it was indeed Kohl Bartholomew.

Harold looked up at me, shaking his head. He texted, **Kohl wants your attention. Stay put. I got this.**

Kohl had wedged his way into the lineup of dads, three persons down from Harold. He'd never shown his face at any of William's games.

"Don't let him steal your joy," Carmella said. "Look at it this way. He was here to see William score his first defensive touchdown."

Kohl stared up at me. His back was to the field.

"Yayyyy!" I screamed. "Get ready, Cornelius! It's your turn!" I stood. Shifted my weight from one heel to the other. Rubbed the tips of my fingers. Our team had to stay in the lead.

"You finally got the upper hand," Carmella said, standing beside me. "Kohl is going to do the fool every chance he gets. Let him. He looks stupid hawking you. Long as you were struggling and miserable, he denied William. Now that you're rocking a Cardi B, hot-ass bod, he's lost his mind."

"You're right," I said, keeping my peripheral on Kohl.

"Thanks for including Cornelius and me on your summer vacation. You know I couldn't afford that and it's all he talks . . . Oh, my! It's my son's turn! Run, baby!" Carmella shouted.

I joined her, keeping my attention on the enemy. "Girl, let's go to the field. I have to make my way down there by Harold before the clock runs out."

As I stepped over the last bleacher, Kohl approached me. "Ramona. I want William to go with me for an hour."

I locked eyes with Harold. Told Kohl, "He has plans with—"

"His father." Harold stepped in and finished my sentence. "You want time after ten years of being a deadbeat? Get the fuck outta here."

I balled my fist in advance, but if my elbows went up, I promised Kohl was going down. I seconded Harold's comment. "Yeah, get the fuck outta here."

William and Cornelius ran to us. "Dad, did you see me score? I did all the things you taught me."

Harold gave William and his friend a high five, then slapped them on the butt. "Great job, fellas. Y'all ready to go fishing?"

Our boys started dancing. William boasted, "If you

think my touchdown was amazing, I'm better at fishing than football—"

"Son," Kohl interrupted. "I'm sorry about everything. Can we hang out for an hour?"

All of a sudden, Kohl couldn't accept rejection.

"No, punk," William said. "Showing up in nice clothes don't make you a man. And it sure as hell don't make you my daddy."

Harold intervened: "Son. Show respect."

"But, Dad!" William exclaimed.

Harold nodded in Kohl's direction.

William heaved a breath. "No, sir. I have plans with my father." Then he mouthed, punk.

" 'Sir'?" Kohl straightened his spine, squared his shoulders. "Son, you can legally call me dad now."

"Go get you and your friend something to drink," I said to William.

Harold told Kohl, "I don't know what kind of game you're playing, but not with my son. You want his respect. Earn it. 'Cause you ain't running shit with my family. You let Ramona struggle with William all his life, and now that's she's married to a baller, you wanna pretend you give a fuck about William? No, son. He's my son."

"I got your son, all right." Kohl raised his voice. "That's *my* boy! I had Ramona first. *First!*"

Ego in full effect. I smirked at Kohl. All I'd gone through and he wanted to play this bitch-ass, disrespectful game. My right elbow went up. Kohl went down. Shit happened so fast, I doubted the coach had time to see me lay Kohl out.

Kohl sprang to his feet. Slipped. Fell. "I'ma see you in court!" he yelled, holding his busted lip.

"Bruh," Harold laughed. "All I can say is, don't get up until she leaves. Carmella, please get my wife out of here." Harold gave her a stack of hundreds. "Y'all go shopping. On me."

I let down my top. Carmella handed me the money.

"Keep it. What you want to do?" I asked my friend.

"Buy a house with all new furniture," she said jok-ingly.

"Why not? Let's do it!" I said seriously.

Now that Harold and I were legal, I wanted my one bestie to be comfortable. We went to a few open houses, put an offer on a modest three-bedroom home, hit Inter-state 10, and drove east to the designer outlets.

CHAPTER 30

Kohl

Day 23

I was a good guy in bad situations.
These head games were giving me migraines.

Typically, I'd hand my keys to the valet attendant at Drago's. Not anymore. Had to rethink my every move. I backed into the closest spot to the exit, on the third level of the garage.

Sitting in my car, I texted Ramona, **I apologize about earlier. Let's work things out for William.**

I texted Lema, **I apologize. Let's work things out. Name your price.**

I didn't want to leave the only place I'd lived. I wanted to be there for Ramona and my son. Couldn't be mad at her for being angry. I deserved that. Deserved her laying hands. Had to find out if she had any love left for me.

Man, she is the type of fine I want on my arm to have bragging rights not only with my crewe but every man alive.

Plus, she always had a good heart. Took a chance, di-

aled her number. Call went to voice mail. Called back. It
rang.

Ramona answered, "What, Kohl?"

"Ramona, listen. I'm sorry. For real," I said. A lump
grew in my throat.

"Apology accepted. Bye, Ko—"

A call registered from Trymm. I declined.

"Wait, Ramona. Don't hang up on me. Don't give up on
me. You know we were kids and I was adopted. I don't
know who my parents are. That bothers me every day. I was
scared when you got pregnant. I didn't know how to be
there for you. My adoptive parents being . . . ," I paused.
Had a difficult time praising either of them. "Christians and
all. I—"

Trymm texted, **omw.**

"Save that bullshit, Kohl. You didn't even try to be
there. You have no idea what I've been through!" Ramona started crying.

Her crying was a good sign. That meant she cared. I
heard a female say, "Hang up on him, girl. He's just trying to run interference."

"That's not true," I lied, then lied again, "I'm happy for
you. You came up. Let's work out visitation for William. I
truly am sorry. Please, can you find it in your heart to forgive me?"

Ramona was quiet.

Spending time with Billy was not of genuine interest,
but I couldn't get to Ramona without bonding with his arrogant behind. "Take your time and think about me."

Ramona sniffled. "We have a court date next week. I'll
have the revised papers served Monday."

Revised? What's in the original wasn't cool?

"We don't need a judge to tell us how to parent our child,
Ramona. That's something Harold wants. You know the old
me still loves you. I'm ready to do the right thing. Can I see

you? Just you? So we can decide what's best for our family?"

No sniffles or weeping. Ramona replied, "What I'm feeling is sorry for you, Kohl. Kohl, I'm a happily married woman, Kohl. I have a family."

Why she kept repeating my name?

"Happily. Married. Woman," background girlfriend shouted.

"Call me when she's not around. I love you, Ramona. Bye." Giving her too much time to question me might turn her pity to anger. Anger to argument. Argument to . . . I ended the conversation.

As I walked into Drago's, Blitz was seated at the end of the L-shaped bar. I heard him say, "All right, babe. I'll meet you later tonight at GW Fins. Bye."

I sat next to him, leaving one seat at the end to my right. The other barstool reserved for the crewe was to Blitz's left. "Fins? You spend way too much on these females."

"You looking sharper than usual," he said. "Who you trying to impress? Your baby mama?" He laughed, but I didn't find the humor.

I was always presentable. For the most part Blitz was, too.

Scoping out the restaurant, I asked, "Where's your Rolex, bruh? Second time I've seen you without it in eight years."

He rubbed his wrist. "Can't find it."

"Sure you didn't pawn it? You might be in over your head, but this bet was your idea and I'm getting my money." If I lived long enough to collect it. I might have to stop doing customers and random chick at my club.

I checked every face at the tables and the other bar across the way. At the bar near the entrance. No one resembled Lema or her goon brothers.

"Never know, might have to smash one of your CEOs," I told him.

"So how's your count going?" Blitz asked with a grin. "Ran out of strippers yet?"

I was no fool. No one had revealed their numbers. Couldn't tell him the game had turned potentially deadly for me.

Dallas approached us, turned the back of his chair to the wall. "What's up, dudes? Trymm coming?"

I answered, "Yeah, said he'd be here shortly."

"One of those chicks probably have his dick tied in a knot," Blitz said, then laughed.

Why is everything funny to him? He's probably in the lead.

Dallas said, "Kohl, you glowin' like Chris Rock after he came all the way up. And before he started cheating on his wife. If you banking on being seven-figures richer in eight days . . ." Sounding like a gangster, doing that upward nod, he added, "Forget about it."

"You still in love with whatever her name is?" I said that to mess with him.

"I got some shit y'all will never believe unless I showed you," Dallas said, unfolding a piece of paper. He slid it to me.

Wow, it took almost thirty years? I had a long list of questions I couldn't ask him right now. Staring at D, I handed the paper to Blitz.

Blitz's face was blank. He was quiet, handed the paper back to me. I placed it in front of Dallas. I wanted to hug him, but that wasn't cool with all the eyes in the room. I clinched his fist, bumped his shoulder. "How you feelin' about this, D?" I patted him hard on his back.

He didn't respond. Sympathizing with him, I understood.

"Nigga, where is your watch?" Dallas asked Blitz.

I looked at Blitz. Waited to see if he'd give Dallas the same response. Trymm walked up.

"Nig-ga, where you been?" Dallas asked.

"You were a straight no-show for our head count last Saturday," I said to Trymm.

Blitz commented, "Ain't seen shit from you on social since Southern Belle. Guess old Clydesdale can't hang."

All of us knew growing up that Blitz had the smallest dick. Couldn't confirm that today. Doubted that had changed. Trymm's manhood was evident from the huge imprint he never tried to conceal.

Trymm placed his iPad on the counter, answered, "Nigga, where is your—"

Dallas shook his head. "Don't ask."

I texted Ramona, **Let's take family pictures. My treat. I'll schedule the date and let you know when and where.**

A text registered from my father, **Hey, son. I haven't seen your tithes for tomorrow. The bank is closing shortly. Don't cheat the Lord.**

My money was welcome, but I wasn't. To hell with him and Paula. Eric and Eleanor, too. They got to stay and I didn't. I knew they depended on my donations to pay the church's and their mortgage. Their car notes, vacations, expensive jewelry. Should've thought about me before handing back my $2,500 in front of the Harrison boys.

I replied, **The pawn shop is still open.**

He responded, **You brought the devil to my door! I never condoned your running a whorehouse.**

I wasn't playing tit-for-tat with him. Nor was I making a deposit without an invitation to worship. The cook doused ladles of sauce—butter, garlic, parmesan cheese—atop the half-shell oysters. The flames on each of the four grills behind the bar shot up six feet high when the cooks hosed water underneath the oyster shells. Rubbing my palms together, I was ready to dive in.

Sent Pastor Bartholomew one more text, **You and everyone in your tabernacle are dead to me.** Why should I be the bigger person? Started to block him. Didn't want to miss a reply.

Trymm sat at the counter next to Blitz. "See y'all left me the seat with my back to the audience so I can't check out the females first," then added, "All I know is each of you betta show your face at my parents' anniversary party at Gallier Hall on the thirty-first. Six o'clock sharp."

I stared at my brother. That was report day. I was double-checking my head count and assembling my package for presentation to the group. Trymm was trying to throw us off. I was quiet. Scanned the entire room again. Dallas and Blitz looked around, too.

Surprisingly, Dallas said, "Count me in."

D must've really fallen hard for that girl. Well, maybe his change of heart was expected, since the Duprees had treated him like family.

"One of y'all say something. Damn!" Trymm stopped our waiter. "Let us get four baker's dozen of them flame-broiled oysters on a half shell and a round of Hen."

"Gotcha," the waiter replied.

My numbers could be on the top or bottom. "I'ma 'bout to trump all y'all. Let's do a count. Write down your numbers," I said, handing each a napkin.

Trymm balled his up. Tossed it at me. "Hell no. All I want eight days from now is proof. Videos, confessions, social posts. All that." He tapped his iPad.

He had it at our first meeting. Probably took it everywhere to take advantage of any situation. Honestly, I'd be glad when all of this was over.

"You're holding out 'cause Walter been on your ass and you in last place," Blitz said. "You ain't got shit on that tablet."

"I'm cool," I said, " 'cause none of y'all put shit on social worth posting." I pointed at Trymm, hoping he'd present proof. Waiting for his response, I ate one, two, three
oysters in a row. I took a huge piece of French bread,
soaked up the sauce with it, stuffed it in my mouth, then
washed it down with liquor.

"Put some respect on it. Ruff. Ruff. Ruff," Trymm
barked, and then pounded his chest. "Southern Belle.
There's more where that came from. A lot more." He tapped
that pad again.

Some random female dressed in denim short shorts, a
man's fedora, and a fitted blouse thrust her cleavage in
Trymm's face. She had big-ass nipples like Ramona's.
Her hair was short, slicked at the back and sides. Lips
greasy.

Dallas kept eating.

"I was at your yacht party. Remember me?" she asked
him all sexy and shit, eyeing his iPad.

Trymm slid his iPad away from her.

When did he have a yacht party?

Trymm looked at her. She eyed his tablet.

"Let that bitch get ghost," Dallas said.

After what had happened to me at church, I agreed, but
didn't comment.

"Yacht, what?" Blitz belted. "I see you, homey. That's
why his ass been MIA."

The three of us could up our game, but I'd have to shut
down my business for eight days. I reached into my plate,
all of my oyster shells were empty. Keeping my eyes on
that female, I devoured two of Dallas's oysters.

"She cool, D." Trymm said to her, "Thanks for coming
over to say hi."

Those oily lips parted; she slid her wet tongue to the
corner of her mouth. Wiggled the tip at Trymm. I saw her
hand go up his thigh. *She's seducing him in front of us?*

She moaned as she said, "I was hoping we could get together again without the other *ninety-nine* females that were all over your big banana boat."

I damn near fell off my seat. *How many?* If that were true, I could concede this minute.

"What the fuck?" Dallas said aloud. "I ain't making that anniversary party, big baller. I don't know about y'all, but that nig-ga is way ahead of me."

Chick put a spotlight on Trymm. Started massaging his dick.

My erection grew. Scooted to the edge of my seat to adjust myself.

Dallas demanded, "Ditch that bitch!"

Trymm moved her hand off of his dick. "You need to back up." Then asked her, "Do I know you?"

She laughed in a weird kind of way. I agreed with Dallas, but kept quiet to see how Trymm was going to handle her.

Trymm moved his barstool back, stared at her.

"'Do I know you?'" she sarcastically repeated.

Oh, yeah. She was crazy.

Trymm told Blitz, "Let's switch seats, homey, before I raise up outta here."

That bitch jabbed the flashlight into Trymm's dick. My brother yelled, "Fuck!" He grabbed his nuts, leaned over, holding his shit.

Dallas placed both feet on the floor. His butt was on the edge of his seat.

When she hit Trymm's left nipple with that flashlight, I felt for him as he fell toward the floor on his shoulder. Slowly he rolled onto his side, curled in the fetal position.

As that female started videotaping, all I could think about was how pissed-off I'd made Gurl 6. Dallas began laughing. I didn't see anything funny, but when Blitz joined in, I did, too.

Blitz recorded Trymm. I wasn't doing that. That was wrong.

"My sister didn't suck your dick for you to degrade her on social media. Thought your lil yacht party was just for fun. Thanks to you, my sister's husband is divorcing her! She has to raise her son and daughter by herself! Had to pull them out of their school because kids wouldn't stop teasing them! You broke up her happy home! I should stun you again!" she said, reaching toward my brother.

Dallas rose up. "That's enough. Trust me. He's sorry." He placed his left hand behind his back, stared at the woman with rage I hadn't seen in a few years.

I needed D to be with me last Sunday.

The woman swiftly pointed the flashlight at Dallas. At the gun range Dallas exhibited skills that reassured me he could knock off anybody in this room with one bullet. When I saw him raise his shirt, grip his gun, then give the woman a daring nod, I moved out of D's way.

Another woman appeared and told the female, "Let's go."

The woman dropped her flashlight into her purse. Dallas was on her immediately. D grabbed her by the throat. Started choking her. Her mouth was wide open, but no sound came out. She started turning red.

The other woman cried, "Help!"

Dallas did not let her go. "I strongly suggest you don't try this shit again. If you do, I'll shoot you." The he said to her friend, "I'll shoot your ass, too. Get the fuck outta here." Shoving the woman as he released her throat, Dallas extended his hand, pulled Trymm up.

"You don't look so good right now, brotha man," Blitz said to Trymm, then yelled out to our waiter, "Yo! Lay four more dozen oysters on us and another round of Hen on me. It's gon' take this nigga a minute to recuperate."

The stuff that could've happened to me at church, if those Harrison boys had fired at me, instead of above my head. I might be dead. I had to become a likable public figure. I could do that by affiliating myself with Ramona and Harold Thurston, as William's father.

Oh, shit!

What if the Harrison boys discovered William Bartholomew was my son? They wouldn't hurt my kid. Would they?

CHAPTER 31

Kohl

Day 28

Tossing and turning, I kicked the covers to the foot of my bed, paced the bedroom. Kneeling at my bedside, I pressed my hands together, positioned the tip of my thumbs on the bridge of my nose, then prayed aloud.

"Lord, You know my heart. You know me better than I know myself. I confess with my mouth and believe in my heart that You will forgive me of all my sins. Lord, I have not been there for my son, but I promise from this day forward, each and every day, I will take an active role in William's life, if Ramona lets me. I pray that I win the challenge. I promise I will personally apologize to every woman I've hurt when it's over. Knowing that no weapon formed against me shall prosper, I pray Lema has found compassion for me, and her brothers are not plotting to harm me. And last, Lord, I pray my father will welcome me back soon into The House of the Lord, that I may take an active role in my church home and serve You. Amen. Oh, and forgive me for threatening my father and his congregation. You know I didn't mean that Lord. Amen."

I wandered into the living room, silently asking the Lord to hear my prayer and grant me favor in the courtroom today. I opened the refrigerator, I'd need to restock for the next nine gurls.

Thought was ingenious but no way Trymm could've done a yacht full of females. Plus, Walter was always on him like flies on horse manure. Less than seventy-two hours remained, I could not wait for the challenge to end. With all the chaos, I managed to maintain my count. I was at eighty-four. Eighty-five if I included Eleanor.

Tired of cooking grits, frying chicken legs, I closed the refrig, filled a bowl with chocolate puffed cereal and milk, went into my office. It was five-thirty in the morning.

Gurl 1 to 84, I double-checked each file for consistency. The ones I hadn't posted to social, I prepared for upload this Sunday, right before the midnight deadline I'd reactivated my accounts, then hit POST. Soon as I was vetted by my crewe, I'd delete all of my Money2930 social pages, create a legit IG, and follow Ramona.

Monday morning when the bank opened, I was collecting all of my funds, but I wasn't going anywhere outside of the city limits. I was born, reared, and would die in the NOLA.

Seven o'clock. Had to arrive at court by 10:00 a.m. Didn't need an attorney to plead my case. Or a judge hounding me with continuances. Driving to Kash In & Out, my car was almost on E. Had enough to make it to my destination. I'd fill up after court. I called Ramona.

"Good morning, Kash," she practically went soprano in my ears.

Hm. I wasn't Kohl today? "Morning." I was feeling confident. In fact, Harold might have to pay me child support when the judge made his final decision. "Will my son be at court today?"

"Of course not, honey," she said. "I know you've

never been involved, William is a straight-A student with perfect attendance. We can't interfere with that to let you practice on being a father, now can we?"

Honey? What was up with all of her sarcasm? She must've forgotten her smackdown video on me went viral. Ramona better be nice. I sighed real heavy into my Bluetooth speaker. I was not playing this game with her.

"Bye, Mama, I love you." I heard a softer side of William.

"Bye, baby. I'll pick you up later." A soft smack, probably on the lips. Had she kissed him on the mouth?

"Bye, baby. I'm dropping our son off at school, then I'm going to Anita's for breakfast. Wanna join me?" Harold was in the background, probably listening to my every word. The sound of another smack sounded in my ears. This one lingered.

"Of course. I'll text you my order when I'm in transit. See you about eight-fifteen. Thanks, babe," Ramona told Harold, then said to me, "My apology, Kohl. What do you want?"

I was no stranger to Ramona; yet she treated me with unfamiliarity. I should show up at that greasy hole-in-the-wall to talk with them. Those women served the best grits, bacon, eggs, hot sausage, pork chops, and pancakes in the city for a ridiculously low price. Most days Anita's closed at 2:00 p.m.

"Is Harold going to be at court?" I asked.

"Of course. He's my *husband*," Ramona answered. I heard the smile in her tone.

This was not Christmas in July. She needed to squash the fake happiness.

Knowing the outcome of the hearing was going to compromise my freedom if I demanded fifty-fifty, I would've been better off maintaining my distance from William and Ramona forever. Too late to put that segment of my life in reverse. "Make sure he stays out of our relationship."

"*We* don't have a relationship. Bye, Kash." My named rolled off her tongue. "See you in court."

I didn't stop her abusive butt from hanging up. Entering the back door of my club, I gathered the mail that was on the floor. "Junk. Junk. Junk . . ." I paused. Hadn't received anything from them since I'd set up my business.

Sliding my finger into the opening of the letter-sized envelope, I read the stationery heading, *Internal Revenue Service . . . Balance Due: $3,346,278.21.*

What the hell? Hold up. There were way too many numbers. This had to be a mistake. I stared at the paper until it slipped from my fingertips, floated to the floor. Picking it up, I dialed my accountant's cell phone, got his voice mail.

"Hey, man. This is Kash. Call me *soon* as you get my message."

I honed in on the amount. Read the notice over. Flipped it over. Tried to find something unauthentic that might prove it to be a scam.

"Lord, please let this be a prank. Please, Lord." I'd done more praying in one day and it wasn't noon yet.

Lema's goons didn't know anything about my finances. She and her brothers had been silent. Hopefully, she'd accepted my numerous apologies and called off her pit bulls. Best to let sleeping dogs lie.

Aw, wow. That's it. The good Reverend Bartholomew reported me. He was known for being vindictive when anything jeopardized the stability of his church. His adopting me didn't keep him from kicking me out, the same way he'd done Ramona. Eleanor just got added to my count. Even the Lord believed in an eye for an eye. I had something to repay those hypocrites. Lloyd. Paula. Eric. And Eleanor.

Afterward, I'd repent. Repentance was like a get-out-of-hell free card and I had a full deck.

I yelled, "Lord, why is this happening to me?! You know everything I did with the gurls was consensual."

It was. Black women were easy. The plus-sized ones were easier. The more they believed I cared, the faster their clothes came off. Discovered strippers were less promiscuous than missionaries.

Heard *eeeeeeeeeeoooo,* then *woop, woop.* The noise stopped. I glanced around my club, the time had come for me to own up to being a father. "Time to go face the judge."

I went outside to get in my car, "Oh, shit!"

Black smoke surrounded red flames. "What in the world? Not my Bentley!"

"Step back, sir." The firefighter continued spraying water on my ride well after there was nothing but steam.

"What happened?" I cried real tears. "You know how much my Bentayga cost?" I asked the firefighter.

Water dripped from his hose, splashed on my shoes. "Man, watch out! You messing up my Stacy's."

A police officer, who was there, answered, "We'll have to investigate the matter to determine the cause."

"Arson!" I cried, looking down my street in both directions.

The upside was my club wasn't damaged. "Thanks, Officer." My voice escalated with urgency. "Complete your investigation. Send me the report. I have an appointment."

He answered, "I need to see your license and registration."

I stared at my unrecognizable vehicle. "It's in the glove compartment, man."

Is he in on this?

"Where were you headed? We need you to stay." A second police car parked on my lot.

I didn't have time for Q and A. They both looked like

they needed to retire. Probably already had double dosages of their donuts and coffee.

Lowering my voice, I explained, "Excuse me, Officers, I really have to be going. Can someone come out this evening, say after seven?"

Getting back sooner was possible, but if Ramona granted me an hour or two to introduce myself to William after he got out of school, that was my priority. *Fuck!* Nothing was going to change the fact that my car was totaled. I'd order a new one tomorrow and wait for my insurance company to cut me a check.

The officer hoisted his belt to his navel. "This won't take long. We need your statement now. Let's go inside."

They had no right to be inside my establishment. "My club is closed." I shook my head in protest. "I'm willing to fully cooperate, but, respectfully, I have less than thirty minutes to get to my appointment," I pleaded.

"What's the appointment?" one of the officers inquired.

Wanted to answer, *"None of your damn business."* Didn't want the situation to escalate and I end up a statistic on the ten o'clock news. I'd never been to jail for any reason. Wasn't sure what would happen if I were a no-show for court, but I knew a few guys who ended up doing time for non-payment of child support. Prayed this cop understood.

"Come down right after you're done with your appointment," the other cop said. "Don't touch the car."

Locking up, I scheduled an Uber. The driver dropped me off in front of the courthouse. Mentally prioritized today's urgent matters. My car. The IRS. Custody.

"*Thurston* versus *Bartholomew,*" the judge announced. I stood. "Here."

Harold and Ramona spoke. "Here."

Taking a long deep breath, I exhaled. Ramona had on a loosely fitted tangerine dress. Her makeup was toned down. Harold had on a tan suit. I was dressy casual. Tan slacks and a printed buttoned-up, short-sleeved shirt.

"Paternity is confirmed," the judge announced, flipping through documents. "Mr. Bartholomew, you are the father. Have you contributed to the welfare of William Bartholomew?"

Dang, she jabbed quicker than Ramona. "I can explain, Your Honor."

She cut me off with, "That's a yes or no."

"Not yet."

"That's a no, Mr. Bartholomew. Children are not free. Your son is a decade old. How much do you make?"

Probably nothing now, if I couldn't get the Feds off of my back. "I'm not sure what my revenue will be." That was the truth.

"I didn't ask you how much it will be. How much does your Kash In & Out net annually? Mrs. Thurston has submitted supporting documentation that shows you own two businesses. Is that correct?"

Sounded rhetorical. I explained. "Yes, but—"

"I'm going to issue an order that you pay one thousand dollars a month until you provided verification of your earnings," the judge said.

Heck, I may never submit verification. Wanting to smile, that was less than what I used to contribute to my father's church.

The judge added, "And another twenty thousand a month for back child support for a total of twenty-one thousand a month."

Shaking my head, I said, "Your Honor, I can't—"

She cut me off again. "If you can't afford the court-ordered support, then I'm sure you'll provide your corporate tax returns soon as possible."

"But what about their income?" Harold didn't need shit from me.

"Mrs. Thurston is currently unemployed." The judge banged her gavel.

My eyes stretched. "But her husband—"

"His income doesn't count." She banged her gavel again, then said, "*Dorgenois* versus *Cagnolatti*."

My life was almost not worth living. "But—"

She yelled at me, "Get out of my courtroom, Mr. Bartholomew! You should've hired an attorney."

Wow! With her attitude, I could catch a case without trying. I was definitely lawyering up next go-round.

Three days remained in a challenge I started chasing with a dream. If I won, I could still lose everything I owned.

CHAPTER 32

Kohl

Day 29

"**D**amn!" Big Gurl 96—shoulda been 69—was putting in overtime eating my bologna.

She held my dick in one hand. Three of her fingers meshed together was bigger than my shaft. Gurl 96 fast jacked me three times. Switched hands, stroked, then sucked three times. Guess that was her or my lucky number. She switched. Fast jacked again. One. Two. Three.

I'd brought her home from my club around six o'clock this morning in my rental car. Was going to take sixty days and a deductible of $29,000 to get a new customized Bentley.

We'd enjoyed an early breakfast. Flattering her with, "You are so beautiful and brilliant," got me spread out like a stick of soft butter.

Next thing I realized, I was lying on the dining table adjacent to the foil pan of fried chicken from Manchu Kitchen.

Watching her perform witchcraft, and pull out two additional inches of introverted dick, my penis was the biggest I'd ever seen it. I asked Gurl 96, "Where did you learn how to do—"

"Oh, no. Oh, no." Methodically she continued. "No talking allowed. Save your strength, Hercules. You're going to need it to eat every inch of me. Think about whether you want to eat barbecue, sweet and sour, or hot sauce out of my pussy."

Eating every inch of her would be the equivalent of digesting 600 seven-ounce rib-eye steaks. I'd lick her juicy vagina. She earned that. No hot sauce.

Opening wide, she reached for a drumette, shoved the whole thing in her mouth. After she eased it out, the skin was gone. She inserted it again, pulled it out, meatless. Cracking the bone, she extracted the marrow. Quenched her palate with an entire twelve-ounce lemon-lime soda.

Burrrrrp.

She didn't bother covering her extended release of air. Better out of that end.

Gurl 96 circled the base of my shaft, squeezed tight, then wiggled the tip of her tongue wicked turbo speed on my frenulum.

"Oh, Jesus!" My nails scratched against the mahogany wood. *Whosoever discovered oral sex, God is good* was all I thought. Had planned on making encores a no-no, but I was locking Gurl 96 into my favorites.

"Aw, sweet Jesus, have mercy on me!"

Sweat streamed down my temples, into my ears. My toes curled. I swore my eyeballs did a one-eighty 'cause everything went black for a moment. I raised to a sitting position, but she pushed me back on the dining table. I did not have the strength to come up again. Was about to lose my nuts.

Talking out of my head, I mumbled, "I'll feed you fried chicken every day if you keep sucking me off like—"

Her hand squeezed tighter at the base.

"Yelp!" I hollered like a pup.

Her other hand slid up and down my shaft real slow. While she gently covered my head with the inner parts of her lips, felt hot, soft, and wet. Unexpectedly, her tongue wiggled.

"Ohhhh! Ohhhhh! Ohhhhhhh!" I could not stop coming and screaming. Just when I thought she'd swallowed all my seeds, she placed her lips around the eye of my penis, suctioned long and slow, drawing out the last nut in the sack.

Maybe I shouldn't feed her again. Another one of these beyond-paradise orgasms and I might end up in the ER. I caressed her arm, an extra layer of flesh covered her elbow. She had to pull me up. I rested on her fluffy shoulder.

Gurl 96 rubbed my back in a circular motion. My eyelids opened and shut. I felt my weight pressing down on her body.

Zzzzzz. Inhaling, I choked. Woke myself up.

I was still on her shoulder. She hadn't moved from the table.

Sun shining through my windows was five shades brighter than when I'd ejaculated. Gurl 96 picked up the last leg, stuck the whole thing in her mouth. The bone came out clean.

I sat up on the table. "What time is it?"

"Noon. You ready for round two," she asked. "My turn."

Taking the bone out of her hand, I waved it high in the air. Sang, "I surrender all." Pivoting on my butt, I exited off of the opposite side of the table. "Rain check, please. I've got to get dressed. What's your address? I'm ordering you an Uber. What's your address?"

"You asked me that twice already," she said, sounding upset.

Picking up my cell, I'd missed a call from . . . William. The voice mail was "Hey, Dad. I have a debate at ten this morning. I'ma text you the address. I'm inviting you. Not my mom."

"Damn!" The first time my son reached out to me, I failed him. "What's your damn address?!"

Her neck jerked backward. "No worries, sweetness. I got it, Kohl." Gurl 96 tidied herself up, got her purse, let herself out.

Being new to this parenting thing, I was clueless. Was I supposed to call my son and apologize? Go to the location, hoping he was still there? For sure, doing what I'd always done was not the solution to my newest problem.

My son had one more reason to hate me.

I dialed Ramona's number.

She answered, "I'm so sorry. You have my condolences."

"It's me. Kohl. I—"

"I know," she paused. "Oh, you haven't heard," she said, sounding sincere.

Hesitantly I asked, "Heard what?"

Calls came in from Dallas and Blitz. If anything had happened to our child, Ramona would be hysterical.

Realizing that wasn't it, I asked, "Heard what?"

"The House of the Lord burned down this morning. Two unidentifiable bodies were discovered inside. Presumed to be the Reverend and his wife. They didn't do right by me, but they were legally William's grandparents."

Ended the conversation with Ramona before I cursed her out; sounded like she was digging for dollars prematurely. I dialed my dad, praying it wasn't true. Got his voice mail. Tried contacting my mom. No answer. Got Eleanor's voice mail.

My dick smelled and felt like chicken. I quick washed

at the bathroom vanity. Dressed. Left the house. En route to the tabernacle, what if Gurl 6 was responsible? All these headaches from sexing her and she wasn't half as good as Gurl 96. My heart pounded. What if the Harrison brothers were expecting me to show up at the church?

I made a U-turn. Went home. Turned on the news.

CHAPTER 33

Kohl

Day 30

Yesterday, after Gurl 96, and after watching the news, after hearing who'd died inside the church, I had a ménage à trois in my private room at Kash In & Out. No one was in a position to financially assist me. Wasn't inheriting any money from my parents. Had to do what I had to do. My club was packed and I was in the back releasing my frustrations inside of random females that were taking tequila shots and competing for my seeds.

Today was a continuation. Not at my club. At my house.

"You're my new man, Kohl," Gurl 101 claimed, wearing a huge smile. The side of her face rested on my pillow as she stared at me.

I felt another warm body pressed against my back. I frowned. I had enough problems. "We're not a couple," I told Gurl 101, then said, "Y'all can put your clothes on and get out of my house. I . . . I . . . please leave. Thanks for a good time but I have business to tend to."

Staring at the ceiling as they exited opposite sides of

the mattress, I cried on the inside. The bodies recovered from The House of the Lord were those of Mr. and Mrs. Lewis. Strange that I hadn't heard from my parents. Almost thirty years of rearing me, I had to mean more than an offering. Tried calling them again. My attempts all went directly to a voice mailbox that was full.

Dallas texted, **Understand if you can't make it this evening.**

I replied, **I'll be there.**

Why not go support D? Wasn't anything I could've done to change the Lewises' situation. Clearly, my dad didn't want me anywhere near him. The Feds weren't going away; my accountant confirmed the notice wasn't in error, but we'd dispute the amount. Might lose my assets and end up behind bars for tax evasion.

Hadn't heard the front door shut. It was too quiet. Bypassing putting on underwear, I stepped into a pair of slacks.

"Hey, thanks for cleaning the kitchen," I told Gurl 101. Gurl 100 peeled back a sheet, sat up on my sofa.

Damn! Who else was in my crib? I roamed my other rooms. Checked my office. Returned to the kitchen.

"You were fun," Gurl 101 said, kissing Gurl 99. "We should get together next weekend. No offense, Kohl, but just us girls."

"I'm definitely down for whatever." Gurl 100 included herself, then powered on the vacuum. *Smack!* Gurl 101 hit me in my face with a wet, dirty dishrag.

Reaching back far, I swung, aiming for her cheek.

"Oh, no you won't!" Gurl 99 snatched me from behind.

The vacuum cleaner stopped. I wasn't in the mood to fight three women, especially not three healthy ones.

Gurl 101's hand was on her hip. Water dripped on my floor from the rag. "That's not what you told me when I was sucking your dick."

What is she talking about?

"She's right. I heard you say you were her man," Gurl 99 vouched.

Lord, why me? How'd they pull a relationship from what I said?

"I apologize, ladies. I got too much alcohol in my system. My fault. Now, please just leave."

"Uh-uh. Don't blame it on the alcohol. You wouldn't have said that if you didn't want me to be your woman." Gurl 101's voice escalated. "I am your woman." She resumed washing dishes.

Gurl 100 said, "Honey, he's low down and dirty. You should leave Kash alone. I'm out."

"Me too." Gurl 99 followed Gurl 100.

"This house needs a woman's touch. I love decorating. I'm going to need three hundred dollars to shop for new things." Gurl 101 started humming.

One way or another, 101 had to get out. Thought about what Dallas said about women when the crewe was at Drago's. What part of "leave" didn't this woman get? I went into my bedroom, called the police. "Yes, I have an intruder that refuses to leave my home willingly."

"We'll send someone out immediately," the dispatcher said.

"No sirens, please. Don't want to alert them or alarm my neighbors." I ended the call, returned to my kitchen. It was spotless.

Gurl 101 held her palm in front of me, wiggled her fingers. "Three hundred, Kohl. I've got to get to the stores early to choose the best items for our house."

If the cops didn't arrive soon, I was shoving her out the front door. "This is not your house. We are not a couple. Please leave," I asked her politely.

"You weren't saying all that when I sucked your dick." Gurl 101 was bold as hell. And certifiable. "You not gonna use me for your pleasure like I'm some kinda ho!"

"Your purse is on the couch. I'll get it for you."

"Don't touch my purse!"

There was a knock at the door. I exhaled. Opened it. "Thanks for coming, Officer. I don't want to cause a scene. I've respectfully and repeatedly asked this young lady to leave, but she refuses."

"I'm his woman. I have a right to be here," she protested.

"Ma'am, is this your residence?" the officer asked.

"No," I said.

She said, "Yes. It. Is."

"May I see your driver's license?" the officer asked her.

"No. What's that going to prove?" she protested.

"How'd you get here?" the cop questioned.

She pointed at me.

"I really don't have time for this, Officer. My father's church went up in flames yesterday. I have business to tend to. I—"

"So you're that guy?" The cop stared at me.

Frowning, I questioned, "What guy?"

"The letter?" he said.

"What letter?" I called him to get 101 out, and he was giving me the third degree.

"The letter that's online. The letter from Assistant Pastor Eric Lewis telling how he was going to kill his wife in the church because she slept with Pastor Bartholomew's son. You just confirmed, you're his son."

Gurl 101 told the police, "I wasn't going to say anything, but he raped me." She cried, but her eyes were dry.

I desperately wanted to call her out of her name for telling that lie.

The officer stared at me. Then told Gurl 101, "Miss, you need to leave."

Gurl 101 backed into me, whaled her arms. "Don't

touch me, Kohl! Officer, I want him arrested! You have to take my report," she insisted.

"Ma'am, if you're lying, I'm locking you up," the officer said.

"Kohl, I need twenty dollars to get home," Gurl 101 demanded.

Gladly, I went inside, returned, handed her a Jackson. "Don't contact me or come to my place of business again. Stay away." Women were treacherous.

The police escorted her away. I went online in search of that letter. Read it once.

"Women talk too damn much. Why did Mrs. Lewis tell Mr. Lewis the truth? Why did Mr. Lewis set the church ablaze? With him and his wife inside? Weak!" I yelled. "Infidelity is no justification for suicide and homicide."

I showered, put on my tuxedo. Had to make it to Dallas's wedding.

"Y'all suited like somebody died," Dallas said. "This is a celebration."

Soon as the ceremony was over, I got in my rental car, went to my club.

What I saw as I parked across the street from Kash In & Out made my blood boil like a sack a crawfish with a pound cayenne was in the pot of water. I couldn't move. "Are you fucking kidding me!" I yelled.

First my dad's church. Then my Bentley Bentayga. Now my club was going up in flames.

Hadn't God heard anything I'd prayed for?

CHAPTER 34

Dallas

Day 1

"**D**rop it, Private!" the drill sergeant yelled. Spit flew from his mouth, landed on my lip.

The skinny black kid, who was literally born in a one-bedroom apartment in the Magnolia Projects, shouted back, "Sir, yes, sir!"

"Pick it up, Carter!" the burly man in fatigues, wearing a Smokey Bear hat, hammered the command down my throat.

I exhaled into hot waves floating in front of my eyes, "Sir, yes, sir!"

This was my first day of boot camp. Lifting 120 pounds, I realized my duffel bag weighed only thirty pounds less than I did.

"Drop it! Get in line for the gas chamber, Carter," my drill sergeant ordered.

"Sir, yes, sir!" Hurrying to the entrance, I stood in line behind other newly enlisted soldiers. For many of us, our next stop after training camp in Fort Jackson was Afghanistan.

I'd just seen countless soon-to-be-deployed soldiers running out of the chamber's exit. Some leaned against trees. Others fell to their knees, prayed to the dirt where they puked until they heaved air. Two passed out.

I shuffled the steel-toed boots strapped to my feet to the door that all boot campers had to enter. No mask. No protection. The handle released, the building with no windows was filled with white clouds so thick each soldier vanished soon as they cross the threshold.

I stood behind a kid I didn't know, dreading my turn to step inside. I had a strategy. I'd shut my eyes tight, hold my breath, until I felt the warmth of the sun kiss my face.

Wumpth!

The door locked behind us.

I was trapped. The poisonous fumes were all I had to inhale. Gas burned my corneas. I swallowed my vomit. Hit the door with my shoulder. Had to survive. I couldn't swallow again. This time a yellowish bile poured from my nostril, then my mouth. Determined to make my mother proud, I yelled, "Arghhh!" Rammed the door repeatedly, until it opened. Stumbling, I gulped the fresh air.

"Mama." I turned. The chamber had filled with water, the boat sailed away. Slowly my mother's lifeless body rose to the top. The more I stretched my arms to rescue her, the farther away she drifted.

My screaming did not save her. Cursing did not bring my mama back. All I had left was suppressed anger that was easily triggered.

"Mama! Mama!" I awakened, fighting the comforter on my bed. Rattled my head. My pillow drenched. Sheets soaked.

I cried out loud.

Picked up my cell. Selected my playlist: *I love my mama*, and I listened to "Your Tears," by Bishop Paul S. Morton and the Greater St. Stephen Mass Choir. He was my mother's number one pastor, and that was her favorite song.

It had been almost eleven years since my mother drowned in Katrina. Seven since my honorable discharge from the U.S. Army.

Getting out of bed, I started my morning ritual. "Hate taking this fucking shit." I swallowed the daily pills to treat my PTSD. These tablets were for anxiety.

When I didn't follow the prescription as ordered the smallest things agitated me. I was what they referred to as a "walking time bomb."

If I did take them, soon as I sat still, I'd doze off like a narcoleptic. Worse, my seventeen-year-old dick pitched a tent the four years I was enlisted, but when the doctor put me on three medications seven years ago, I became flaccid.

Had a different drug for nightmares, another for flashbacks. Same muthafuckas that manufactured all that shit produced male enhancements. In order to satisfy a woman, I needed to take that, too.

Scrambling three eggs, I mixed enough batter for four pancakes, then put six strips of bacon in a skillet. I stacked my plate with everything I'd cooked, poured a tall glass of milk on ice, opened a can of Steen's cane syrup. Sat naked in front the television. Watched back-to-back episodes of my favorite, *The First 48,* while I ate. Midway through the third show, I dozed off.

A pic from Blitz with text, **Met this CEO on a dating app,** woke me up.

She was cute in the photo. He'd betta hope that shit wasn't from ten years ago. I refused to pay to be on a dating site. Too many fine women living in my city, plus all that **gm, hyd, wyd, gn** back-and-forth shit was a waste when I could talk to her in person.

I replied, **Cool,** imagining he'd sent the same to the crewe.

Close to noon I popped in a XXX DVD. Having gone eighteen months of my four years in the military without seeing a woman I didn't have to kill during combat, I never tired of watching naked ladies, porn, or eating pussy. Stroking my dick for a half hour felt good, but those fucking meds had kept my shit flaccid.

Smacked my dick five times. Cursed it out. "Motherfucker!" Choked the head. Flung it against my thigh. Left it alone.

I cleaned my kitchen. Restored everything as though I hadn't cooked. Every single item in my house had its rightful place, and if anyone touched my stuff, I noticed it.

Opening the app on my phone, I viewed my four bedrooms, four bathrooms, living room, and theater room. The back and front yards were quiet. A few cars drove by. Had this setup for seven years. Everybody was the enemy, especially these thugs in the NOLA.

Hadn't quite wrapped my heads around what I'd agreed to, but I was prepared to capture footage of these women, starting today. Having killed countless men, women, and children to protect the men, women, and children in the United States, money and material things didn't excite me. I was in the challenge with my crewe for my love of competition.

All these wannabe gangstas packing pistols would scream like bitches if they had to do a fraction of what I'd done to protect their asses. I secured peace and liberties for white folks who still called me boy. One called me a nigga to my face. Almost squeezed his last breath out of him. Recruiter convinced me joining the military was a good way to control my—what he'd referred to as—anger management.

Now that ungrateful motherfucker Uncle Sam had moved on to the next group of recruits to fuck up their minds and dicks, without giving a damn about me. Well, fuck that nigga, too!

I took my enhancement drugs. Showered. Got fresh in my rust-colored slacks, a black T-shirt, black leather loafers. Gold chain, twenty inches, 18k. Wore pinky rings in case I had to bust a dude in his mouth right quick I'd split that lip wide open.

Secured my gun behind my back inside the waistband of my pants. Shoot-outs in the Big Easy could happen anytime, anywhere. Combat was a sport. I missed the hunting, the fighting, blood splattering on my uniform. Torturing someone excited me. Knew how to leave a man for dead by tying his hands around a post, tucking one foot behind his knee, then placing him in the squatting position.

Making my way inside the Ernest N. Morial Convention Center, I checked out the sexy women strolling Hall A as I stood in line.

When it was my turn, the woman behind the glass asked, "How can I help you?"

"Let me have six super-lounge tickets. Two for each night," I told her.

Super lounges were more fun than being cramped on the main floor restricted to a seat where you had to step over motherfuckers to go take a piss. Plus, the lounges didn't have chairs. I could get as close or far from the stage as I wanted, and the cost to see the artists wasn't no $200 to $4,000 per ass like on the floor.

Putting the passes in my pocket . . . I entered the exhibit section in search of my date. Hundreds of vendors from Coke to Walmart to African clothing, to jewelers, to food stands spanned from Hall A to H.

Spotted date number one, a pretty, brown-skinned sistah trying on sunglasses. "Those look nice on you," I complimented her.

A gold rack capped her top six teeth. Ordinarily, that would be a turnoff, but long as she took them off before sucking my dick, I was on a mission to win the competition.

"You think so?" she asked, admiring herself in the mirror. Did the extra to show her uppers. "You handsome, daddy."

Couldn't lie. Her compliment made me feel good. "You going to the concert tonight?" I asked.

Taking off the glasses, she answered, "I want to, but I don't have tickets."

Showing her mine, I said, "Well, I do, but I don't have a date. First I need to know how old are you?" Before I could formally invite her, two other females slid into our picture.

One scanned me up and down. "You're tasty. Love your tats." She touched my bicep, then rubbed my neck.

I twitched, snatched her wrist.

She pulled away. "My bad. Didn't know you were sensitive," she said, then asked her friend, "Where'd you meet this one?"

A "may I touch you?" would've been in order. That way I could've told her no. She'd better be glad she didn't touch the image of my mother that was high up on my left arm underneath my sleeve. Nobody felt Mom without prior permission.

"I'm twenty, soon to be twenty-one," the female I was interested in replied.

"Gurl, you always meeting some man. Who's this?" Her girlfriend seemed annoyed.

Introducing myself, I extended my hand. "I'm Dallas." She was legal, so her age wasn't a concern for me. Young girls didn't require much, and most of them enjoyed sex.

"Dallas, I'm Keisha," the one with the gold teeth replied, shaking my hand. "Do you have concert tickets for all of us?"

Damn. I hesitated. Women who traveled in packs seldom put out.

Keisha's girlfriend, the one that was hating, lowered her eyes to my dick, then back to my face. "Well? Do you?"

Her friend was so thirsty, I could bend her ova, fuck her for free right here, then leave her with a wet ass. My standards was never higher than a woman's.

I told Keisha, "I will give these two tickets to you for your girlfriends . . . *if* you accompany me back to the box office so I can get our tickets. We, you and me, can hang out and meet up with them at the Superdome later."

The friend who'd been quiet spoke. "What's your cell number, Dallas?"

The hater placed her phone in front my face, snapped a picture of me. I couldn't take a bitch like her out. I wanted to choke her disrespectful ass with one hand.

"Five, o, fo." As I said the remaining numbers, each of them locked me in.

Taking a chance on dipping inside of Keisha after the concert was not happening. I kept my word, got our tickets, then took her straight to my place.

Putting my gun in the drawer of my nightstand, I asked from my bedroom, "What do you want to drink?" I hung my clothes in the closet, kept on my underwear, pissed in the half bathroom that was off of the living room with the door opened.

"You got any Cîroc?" Keisha flipped through channels. "You have a nice home. Where's your girlfriend?"

Noticed she'd moved one of my seven white candles on the mantel. After my mother died, I collected money from the state and city governments, rehabbed the home she'd died in, rented it out to a single mother with two kids. Used my VA loan to purchase my spot uptown off of Magazine Street.

Fuck getting paid a dime of retirement or disability. Should've listened to Mom and never joined the military. I didn't mind serving. It was my country's abandonment after pledging my loyalty, putting my life on the line every day for years for my government, and the uncanny ignorance from clueless motherfuckers in the United States that made me keep my artillery polished.

"Coconut, vanilla, pineapple, amaretto, red berry—"

"Dang, I shoulda brought my gurls over here. Let me sip some of that red berry straight."

I poured her drink over ice. Hen for me. Sitting on the couch, I cupped Keisha's breast, closed-mouth-kissed her really quick. "Sorry, I couldn't resist those lips."

"That's okay, daddy," she said, then sipped her drink. "I thought we were going to dinner." She stared at my boxer briefs, exposed her grill. "Nice imprint."

That muthafuckin' rack had to go. I got up, brought her a small china plate with gold trim. Placed it in front her. "Your mouthpiece will be safe here."

I sighed relief as she carefully removed them.

Sipping her drink, she swished the vodka, then swallowed.

"I didn't want you to get sleepy on me. We're going to eat right before the show. Anywhere you want to," I paused, placed my hands on her shoulders. Gave her a massage.

"That feels good, daddy." She closed her eyes.

Pulling her panties to the side, I sipped my drink, then licked her pussy.

"Oh, daddy. You the man. I have to thank you first." She released my semierect dick through the opening.

The red berry in Keisha's mouth splattered on my lap, stained my suede sofa.

It was clear liquid. Nothing wipes couldn't clean up. I smiled, pulled back my foreskin. "Suck him."

Raising her hands like there was a stickup, and my dick was an assault rifle, she rattled her head, scooted back quickly.

Enhancements were in full effect. My shit was huge. Could understand how I must've frightened her but I was ready to blow cum in her face. Get my first count on record.

"Don't be scared. He's bigger than his bite," I reassured her with a grin as my dick got harder. "But I'm going to nibble on your nipples." I wasn't joking as I reached for her hand, pulled it toward my swollen head, leaned in to kiss her breast.

She jumped up, then shouted, "Ugh! It's nasty! Your dick looks old. Why do you have so much loose skin? I've never seen that. I feel like I'm gonna throw up." Keisha put down her drink, snapped in her grill.

Bitch! I stared at her. Slowly my face grew tighter. I couldn't stop the rising tension. Best if she left right this fucking minute. My eyelids narrowed.

"I'm sorry, daddy, but I've never seen anything like—"

Snatching that bitch at her throat, I tightened my fingers. I made sure she swallowed her next words.

Dumb ho! I wasn't the biggest and thickest, but I had

above average length and girth, and I ain't never had no complaints.

Didn't she know, once this dick was inside her pussy, she wouldn't feel the foreskin?

Well, Keisha was about to find out.

CHAPTER 35

Dallas

Day 3

*A*n American flag was not going to get delivered to her
mother's home. "Grab my hand! I got you!" My fingertips touched hers.

Trembling, she started crying. "I'm trying!" Her elbow
bent slightly.

"Don't you dare give up on me, Private!" I commanded,
choking on the cloud of dust surrounding us. "Try harder! I
stretch! You stretch!"

Giving it all she had, she grunted, "Ughhhh!"

"That's it. I got you! I got you!"

A boulder fell inches from us, a cluster of rocks rained
down on our back. Each blast shook the foundation.
More dust rose from the ground, covered our air space,
choking us. Gripping her wrist with both hands, I could
hardly see her face. I grabbed underneath her armpit.
Another boulder descended moving the earth beneath
like a quake.

"Hurry, Carter!" She shoved her body toward me.

I yanked her closer. "That's it! Keep coming!"

"I'm stuck!" she yelled.

Boom! *Rocks descended like golf balls of hail.*

"Ahhhhh!" She tried to break our grip.

I refused to let her go.

I'd heard that sound before—the kind that roared from the gut, releasing the soul from the flesh. Blood squirted out her mouth.

If I pulled again, her pain would worsen. If I gave up, she'd lose hope. If I left her there, she'd die. Not on my watch. I mustered the strength to free her body, maneuvered her onto my back, then ran fast as I could, carrying her deadweight.

"Mama! Mama!" Boxing with the comforter on my bed, I rattled my head until my eyes opened. My soldier's face flashed before me. My pillow was drenched. Sheets soaked.

I cried. Picked up my cell, inserted my earbuds. Listened to "Your Tears."

"Are you okay?" the naked woman in my bed questioned.

"Nah, I'm never going to be okay. Ran into my daddy at the concert."

I wanted to kill him with my bare hands. Wouldn't have been my first time choking a man until his eyes popped out of his head. Didn't have hatred for my sperm donor's wife, Noelle, but had no love for her, either. Took her cell number because she wasn't the only one who had things to talk about. It was time for me to get answers to why Hawk left my mama for dead.

"Which one was your dad?" she asked.

Staring at the ceiling fan blades going round-and-round, I shook my head. Exhaled. Answering her would make me show her a side of me that I was sure she wouldn't like.

Noelle's boys were my half brothers that I'd never said hello to. Why the fuck she waited until I was damn near thirty to share her fucking contact? Didn't matter when I was in elementary school, they all lived four doors down. They wouldn't feed me, but her ass knew there were days when my mother couldn't make ends meet.

Sitting up, I asked the strange woman in my bed, "You hungry?"

She had green eyes. Her weave was tangled. I liked her womanly figure, curvy hips, big ass, and fake, beautiful breasts.

"Depends. On what you have to eat," she said real sexy, then spread her thighs.

Diving into her pussy, I lapped her lips like a dog feasting on a bowl of milk. Instantly my dick got brick-hard. Couldn't recall much of what happened after we got in from the concert. Didn't want her to disrespect me the way that twenty-one-year-old had done.

I flipped her onto her stomach, penetrated her doggie-style. Ramming her from behind, I yelled, "Take this dick like a soldier." I made the crown of her head hit my royal-blue plush board.

"Uh, uh, uh, uh," she repeated.

Not sure and not caring if she was trying to say anything else, I elevated to turbo speed. Sex for me was more about feeling the inside of a woman's hot, juicy flesh. I replayed a porn video in my mind (that was the good flashback), started slapping her ass, yanking her hair. She grabbed my wrist.

"Don't touch me!" I yelled, slinging her arm toward the mattress. "You asked for it. Take, all, this, big, dick," I said, thrusting hard as I could.

"Stop!" she screamed. "You're hurting me!"

None of my neighbors were close enough to hear her cry. Her screeching excited me. I hoisted her pretty ass up, French-kissed her asshole, then ate the cream off her pussy lips. My dick was at attention again. I put him back inside her.

"Uh, uh, uh, uh," she repeated.

I wanted to ejaculate so badly I became tensed. Even with the enhancement meds, it was hard for me to come. Before enlisting, if a chick blew on my dick, I'd bust one in her eye. Fucking felt amazing. I could go as long as my erection lasted. Nothing came out. My balls smacked her labia as though they were in a National Open and this round was for the win.

Her body slid flat against the mattress. Breathing heavily into the sheet, she said, "Dallas, that's enough."

Suddenly I realized I couldn't remember her name. Probably best, since I was posting her video on social soon as she left. She'd earned a break but she had to finish the job.

"Okay," I agreed. "Take fifteen, soldier."

CHAPTER 36

Dallas

Day 4

"*Baby, please don't join the military. I'll take out a second mortgage, refinance the house, whatever it takes. Those people at Tulane University accepted you, Dallas. Mama wants you to go get your degree.*"

"*Serving your country will put that anger for your father not being in your life to good use, boy. Unlike your daddy, Uncle Sam needs you. You can save your money, get your degree, and buy your mama a bigger house with your VA loan after you get out, and . . . you can buy that house far away from that deadbeat daddy of yours, anywhere in the country.*"

The recruiter looked nice in his dress blue. His shoes were polished spotless. I had clean clothes in high school. The best mama could afford from the Goodwill, but I couldn't dress like Trymm, Kohl, Blitz, or the dude who was convincing me I was needed.

"*I know your mind is made up. Promise me you'll never reenlist, baby. Once they got you in, they try not to let you out for twenty years.*"

I was seventeen. I was a man. I was also my mother's only child. "I promise, Mama."

"The army is the safest place for a young black man. Especially one in New Orleans," the recruiter convinced me. "We'll protect you. We'll provide for you."

"The military ain't no place for a young black man, Dallas. Baby, it's worse than prison. Going to college is better than killing peoples or having somebody shoot at you, or being locked up." Mama's eyes had filled with tears.

Nothing was worse than seeing my father play daddy to Noelle's boys every day. Take them fishing in his boat on the weekend. The boat that saved his family. Heard there was room for my mama, but . . . The hate inside of me wasn't normal for a kid.

"Your mama can't afford to send you to college. If she misses too many payments, both of you will get kicked out. Why take that chance? This ain't no city to have idle time on your hands. The army will treat you with respect. You won't get that from a prison guard. That's for sure," the recruiter reassured me.

"Men come outta prison and turn their lives around. Military trains you to kill. Kill peoples you don't know if they'z good or bad. I don't know one person that come out in their right mind. They don't talk about what happened, but they forever crazy in they mind. They don't tell nobody nothing. Think nobody can tell. I seen what it done to your daddy. He has a good heart. It's his head that was bad when he come back home to me."

"You can learn a skill in the military, come out, and have an amazing career," the recruiter said enthusiastically. "Let's get you in one of these uniforms, boy. Sign right here."

"Baby, whatever you do, don't let 'em trick you into

signing dem paypas. They tell you all the right things, but once they got you, you never see them again. They on to trick somebody else's child. Dallas, please don't leave me."

"Mama! Mama!" Rattling my head until my eyes opened, I was cocooned in the comforter. My pillow drenched. Sheets soaked.

I cried. Picked up my cell. While I showered, listened to "Your Tears" on the Bluetooth speakers throughout my house.

Tan cargo shorts, black T-shirt, tennis shoes, tied left, then right shoestring. I shoved my gun in my pocket, put on my fisherman's hat and sunglasses, skipped my meds, downed two enhancements for my manhood, then headed to Li'l Dizzy's Café for breakfast to meet up with Blitz.

Sitting in the corner at a table for two—four days in— I wondered how I was going to win the challenge if I couldn't be sure I'd stay hard enough to fuck a girl a day. Couldn't keep skipping my meds. Couldn't keep poppin' pills to keep my dick hard. Side effects and stress of it all, shit might give me a heart attack.

My official count was one and I couldn't recall her name. Couldn't force myself upon Keisha when she started crying and pleading for me to just let her leave. I did. Plus, her girlfriends had my number, photo, Keisha may have done a pin drop with the location of my house. Police could've showed up and arrested me for sexual assault.

Serving in the military, I'd done tons of morally questionable things, but raping a woman was not one of them. Was not going to start with Keisha. I had to let her go. Didn't want my mama turning over in her grave.

Wow! A gorgeous lady sashayed in my direction. That left hip moved in slow motion to the side, then she lowered her ass to the luckiest seat in the restaurant. I pictured her on my lap. Damn, my arousal caused blood to flow to my shaft. Desperately wanted to squeeze my head before it became engorged, I decided to press my thighs together to avoid feeling like some sort of pervert.

She tapped on her cell. Pretending I was scanning my phone, I focused on her every move, waiting to see if some dude was trailing. Two minutes passed. Five. I motioned for the beautiful lady's attention.

"Would you mind joining me?" I asked.

She glanced over her shoulder and back, then made eye contact. "Me?" she mouthed, pointing at herself.

Smiling, I nodded, praying she'd accept my offer. *Fuck Blitz.* He could find his own table and chick when he showed up.

She picked up her purse. I would've gotten up to pull out her chair, but my dick was hard as shit and not close to going down. Not even a little bit. Fuckin' enhancement drugs needed better timing. Never knew if my shit was gon' stay hard four hours or four minutes.

"Thanks for your company. I don't normally do this, but you look amazing and I didn't want to eat alone . . . again," I threw in. "Order whatever you want, it's on me."

The waiter placed a bread basket in the center of the table. She asked for shrimp and grits. I had a juicy medium-rare T-bone steak, with grits and eggs over easy. We both requested OJ.

I extended my hand. "My name is Dallas," I said, intentionally not giving her my last. Everyone in the NOLA assumed if you had my last name that you were related to Lil Wayne.

If I ever had a daughter, I'd teach her how to get all of a man's pertinent information before telling him anything about herself, especially her full government name. And I'd quiz her on how well she surveyed every room she entered and every person in it.

The FBI agent was diagonally across from me. His gun was strapped to his ankle. The man with a wedding ring on wasn't grinning in his woman's face, which meant she was probably his Mrs. The gang member with the teardrop next to his eye was chillin' by himself. The councilman had handed over his government credit card, although he'd eaten alone.

"Hi, Dallas. I'm Debbie Schexnider. Are you from around here?" she asked. The tip of her tongue extended to the rim of the glass. My gazed lingered when juice flowed into her mouth.

Something about Debbie was different. Her presence had an instant calming effect on me. "I am. Did four years in the army. Graduated TU two years ago. How about you?"

The beacon in her eyes was bright as her beautiful smile. Dark lips, chocolate gums. No gold caps. Thank God. White teeth a little uneven at the bottom, but I liked that. Her breasts were small in comparison to her butt. She had a sexy hourglass waist, flat stomach. Short blond hair, barely long enough to grip with my fingertips.

"I work for the housing authority. HANO. Been there for three years. Excuse me." She bowed her head for several seconds, placed her palms up, said grace, then started eating a piece of cornbread.

"How old are you?" I asked.

"Twenty-five, and you?"

"Twenty-nine." I admitted the truth. "I don't like being alone. Having a hard time finding someone to date," I lied, then told the truth again, "Women here, once they see my spot, they ready to move in. Looking for me to take care of them financially. When they find out I don't have discretionary income, they move on."

Placing the plates of food in front of us, the waiter walked away. I was glad he hadn't interrupted.

Debbie nodded. Her eyes shifted to the right. I imagined she was processing what I'd just told her.

"So what was your major at Tulane? Do you at least have a job?" she inquired, steadily raising her fork to her mouth.

"Communications. Thought it would help me deal with people better, but the military kinda . . . Let's just say I'm not ready for a nine-to-five. I own property and a lil piece of land, but I'm trying to purchase another rental if the numbers add up." Basically, if I won the challenge, I was investing it in real estate. "Just moved some things around. Can't alter anything else right now." That was real.

"What was the military like? Did you deploy? Did you have to kill anyone?"

She'd asked too many fucking questions! There was a code of silence that soldiers honored. I had not shared details with my crewe or anyone. I was quiet for a moment. Had to regroup. Scanned the room. Redirected my attention to Debbie.

"Whatever I want you to know about my time in Afghanistan, I'll tell you. Don't ever ask me no shit like that again," I said.

Her eyes grew wide. She perched her lips to the side, put down her fork, picked up her purse. Stood. "Sorry."

Black women were overly sensitive. My response was about me, but Debbie immediately took offense. But I liked her and didn't want her to abandon me.

I held her wrist. "That didn't come out right. Please sit." I carved my first sliver of beef. It was warm. Eggs not as much.

Slowly lowering her hip to the left, she exhaled, then resumed eating. Her eyes darted to the ceiling. Back at me. "I'm sorry. It's not you. I just broke up with my boyfriend. We'd been together since high school. Ten years. He didn't want to work, wasn't looking for a job, always driving my car, but couldn't fill it up with gas. It's hard to meet a man my age that's about something. At least you own property, have a degree, and served. I can work with a man with potential."

Hmm. Potential? She'd concluded that was what I had. My dick became flaccid. I shouldn't say thank you for her underestimation of my accomplishments. I'd been pinned with more medals than the number of years she'd lived.

"If it's okay, I'd like to invite you to my house tonight and cook for you. Maybe we can get to know each other better."

First she frowned. A slow, playful smile grew halfway, but the true shine, she couldn't contain, was in her hazel eyes.

"I'd like that, Dallas," she said. "Lock in my number. I've got to get to work."

CHAPTER 37

Dallas

Day 8

Showering, I put on a pair of silk leopard boxers, took my meds, cooked pancakes, bacon, scrambled eggs, in my favorite butter-flavored Crisco. Poured myself a tall, cold glass of milk, over ice, watched back-to-back episodes of *The First 48*, until I dozed off on the couch.

"Shoot him! Again! Again! Unload! Reload! Let's go!"

Six months in, training camp equipped me physically, but nothing prepared me mentally for my first killing. Seventeen years old, with an assault rifle in my hands, I was scared shitless, but I wasn't ready to die.

Dhak! Dhak! Dhak! Dhak! Dhak! Dhak! Dhak!

"Carter! Let's go!" my superior shouted.

We were not retreating. We were pressing forward. Long as the enemy was firing back, our mission was not accomplished.

Dhak! Dhak! Dhak! Dhak! Dhak! Dhak! Dhak!
Dhak!

Dhak!

Dhak!

Dhak! Dhak! Dhak! Dhak! Dhak! Dhak! Dhak!

Gunfire was deafening. I'd done as instructed. The faces of my targets, I imagined each one was Hawk Carter; then one day I stared in the eyes of a kid that must've been barely thirteen, fighting for his country. For a split second I froze.

"What the fuck? Shoot him!"

Dhak!

Dhak!

Dhak!

It was the boy or me.

"Mama! Mama!" Rattling my head until my eyes opened, I slammed the decorative pillow to the floor. Stomped on, then kicked it.

I cried.

Wasn't my last time. Some were younger. Couldn't lie. Would rather blow 'em up with a bomb than to look 'em in the eyes, then take their breath away.

They said everyone's days were numbered. Wondered how many more I had to go. I picked up the dishes. Carried them to the kitchen. Hadn't realized I'd missed the sink until the china plate—salvaged from my mother's belongings—crashed on the tiles.

All of my baby and other pictures growing up were destroyed. Had a few photos of me with my mom in my cell that weren't backed up anywhere. Since I couldn't take my cell to boot camp . . . they were erased by water damage.

I cleaned up the broken pieces, picked up my phone, silenced the television, sat on the sofa. Listened to my mother's favorite song.

After the third replay I called Debbie.

"Hey, handsome. How you doin'?" Her voice was soothing.

"Had another crazy dream. Don't think they'll ever stop. You have no idea." Made my way to the kitchen. Poured a double Hen. Downed two enhancement tabs with the liquor. Dying of a heart attack with my dick inside of a woman, that would be a nice way to go.

"I know you don't wanna talk about it, but if you ever change your mind, I'm here. And I promise not to ask any questions," she reassured.

"I just want the nightmares to stop."

"They will, baby. It's not your fault. You want some company? We could eat popcorn, drink, chill, and watch *For My Man*." She laughed.

I did, too. Not many chicks enjoyed seeing people die. The more violent, the better. Some thought, *Dat nigga crazy*. A different kind of crazy from the females slashing tires. It was easier to go from civilian to soldier than back.

Fuck Uncle Sam! Fuck Hawk Carter! I wanted the one thing I couldn't have. My mama.

"Thanks. Not tonight." Had to up my count. Had to get out there and find another sex buddy. "What you doing Monday?" I asked.

"Monday is cool. Dinner?" she asked. "That way I can stay the night. That is, if you don't mind."

"Woman, if I had the money for a wedding and a ring, I'd marry you today," I told her, knowing damn well I was not marriage material. I wanted to be. Actually, the good side of me, the little boy raised by an unconditionally loving, single mom, the child that grew up in the church, I was worthy of having a family of my own. Leaving my assets to my wife and kids would make me feel like a man.

"I have a few dollars saved up. Let's talk about it face-to-face when I see you Monday?" I told her.

Women liked when a man showed his sensitive side. Why not marry Debbie?

"I don't care about how much money you have, Dallas. I don't have much either. I like you," she said in her angelic voice.

Did my mother send Debbie to me? God? If there was no bet, I would've still invited her to eat with me at Li'l Dizzy's Café.

"My mother would've loved you." *She really would have.* "Stay out of them streets. Don't want my future Mrs. hanging in bars. Get some rest, I'll call you in the morning," I told her, not wanting to see her wherever I was headed.

I showered again, snatched my piece, headed to Bertha's, arrived at ten o'clock. "What's up, Brenda Jackson?" This was her home away from her crib. Brenda was beautiful with her wide hips, big butt, and gorgeous smile. Had that real Southern hospitality. She'd rejected all of my advances over the years.

"Hey, Dallas. You lookin' extra fresh tonight," she said.

I sat at the bar facing the door, ordered two drinks, placed one in front the barstool beside me, covered it with a paper napkin, leaned the chair against the counter. In another hour the small joint would be packed wall-to-wall and my future smash piece would be looking for a place to rest her feet as I invested in a place between her legs to rest my head.

CHAPTER 38

Dallas

Day 9

"*I hate your fucking ass!*" *I shouted at my sperm donor.*

"*The feeling is mutual. I'm not your daddy, boy!*" *Hawk claimed.*

I wasn't the product of what I'd heard men in my infantry bitch about. How the baby wasn't theirs. How their woman got pregnant when they were deployed. Or how their wife had a baby while they were away. My mother was not that type of woman. My mom would never lie to me about who my daddy was.

Shaking my head, I saw my hand was steady. I pointed my gun between Hawk's eyes.

"*You think I'm scared of that. After all the shit I done seen in the military, boy? I kill in my sleep! Do me that favor,*" *he said, pressing his forehead against the barrel.*

"*Why the fuck you deny me all my life?*" *I asked.*

He didn't move his head. I hadn't moved my hand.

Calmly he answered, "You don't want to know the truth."

"Why didn't you save my mother? You could've let her get in the boat with your family." Tears burned my eyes.

As he tightened his lips, his face twitched to the left, then back to the right. *"So Noelle and Lalita catfighting could've drowned all of us? My wife came first."*

"What really happened?" I yelled, *"You playin' me for a fool?"*

Soon as he opened his mouth . . . Pop! Pop! Pop! Pop! Pop! Pop! Pop!

"Mama! Mama!" I rattled my head until my eyes opened; my body was wrapped like a mummy. My pillow drenched. Sheets soaked.

I'd heard the rumors. "You know that's not your real daddy. Your mama and Noelle used to be best friends."

Silently I cried. Picked up my cell, put in my wireless earbuds. Listened to Bishop Paul S. Morton and the Greater St. Stephen Mass Choir.

"Are you okay?" the woman in my bed asked.

Sun rays illuminated my drapes. Staring at her, I couldn't remember if we'd had sex. I slid my hand between her legs, stuck my finger inside of her. She was slurping wet. I had to have inspired her juices.

"How many times did I make you come?" I asked, seeking confirmation.

She started smiling and stroking my shit. "You're an animal. Fuck the shit outta me again. I loved it." She almost growled.

Damn, I was glad I didn't have to make these women fall in love. Otherwise, I'd have to restart my count. "How'd you get here?"

"Stop playing, Dallas. You drove me," she said, straddling my knees. Opening her mouth, she leaned forward, feasted on my head vulture-style.

I told her, "Don't do that." Wasn't as though the shit didn't feel orgasmic. Wish I could come, but I had nothing left to give her.

Yank. Suck. Lick. Stroke. It was as though I hadn't said a word.

I frowned. Looked down. My shit was limp. Instantly the muscles in my face tightened. *Fuck!* Took the drug less than twenty-four hours ago. I should have a decent seventy-two hours before dealing with this impotent motherfucker. Not being able to get it up was not the side effect I wanted.

Smack! Smack! Smack! I knocked that nigga upside the head for being weak. This chick no longer turned me on. That was it.

"What's wrong with big daddy?" she asked, pulling on my dick like she was trying to jump-start an old lawn mower. "He jackhammered my pussy all night long. And you fell asleep on top of me. Get hard," she begged, then smacked my dick several times.

"Bitch!" I shoved her aside, squeezed her titties, not caring if them implants exploded like an IED. "What the fuck wrong with you? How you like it? Huh?"

"*Ow!* You're crazy! Let my titties go!" she cried, covering my hands, which were still attached to her breasts.

I released them.

Easing out of bed, she stared at me while examining herself. "Something is wrong with you. If they're leaking, I'm suing you."

And was I to countersue if that bitch injured my dick? I got up, threw her clothes to her. "Get the fuck outta my house." If I opened my nightstand drawer, the next nightmare would be her reality. I was shooting her ass.

Dumb bitch!

She gathered her phone, purse, shoes, dressed, then left. Saved me from having to physically throw her out. I was tired of women calling me crazy. Guess we both had too much fun drinking and partying at Bertha's last night.

I laughed.

Showering, I put on boxers, made my usual breakfast, called Debbie. Two more days before I'd see my boo boo.

"Top of the morning to the man of my life," she answered.

Debbie had no idea how much hearing her voice made me happy, if only for the moment. "You ready to change your last name to Carter?"

"If you're serious, yes, I am. Let's discuss it Monday. I've been looking at rings."

I was tired of sleeping alone. Waking up to strangers was starting to piss me off. Debbie had a good job. She was fine as hell. My dick got hard imagining being inside of her. I smiled, then frowned.

What woman would want to see my face every day? I couldn't add Debbie to my count. I was technically near zero. Should opt out of the nonsense, request my money back. My ego got me into this bullshit.

"I say what I mean, and mean what I say. On my mother's grave I'm dead serious." That was how I felt in the moment. Finished eating, I placed all the dirty dishes in the sink.

A text registered from Blitz, **Jax Brewery, noon, brother.**
Clang, clang, clang resounded loud in my ears.

I ducked below the counter, opened the kitchen drawer, got my handgun, released the safety. Crawled to my front door. "Sssh. Be quiet," I told Debbie.

"Oh, sorry. I dropped a pot. Getting ready to make oatmeal. Next time I have to cook for you."

Dumb bitch! Betta be glad you weren't near me.

Falling onto the floor, I replied to Blitz, **Cool,** then told Debbie, "I'ma call you later," ending our call before I blasted off a round of profanity. I cleaned the kitchen, then headed to the French Quarter.

* * *

Found Kohl and Blitz upstairs, outside on the deck. I squatted next to Kohl, Blitz was across the table facing us.

"I don't know about y'all, but this dick-and-dump shit is hard as hell. Plus, it doesn't seem right," I confessed, knowing if my mom was alive, I'd rip a dude's head off with my bare hands if he embarrassed her on social the way I'd done the girl after Keisha. Which reminded me, I had to blast ole broad with the deflated tits later.

"I'm having fun," Kohl said, grinning.

"Don't get me wrong. Bitches are easy. Talking a chick into giving it up is a cinch. Throwing them outta my bed, I hate doing that shit. Plus, one of 'em"—I bit my bottom lip, thinking about Debbie—"I can't do her like that."

I ordered a round of flights.

"Don't tell me your ass met somebody you like," Kohl said, then started laughing. "Put her on hold for the next three weeks, or you might as well sit this challenge out."

The challenge had taken the fun out of chasing pussy. Shit felt like a split shift.

"Nah, the deal is, the brother is having difficulty keeping it up." Blitz balled his fist, bent his elbow, flexed his biceps.

I leaned back, squeezed my dick. "That's the least of my concerns," I lied. "Round-the-clock breaking him out, I'm willing to admit, my dick hurts and that nigga is tired."

"You not getting your money back," Blitz insisted. "Dick. Date. Dump. Proof. No exceptions," Blitz said. "Winner takes all."

Then Blitz tapped the table. "I'll give you a side challenge. Whoever that bitch is, the one you like, do something publicly outrageous to embarrass her ass and . . . if I win, I'll give you back your two hundred and fifty."

With twenty-two days to go, I had a way to at least get back my contribution. Another woman like Debbie could come along.

Maybe.

"I wouldn't give his ass shit back," Kohl said, downing a shot.

Blitz laughed at Kohl. "Bruh, you act like you behind on your bills."

Kohl choked, cleared his throat. "I'll make you the same proposition that Blitz just made."

If I could convince Trymm to do the same, the only thing I had to lose was my relationship with Debbie.

"Whoa!" Staring at my cell, I saw a video that had to have been posted by Trymm. "Hashtag Clydesdale2930 on social," I said.

Seeing that chick on her knees praising his . . . I wasn't gay, but I'd dammed near forgot how Trymm was hung like a horse. Whoever she was, she tried, but she couldn't pack all that meat down her throat. I'd give her an A for effort. My dick got jealous. Rose to an occasion that wasn't available to him.

Blitz and Kohl held their phones in one hand, covered their mouths with the other.

Trymm walked up. Bet dude was in the lead.

Blitz greeted him with, "Nigga, you cold-blooded, my brother."

"His ass always been the most scandalous," I said. "I got something for y'all tomorrow." My shit wasn't nearly as wild, but for the sport of it, I was uploading the chick from this morning to DDD2930. That way they might think I was a chick.

Trymm stroked his chin, tapped his iPad. "If I told you my official smashdown that's right here, you'd think I was lying."

"Man, this challenge opened my eyes to how small

this city is. Even during the festival all I met was local randoms. My face is starting to become too familiar." That was true.

Trymm smiled. "New faces require new places, D. Upgrade your locations. What's up with you, Kohl?"

One side of Blitz's mouth twisted to the left. He squinted at Trymm.

Bouncing in his seat, Kohl said, "Ain't never a shortage of big gurls in the South. They come to me. I feed 'em, then fuck 'em, and if they let me fuck 'em first, I might not give 'em a po'boy or a daiquiri."

Not sure how to handle Debbie. "Gimme some," I said, slapping Kohl's hand.

CHAPTER 39

Dallas

Day 11

"Hey, boo boo. How was your day? Let me take that." I took Debbie's bag, put it in my bedroom. "Make yourself comfortable. My house is your home." I had to kiss those glossy lips.

"I missed you all weekend. Did you make it to any of the concerts?" she asked. Debbie snapped her finger. "Dang, that's what we should've done! Next year." Following me from the bedroom to the kitchen, she inquired, "What did you do this weekend?"

Bitch, I heard you the first time. "Stay right there." I opened my linen closet, got a scarf.

"What's that for?" she asked.

"You. Turn around." I blindfolded her, opened the refrigerator, removed five plastic containers, then untied the knot. "Boo boo, look what we have for dinner."

The smile on her face showed approval as I uncovered each one.

"Fresh catfish, scallops, shrimp, oysters, and soft-shell

crabs. This is what I've been doing. Shopping for my future wife," I said, initiating a kiss.

Debbie laid a wild and wet one on me. "My ex never cooked for me. You're different."

"You got a real man to take care of you. I told you, this is what I've been doing all weekend. Getting ready to make my boo boo the biggest seafood platter you've seen. And . . ." I raised the tops off of my special red beans and rice, with andouille sausage. I took out the gallon of 190 octane I'd gotten from the drive-thru daiquiri shop.

She bounced that ass like a basketball, but her small titties barely moved. Debbie filled a pair of twenty-ounce Styrofoam cups, secured the lids, inserted the straws. She suctioned her drink slow, swallowed. "*Ooh-wee!* I might have to call in sick tomorrow if I finish this."

Rubbing her hair, I said, "Cool with me," stealing another kiss from that pretty mouth.

Washing her hands, she said, "Let me help you."

I had something for Debbie to do later. "You gon' need your energy to bless the cook."

The female I'd met on a free dating site had left this morning. Trymm was right about new locations, and I now understood why Blitz used apps. All that chick wanted was to fuck.

"Go take a shower. I have shampoo, conditioner, extra toothbrushes, toothpaste, shower caps, fragrance body oil, lotion, spray, and lots of scrunchies under the counter. If you need a scarf for your hair, I got lots of those, too. You better put one on. If you don't, you gon' have huckleberries around your edges."

She laughed. "Why you have so much stuff for women?"

That was nothing. I had women's socks, shorts, tops, panties, with tags on. Had one of those expensive gold designer purses a chick left. I refused to give it back.

Waited for the right female to gift it to. Anything anybody left in my house instantly became my property. My possession.

"Woman, who over here? You! Go wash your ass!"

My future wife entered my bedroom. I closed the door to give her privacy. I felt calm. Happiness struggled to break my emotional barrier. A half smile was all I mustered, but on the inside I was superexcited about Debbie. Downing two enhancement pills, tonight we might consummate our relationship. That was, if Debbie was ready.

Dumping an entire box of Zatarain's fish fry into a brown paper bag, I coated the seafood, shook it several times. Turned the bag upside down, then right side up. Sat it on the counter. I layered a metal pan with torn pieces of a brown paper bag. I opened the patio door off the kitchen, stepped outside, closed the screen. Floating the fish into the deep fryer filled with lard, I sprinkled my French fries with Tony Chachere's.

I cleared the coffee table, draped it with a red-and-white checkered tablecloth. The platter I placed in the center was better than one of my favorite restaurants in Metairie, Deanie's Seafood. I topped off our 190.

Plates. Napkins. Beans and rice. Tossed two plush sofa pillows on the floor. Loaded *Training Day,* with Denzel Washington into my Blu-Ray player.

We were set!

"Oh, my God." My chin dropped.

Soft and simple. A sleeveless white dress clung to every curve. Her makeup was fresh, blond hair was wavy. The lashes were new.

"Behold the most beautiful boo boo in the world. This is our first date. Mark this as our anniversary." Had to remind myself to breathe.

Inhaling sweet perfume, I kissed Debbie on her lips, neck, collarbone. Drew her closer, shoved my tongue far as it would go into her mouth, then wiggled it around. Suctioned her tongue into my mouth, sucked it hard. I had to stop myself, but it was too late for my dick. He was on the verge of having a fracture.

She placed her palms on my cheeks. Pressed gently. Her eyes were wide. She exhaled. No woman had handled me with her level of care. There was love in her every touch.

"I'm glad we're taking our time, baby. The food looks amazing. Thank you."

Fuck the food! I wanted to bury my face in her sweet pussy. She smelled fruity. I led her to the living room, said grace.

"Thank You, Lord, for blessing us with this opportunity to come together and enjoy this seafood, the libations, and great company. Amen."

"Amen," she repeated.

I pressed PLAY on our movie. My favorite part was the ending. Denzel went down like a real man. That was how I would've gone out if the enemy had opened fire on me.

"You want kids?" Debbie asked, after the movie had ended.

"Noooooooooo . . . more than two," I answered. The eyes of that thirteen-year-old flashed before me. "Go to bed. I'll be in shortly." She'd ruined my appetite. Wasn't her fault.

Clearing the table, I restored everything back to its original state. Would I be a good father? What would I do if the baby screamed or cried all the time? Having a family seemed like a good idea, but if I had a daughter and any fool mishandled her, he wouldn't live to do it again.

I showered, slid back my foreskin, scrubbed under my corona. Couldn't take any chances that my . . . whatever Keisha had called it . . . had the same negative impact on Debbie. Slipping on boxer briefs, I peeled back the cover.

"Just let me taste her and I promise I'll let you get some rest."

Debbie didn't resist me.

A smooth strip of hair led down to nice, plump licorice-colored outer lips. Carefully I spread them. *Wow!* Pretty red flesh covered her clit, her wing tips, and the entry to her pussy.

I sucked her clit real soft.

"Mmm," she moaned along with me.

Juices streamed into my mouth. I craved more. Licked her from the opening up to her clit, then suctioned harder.

"Mmm." This time we were louder. I'd followed her lead.

Inserting my middle finger in her hotness, I did a come hither, kept eating her out. I squeezed my dick. It was the hardest I'd felt it in years.

"Can I put it in?" I asked, eager to feel her flesh.

"I'm not on anything," she said. "I stop taking the pill after I broke up with my ex."

Shocked, but not willing to miss this moment, I told her, "I'll get condoms next time."

Truth was, I had a drawer full of condoms, but I hated wearing them.

"Okay, just this one time," she said, then spread her thigh.

Pulling back my foreskin, I eased the head in. "Ah," I exhaled, penetrating her deeper. "Oh yes! You are the best, boo boo. I swear."

Debbie passionately thrust her hips toward me, squeezed her vaginal muscles.

My entire body trembled.

She squeezed tighter.

"Oh, shit! Oh, shit!" I said, shaking.

Her pussy throbbed to the rapid beat of my heart.

"Aw . . . shit! I'm fucking coming! I'm coming!"

Seemed as though I was a teenager ejaculating for the first time. The load was heavy. I couldn't stop coming.

I couldn't pull out. Collapsing on top of Debbie, felt like someone had freed me from a foxhole I'd been buried in for seven years.

CHAPTER 40

Dallas

Day 14

"**P**ut him six feet under, Carter!"
Hunching, I balled my fists, flexed my biceps, hiked my shoulders, felt my veins pop out in my neck. Killing had become our entertainment when the situation allowed. I growled, grabbed the dude over his shoulder and between his legs. Hoisted him in the air, then slammed his body into the jagged mountainside.

He fell on his back. I could cut his head off or worse.

"Finish him, Carter!"

Pulling out my pistol. One to the head. He was done. An extra bullet could cost me my life. I had no remorse. All in a day's work in a hundred-degrees weather. Helmet, T-shirt, jacket, pants, boots, and a backpack stuffed with ammunition.

"Ambush!" someone yelled, and just like that . . . it was showtime.

We were outnumbered. Outgunned.

Shoop! Soldier down. Couldn't abandon the body.

Firing at the enemy, I dragged our wounded sergeant with my other arm.

Shoop! *Another one of our men fell.*

Soon there were more soldiers down than we had men to carry them. Use the dead to shield my body, or die. I reloaded. Resumed combat. Six of us fought off what seemed like a hundred of them. The last enemy soldier went down. More resurfaced out of nowhere.

Fuck! *I was shooting blanks, had no more bullets. Determined this was not going to be my last fight, I threw my hand grenade.*

"Mama! Mama!" Rattled my head until my eyes opened. My pillow drenched. Sheets soaked.

I cried.

Picking up my phone, I played my song. Releasing my pain, I realized Hawk's wife, Noelle, asking for my number was an olive branch.

I texted Noelle, **Let me know when and where you'd like to meet.**

I was almost thirty, about to get married to a woman I hardly knew. Hell, that was the case for most people getting hitched. Time for me to stop holding on to hate, even if I didn't find true love. If Debbie could make a positive change in my life in a matter of days, I could try.

Shower. Meds. Pancakes. Bacon. Eggs. Steen's. Back-to-back episodes of *The First 48.* Dressed. Gray tank to expose my tats. Black jeans and tennis shoes. Gold chain. Two male enhancements. Gun.

With no destination I drove along St. Charles Avenue to the Riverbend. Doubled back to Poydras Street, parked, chilled solo at a bar inside Harrah's Casino, plotting my next move.

Squinting, I thought that looked like Blitz at the craps table. I stood to make sure.

"I know you're not leaving already. You look like you could use a friend." A strange woman smiled at me, then asked, "Is this seat taken?" holding the back of the chair next to me.

I nodded, sat down thinking, *I'm taken.*

"What brings you here, soldier?" she asked.

I was quiet.

"I'm in town for a few more days," she said real seductively. "Want to hang?"

"Forty dollars, my place, right now," I told her.

She countered, "Sixty."

"Fifty. Take it or leave it."

"Can I get a drink first?" she asked, touching my thigh.

I took that trick by the hand. "Let's go."

Soon as I closed my front door, I poured two Hens over ice, gave her one. She took it like a shot, refilled her own glass.

"Let's go," I said, leading her to one of my three guest bedrooms. Didn't want another woman in my master bedroom. That was reserved for my boo boo, Debbie.

My dick was hard as fuck. I put on a condom, bent the trick over, pulled her dress over her hips. *Bam! Bam! Bam! Bam! Bam! Bam! Bam! Bam! Bam!* I went straight in her asshole.

"Say you like it," I demanded, still pounding in fast motion.

She glanced over her shoulder.

"Say it!" I told her.

"Sixty dollars," she said, not fazed by my strokes.

"How about forty?" I answered, pulling out.

"Okay, I like it." She pulled down her dress, held open her palm.

Handing her two twenties, she snatched them. Made a

call. "Girl, meet me at . . . ," she paused. "What's your address?" She wasn't all friendly and shit the way she was an hour ago.

"Whatever corner you standing on. Get the fuck outta my house," I demanded.

"Aw, don't be like—"

"Bitch! Don't make me ask twice." I picked up my gun off the floor.

She was out the door in five seconds. I stripped the sheets from my bed, tossed them in the washer, disinfected my room, showered.

A text registered from Noelle, **Can you meet now in emergency at Tulane hospital?**

omw, I replied.

I rushed to put on slacks and a short-sleeved buttoneddown shirt.

Thirty-one minutes later I walked through the sliding glass doors of the ER.

She rushed to me, "Thank you for coming." Her upper and lower lip had sutures.

I could've assumed the deadbeat had done it, but either way, wasn't my battle. She was walking, breathing, obviously she wasn't the patient. "What's up?"

"One of my sons was in an accident. Can you please donate blood for him?" She started crying.

The woman who let me starve as a child now needed me to give my blood to her flesh and blood? I'd taken so many lives. This was an opportunity to save one. I did her that favor. We went into a small room. I lay on my back.

As the needle entered my arm, Noelle asked, "You don't want to know what happened to me?"

Is this bitch serious? I shook my head. "No. I don't."

"Okay, but you should know. Your mother was an honorable woman."

"Tell me something I don't know about my mother," I said. The bag couldn't fill up fast enough. I had shit to do.

Noelle's voice lowered. "Lalita and I were best friends," she said with a melancholy tone.

I inhaled. My chest expanded. "Where the fuck you going with this? Was this donor request to pin me down?" My eyes narrowed to a slit. "It'd better not be to save Hawk 'cause I'll beat your ass, too. Are you trying to clear your motherfuckin' conscience?"

If I rose up, Noelle was getting busted, fuck her lips, upside her fucking head. For real. My mother was the only person who loved me unconditionally. Tears clouded my eyes.

"Just hear me out," she insisted.

I swear if she started talking bad about my mother, this needle was going in her neck. I sat up. The nurse removed the IV. "Let's take this outside," I insisted.

We entered an empty waiting area. Noelle sat next to me.

"Hawk loved your mother. Le—"

I jumped up. "That's a fuckin' lie and you know it! You don't let somebody you love die when you could've saved them. He . . ." The rest of my words were stuck in my throat. Tears burned my eyes.

"I can't imagine how you feel." Noelle's eyes were dry.

I cut her off. "Imagine how I feel about what? Your ass was in the boat."

Noelle dug into her purse, handed me a stack of photos of my mother.

"You've never met Leroy. That's Hawk's brother. Leroy has been living in New York for thirty years now." Separately she gave me a photo of a man that I resembled more than Hawk Carter.

Staring at the pictures, one by one, I rotated the five by sevens. When I got to the photo of my mother holding me in her arms, she was in a hospital bed. I was a tiny baby wrapped in a blanket. Her lips were pressed against my forehead. Tears soaked my shirt. Snot rolled out my nose. Burying my face in my palms, I didn't give a fuck about that "men don't cry" bullshit.

"After you were born, Leroy begged Lalita to go with him to New York, but Lalita was, by then, dating Hawk."

I looked up at Noelle.

"Lalita was the one all the men wanted. So when she and Hawk became an item, I started dating Leroy." Noelle became quiet. "But he was always in love with Lalita."

"Go on," I said, wanting to be clear on where she was going with her story.

"Being that Lalita was my best friend, she confided in me. She was scared to move to a big city. Hawk went into the military, but when he came back, he wasn't the same in the head. He's never been the same. Lalita left him. But secretly I loved Hawk. When I had the chance, I married him, had his two sons."

"So because my mother left him, you took up her left-overs and let Hawk abandon me?"

Noelle placed her hand on my thigh. I moved it. "Don't touch me."

"Dallas, Lalita left Hawk, not because he had PTSD. I've never told Hawk this, and your mother swore me to secrecy. But you deserve to know. Hawk is not your father. Leroy is your father, but he doesn't know that."

Staring at Leroy's picture, I was really fucked up in the head now. My mother wouldn't do this to me.

"One last thing. Your mother wasn't happy that I'd married Hawk. I told her, 'He's my husband now. He's not Dallas's father. Let it go.' But I'd never turned my back on her. She was the one who ended our friendship. I begged Lalita to get in the boat. She refused." She slid her pointing finger from her throat to her stomach, then dragged it from breast to breast. "Hope to die."

Cross her heart hoping to die. That was for kids. I didn't know whether to believe Noelle or not.

"I know," she said, then handed me a piece of paper.

"Leroy Carter, your father, is a very successful man. Here's his number. Call him, Dallas."

"The—"

Noelle interrupted with, "Yes, *the* Leroy Carter."

"Thanks" was all I could say at this moment. *My dad is the famous actor?*

"One last thing." Noelle stood, handed me one more picture. "That's Leroy when he was in the navy. If you need me, I'm here for you. Take care."

I must've sat alone for hours trying to piece together my life. I saved Leroy Carter's number in my cell. Dialed him.

"Leroy Carter here!" he answered.

I was quiet.

"Hello!"

I couldn't speak.

"Hello," he said a third time. I ended the call.

CHAPTER 41

Dallas

Day 15

Pillow, dry. Sheets, crisp. Hadn't slept all night.

"Tracy." I nudged her. "Wake up. You hungry?" I asked, spreading her legs.

Closing her thighs, she said, "You've eaten my pussy enough, and, yes, I'm starved."

Cool if she felt that way. "Go shower. By the time you're done, breakfast will be served."

I headed to the kitchen, put Crisco in the skillet, admired my mother's picture on the wall beside the refrigerator. I'd framed all the photos Noelle had given me and hung them throughout my house.

Texted Noelle, **Thanks.**

Wondered if Leroy loved my mom the way I did Debbie. Mixing the batter, I set it aside, scrambled eight eggs. Slowly pouring batter onto my stovetop grill, counted, "One, two, three, four, five, six, seven, eight," then stopped, flipped the bacon.

My cell rang. "Hey, boo boo, top of the morning. You

at work?" Debbie having a steady job was perfect for me, except when she worked out of the office.

"No, I'm outside. Brought my fiancé steak and eggs from Li'l Dizzy's. Open up, baby. My hands are full."

Fuck! "Hold on. I'm coming."

I glanced at the monitor. *Damn!* She wasn't kidding.

Muting my phone, I set it on the counter, turned off everything on the stove, dumped it in the trash. Febreze the kitchen. Went to the bathroom.

I got my gun from the nightstand, entered the bathroom, pointed the barrel toward the floor, pulled back the shower curtain.

Whispered, "Tracy, get out the shower. Do as I say, and I won't hurt you. I've got a situation with my girlfriend. Need you to stay in the bathroom. Lock the door. Don't open it unless it's me. Chill out. Don't come out until I come get you. She's crazy. If you hear gunshots, hide flat on the floor in the linen closet."

Tracy's eyeballs protruded. She started trembling all over. Her brows rose, then grew close together.

I kissed her, then whispered, "I know. Don't be scared. Sit down. I'll be back. Do not come out of the bathroom. Stay put. Lock the door. And be quiet." I kissed her again.

Putting my gun back inside my nightstand drawer, I blasted Q93-FM, closed the bedroom door, unmuted my cell, opened the front door.

"What took you so long?" Debbie asked. "Our food is probably cold by now. But it's . . ." She paused. Stared at the stove. Sniffed the air.

"I dumped the food I was cooking for myself in the garbage. Next time, call ahead." I meant that shit. If she tried me again, I'd introduce her to whatever woman was in my house.

Debbie smiled while arranging our food on plates. Slowly she uncovered shrimp and grits. "I can't call and surprise you. What am I supposed to do when we're married? Can you turn down the music? I can barely hear myself," she said, setting silverware next to our meals on the table.

Thanks for reminding me why I'm single. One, she was inconsiderate. Two, demanding. Three, she hadn't noticed a single framed photo of my mother and me.

Not giving a fuck at this point at her staring at me waiting for a response, I told her, "You turn it down," opening the bedroom door.

Got a text from Noelle, **I'm mailing you something important in a few days.**

Hit her back with, **I forgive you.** Felt uncomfortable. Noelle made my heart soften. A little.

"Dallas, why is the bed all messed up on both sides?" Debbie asked.

"Because I slept in it."

"But both sides are ruffled." Her eyes beamed like lasers in every direction.

"I slept on both sides." Four, she was too damn nosy.

Debbie turned the bathroom doorknob. Jiggled it. Put her hand on her hip. "And why is the door locked from the inside?"

Her eyes filled with tears. Debbie followed me back into the kitchen. "Dallas, is there something you need to tell mc?"

"Actually, there's two. Let's eat, or you can leave now."

Soon as we were done with breakfast, Debbie had to get out.

CHAPTER 42

Dallas

Day 19

Lying in bed next to Dawn, I got up.
I crept to her side, stood over her, watched her sleep.

One arm was tucked under the pillow, the other elbow was buried midwaist. Knees slightly bent in a nearly fetal position. Back to me. Her breathing was calm.

I wish I could have just one night of rest without a med-induced crash or nightmares. Leaning closer, I wondered what was going through her mind. What kind of shit normal people thought about? Dreamt about?

My going from the queen-sized bed my mother bought me when I went to high school, to a bunk in boot camp, to a metal container that was smaller than some prison cells, I had the biggest king-sized bed I found at Comeaux Furniture. And I had a beautiful woman in it.

Dawn's eyelids fluttered. Slowly she rolled in my direction.

"Ahhh!" She screamed and kicked at the same time, then shouted, "What are you doing? You scared the day-

lights outta me." She sat up. Grabbed her phone. Her breathing was heavy.

She slept like a baby. I was admiring and envying her. I backed up. Replied, "I'm getting ready to fix breakfast. You hungry?"

"No, I'm good. I need to get going," she said, clutching her cell. Never letting go of her phone, continuously glancing at her screen, Dawn put on her clothes, then picked up her purse. "Thanks for a lovely evening. My Uber is outside."

No "call me later" or "I'll text you when I get home," or wherever she was going. She left me before I could smell or taste her morning pussy. Fruity and sweet was okay, but I loved the stench of a marinated vagina.

My nose wasn't sensitive, like most Americans'. A person fart and they go frantically fanning. Try living day in and out where every inhale was that of being trapped in a sewer 'cause everyone was shitting in the field. Where you learn to live with your own shit after taking a dump because you can't properly cleanse your ass. Or you shit in your drawers in a kill-or-be-killed environment.

Fucking weak-ass civilians.

Shower. Meds. Pancakes. Bacon. Eggs. Steen's. One episode in of *The First 48,* a text registered, **Morning, baby, I'm on my way.**

Really? After finding Tracy in my bathroom. I didn't deserve Debbie, but I needed a woman like her who would give me another chance. I restored my kitchen to its original state. Dressed. Green T-shirt, black slacks, casual leather shoes. Gold chain. Time to reload. Male enhancements. Two. Gun.

Met Debbie in my driveway. Opened the passenger door for her.

In transit she asked, "Did you sleep well last night?"

"You could say that," I replied. "You look nice. Smell good, too."

"We can't keep ignoring the fact that you need help." Debbie held my hand.

I was quiet. What good was help without a cure? Scientists couldn't cure the common cold. The ounce of prevention was not to join the fucking military. What in the fuck were doctors going to do for my PTSD? Meds and more meds that required me to take . . . more meds.

She had on a white maxi sundress with spaghetti straps, rhinestone-covered sandals. Starting to think white was her favorite color. I parked in the lot, opened her car door, placed my hand on the small of her back as we entered the store.

"Welcome." The guy behind the counter greeted us with a wide smile and an Indian accent.

"Let me try on a size seven." Debbie proudly held up her left hand as though she'd practiced this a gazillion times.

"A size ten for me," I told him.

The jeweler removed a set of plain silver wedding bands from the case, eased Debbie's ring on her finger. "Sir," he said, pinching mine as he held it in front of me. "This is a very special set. But if you prefer something more elegant—"

Did I appear to be a nigga that gave a fuck about elegance? I cut his up-sale off with, "This is good, dude."

How the fuck he come here from India and get his own jewelry store selling all this shit to blacks? Wouldn't be my money. I'd have custom-made pieces from the black dude who exhibited at the convention center during Essence. Had his card, but since I wasn't buying, I was here to do what Debbie could afford.

I took mine from him, tried it on. "Cool. It fits." That was all that mattered to me.

Debbie clicked pictures of her ring while it was on her hand. She held it next to her cheek, smiled, took selfies. "Let's get some together, baby."

Fuck no! That was her shit. "Can't spoil the surprise for my crewe. Still have to ask them to be in the wedding."

"Okay. So you like these?" Debbie asked.

"I like whatever you like, boo boo." Honestly, I didn't care. I wasn't buying or wearing it. Hated people identifying things about me without saying a word. Not that most women gave a damn if a man was married. Trymm proved that every day.

Debbie pulled out her credit card, gave it to dude. I stared that happy motherfucker down. I'd fought for his ass to suction food out of black people's children's mouths, make them late on their rent, all kinds of shit, just to sport some jewels that didn't mean shit but probably came from the motherland. And I was sure that he took tens of thousands of dollars a week back to his community and his country.

Dude put the blue velvet boxes in the same bag. "Thank you, madam. Sir. Next time you come back, I'll give you a really good discount."

Wouldn't be no fuckin' next time for me.

"Now it's off to City Hall to get our certificate," Debbie sang as she wiggled her body next to mine.

Kissing her cheek, I understood why dudes fucked as many bitches as they could the night before tying the knot—fuck a knot—the noose around their necks.

"Cool, boo boo. How many people you invite?" I asked, driving us to point B.

"On such short notice, that reminds me, are we going with Saturday, July thirtieth, or Sunday, the thirty-first? Saturday is better, since we're having it at my church."

The Dupree's anniversary on Sunday. I hunched my left shoulder. "Saturday it is."

She frantically tapped on her cell. "There, the pastor knows. And I group texted my family. I should have about seventy-five. How many for you?"

Damn, she must've included everybody from her job and her entire family. "Three."

"Okay, that'll round up to about eighty people for my family to cook for. The reception will be at the church immediately following the ceremony."

If I didn't have 250 g's riding on this wedding, I'd reach across her lap, unlock her door, and push her the fuck out of my Lexus. I parked in the garage, locked my gun in the glove compartment, opened her door.

"Here we are," Debbie said, skipping through the corridors of City Hall. "We'd like to apply for a marriage certificate," she said, cheesing ear-to-ear.

The lady assisting us was hot. She smiled at me. Gave the form to Debbie, then said, "Fill this out. I'll need your driver's licenses, certified birth certificates, and Social Security numbers. Have either of you been previously married?"

Debbie and I said, "No," at the same time.

"Good," the clerk said. "Come back to my window when you're done completing the application."

Handing my documents to Debbie, I let her write down my information. She turned in our application. She got our certificate.

"I'll hold on to this, baby." Her adding, "I need to shop for my dress" was music to my ears.

I parked in my driveway, got my gun, escorted her to her car, opened her door.

Just like Dawn, no "call" or "text me later" was mentioned to Debbie. Entering my house, I placed my gun on the nightstand.

"What the fuck are you doing?" I yelled.

If I were suicidal, I'd shoot myself in the head.

I thought about reaching out to Leroy Carter. Changed my mind. This wasn't a good time. I was too mentally frustrated.

CHAPTER 43

Dallas

Day 22

"Mama. Mama. Can you hear me?"

"Baby, there is a hurricane headed our way. I don't know what to do."

"It's not headed to New Orleans, for sure. That's the last news I saw."

"This one seem different, Dallas. Can you come home?"

Weather people were always getting shit wrong. They'd been tracking Katrina for several days. Boot camp was closer to the end than when I'd started. Was definitely going home on my ten-day leave before reporting to my unit, which had already deployed to Afghanistan.

"Dallas, please," Mama begged.

"It's not that simple. I only have one more week and, I promise, I'll be there."

"Private Carter! Are you on a phone?"

"Love you, Mama. Gotta go!"

Praying I wouldn't be set back for weeks, I answered, "Sir, yes, sir!"

"Vacation denied. Next week you report directly to your duty station."

One day later, August 28, 2005 . . .

"Private Carter. Request permission to phone home."

"Denied!"

I'd heard conditions had gotten bad at home. Stations ran out of gas. People were evacuating by the thousands every hour. Needed to hear my mama's voice.

Two days later, August 29, 2005 . . .

"Private Carter request permission to phone home."

"Denied!"

Three days later, August 30, 2005 . . .

"Private Carter request permission to phone home."

"Granted"

"Hi, this is Lalita Lavigne. Please leave a message and have a blessed day . . . If you'd like to leave a—"

I redialed. Ended the call. Redialed. Ended the call.

"Time up, Private Carter. Back to work."

I redialed. Ended the call. Redialed. Ended the call.

"It's pretty gruesome in your hometown, Private Carter. Vacation reinstated."

Got a glimpse of the news. People were stranded on rooftops. The Superdome was filled with homeless people. Dead bodies floated in muddy waters.

"Mama! Mama!" Rattled my head until my eyes opened. My pillow was drenched. Sheets soaked.

I cried out loud.

Picking up my lamp, I slammed it to the floor, punched a hole in the wall, cried into the carpet. "I don't want to live like this, Lord!" Civilians were fucking clueless. I couldn't believe my mother would choose death over getting in a boat with Noelle and Hawk.

I'd captured the enemy, but I was the one held hostage

in my mind. The ransom was death, and I was ready to be reunited with my mother.

I hummed the melody of "Your Tears," then played my song.

Showered. Meds. Pancakes. Bacon. Eggs. Steen's. Back-to-back episodes of *The First 48,* until I dozed off on the sofa.

Tap. Tap. Tap. I jumped up, scanned the room.

Tap. Tap. Tap. Resounded from my front door.

I got my cell off the coffee table. Viewed my house from the outside. A man dressed in a navy-blue shirt and shorts, holding an envelope, made an about-face with the package in hand.

Opening the door, I asked, "Hey, dude. You got something for me?"

"Yeah, man. Thought nobody was home. Sign here." He extended an electronic pad.

I scribbled. Closed my door.

Debbie's text **Can you find one more groomsman? I want my first cousin in the wedding** posted.

Every damn day, all day long. Damn cert gave her a license to stay connected.

I tossed the envelope on the dining table, then replied, **No, boo boo, you've spent enough.**

What was I going to do until it was time to go out and find chick number twenty-four? I reclaimed my spot in front the television, logged onto my page, DDD2930.

Got a message that my page was blocked for forty-eight hours. I didn't care. Long as it was back up on the thirtieth, I was cool. I checked Clydesdale2930. Trymm didn't have any recent posts. Maybe his shit was shut down for posting, too. An incoming call from Debbie interrupted my viewing Blitz's social.

"Hey, boo boo. How's everything coming along?"

"Hi, baby, I called to ask if you could contribute a hundred dollars for the balance to the caterer? That's the last thing that needs to be paid and we're all set. The dress my mother made is so beautiful on me. You want to go out tonight? Bertha's at ten."

Debbie had a way of answering her own questions.

I told her, "No, and no."

Silence lingered. I heard her sniffle.

"You don't have a hun—"

Of course I did. Her wedding. Her debt. She should've let me take the lead.

"What part of *no* didn't you get? I can't move my money until after I close on my next property. You're not marrying a rich man, but if it's costing you too much, call off the wedding."

"She accepts credit cards, but mine are all maxed out." Debbie's voice was filled with desperation.

Debbie needed to fall in line sooner than later. Either she was going to let me be the man or have it her way. I was quiet.

"Okay, baby. I'll take out a loan or borrow it from my mom. We'll be fine. We don't have to go out. You want company?"

"Let me catch this. I'll call you back, boo boo." There was no incoming, I just wanted to get off the phone with her.

CHAPTER 44

Dallas

Day 23

"Thanks for an exciting night. You were amazing," Nancy said before she kissed me on the lips. "I wish I didn't have to work today, but if you want to get together later, text me."

"Okay. Drive safe," I told her, heading back inside for my routine.

Shower. Meds. Pancakes. Bacon. Eggs. Syrup. Back-to-back episodes of *The First 48*. Dozed off. Woke up to ten missed calls, and twelve text messages from Debbie.

Dressed. Collared, buttoned-down, short-sleeved cerulean shirt. Matching slacks. Diamond studs in each ear. Feeling myself. Dark sunglasses. Gold chain. Piece.

I couldn't lie, I was excited driving to Drago's to see my crewe. Parked in the garage by the Hilton, trotted across the street. Kohl and Blitz were already there.

"What's up, dudes? Trymm coming?" I asked. Turning the back of my stool to the wall, I sat facing everything and everybody in the room.

"Yeah, said he'd be here shortly," Kohl answered.

"One of those chicks probably have his dick tied in a knot," Blitz said, then laughed.

It's long enough, I thought, having a pleasant flashback to Southern Belle. Kandy was the shit, too. How come my chicks didn't get down like that? None of them licked my asshole. Trymm was a magnet for freaks. Maybe after I started wearing my wedding ring, women would treat me better.

Kohl's attire was church ready as usual, but damn. Had to say, "Kohl, you glowin' like Chris Rock after he came all the way up. And before he started cheating on his wife. If you banking on being seven-figures richer in eight days, forget about it."

He fired back with, "You still in love with whatever her name is?"

Fuck yeah. "This game might have done me one solid." He knew her name was Debbie Schexnider.

"I got some shit y'all will never believe unless I showed you. Hawk's wife told me this is my real father." I took the piece of paper with my dad's name on it, slid it one space over to Kohl.

He stared at me, handed it one space over to Blitz. They'd saved Trymm the seat facing the grill. Blitz's face was expressionless. He was quiet, handed the paper back to Kohl.

Kohl placed it in front of me, clenched my fist, bumped his shoulder to mine. "How you feelin' about this, D?" He patted me hard on my back.

I opened the photo app folder *Lalita My Love,* gave my cell to Kohl. "Saved these a few days ago."

A smile grew on Kohl's face. "You were skinny, D." He showed Blitz, making dude laugh.

"Nigga was scrawny! I never thought about it, but you do look like Leroy Carter," Blitz said. "I'd forgotten how beautiful your mom was. My condolences all over again, man."

Shaking my head, I took my phone from Kohl, then said, "Noelle laid a lot on me, all of those. Debating if I should reach out."

"That's what's up. If you good with it, I am, too," Blitz said as Trymm walked up.

"Nig-ga, where you been?" I asked Trymm.

"You were a straight no-show for our head count last Saturday," Kohl said to Trymm.

Blitz commented, "Ain't seen shit from you on social since Southern Belle. Guess old Clydesdale can't hang."

What was up with Blitz's lil-dick ass always talking about how we can't hang? "Don't let this dude order shit. He full from"—I looked at Blitz—"eating pussy."

Had to admit we were all looking better than we did three weeks ago. Blitz's nails had a good buff. That was new. His teeth were whiter, too. Clothes were cool, but first thing Tuesday, I was lining up facial, manicure, and pedicure appointments to look like that mil had already been deposited into my account.

Placing his iPad on the counter, Trymm answered, "Yeah, that's it, homey. Cialis hijacked my shit, had it on swole five days in a row. Now I can't get it up." He faked a dry cry.

Is that true? No way I'd ask, but Trymm might not be joking. A text registered from Debbie, **Are you at Drago's?**

She sent another message, **My cousin said you're there now.**

A third came in from her: **Are those three guys your groomsmen?**

A fourth, **Can I come by and meet them?**

I replied, **No!**

What the fuck is wrong with her? I'd never met her cousin, and I wasn't dat dude to deal with, or answer to, women or their nosy, eye-spying, man-hating single girlfriends. Debbie's cousin could suck the shit outta my ass-hole and swallow. I didn't give a fuck about her.

Those sizzling oysters on the grill had my name on thirteen of 'em.

Trymm sat at the counter next to Blitz. "See y'all left me the seat with my back to the audience so I can't check out the females first," then added, "All I know is each of you betta show your face at my parents' anniversary party at Gallier Hall on the thirty-first. Six o'clock sharp."

We all stared at that nigga. *Is he serious? Determination day we supposed to be at . . .*

Mr. and Mrs. Dupree—unlike Blitz's and Kohl's parents—had been there for me after my mom died.

"Count me in," I said.

If these dudes knew I seriously wanted to get married a week from now, that might be grounds for disqualifying me for the challenge. For that reason alone, losing out on a million dollars, I couldn't say, "I do," but I had another idea. "I want you guys to be my groomsmen."

One, two, three heads turned toward me.

"It's not real, dudes. I'm just letting her think it's real," I said.

I texted Debbie, **Boo boo, I'm sorry. Don't be mad at me, but I can't deal with people watching me. I love you.**

Debbie replied, **I understand. Won't happen again. I love you, too, baby.**

I scanned the sweeping dining area, the bar in the center of the hotel, and the other bar at the entrance of the restaurant for a chick to take home. Seemed as though Kohl and Blitz were on my page.

"One of y'all say something. Damn!" Trymm stopped our waiter. "Let us get four baker's dozen of them flame-broiled oysters on a half shell and a round of Hen."

"Gotcha," the waiter replied.

Kohl said, "I'ma 'bout to trump all y'all. Let's do a count. Write down your numbers." He handed each of us a napkin.

"Hell no," Trymm objected. "All I want eight days from now is proof. Videos, confessions, social posts. All that." He tapped his iPad.

"You're holding out 'cause Walter been on your ass and you in last place," Blitz said. "You ain't got shit on that tablet."

My count was low. Couldn't include Debbie even though I had proof.

"I'm cool," Kohl said, "'cause none of y'all put shit on social worth posting." He pointed at Trymm, then devoured three oysters, then stuffed his mouth with butter-soaked French bread, washed it down with liquor.

"Put some respect on it. Ruff. Ruff. Ruff." Trymm gave three deep barks, pounded his chest. "Southern Belle. There's more where that came from. A lot more." He tapped that pad again.

A female dressed in denim short shorts, a cute fedora, and tight blouse, with big-ass nipples, thrust her cleavage in Trymm's face. Her hair was short, slicked at the back and sides. Lips glossy.

Lucky motherfucker. I sucked the largest oyster right out the shell.

"I was at your yacht party. Remember me?" she asked him all sexy and shit, eyeing his iPad.

Trymm slid his iPad away from her.

Good job, dude.

I knew my boy. He either didn't remember that chick or he didn't know her. She was cool at first, but . . . *What is this bitch up to?* She kept staring at his tablet.

"Let that bitch get ghost," I said.

Blitz's eyes stretched wide. "Yacht, what?" he belted. "I see you, homey. That's why his ass been MIA."

All of Kohl's oyster shells were empty. He devoured two of mine while gawking at ole girl.

"She cool, D," he said. Then, "Thanks for coming over to say hi," Trymm told her.

Her shiny lips parted as she swiped her wet tongue to the corner of her mouth. The tip wiggled like a snake's at Trymm. Her hand slid up his thigh. She said, "I was hoping we could get together again without the other *ninety-nine* females that were all over your big banana boat."

"What the fuck?" I said aloud. "I ain't making that anniversary party, big baller. I don't know about y'all, but that nig-ga is way ahead of me."

Chick shined a flashlight in Trymm's face. Started massaging his dick.

This nigga was being too nice. "Ditch that bitch!" I told him.

Trymm moved her hand, the one massaging his dick, then asked her, "Do I know you?"

She laughed.

I felt uncomfortable for my boy, but since he ignored me, I wasn't making a move. He scooted his barstool back, stared into her eyes.

"'Do I know you?'" she sarcastically repeated.

Looked in her eyes. Oh yeah! That bitch was on something.

Trymm told Blitz, "Let's switch seats, homey, before I raise up outta here."

Ole gurl jabbed the flashlight into Trymm's head. He yelled, "Fuck!" Screaming like a bitch, he grabbed his nuts, bent over, held his shit.

I wanted to choke that bitch, but if I got up out of my seat, I was going to shoot her.

She shocked Trymm's left nipple. He slowly descended toward the floor, landed on his shoulder, then rolled onto his side in the fetal position.

Ole gurl and people around us started videotaping. Suddenly I started laughing uncontrollably. Blitz and Kohl were laughing harder.

Blitz aimed his phone at Trymm. Now, that was cold-blooded.

"My sister didn't suck your dick for you to degrade her on social media. Thought your lil yacht party was just for fun. Thanks to you, my sister's husband is divorcing her! She has to raise her son and daughter by herself! Had to pull them out of their school because kids wouldn't stop teasing them! You broke up her happy home! I should stun you again!" she said, reaching toward my boy.

I got the fuck up. "That's enough. Trust me. He's sorry." I placed my left hand behind my back, stared that bitch down. I swear if she did it.

The woman swiftly pointed the flashlight at me. I became quiet. In slow motion, not moving my eyes, I shook my head, raised my shirt. Nodded at that bitch.

"Let's go," another woman said.

Calmly the woman dropped her flashlight into her purse. I was on that bitch in two seconds. Grabbed her by the throat. Started choking the fuck outta her. I was sure she wanted to say something, but couldn't speak. Her face turned red.

The woman's friend began crying, "Help!"

Something got a hold on me and I couldn't let her go. "I strongly suggest you don't try this shit again. If you do, I'll shoot you." I stared at her friend. "I'll shoot your ass, too. Get the fuck outta here." Releasing the woman's throat, I extended my boy my hand, pulled Trymm up.

"You don't look so good right now, brotha man," Blitz said to Trymm, then yelled out to our waiter, "Yo! Lay four more dozen oysters on us and another round of Hen on me. It's gon' take this nigga a minute to recuperate."

"Fuck you, Blitz. I'm still ahead of you," Trymm said, leaning on the counter.

Blitz smiled, "Not for long, my brother. Not for long."

Quietly I stared at Blitz. Saw a side of him I hadn't seen before. Kohl didn't do shit, because I handled her. But Blitz? He was on some "the money means more"-to-him-than-Trymm bullshit.

Blitz had better hope he never needed me to have his back.

CHAPTER 45

Dallas

Day 29

Bachelor party?
Rehearsal?
Bachelor party?
Rehearsal dinner?
Bachelor party.

"Boo boo, what's there to practice about walking down an aisle? My crewe will be at the church thirty minutes before the ceremony."

Debbie explained, "Baby, that's not enough time. Can they come for thirty minutes tonight?"

"Make it enough." I wasn't asking.

"So the first time you will meet my mother is going to be at the wedding, Dallas?" Debbie stated, then started sniffling.

"I really don't have to meet her at all," I said, then raised my voice, "I told you—"

"Okay. Okay. But please. Make sure they're on time." She spoke with authority.

I'd let her have that. "Boo boo, I gotta go. I'll see my baby tomorrow." I ended the call.

I group texted Kohl, Trymm, and Blitz the address to the church and time to be there: **Five thirty.**

Bro, you really going through with this #fakewedding, Blitz texted.

Outside the group I reminded his fake ass, **If you win, I gets my two-fifty back.**

Kohl rebounded with, **I wouldn't miss this for nothing.**

Trymm replied, **Lucky I owe you one, but you betta start on time. 8:00 I'm out, not 8:01.**

I responded, **Cool.**

I put on black everything: slacks, shirt, shoes. No jewelry. Packed my piece. Locked it in the armrest compartment. Weapons weren't permitted inside where I was going. Security at the sex club did their job well.

Before I got out my car, I put all calls on DO NOT DISTURB, then locked my cell in my glove compartment.

I stepped onto the red carpet; it was Pantyless Friday. I had a bottle of pineapple Cîroc in one hand and Hennessy in the other. Stopping in the changing room, I removed my clothes, oiled my body, jacked my dick really hard to make him point north. I pulled back the foreskin, took my alcohol upstairs to the lounge, requested they set me up. Immediately the thirsty females gathered around me.

A few women traded off, stroking my erection. "I'm having an after-party at my place if any of you want to come by," I said, cursing myself out in my mind for not doing this sooner. They would only count if I could prove I had sex with them.

"Oh, I'd love to," the petite one said, then licked my nipple.

Two others requested my number, claiming they'd be there. "Bring a friend. Not a dude. I've got to run." I left the liquor for their enjoyment.

Getting in my car, I drove home. Got my gun and cell. My voice mailbox was probably full of messages from Debbie. I'd check later.

Made my own setup. Closed all my bedroom doors. Left access to the half bathroom. Minutes later, *tap, tap, tap*, at my door. My driveway was filled with cars. An overflow was curbside.

"Damn, come on in, ladies."

They formed a single-file line. When I was done counting, I had seventeen women in my living room. "Help yourselves to cocktails and my cock, ladies."

The one playing with her pussy, I ate her out first. "Mmm, you like pineapple," I say, sucking her clit firm.

"Oh . . . yes," she said, playing with her titties. "Eat out every day."

I felt a finger at the tip of my asshole. Reaching back, I grabbed a wrist. "My ass is off-limits." Never have and never will let hand, dick, dildo, butt plug, none of that shit, go past either of my sphincters.

Burying my face in the bush of the chick, next to the chick that I was eating, I was interrupted. "I'm next, big daddy."

I told her, "Hold on and spread it open for me."

Didn't mind pubic hair. Hated when I swallowed a hair. Felt a hand massage my balls, another stroked my dick. Made me question if I should walk down the aisle in less than twelve hours.

The break of dawn peeped into my living room. I did a count and all seventeen of them were still there. Some had passed out. Couldn't remember whom I'd eaten out or fucked but my mouth and dick were exhausted.

When I looked down, one eye was staring up at me. My meds hadn't failed me. "Come here," I told the pretty petite one, turning her around. "Bend over."

I wasn't asking as I shoved her breasts toward the back

of the sofa. Slipping on a condom, soon as I tried to shove the head in, instantly I went soft. This was not happening.

"Fuck it!" I yelled, waking a few of the sleepyheads.

"It's okay," one of them said. "Relax. I'll get you right back up."

She lightly scraped those long nails all over my back. Then she trailed kisses down my spine. The closer she got to my asshole, the harder my shaft became. Soon my dick was hard enough to put on a new condom.

"What the hell? I'm coming!" I screamed as a finger slid into my ass.

Yanking it out, I felt my hole tighten. I came again. Harder this time. More extreme than ever before.

Quickly regaining my composure, I told the ladies, "Okay. That's enough. Thanks for coming. Gather your clothes. Party over."

Everyone politely left. Some with their clothes in their hand.

Restoring my house to its original state, I scrubbed every inch of my sofa with disinfectant wipes, cleaned the coffee table, vacuumed the living room, washed the glasses, tossed out the empty liquor bottles.

Normally, I'd be awakening at this time. Better take Debbie off of DO NOT DISTURB. On second thought I'd better get a few hours of sleep.

I left Debbie Schexnider, soon-to-be Carter, on DND and went to bed.

CHAPTER 46

Dallas

Day 30

M y cell rang. I checked the caller ID. It was Trymm. "Nigga, you gon' be a no-show?" he asked.

I looked at the time. "Fuck! I'm on my way."

Getting ready in military time, I showered in two minutes. Brushed my teeth, downed my PTSD meds, skipped the enhancements, stepped into the tuxedo I had for three years, slipped my cell in my pocket. Started to leave my piece. Changed my mind on that. Was out the door and at the church before my boys finished their half-hour rehearsal.

Blitz took one look at me and laughed. "Your eyes red as hell. You must've had a hell of a night."

"Other than that, nigga, how I look?"

"Man, you really going through with this?" Kohl asked. "I know I said do it, but this ain't right, D. Let's just leave now."

"And walk away from the quarter of a mil you promised me if *you* win?" That wasn't happening. "Same goes for you, Blitz."

My crewe was sharp, but those niggas were dressed in black. "Y'all suited like somebody died."

"If you follow through with your plan, you might be signing up for your funeral," Kohl said.

The good Reverend Bartholomew's church burning down, there wasn't shit Kohl could do. That was what insurance was for. The church was old. White flaking paint, wood trim on the windows were rotting. Might be a blessing that they get to rebuild. Southern Christians were superstitious. Eric and Eleanor Lewis might haunt the congregation forever.

A lady came outside, announced, "Places, everyone."

I stood at the altar, facing the door. My crewe strolled in and escorted women, whom they didn't know, to pre-assigned places; then they claimed their positions in front of the first pew. White ribbons were tied to the end of each bench. A large arrangement of magnolias was in a gigantic vase on a table behind the minister.

The organist played the traditional "Here Comes the Bride" tune. I clamped my hands behind my back.

Doors opened to the most beautiful woman I'd seen. Debbie's white dress didn't have one of those long trains dragging behind her. It stopped at her knees. Long sleeves, loose-fitting. A simple veil covered her face.

My boo boo was classy. Mama would've cried. Not for Debbie. To see her only child getting married would've made her happy . . . and sad, I imagined.

As Debbie faced me, I noticed the veil had tiny pearls on it. I peeled it back. A simple, sweet chocolate lip color, and light makeup. Her blond hair was freshly trimmed.

The pastor, I'd never met, asked her, "Do you take this man . . ."

"I do" softly escaped Debbie's lips.

Insisted on her going first for a reason. I slid her ring on her finger. Tears streamed down her cheeks. I should do the proper thing.

Kohl was right. This was wrong. But most marriages didn't last, anyway. I did have undeniable feelings for Debbie. She was a nice girl. But was *nice* enough for me? Definitely didn't need a crazy wife. Debbie had made me come. But so did that woman last night.

The pastor said, "Do you take this woman . . ."

Less than thirty days . . . I barely knew Debbie. Did I want her to be the mother of my children? She'd be a great mom, I guess. How the fuck would I know?

I looked at my boys, nodded my head toward the door. One by one, they walked in a single-file line.

As I followed, people gasped. Mumbled.

"Where's he going?"

"Is he coming back?"

"He can't be serious."

"This had better be some sort of joke."

The one thing nobody did was laugh.

Heard the pastor ask, "Son, where are you going?"

His saying, 'son,' tugged at my heart. Was that how Leroy Carter would've spoken to me. Felt as though if I looked back at Debbie, I'd turn to a pillar of salt.

"That's fucked-up, D," Kohl reminded me. "Hope it was worth it."

"Nigga, if you win, I want my money," I said, feeling like shit for embarrassing Debbie.

"Dallas," Debbie said. "What are you doing?"

I could change my mind, go back inside with her and make it right.

Without answering her, I got in my car, drove home, opened a fresh Hen, drank straight from the bottle.

"Fuck this bet. I want my woman." I needed Debbie more than she needed me. Getting back in my Lexus, I returned to Debbie's church. Saw an ambulance out front. Debbie was strapped to a gurney.

"Fuck! I fucked up." She couldn't hear me say, "I love you boo boo." I kept driving.

A text registered from Noelle, **Heard on the news a few minutes ago. Leroy Carter was killed in a car accident. Had you contacted him?**

I was waiting for the right time to contact him. Didn't want him thinking I was after his money. What the fuck was I to say over the phone after almost thirty years of not knowing my dad?

I didn't respond to Noelle. Seen enough death. Didn't affect me the same. Driving to my house, I called Debbie.

A woman answered, "This is Debbie's mother."

"Ma'am, this is Dallas. I-I-I'm so sorry. Can I please speak with Debbie?" I begged.

"Young man," Debbie's Mom spoke softly. "I'm going to pray for you. But as long as you live, stay away from my baby," she told me, then ended the call.

'As long as you live,' echoed in my head. I couldn't blame her. I didn't know Debbie's mom's name.

Bypassing my home, I cried out loud. I drove across the train crossing. Doubled-back. Parked my car on the tracks. Staring up at the sky, the sunshine blinded me. A train would come eventually. If I tired of waiting for the unknown, I had options. I held my gun in my hand.

Had demons to fight. I could blame my abandoning Debbie at the altar on the game I was playing. I could blame it on PTSD. What I couldn't do was fault Debbie.

Debbie was the closest I'd come to loving a woman.

I pointed the barrel at my temple. "God I can't keep living this way every day."

CHAPTER 47

Blitz

Day 1

"What can I do to make sure *I* have complete control of this account, my brother?"

I arrived at my bank before the crewe to discuss the details and options that would grant me sole access to the funds anytime I wanted. Shitz, I could work miracles with a million dollars.

Giving my banker the challenge overview, I explained, "This shit is no different from what I normally do. I just have to do more of it in a shorter period of time. But realistically"—I had to keep it one hundred with myself—"there's no way I'm going to date, dick, and dump more chicks than Trymm in thirty days, but it was his idea, ya feel me. And you know my financial situation."

"That's a lot for a bet. Yet, alone, one that's uncivilized." Ralph's already-good posture became perfect as he elongated his spine and his neck. "You running some type of scam like your shady daddy?"

How dare this lil nigga question my integrity! "You best be joking. Don't forget who got you this job."

There was plenty of false accusations about how my dad had ripped off Katrina victims in his district. Done under-the-table deals with government and independent contractors who'd paid him in cash. Nobody bitched when former Governor Edwin Edwards allegedly did the same. In fact, people in New Orleans loved Edwards's dirty drawers. The only difference with my dad was he was black. Regardless to what really transpired after the hurricane, Henry Roulet, House Representative for over thirty years, taught me, peanuts were for pussies, always get the lion's share of every deal.

Fuck what is fair!

"The fact that he recommended me for this position is what's up, but I have a wife and two kids to feed!" he exclaimed.

If that was the way Ralph saw it, so be it. And I imagined he'd want to continue putting bread on his table. Ralph was going to help me, or he'd be unemployed by whatever time he was scheduled to get off today.

Ralph was all of twenty-five, been working at the oldest bank in Louisiana almost a year. That was why I'd waited an hour to speak with him. All the seasoned staffers knew me too well. Not one of them would let me have my way.

"Stop wasting my time on the frivolous, youngster. I got your back. Transfer two hundred fifty thousand from my joint account ending in 0069 to a new—"

Ralph's shoulders slumped forward, causing his back to hunch. "You mean from your parents'—"

My voice deepened with authority: "It's my family, my brother. Not yours. I'm legit on there, too."

"Yeah, but no one is to take money out of it. That's what your dad told me when I started—"

I knew what my father had said to my mother and me and everyone that worked here at the bank. That was why I would have to ask for forgiveness when he found out.

Once I disclosed the reason and the return, my dad would praise me.

Henry Roulet had warned me to never make a deposit or withdrawal from 0069 until after my mother and he were deceased. Assuming I'd outlive them both, why wait?

"You're going to fuck up for peanuts?" Ralph asked.

There this young buck went, smelling his own piss again. "Listen here, pretty Creole boy, with your crystal-gray eyes." That were the same color as mine. "How much of an incentive do you need to do what I ask?"

I had a few dollars left in my other accounts, but that wasn't enough to bring my gambling and other debts current. All the fronting I'd done over the years—buying women expensive shit—was to impress my crewe. Truth was, creditors were on my ass every day. Wish I could re-possess all the gifts I'd given to those females. Even if I hadn't come up with monetizing the bet, I desperately had to get money from somewhere to repay the near 750 g's, plus interest, I owed the casino. I had to wear a disguise just to get past the people checking IDs at the door.

Payday. Thirty days from now, it would be in one hand, out the other. But most important, I'd have a clean slate.

Ralph frantically loosened his tie, unfastened the first two buttons on his shirt. He pressed a button on his phone. A dial tone followed. "Just let me get clearance from my boss."

I reached across his desk, snatched the receiver, slammed it on the base. "What the hell are you doing, man?"

"Calling for—"

I was seconds from slapping my brother upside his head with his own handheld. "If you don't do as I instructed, I'll make sure this is your last day working here, and all your family will have to eat will be peanuts. I don't need permission." I reiterated, "I'm on the account."

As he tapped on his keyboard, sweat beaded on his forehead. He swiped it away, then rubbed his palm on his navy-blue slacks. One last peck before staring at me. "Done. Transfer complete. New account is open."

I handed him Trymm's cashier's check. "Two more deposits are coming soon as my other brothers get here. Now, back to me having exclusive control. Make that happen right quick."

Ralph didn't blink, didn't move his head.

"I know you're new at this. I'm not." I also knew that my dad had been fucking Ralph's mom for years and that was the real reason Ralph was on payroll. To make up for my father's nonpayment of child support and for Ralph and his mother to keep their mouths shut. "I wouldn't let anything happen to you or your job. Somebody has to have the authority to *close* the account. Right?"

Silence filled the air space between us.

Ralph exhaled heavily. Wrote on a piece of paper. Slid it across his desk to me.

I read: *dollar sign, one, zero, zero, zero, zero, in cash.* Then responded, "Cool." Mentally he was slower than I'd thought.

"There is one way, I will give you control," he finally agreed.

Everybody in my town had a price. Most would do more for a lot less. Slapping my hands together, I smiled. "My brother. You are the man. I'll have that in your hands at the end of the thirty days."

No way I was paying him up front. For what? Ralph had just entered the big boys' league and didn't know it. My dad was going to have Ralph's head on a chopping block, but that was not my problem.

Ralph countered, "Half now. Half later."

"Cool. Let's see this set up all the way through first," I said, knowing he wasn't getting a dime. Not now. Not later.

Dallas tapped on the glass. Before they entered the office, I told Ralph, "That's my crewe outside the door. Make it happen and I got you, but you have to keep this shit between us, yeah."

Dallas sat to my right. Kohl on my left.

Ralph regained his professional posture and greeted them. "Welcome, gentlemen. I'm Ralph Leimert. The investment account is set up. All I need is your deposit and your signature."

Anxious to make my next move, I assumed a poker face.

"Investment? Who said anything about investing?" Dallas held his cashier's check firmly in his hand.

"I don't know," Kohl replied. "That might actually be a better idea. We invest in something safe. Winner takes all of the interest and we each get our initial back in thirty days."

Dallas nodded.

"Not enough of an incentive," I insisted. "Plus, Trymm's not here and his money along with mine is already deposited. But we can discuss that as an option and convert the account later, if agreed."

I wasn't changing shit!

"That's true," Ralph agreed. "Let me add you guys on. Driver's licenses, please."

My banker keyed in the information, handed Dallas and Kohl back their identification, along with their deposit receipts, and copies of their executed documents.

I confirmed, "I'll give Trymm his package today and have him come by tomorrow with his ID and sign-off."

"Great, gentlemen. Enjoy the rest of your day," Ralph said.

Dallas paused in the doorway. "Y'all know I don't have any other friends. Don't let this shit come between us"; then he walked out.

"I second that," Kohl said before he left.

I was the only one left sitting with Ralph. "How soon will I have access?"

"Immediately. But keep in mind, if they set up online, they can view the balance at any time."

"Shit, bro. Why'd you add that feature?"

"It's automatically included," he said. "Long as they don't sign up, it won't matter."

That nigga inserted a snag in my protection plan. I could make a move, but not without the crewe potentially knowing. "Find a way to block that feature. I'm out."

As I stood in the lot by my BMW, my cell rang. **No Caller ID** registered.

I answered. Remained silent.

"Hello, Mr. Roulet?" she said.

"Yeah. That's me."

"Is this Mr. Blitz Einstein Roulet?"

"Bitch, yes. What's up?"

"This call may be monitored for quality-control purposes. Your account is two months delinquent. If it's not brought current by the second of next month, we may start the foreclosure process. When can you bring your account current?"

I knew the rest of her spiel. Payments were contractually due on the first of each month. Late by the second, not the fifteenth. The extra days to pay was a privilege, not an entitlement.

"I'll bring it current in thirty days. Please stop harassing me."

"Can you make one pay—"

I hung up on that bitch.

CHAPTER 48

Blitz

Day 1

Trymm parked in front my home, lowered the tinted window of the black Benz he got a year ago. His GLS, Ferrari, and his Range Rover were paid in full before he drove them off the lot.

Digging in my back pocket, I approached the passenger side, handed him an envelope with his deposit receipt inside, along with documentation verifying the balance in the account with each of our names on it. I'd left inside the additional paperwork that benefited only me.

Trymm ripped the seal, peeped inside. "This kinda light. Where the rest of the deets?"

"Nigga, don't get new over a bet you're going to lose. Oh, text me a copy of your driver's license. My banker, Ralph, needs it for the file," I reassured him.

"Fuck that. I'll drop by the bank early Monday to make sure everything is in order. I'll give it to him then," he said.

"I got a few female intellects lined up while you . . . at

work." I smiled, flashing my stopwatch in his face. Pressed START. "Your ass late, bruh."

Then I lied and told him I'd run into his ex, but truth was, I was hooking up with Atlantis tomorrow.

Turning off the water hose, I texted my bartender friend at Trenasse, **Reserve two seats at the bar for me. Omw for lunch,** finished sprinkling my front lawn before going inside to shower.

Checking my cell, he'd replied, **np.**

Being the son of Henry Roulet afforded me perks at all the five stars in the NOLA. Valet-parked my ride. Strolled through a sea of beautiful sistahs.

"Haven't seen you in a while, Blitz," the bartender said. "You want your usual?"

"Two glasses of water for now," I answered. Had to pace myself. Reel in the right woman.

"Here you go."

Resting the seat next to me against the counter for whoever appeared an easy lay, I watched women gather in groups. Some had more swing in their hips than others. I'd hold out for the loner. She was generally the easiest to persuade to bed.

I placed one glass in front of me, the other by the empty chair. As the bartenders began taking orders, the only available of the eight spots at the bar was the seat next to me. That was exactly how I wanted it.

Quenching my thirst with a sip, I chilled.

"Excuse me." A friendly voice resonated in my ear. "Is this seat taken?"

Glancing back at her, I saw she wore fitted jeans with slits at the knees, a T-shirt tight enough to be a second skin. Her hair was in a ponytail. That was okay. What wasn't kosher was her hair was matted.

It was a definite lie of "Yes. My girlfriend is on her way."

Turning in the opposite direction, at a ninety-degree angle, I noticed a plus-sized, curvaceous woman heading in my direction. She stood behind the stool, placed her hand on her hip, stared at the glass of water. Sliding her sunglasses to the top of her head, she glanced around the room as though she was looking for someone, then picked up the menu.

Extending my hand, I said, "My name is Roulet. What's yours, sweetheart? Can I buy you a drink?"

I wasn't so down on my finances that I couldn't pick up tabs on credit cards, I'd planned to pay off by the first. My balances were thousands here and there, five figures to satisfy my delinquent mortgage and car notes. My declining stocks, I'd have to take an "L" to trade.

"Looks like someone is sitting here," she said, eyeing the glass.

"You are." I handed the water to the bartender, pulled out the stool for her, extended my hand, reintroduced myself.

A fresh glass of water appeared without my asking.

"I'm Lema. Lema Harrison," she said, sounding as though she were running for office. Placing an oversized designer handbag on the countertop next to the wall, she tugged the hem of her thigh-length dress.

Really? "Are you related to"—I wanted to say *"the notorious,"* but didn't—"the Harrison brothers?"

She smiled. "Don't be scared. I'm harmless. I'm their baby sister."

Let the games begin!

Lema seemed sweet, but she couldn't possibly be harmless with her family's history. Drive-bys. Murders, with an *s,* by execution. Drug trafficking. The eldest brother was awaiting trial for beheading someone that had allegedly cheated him out of a dollar. The other brothers were known for putting hits on witnesses that were scheduled to testify against their brother. Already I was on track to eliminate my competition. Lema, minus her affiliation, was undoubtedly Kohl's type. A little intimidation to minimize his count, throw Kohl off his game, was all I needed.

"Give this lovely lady, Lema, whatever she'd like. And I'll have a Hennessy on the rocks."

"I'll have the same," Lema ordered, "and a dozen oysters on the half shell."

"Make that two dozen," I said, imagining a thank-you was coming from her any moment. Not.

I spoke to the woman on my right. She glanced at Lema, looked at me, turned away without responding.

"That was rude," Lema said. "Let that bitch do it again. I dare her."

Defusing the situation, I told Lema, "You know you women are catty like that. See another woman and automatically assume we guys are in a relationship."

Lema ordered more food. Thought she was done.

One hour, four cocktails, conversation, and twenty-four oysters later, felt comfortable enough to present my proposition. "I have two hundred dollars in your hand right now if you help me play a trick on one of my boys."

She hunched her shoulders. "Cool. Do I have to fuck him?"

I nodded.

Another round followed by a salad with grilled chicken was placed in front of her. "Five hundred," she demanded.

This was an investment. "Four?"

"Let me see a pic." Swallowing, she said, "Deal. Now give me the deets." After she slid her leafy greens aside, her hamburger arrived.

"He owns a hookah slash strip club on—"

"Let me see that pic again," Lema interrupted. Her smile was wide. "Kash In and Out in the East. That's Kohl." She squirmed on her seat.

I smiled. "Okay, you're familiar. The owner is my crewe. Be yourself, but put it on him real nasty. Then have your brothers scare the hell out of him. Threaten to do him in . . . but don't take it that far."

"Gotcha. This will be fun. I would've done him for free, but the deal is done. Where's my money? All of it." She extended her hand.

I counted four $100 bills into her hand. My cell rang. A number, no name, registered. I sent it to voice mail.

"I got you. Tomorrow night," she confirmed, eating the remainder of her fries like she was in boot camp. "Nice meeting you, Roulet. Lock in my number."

Damn, I'd almost forgotten to get her digits. I gave her mine. Lema left. The bartender cleared the empty dishes.

I requested, "Two more glasses of water, man," then tilted the chair.

Sitting alone, I searched social pages for Trymm's ex, Atlantis. Came across her profile. DM'd her, **How you doing, Atlantis? Looking good.**

Wow! Strange hearing from you. How's my guy? she replied.

You have time for a cocktail tomorrow. Polo Club Lounge? 3:00 p.m.? I had to get all the specifics out.

She replied right away, **Sure!**

Cool. CU 2mrw. I set my cell on the bar.

Two down. One to go. Have to create a distraction for Dallas.

A cutie suited in a light blue blouse, navy pencil skirt, and closed-toe pumps approached the bar. "Please sit here. The person just left."

She smiled. "Thanks."

Time to make her palate and her panties wet. Figured if I got one-point-five lays a day, my numbers would be legit, and no matter how many drawers dropped for Clydesdale, I had something that was going to put his dick six feet under.

"You from here?" I asked her, then told the bartender, "Put whatever she's having on my tab."

"Who says chivalry is dead, huh? You're kind," she said, then ordered. "I'll have a mojito and a cobb salad."

In a friendly tone I inquired again, "You're from . . . ?"

"Washington. Seattle. And you?"

"Here. Native."

The first thing out of her mouth was "I hope Katrina didn't leave you and any of your family members stranded on a rooftop. The footage was horrible. I couldn't imagine. Did you lose everything?" An eatery setup followed by a black cloth napkin, which was spread in front of her, didn't silence her monologue.

"Was your home underwater? Did you have to sleep in the Superdome? Did you leave town before the flood?" A large bowl was placed in front of her. Dressing on the side.

"Bartender, give me the check," I said. "We're done."

"Oh no! I'm sorry. I didn't mean to offend you. Bartender, please give me the check. And whatever he wants is on me."

In that case I'd listen a little longer. "That's extremely considerate. Thank you." I ordered, "I'll have a Hennessy, my brother."

Although Katrina had hit more than a decade ago, people who'd never lost everything didn't know what to feel for New Orleanians. I understood her compassion, but if she were a chatterbox, I might have to stick my dick in her mouth.

Lalita, Dallas's mother, was the closet person I knew that had died in the aftermath. Hard for D to have real closure when they'd never recovered his mother's remains. What if she was alive in a nursing home with memory loss? Or somewhere in a coma? Dallas had never mentioned that, nor would I ever bring up no shit like that.

Lots of people died due to grief, stress of losing their loved ones and their property. The government and insurance companies were the real assassins. With my dad being a politician, I cashed out better than most. Bought expensive purses and jewelry for females. Gambled at the casino, trying to hit the jackpot. When I won the bet, I wasn't fucking up again.

Taking advantage of the woman seated next to me, I said, "We're better now. My parents are back to work." They'd never had time off. Mom was an oceanographer. The demand for her field had increased. Dad was taking calls from his constituents around the clock. "I finally restored my house off of St. Charles Avenue." That was true.

Her fork was midair. Eyes wide. "You own one of the historical haunted homes?"

Historical, yes. Haunted, hell no! Black people didn't cohabitate with dead people. I nodded. "You should see it. When are you leaving?"

"Tomorrow afternoon," she said.

"Say, dinner. Tonight. Seven. My place." I'd offered little in exchange for what I wanted from her. "Excuse my manners, I'm Roulet. What's your name?"

She had the most brilliant smile. "Aurora. And I accept your invitation. Here's my number. Text me your address."

I locked her in. "Crawfish are out of season. You're not supposed to eat oysters in a month that doesn't have an *r*, though we natives do it all the time, but I try to only do the flame-broiled ones June to August, inclusive. I'll get you some blue crabs, make a jambalaya, and pick up a doberge cake from Gambino's."

"Oh, you're handsome *and* you can cook? I'll bring the wine," she insisted, then handed the bartender her credit card, closed out our tab (and Lema's) without X-raying the bill. "I have to get back to my conference. Great meeting you, Roulet."

Aurora exited the bar. A woman dressed in fitted slacks, a buttoned-up, long-sleeved shirt, with the top three buttons undone, sat next to me.

I told the bartender, "Put whatever she's having on my tab."

She frowned. "Thanks."

"Hi, my name is Roulet. And you are?"

CHAPTER 49

Blitz

Day 2

"Bruh! That's my space," he said, jumping down out of his 4x4. Brother man left his engine humming and his door open. Stood six feet in front of me, pulled up his pants. In one continuous motion, they fell below his waist. His car blocked mine in, as if I gave a damn about him, the upper and lower gold grills in his mouth, his black wifebeater, rope chain, or his sagging jeans. What the fuck was the belt for? Needed to snatch it off of him and beat his ass the way my dad did me growing up.

Wasn't about to get into a fight over a spot. Wasn't moving my BMW. Wasn't explaining that I'd circled each floor of the garage four times. Clicked my remote, locked my doors.

"Nigga, you leave, trust and believe your shit gon' be missing when you get back," he said, sucking his teeth. "You know who I is, nigga?"

On that "is" note, I was done wasting my time.

I'd worn a nice short-sleeved, buttoned-down white shirt, blue tailored slacks, navy leather loafers, no socks.

My platinum diamond-face wristwatch was my only jew-elry. Got a fresh haircut this morning for my face-to-face with Trymm's ex-girlfriend.

"Nice Rolex, nigga. Let me hold it," he said as though we were familiar, then slid his tongue inside his upper lip.

My heart pounded against my chest worrying if I were about to get jacked during daylight. The closest couple and the elevators were approximately one hundred feet away. The one thing I didn't do was doubt that this dude would make good on his threat in reference to my vehicle, but I was not taking off the sentimental graduation gift my parents had passed on to me from my grandfather's collec-tion.

A dude in the passenger seat—damn near looking like dude's twin—got out, twisted his hand sideways, pointed the barrel of a gun at me. "What's taking you so long to unleash the fucking watch?"

Should've left when the first guy accosted me. Now there were two. Used my peripheral to view my sur-roundings. I was from a generation that respected their el-ders. These teenagers were on some "I don't give a fuck about nothing and nobody" bullshit.

Texted Atlantis, **Running fifteen minutes late.**

No worries. Got here early. Saved you a seat. To your left at the bar when you enter the lounge, she replied.

"Nigga, you wanna release that phone, too. I'z ain't got all day."

Both dudes stared me down. As I walked toward my sedan, I memorized their license plate, make, and model. Opening my door . . . *wham!* I grabbed the side of my face; my knees buckled.

"Lay the fuck down, nigga," one of them demanded.

Material things were generally replaceable. Was taught by my dad, nobody is going to give you what you deserve in this world. I remained in a kneeling position. I was within reach of my armrest compartment. Placed my hands in the air, praying someone would pass by and these fools would run. Dude with the gun unfastened the latch, slid fifty grand over my hand, and locked it onto his wrist. They laughed.

Wasn't shit amusing. At this point I feared they'd shoot me for the sport of it.

As they walked away, I heard their conversation.

"Can't be nice to niggas these days."

"That nigga lucky you didn't pista-whup him."

"Or bust that ass wide open . . . with my dick!"

"You right, yeah."

They joked back and forth, got in their truck. After they sped off, I knew I'd never see my grandfather's keepsake again.

I crawled into my sedan, locked all four doors, drove to valet at the hotel across the street, where I should've gone initially instead of trying to save a few dollars on parking.

The attendant greeted me with "Are you checking in?"

"Yes," I lied. My pants legs were scuffed in front my shins. Brushing away the dirt, I was relieved my white shirt was spotless.

"Last name?" he asked.

Wasn't as though they'd ever request identification. "Johnson" never failed with festivals of this magnitude, there was always at least one.

"First initial?"

"T," which could've easily registered as a *d, p,* or *z* the way I'd said it. Taking the ticket, I told him, "Thanks."

"Need help with your luggage, sir?" he asked.

"Airline lost it," I told him, pointed at my cell, then spoke into my Bluetooth, "Hey."

"I have to inform you that this call may be monitored for quality-control purposes. Is this Blitz Einstein Roulet?"

"Bitch, record this. I just got robbed. I don't give a fuck about you right now." Had to stop answering without looking. Thought it was Atlantis. I had more important business. If there wasn't a line of people getting out of and waiting for cars, I would've cursed her out loud enough to awaken Marie Laveau.

"Your car note is overdue, sir. You're behind three months," she said, then asked, "Can you bring your account current today?"

"Bitch, if I could, I would. I can't deal with your shit right now. Did you hear me say, 'I just got robbed'?"

"Then you'll know what it feels like when we repossess yo' shit," she retorted.

Unprofessional ho sounded as though she could be related to the motherfuckers that stole my piece. I asked her, "What's your first and last names?"

A group of women stepped off the elevator. I opted to climb the stairs one level up to the Polo Club Lounge, as I told the ratchet collection agent, "I'll take care of it. Just give me one more month and I'm paying it off."

"If we repo it, you'll have to pay it off to get it back. A loan is a promise to repay, sir. Stop signing shit without reading it first. This was a courtesy call."

She could work for the casino's debt collection department. Squeezing between a pack of happily chattering females, I saw Atlantis waving at me from the end of the bar. I made my way to her.

"Hey, you," she said, spreading her arms.

"Can you make one pay—"

That bitch hadn't hung up. Ending the call, admiring Atlantis, I didn't know who was hotter: Trymm's ex or Kohl's ex? Ramona's pics on Instagram, but given the opp under the "date, dick, and dump" challenge, I'd fuck both. Dallas never really stayed with a woman long enough to put her in the girlfriend category. Neither did I.

Atlantis wore a printed maxidress with a split that stopped above her navel. The fitted boy shorts underneath revealed her camel toe and shapely thighs.

"You look amazing." I hugged Atlantis longer than Trymm would've approved. Slowly slid my fingers to her lower spine, stopped a fraction of an inch above the crack of her booty.

"What are you sipping on?" Should've asked what perfume she was wearing. Bet I could eat her pussy better than Long Dick Silver.

"A girly cocktail. Ruby Red martini. It has coconut rum, peach schnapps, vodka, cranberry, and lime," she said. Thrusting her breasts forward, she pulled up her top.

She knew what she was doing. I got a glimpse of her nipple. "Excuse me, beautiful, real men do drink martinis." The high pitch in my voice made me clear my throat. I wasn't sure if her enthusiasm was sparked by my presence, but I went in for hug number two. "It is so good to see you, girl. How long has it been since we last ran into one another? Two or three years?"

"Essence. Two years ago. On the floor." Atlantis did a sexy side-to-side swerve, running her fingers through her hair.

Trymm played basketball for LSU. Atlantis and I occasionally bumped into one another on campus at Grambling. She was always bad.

"Your usual, Blitz?" the bartender Jason asked.

"I'll have what she's having." I slid my stool close enough to Atlantis to straddle her leg.

I scratched my arm and wondered what those thugs had done with my fucking watch. A police report was being filed as soon as I was done with Atlantis. I could easily identify those fools in a lineup. Meeting with Atlantis wasn't more important than filing a police report, but both outcomes was potentially lucrative, and there was no point in canceling. First things first. I'd file a claim for my watch later. Might toss some extra shit in the lineup.

"When was the last time you saw our boy?" Atlantis asked, extending the tip of her tongue to the rim of her glass.

"Yesterday. He mentioned you. That's why I hit you up. He's always talking about you. You should call him. He'd like nothing more than getting back with you."

"I don't know. After all these years I still love him. I will always love Trymm. But we both know Trymm will never stop sleeping around." Her excitement dimmed to sadness.

Damn. Is this brother's dick dipped in gold?

They were high-school sweethearts over ten years ago. He'd been with her replacement for nearly that long. The one thing about men, women could easily throw us off our game. And equally so, we could win them back.

"You know we don't mature as fast as women. Men are not complicated. If you really want to know if Trymm feels the same way about you, I can help you. He does not love Francine. Treats her like shit. If he truly cared, he would've married her by now. Y'all belong together."

Atlantis tried concealing her excitement. A reserved smile grew wider. "What do you mean by 'I can help'?"

"Might sound crazy, but buy yourself an engagement ring."

Jason placed my drink in front of me.

Atlantis sat up straight. Gave me her undivided attention. "I'm listening."

"Get it from Sam's . . . scratch that. Make it Costco or somewhere you can take it back afterward with no questions and get your money back. Don't tell my boy you're engaged. Make sure he sees the ring when the two of you meet up. If he fights for you, or starts saying shit like, 'I don't want you to marry him,' or 'I missed out,' he's figuring out his next move with you and he still has feelings. If he's simply trying to hit it one more time, he doesn't give a damn about you, per se, but we know better. Us men believe once we date you, your pussy belongs to us. Always and forever. If he doesn't make any moves, still doesn't means he's done. You got that nigga thinking."

Most of the times I was done pursuing a woman before I started. I was in it to show her a good time, ejaculate once or twice, then lick her dry. Not necessarily in that order, but that was it.

Atlantis sucked her drink a long time, then said, "I've sabotaged several relationships comparing each guy to Trymm. None of them measure up."

A Clydesdale is not in every stable. Hell, not in every city. I wondered if her vagina was loose enough for me to fist her.

Atlantis's emotions must've been swirling in her glass, where her focus was. "I'm always going to love him, Blitz. If this doesn't work out—"

"But it's worth your trying," I said. She had to do this for me. "You got his number?"

"No. Deleted it years ago. I shouldn't open Pandora's box."

"Put his number in your phone," I insisted. "Call him today. Go out with him. Keep me posted. You work on him from your end, and I'll get him on mine. And tell that nigga you posted up with you future. That way he can't get comfortable at your spot."

"You're right. What have I got to lose?" she said. "The guys out here are all playing games. I've got to get ready for the concert tonight. Thanks, Blitz." Atlantis placed a twenty on the bar.

I handed it back to her. "On me, beautiful." *Trymm is a fool for holding on to Francine and letting Atlantis go. Nah, make that, like so many other women, Francine is the fool for staying with that nigga.* "Skip the concert. Heard Trymm is having a yacht party. You don't want to miss it."

Time for me to transition to triple-d mode. A woman draped in a strapless jumpsuit approached the bar. I pulled out the stool Atlantis had recently abandoned.

I told the bartender, "Put whatever she's having on my tab."

She frowned at me. Gave me a partial smile. "Thanks."

"What's up with the face? I'm trying to be a gentle-man." I extended my hand. Thought about my watch. I was definitely filing that report, today. "My name is Roulet. And you are?"

"Please to meet you, Mr. Roulet." Her grip was firmer than mine. "I'm Viola Chambers."

CHAPTER 50

Blitz

Day 2

"Besides Essence Festival, what brings you to my sin-fun city, Mrs. Chambers?"

Viola removed her sunglasses, placed them in a Versace case. "I'll have an old-fashioned." She spoke to me. Relaxed on her stool. Eased her top above her cleavage. Crossed her long, luscious legs.

"I got it, boss," Jason answered. He removed my old bill, replaced it with a new tab.

"I run a Fortune 500 company. My business here is done. Tomorrow, so am I." She slayed with confidence. In three seconds she overtly gave me a head-to-toe once-over. She dangled her shoe on the tip of her toes, and her feet were impeccable. Clean French pedicure.

Had to smile. "Where're the last places you've traveled . . . for pleasure?"

The bartender placed her drink on a coaster. She picked it up. I admired her manicure as she held her old-fashioned areola level.

"London, Sydney, Rome, Budapest, Cusco, Hong Kong, Barcelona, Cape Town." She winked her right eye, added, "New Orleans. That's within the last six months." Viola sipped her cocktail. "You?"

Damn! Eight countries? All of that couldn't be on her dime. If it were, she might be my golden ticket to becoming debt free. Or at least I could be her traveling companion if her husband wasn't in tow. Wanted to ask what company she worked for. "Montego Bay, Dominican Republic, Cozumel, St. Thomas." That was the last six years.

"At least you possess a passport," she said, sipped, then continued, "And you like sunshine and gorgeous women. Probably never married. Committed to your coins. Not women. Just a hunch. You own or rent?"

To that, I had to drink up. Requested a Long Island this time. Soon as I said, "Own," my cell rang. No number registered. I declined the call.

"House or condo?" she asked.

"House."

"Good. Let's not waste precious time. I have a four-hour window before the concert. Put my number in your cell. Text me your address. See you in thirty minutes. Oh, and put on something worth my taking off."

Viola gave me her number, snapped a picture of me, then left. I watched her walk away. Bit my bottom lip. Brilliance and beauty. I closed out my tab. Texted her my address. Got my car from valet.

Heading home, I was wondering what to wear. No woman had asked—make that *told*—me to put on something enticing.

Damn! My dick and my tongue got hard.

CHAPTER 51

Elizabeth

Day 2

Men didn't need to know everything about me, but in my line of work, there was nothing I couldn't find out about a man.

Had one phone and two numbers. One for business, the other, which I'd given to Roulet, was strictly for disposable dick. I'd never shared my sexcapades with my staff, and I had one really close girlfriend—we were opposites—that knew me well.

I wasn't married, but I wore a wedding ring to attract men—like Roulet—looking for what I wanted when I wasn't working, and that was a good time without attachments. Never invited a man to my hotel room. I had too much to lose if a backstabbing employee saw a guy walking out my door at sunrise. I didn't carry much cash but a Casanova could creep out in the middle of the night along with my valuables—laptop, camera, jewelry.

Most importantly, I always had sufficient information to verify a man's identity before I opened my legs.

Viola Chambers was my alias. Elizabeth Dawson was my government.

I'd Google searched Roulet's property. Learned his name was, in fact, on the mortgage associated with his address. His government was Blitz Einstein Roulet. Loved his middle name. Searched his first, middle, and last names. Discovered he was twenty years younger than me. His dad was a politician. Mom an oceanographer. He'd never held a nine-to-five. Did a background on his cell number. Cross-references were confirmed.

Parking in his driveway, I spritzed perfume in my hair, on my red, green, and gold metallic bikini top, with the matching bottom. Added a tad of sweetness on my wrists, neck, ankles, and feet. In case he had a Jacuzzi or over-sized jet tub, I was prepared. My long red skirt, with the slit up to my hip, that bow-tied at the waist was for his enjoyment. Men loved untying things.

I texted him, **I'm outside. Walking up to your door.**

Intentionally, I made him wait three minutes in his doorway before stepping out of my rental car in my "come, fuck me" high heels. The humid breeze created a silhouette blowing my skirt up and back, exposing my glistening legs. I approached Einstein in slow motion.

"You look amazing," he said.

As promised, "Here's the wine. You look nice as well." I never over-complimented a man. I was no guy's cheer-leader.

Other than a change in color, his attire was similar. Black buttoned-down shirt. Black slacks and leather loafers, no socks.

"Make yourself comfortable," he said.

The living room was spacious. White leather sofa, love seat, and oversized chairs. Contemporary. Cute. His cell rang.

"Sorry about that. Let me put this on do not disturb."

"You have a lovely, historical home. I don't have much time. A tour would be nice," I said. Not waiting for his approval, I led the way.

Opening the sliding glass doors, I stepped into his backyard. To my surprise, I found there was a large pool secluded by oak trees. "Can you pour us a drink? I'm thirsty and ready to get wet."

I dug out my cat-o'-nine-tails and handcuffs. Placed my tote on the poolside lounge chair.

Einstein returned wearing sky-blue boxer briefs cut trunks, carrying two glasses of red wine. I kissed him. Removed his swimwear. Whacked him on the ass several times.

"Aw, damn. Take it easy," he said, splashing wine.

"Easy is for underachievers." I twirled the handcuffs. "You? Or me?"

"Let's take this inside," he insisted, retreating to the other side of his patio doors.

Time permitting, I could skinny-dip when we were done fucking. I retrieved my bag, followed him to his bedroom. Took a sip from my goblet, pulled out my hot vanilla massage oil.

"Lay down. On your back," I told him.

Layering oil all over his body, I straddled him. Began vigorously massaging him with my pussy, making his temperature and his dick rise.

Einstein stared up at me. "You are amazing. Who did you say you worked for?"

I didn't. Nor was I telling him now. "No questions," I said. Putting a condom on his dick, I sat my pussy on his mouth. I'd get on his stick momentarily.

Ladies first.

He nibbled. Sucked softly. Placed the tip of his tongue on my clit. Flickered. Nibbled some more.

Cuteness needed assistance.

I spread my lips. Held them open for him. His tongue penetrated me to my G-spot. That was impressive and a first. My muscles tightened. "That feels delightful," I said, swaying my hips back and forth. "Mmm. That's good. I need to feel your dick inside me. Don't move. I'll do all the work."

I didn't get to the top relying on a man. Aligning his head with my vagina. His penis was smaller than average. But it was hard and the perfect length to hit my G-spot. I did a one-eighty, hugged his knees to my breasts, then rocked back and forth for ten minutes.

Letting go, I did a half spin on his dick, pressed his sides to the mattress. Grinding hard, I let him know, "I'm about to come. You ready?"

Einstein nodded. As he barely ejaculated, I gushed all over his stomach and drenched his bed.

"Aw, shit!" He pushed me off of him. Felt his sheets. "I didn't know you were a squirter. *Fuck.*"

Stripping his bedding, he balled up the linen, left the room. He turned on the ceiling fan. "This is fucked up." He scrubbed his mattress with a large towel.

Putting on the clean dress I'd packed, I picked up my tote. Not caring about Einstein, I said, "I'll see myself out."

He wanted to fuck. I wanted to come. I wasn't scheduled to be back in New Orleans for a year. Like the majority of the men I'd bedded, I'd probably never see him again, nor did I want to. Didn't need the damn headaches, drama, or deviant behavior users came prepackaged with.

Fuck Larry, Moses, Jerry, Philip, Casey, Donovan, Ernest, Upshaw, Leonardo, and Blitz! Men like you taught me how to not care.

Fair exchange is just that . . . fair.

CHAPTER 52

Blitz

Day 3

Viola. That arrogant bitch.

Took two fans and all night to dry out my mattress. I opened my laptop this morning, downloaded, then uploaded Mrs. Viola Chambers to my social pages, CEO2930, with pleasure.

A few minutes later, a text came from Trymm, **Damn, homey. Your tongue almost longer than Clydesdale.**

That was a damn lie! Kohl hit me with, **God almighty. Let the vagina say Amen! You, bruh, are an orator for sure.**

Dallas followed up, **I need a cigarette, yo.**

That nigga didn't smoke, but he was going to be on fire when I was done with him. Heading to The Ritz on Canal, I scanned the faces at the bar, sat next to a pretty young thing I knew Dallas would hound immediately.

"Put whatever she's having on my tab," I told the mixologist, then introduced myself, "I'm Roulet."

"Oh, that's not necessary," she said, handing him her

credit card. "This meal is on the government. I'm on official business today."

"What agency?"

"Education." She signed her receipt.

"Where?"

"New Jersey," she answered.

She was too far away to use her to execute my next plan. "I'd be happy to show you around later. Lock me in. Let me know."

After keying my number into her cell, she said, "That would be nice," then exited the restaurant.

"Let me have a Hennessy, man."

Just as I'd ordered, I'd heard, "Is this seat taken?"

Cuter. Younger. "It is now. I'm Roulet. And you are?"

"Debbie," she said, smiling brilliantly. "Schexnider."

I knew of quite a few people with the last name. Wasn't digging into her family tree. Had to inquire, "You live here?"

"All my life," she said, smiling wide.

"That's awesome." I could tell Debbie's personality was nothing like Viola Chambers's. Debbie was way too trusting. "Debbie, sweetheart, I could use a friend."

"Well, everyone says I'm friendly."

"But are you single?" That part did matter. Some of the dudes in the NOLA wouldn't hesitate to shoot anybody that messed with their woman. Dallas was not one to be fucked with.

"Kinda. Just broke up with my boyfriend," she said, not sounding heartbroken in the least.

"Then you must allow me to not only buy you a drink, but to also treat you to lunch."

Debbie was perfect for Dallas. We laughed. Shared relationship stories. Mine were complete lies. Imagined hers were some version of her reality. Nothing she said mattered.

"That's the nicest thing a man has done for me," she said. "Thank you, Roulet."

Shifting my eyes to the side in disbelief, I told her, "Cool. I need you to position yourself to meet my boy. But don't let him in on our plan. Be sure to allow him to make the first move. Over the next four weeks, be clingy, needy, attentive, but not too assertive. Can you do that for a hundred dollars?" What I was really asking was, could she handle the situation without fucking it up?

"Basically, you want me to distract him."

Close enough. More like *dick*-stract. "Exactly."

"What if I start to like your friend?"

Debbie's short blond hair was sexy. Wanted to touch it. That would be inappropriate. "This charade ends in about a month. After that, it's up to you."

"A hundred dollars?" she asked. "To go out with him for a month?"

"Yup. That's for you. Let that nigga pick up the tab. Li'l Dizzy's Café. Tomorrow morning."

Debbie wasn't as clever as Lema, but I gave her a 50 percent deposit at the bar. We exchanged numbers. I texted her a photo of Dallas.

She held a pen in her hand, placed a white paper napkin in front of her. "Am I supposed to approach him?"

Got the feeling Debbie was going to do things her way. Long as they met that was all that mattered. "Wear something nice. I'll text you when he's inside. Sit at a table close to him if you can. If you can't, make sure you pass by him. Make eye contact. And put that pretty smile on him," I told her.

She flashed wider. I noticed her bottom teeth were slightly crooked. Trymm would care about that, D wouldn't give a fuck.

I texted Dallas, **Meet me at Dizzy's in the morning. Won't take long.**

CHAPTER 53

Elizabeth

Day 4

"I want your life," my friend Nefertiti said over the phone as my driver parked in my private space at the office building on Geary Street.

Nefertiti was a fifty-year-old technology genius. She created apps for major corporations and small companies, but her brain did not compute when it came to dating men. Married four times. Divorced four. She'd won custody of the kids from her first husband, but had lost her cat, who was like her baby, to her last ex.

"Give me a moment," I said to my chauffeur, waited for him to get out of the car and close the door, then told her, "Gurl, you know I always say, you'll wear wedding gown number five before I put on one."

"You're jaded," she said.

By what? "Why is it that when a woman dates like a man, other women think we hate men? I love dick and I've got my own dollars. Einstein's bed was like a soaked sponge after I gushed all over him." Men patted themselves on the back when they made a woman squirt.

"Not the gush!" she exclaimed. "Tell me again, how do I make myself squirt?"

Nefertiti's status reverted to single a year ago. She was too trusting of men. Always letting them determine her worthiness and her sexual satisfaction, or dissatisfaction. I knew what I wanted from a man like Einstein, before I said hello.

"Stop relying on a man to make anything happen for your body. Practice your Kegels. I'm going to send you another G-spot gift package, and you'd better use everything in this one. I've got to go. I'll call you when I get to Beijing."

"Wait. On the final leg of your trips, bring me back a tall, sexy Barcelona man, with that shiny black hair and an olive complexion," Nefertiti said. "At least six-two and looking for a wife."

She could do that herself, if she'd meet me in Spain. It was a fact. Spanish and Italian men adored black American women. The only reason a black woman in America dealt with the bullshit African-American men put them through was because most sistahs had no idea how much they were loved by men around the world, since they'd never traveled outside of the country.

"Women who live by the dick, they die by the dick," she said.

"Absolutely. You know my motto. A man can never outfuck a woman. Life is short. . . . Dicks are shorter. Men who defined themselves by their dicks ain't shit. Women must live to the fullest." All of these things were true, but trying to convince women they were sexually superior was like beating life into a rock.

"Bye, Elizabeth. I love you. Text me when you land," Nefertiti said.

"Love you, too," I said. I wasn't trying to change her, and she wasn't judging me.

* * *

"Good morning, Ms. Dawson," my assistant greeted me. "I've e-mailed and uploaded your itinerary to Slack, checked you in for your two o'clock from SFO to Beijing. Your driver will be back here at eleven o'clock to pick you up."

"Thanks," I said closing my office door. I heated water, inserted a mint tea bag, stirred in lemon and honey, then powered on my monitor. Scanning the images at the bottom of the screen, team USA, China, Emirates, Egypt, South Africa, and India were logged on for my Monday meeting.

"Team China, report first."

The twenty-two-year-old Asian graduate out of UC, Berkeley, based in Beijing, was one of my shining stars. I'd see her face-to-face tomorrow.

She answered, "Next week's gross revenue projections are to increase by nine percent."

"How're we doing on human-hair bundles?" I asked.

"Up by sixty-two percent overall. The United States is still our largest consumer. The majority are repeat customers between thirty-five and fifty. Need to incentivize new African-American consumers twenty-five and younger. A lot of them are going natural. We also need to target non–African-American customers in that same age range. A hair app could be beneficial, where they can upload their picture, see themselves in any style. Braids, ponytails, bringing back the oversized Afros could become trendy if we can get it to go viral via a celebrity that's gorgeous, young, and cool. A fresh face could work well also. One of the gymnasts, or musical competition finalists."

I finished my tea. Even when I liked their report, I seldom complimented my employees. That way they stayed motivated. "Maybe." Powering on my coffee machine, I plopped in an Ethiopia dark-roast pod. "Send me a more detailed strategy in an hour. Canada, report."

The president of the board opened my door without knocking and stepped into my office. "Hold reporting, team Canada," he said. "I'll get back to everyone within the hour. Elizabeth, I need for you to end the call. *Now.*"

I'd dealt with all types of crises on an almost daily. Learned most issues weren't as serious as they initially seemed, but how dare he interrupt me! "Do you want to sit in on the rest of the team meeting, then we can speak?"

"Now," he repeated.

"Everyone, I'll send you an e-mail to reconvene."

Powering off my monitor, I stood. "This is a surprise," I commented, hoping his urgency was regarding a new acquisition. That could make up for his inconsiderate behavior. "I have to catch a flight shortly."

"I know. Come with me to the conference room."

Trailing him, I said, "I'll have to continue the meeting after I land in Beijing." He remained quiet. Peering through the glass window, I noticed the entire board of directors was present.

"Sit next to me," the president said, then picked up the remote, pointed it at the screen on the wall. There I was, spread wide open, riding Blitz's face.

"Is this you, Elizabeth?" The president stared at me.

I wanted to lie. Tell him no. But clearly it was me. I glanced at each of the members, then nodded.

"Respectfully, what you do in the privacy of your confinements is your prerogative. When a sex video of you goes viral, it's our obligation to our shareholders to protect their interest. We have to let you go. Immediately. To protect the corporation, we won't confirm or deny to our clients that this is you. No severance package. You can clear out your personal things only. Don't touch the computer. Turn in your phone, tablet, and laptop."

I went to my office. Three security officers stood by as I emptied my drawers.

Retrieving my luggage from the chauffeur, I exited the building, ordered an Uber on my phone, went directly to the airport, hopped the first nonstop flight to New Orleans.

CHAPTER 54

Blitz

Day 5

A ring at my front door got me out of bed at 10:00 a.m. I looked outside, no one was there. At my feet was an express package. Opened it. Read, *Acceleration of Mortgage*. The entire balance to pay off my home was due in fifteen days, or the bank was starting the foreclosure process.

Slammed the door. "I told that dumb bitch I was paying it off!"

A call from an unidentified number flashed on my phone. I answered, "Hello," hoping it was someone from the bank with sense that I could work out some kind of forbearance agreement with.

"Listen, Blitz. We need a good-faith payment on your debt at the casino. Two hundred, in two weeks," he demanded.

"Three weeks and two days and I got you," I told him.

Silence.

I said, "Hello? Hello?"

A call from Viola registered on my cell.

I sent superbitch to voice mail.

She called right back.

"Hey, what's up?" I asked, with more pressing things on my mind. Squeezing toothpaste on my brush, I vigorously scrubbed up and down.

Calmly she said, "I'm in New Orleans. We need to talk in person about the defamatory post on your social."

I spat in the sink, rinsed my mouth. "Oh, that."

"'Oh, that'?" She paused, then repeated, "'Oh, that'?"

"I heard you the first time. Looka here, I have more important business to tend to, Mrs. Chambers. Talk to you la—"

She rudely interrupted, "No, you're going to talk to me today. Face-to-face, Mr. Roulet. When and where can we—"

I ended the call. Put that bitch on BLOCK, then got dressed. She should've said some shit to hold my attention, like offering to replace my mattress, and she best not show up at my house. I know she didn't come back to the NOLA over a post.

Getting in my sedan, I stopped at my bank. Didn't bother signing in to speak with the only man that could assist me. I stood in his doorway.

"Hey, Blitz. How you doing, man?" Ralph waved at me with a come-hither gesture.

"Everything is everything," I said, stepping into his office. I gripped the wooden arms of the chair, picked it up, set it down as close as I could to his desk. Leaning forward, I got straight to the point. "I need to withdraw five hundred grand."

Ralph closed his door. His head moved left and right as he reclaimed his seat across from me. "No can do."

"Why the fuck not? Let me borrow against my contribution, plus a little extra," I demanded.

He shook his head. "Partial isn't how it's set up. You wanna close it? I can do that now. But just so you know, everyone will be notified."

Fuck no! That was my crewe. Wasn't going to betray them, but my ass was about to become homeless. Reconsidering the option, I was tempted to shut it down. I could reopen a new one, with half the amount and a different number.

"Give me a minute." I was heated. My cheeks filled with air, then deflated. I couldn't do that without jeopardizing having them cancel the challenge. Then I wouldn't get shit.

"I'm drowning in three feet of water. I just need five hundred g's, I'll put it back before July thirtieth. Throw me a life preserver, man. No one will notice it's missing if I borrow against it. Just this one time."

"No, Blitz. I told you not to bring no illegal shit here, ya heard me."

"I told you!" I paused, lowered my voice. *Fuck!* I wasn't about to disclose my gambling situation. "Listen to me. I need this money."

Ralph stood, removed his blazer from the coat rack, eased it on. "I need my job. And don't even think about making another withdrawal from 0069. I won't do it unless we let your father know in advance. Otherwise, you'll have both of our heads in a guillotine at the same damn time. The best I can do is connect you with Irene Pitts. She's a reliable source that does short-term, high-interest-rate loans."

Quickly I asked, "How high?"

"Thirty days. Double return, something like that. I have to go. I have a lunch meeting. You should've taken a million instead of a quarter of a mil from 0069, and we wouldn't be having this conversation. You want the number for the loan or what?" Ralph said, opening the door.

"Sure. But if this doesn't work out, I'm going to close the account and open one under my name the same day?"

"With half the original?" Ralph asked. "But you, not me, will have to deal with your boys and possibly the IRS if they audit your ass. Point your friends to the terms and conditions they executed giving you signature authority to shut it down. Not sure what you'd tell the government, but damn sure nuff don't mention the unscrupulous game y'all playing on females out there. And get yourself a lawyer. Maybe two."

Ralph may have never wilded out on our level, but I was certain he, like us, was no stranger to fucking over females. I locked in Irene's number, left, drove to Jax Brewery to meet the crewe. Five days into the competition, shit was going south quick for my ass. I didn't want to cross the fellas, but I might have to. I wasn't losing my possessions, and I had to buy a new Rolex soon. I wore that watch every day.

Logging into the investment app, I saw my portfolio was performing worse than an escort that refused to spread her ass. Usually, when one stock was down, the other was up. Had no liquid resources that would make a significant change in time to bring my bills current. I was surviving off of my credit cards. Dad had taught me never to pay debt with debt.

Might have to dip back into 0069.

CHAPTER 55

Blitz

Day 9

Posted up at a table for four on the terrace at Jax Brewery. I was the first of the crewe to arrive. Dreading utilizing my next option, I took a deep breath, exhaled, dialed her number.

"There you are. Where've you been? We didn't see or hear from you last weekend," Mom answered.

"Sorry, Mom. I got caught up with all the concerts." Truth was, my jaws were tired from eating one-point-five pussies a day. "I'm okay. Kind of got myself in a bind. Could use your help," I said, taking in all the fresh air my lungs allowed.

Exhaling, I told the waitress, "It's humid as hell. Let me get four glasses of ice water."

"What is it? Did you come across an IPO you're interested in?" my mother asked.

If I said yes, she'd give me whatever I wanted today, but I didn't want to lie to my mother. There was no company with an initial public offering that I was considering buying shares from. I was supposed to be debt free, living off of my investments. I probably could've made money day trading the million, but that shit was like putting everything on a craps table.

The waiter brought the water quickly. Condensation was already beading up. I pressed my glass to my temple.

"Mom, please don't tell Dad," I begged her, speaking low into my phone. "It's not to generate new business. Consider it a short-term loan to keep me breathing. Four weeks and I promise I'll pay you back in full. I only need a half a mil—"

"That's too much. For what? Your house and car are paid—"

"Mom, please. I refinanced my home loan instead of paying off the mortgage like Dad had told me." Didn't listen when he said to buy a used car, cash; a new car would depreciate the second I drove it off the lot.

"Blitz, this is horrible!" she exclaimed.

"I know, Mom. Please do it."

"Well, you know I can't take it from 0069. That could have all of us behind bars. Let me call my banker and I'll get back to you, Blitz."

Whenever she ended a sentence with my name, Mom was disappointed in me. *Jail? All of us?* The first thing I had to do was redeposit the money I'd borrowed from 0069. A few more weeks and I'd make her proud. "Thanks, Mom. I love you."

"I love you more," she said.

"Who's that?" I overheard my dad ask in the background.

"*Your* son," Mom said.

"Hey, son! Call me on my cell," my dad shouted. "Got some start-up companies I want you to invest in."

"Honey, he's busy right now. Bye, Blitz," Mom said.

Ending the call, I accidentally answered an incoming caller. There was the all-too-familiar no caller identification. Confident that Mom would come through, as usual, I answered, "Hello."

"This call is being monitored for quality-control purposes. Is this Blitz Einstein Roulet?"

"Let us have two flights," Kohl said to the waitress as he walked up behind me.

I told the bill collector, "Let me call you back."

"Mr. Roulet, your account is seriously de—"

Terminating the conversation, I said, "What's up, Kohl?" I gripped his hand, bumped his shoulder with mine.

"It's all good." He sat directly across the table from me, then immediately asked, "How long you been following Ramona, bruh? Y'all friends? I mean off social."

Ramona? Lema is the one he needed to be more concerned with. Atlantis and Debbie, I had started following on social, too. The waitress placed our flights on the table, then left. I hadn't planned on my befriending Ramona getting him off kilter. This was a bonus.

"With your joint, why you not on social?" I asked, downing the first of five beer samples.

"Don't have time for the social foolery." Not blinking, Kohl squinted. His forehead compressed. "But doing one another's exes is forbidden."

I tossed back beer flavor number two. Kohl caught up. Followed an ale with an IPA.

I told his ass, "Too late for add-ons, Kohl. What nigga you know wouldn't hit that? I mean, six, seven months ago, hell to the no. Ramona was big as a whale. Now, shitz. I check her page three times a day."

Ramona went from blab to fab posting pics in swimsuits and spandex on her page. I was confused how she snagged a baller before she got plastic. My tongue started getting hard as a motherfucker looking at her post. I flashed Ramona's pic in Kohl's face.

"You can only eat so much coochie before you throw up, my brother. You might as well be lesbian and strap on."

I laughed. Tossed back number three. It was bitter as the words that had escaped Kohl's pussy-shaped lips.

"Ha-ha, my behind. Once upon a time Ramona and I were in love."

Exhaling between clenched teeth, I decided not to spare his emotions. "Drink and listen up, potna," Straightening my spine, I told him, "One, according to you, Billy boy ain't your son. Two—"

"I don't know that for a fact!" He finished his next beer. Suctioned in his lips.

Fuck that wannabe, fake-ass, Christian, sex-club-owning Negro. "Take the damn test then, nigga! . . . Billy boy looks exactly like your ass. . . . I don't blame you for disowning him if Ramona stepped out like you said. And you shouldn't care who smashes her. I'm serious. If Harold blinks, I'm all over that new body." Kohl could foolishly side-bet that I wouldn't hit it and give away some more of his money.

Sucking up number four, I tagged on, "You think she got her vagina rejuvenated? I heard that's the in thing for females nowadays. If I find out, I'll let you know." I tugged on my collar, picked up my last sampler, then smiled at Kohl. "Cheers, my brother."

Holding the beer in my hand, staring at Kohl, I bet Ramona tasted sweeter than cane sugar.

"On second thought . . . cheers." Kohl lifted one of his glasses. "If you hit that in your count, get proof, post it to your social, and tag her. If I win, I'll give you back your quarter of a mil."

I swallowed my last in one gulp. "Bet. Text that to me, my brother."

Kohl caught up on his final beer. The waitress cleared the table. None of us drank the water served at restaurants. Not that it wasn't safe, we used the glasses to hold seats.

Dallas walked up, claimed the spot next to Kohl. I was across the table facing them.

"I don't know about y'all, but this dick-and-dump shit is hard as hell," Dallas confessed. "Plus, it doesn't seem right."

It wasn't, but some black women, like Viola, needed to be knocked down a peg or two. When did any of us treat women right? Trymm had been in the longest relationship and he treated Francine like shit. Dallas was too serious. Our playing rapid fire with chicks was just a game.

"I'm having fun," Kohl said.

I texted Lema, **Time to execute plan B for Kohl.**

She replied, **Fuck Kohl! & U2!**

Wasn't sure what that was about. I replied, **I'll call you later.**

Don't bother! U never said anything about him putting me on social media. Whatever happens to Kohl is outta my hands, she texted.

Why the fuck was she tripping? I'd paid her ass. In advance. I replied, **Deal direct. I have nothing to do with that,** along with Kohl's number.

"Don't get me wrong," Dallas said. "Bitches are easy. Talking a chick into giving it up is a cinch. Throwing them outta my bed, I hate doing that shit. Plus, one of 'em . . ." Dallas paused, bit his bottom lip, but then continued, "I can't do her like that."

Blackjack! I could tell Debbie was reeling Dallas in already. I smiled on the inside.

Texted Debbie, **You must have that voodoo. Got my boy all soft ova here talking about you.**

She responded, **I like him, too. Might have to refund you your $100.**

Keep the cash. Keep up the good job. 3 more weeks and he's all yours. I'll call you later.

We ordered a round of beer samplers with Dallas.

"Don't tell me your ass met somebody you like," Kohl said. Then that nigga started laughing. "Put her on hold for the next three weeks, or you might as well sit this challenge out."

"Nah, the deal is, the brother is having difficulty keeping it up." I said that to piss Dallas off. For added effect, I balled my fist, bent my elbow, then flexed my biceps.

Dallas's face pickled. He grabbed his nuts. "That's the least of my concerns. Round-the-clock breaking him out, I'm willing to admit, my dick hurts and that nigga is tired."

"You not getting your money back," I insisted. "Dick. Date. Dump. Proof. No exceptions," I reminded them. "Winner takes all."

Tapping the table, I added, "I'll give you a side challenge. Whoever that bitch is, the one you like, do something publicly outrageous to embarrass her ass and . . . if I win, I'll give you back your two hundred and fifty."

"I wouldn't give his ass shit back," Kohl said, downing a shot.

Seeing that my laughter agitated Kohl earlier, I did it again. "Bruh, you act like you behind on your bills." Figured if I threw that out, no one would suspect I was deep in debt.

Kohl told Dallas, "I'll make you the same proposition that Blitz just made."

"Whoa! Hashtag Clydesdale2930 on social," Dallas said. His eyes were fixated on his screen.

I found the post. That bitch was insane. She had to be

somewhere in ICU fighting to keep her tonsils and her thyroid.

Trymm strolled toward us, dipping his left shoulder with each step.

"Nigga, you cold-blooded, my brother," I told him.

"His ass always been the most scandalous," Dallas said. "I got something for y'all tomorrow."

I doubted Dallas had anything worthwhile.

Trymm rubbed his iPad like it was a woman's ass. "If I told you my official smashdown that's right here, you'd think I was lying."

Dallas said, "Man, this challenge opened my eyes to how small this city is. Even during the festival all I met was local randoms. My face is starting to become too familiar."

Trymm said, "New faces require new places, D. Upgrade your locations. What's up with you, Kohl?"

I stared at Trymm. He was right, but I didn't want Dallas popping up at the upscale bars where I met women.

Kohl commented, "Ain't never a shortage of big gurls in the South. They come to me. I feed 'em, then fuck 'em, and if they let me fuck 'em first, I might not give 'em a po'boy or a daiquiri."

I jumped in with, "Changed my mind about fucking your ex, Ramona."

"Shitz, I'd do her right here. Right now," Dallas said. "Those pictures she be postin' puts me on swole."

Kohl looked at Trymm. "You follow her, too?"

"Hell yeah. She's got something like eight hundred thousand followers," Trymm said.

"That's tripled since Harold announced their engagement on television," I confirmed as I liked her recent pic. "Check this out." To set my boy off, I showed Kohl a photo of Harold Thurston leaning against his Ghost with

Ramona by his side. Then I flashed Kohl a picture of the old Ramona on her knees with an old man's dick in her mouth.

"Text that to me, bruh," Kohl said.

I wasn't revealing my source, but for the right price my boy could have it and the cum shot photo that I hadn't let him see.

CHAPTER 56

Elizabeth

Day 12

Here I stood, in the heart of Chinatown, in front of Tosca Café. Across the street, in red neon lights, there was a sign that read: PSYCHIC READINGS. LOVE HAPPINESS SUCCESS. FORTUNE TELLER PAST PRESENT FUTURE. TAROT CARD READINGS. Only a fool would walk through those doors and pay a person to predict the outcome of their lives.

My favorite host greeted me at the entrance, "Nefertiti Parker-Brooks is in your reserved private dining area, Ms. Dawson."

"Thanks." I took my time going up the narrow hardwood staircase, which led to another stairway, then entered the room where heartless gangsters once gathered to eat, gamble, smoke cigars, and determine which double-crossing backstabbers wouldn't live to see the sunrise on the Golden Gate Bridge.

My sole purpose for being here was to implement a plan to castrate Einstein.

Perhaps my misfortune was considered karma to some.

No way in hell had I deserved this. "Nefertiti, thanks for meeting with me, girlfriend." I tossed my purse on the seat next to hers, scooted in the booth.

Nefertiti's brilliant red lipstick illuminated her brown eyes. Long black locks were gathered into a ponytail. Bronzer coated her face, neck, and cleavage.

I gripped her hand. "I really need your support."

Nefertiti squeezed my fingers. "You've got it."

"Good evening, Ms. Dawson. May I start you beautiful ladies off with something to drink?" the waitress asked.

I ordered. "Let us have a bottle of brut rosé champagne. The Dungeness crab salad, beets, grilled polenta, the roasted chicken, grilled twenty-eight-day, dry-aged prime strip steak medium, and the *bucatini.* For dessert, tiramisu and your peanut butter cup."

"Certainly, Ms. Dawson," she said, then exited the room.

Giving my undivided attention to Nefertiti, I asked, "You remember the guy I fucked in New Orleans?"

"The one you squirted—make that *gushed*—all over? Let me guess." The right side of Nefertiti's lips curved up. "He wants you to buy him a new mattress?"

"I wish that were all, although I wouldn't. Brace yourself." I showed my girlfriend the video that was posted on CEO2930. As Nefertiti watched with her mouth wide open, I added, "And I was terminated by the board, from my position, a week ago."

A five-hundred-thousand-dollar position. Gone. Over a piece of ass?

"I could ask why are you just telling me this, but . . . aw, hell no! This motherfucker is going down. I'm about to make sure of it." Nefertiti reached into her bag, retrieved her laptop. "Text me everything you have on him."

The waitress filled our flutes, placed the champagne bottle in an ice bucket, and left. Nefertiti moved her and my purses to her left. Slid closer to me.

I shared his contact info, which included information on his parents.

Nefertiti's eyes grew wide with excitement. "His dad is a politician. They always have buried bones. This ought to be a great dig."

Her brows raised, lips curved. "Oh, really," she said. Nefertiti's fingers darted all over her keyboard.

"I tried amicably resolving this. Went to New Orleans to meet with him and he acted as though exposing me was no big deal. Hung up on me. Then he had the audacity to block me."

"Totally outlandish," she commented. "Do you have any idea why he'd put this up? And after you found out and contacted him, he refused to remove it?"

"None. And that is correct."

I watched Nefertiti enter a user name and password for her account. My girlfriend viewed screen after screen. Opened several new windows.

"Einstein will pay you restitution. By the time he realizes what's happening, he won't be able to reverse any of this." Nefertiti typed, paused, then pivoted her screen to me. "It's gone," she said.

"What?"

"Your video link is deleted."

My concern was "Can he repost it?"

Nefertiti's mouth was tight. "Yes. For now. But don't worry. Once I gain access to his computer, I'm erasing everything on it."

"How?"

"That information I can't share," she said, "but I'll keep you updated."

Never would I have thought Einstein, or any man I'd

fucked, would've done this childish shit. "Thanks for deleting the video."

Nefertiti stared at me. "Wow. Watch this." Typing *#CEO2930,* *@CEO2930,* and *CEO2930* into her search engine, nothing came up.

I frowned. "Are you serious?" I tried various combinations on my phone. No exact matches.

"You have no idea what I'm capable of. I'm just getting started."

Nefertiti's enthusiasm reminded me of my team leader in Beijing. The board would make another terrible decision if they didn't respect her leadership.

Nefertiti was right. I didn't have a résumé on my girlfriend. Hugging her, I fought the tears trying to escape my eyes. I was a damn good leader. Hard to walk on others when you're at the bottom. I felt powerless.

"How can we get the board to give me back my position?" I drained every bubble in my glass down my throat.

Nefertiti sipped her champagne. "I got you on that, too, but I can't make any guarantees. But . . . if they rehire you, I want you to give me a six-figure contract."

Men did that all the time. "Deal."

Our food was placed in the center of the table. Half of a chicken meant head, neck, and one foot was on the bird.

Nefertiti leaned back. "I know you're accustomed to all this exotic culinary cuisine, but can we—"

"Waitress, please have them remove everything above the breast and below the leg."

"Certainly," she said, taking away the roasted chicken.

"I have enough information to start giving Einstein the blues. While we're eating, I'm going to hack into his cell, and if his Bluetooth is synced with his computer, we've got access to all his information." She eased her fork into a slice of precut steak.

"It can't be that easy."

Nefertiti smiled at me. "Simple as Siri, Alexa, and Google Home. Those devices eavesdrop. How do you think they respond to voice commands? The program is listening twenty-four–seven. We will hear and record every word of every conversation he has, even when his phone is powered off. You will know his location at all times. Any app on his phone, from social pages to e-mails to banking, if his passwords are stored in his phone, we're shutting all that shit down. I will give you access to account numbers, balances. If his taxes are in an attachment, we can download those, too, to see how much he makes. We are going to fuck him so far up his ass, his dick will be on top of his tongue."

Men could never outsmart women. The stupid ones believed they could. Realistically, the weakest woman had more power than her man if she played the game well.

"Let the side show begin," I said, laughing. "Question."

"Ask," Nefertiti said, garnishing her plate with a little of everything.

The waitress entered and placed our chicken on the table. "Can I get you ladies anything else?"

"A fresh bottle of champagne and glasses," I said. "We have to toast to this."

"Certainly. I'll be right back with that," she said, leaving.

"What's your question?" Nefertiti asked, cutting the poultry into six pieces.

"Is this going to get us five-to-ten in the pen?" Wasn't doing time over revenge on an asshole.

"You know as businesswomen we always have what?" she asked.

I answered, "An exit strategy."

Nefertiti snapped her fingers. The waitress removed the old and set up the new.

We raised our flutes.

"A toast," I said.

Nefertiti added, "To burying that son of a bitch, Blitz Einstein Roulet, sixty feet under."

"I'll drink to that."

CHAPTER 57

Blitz

Day 14

A white wooden sign with the words LAW OFFICES hung above the black VOODOO BAR plaque. Wondering which was her place of business, I stood on the porch. *Is this the way I want to get out of debt?*

My cell rang. It was the third unidentified caller of the day, and it was only ten in the morning. I entered through the door, with peeling paint lining the trim.

The hallway had suites on both sides. I found her number. VOODOO QUEEN was on a dream catcher that swayed over the peephole.

I tapped three times, took a step back.

"Hi, Blitz Roulet?" she said, standing barely above five feet. Her waist rounded to her hips. Her body rocked side-to-side as she walked. The dream catcher chimed long after she'd closed the door.

"Yes. You must be Irene."

A porcelain statue of a black man with shackles on hands, feet, neck, was in the center of the room. I walked around him. Felt as though his eyes followed my every move.

"Aw, don't mind, George. He keeps me grounded. Never want to forget where I come from," Irene said. "The moment you forget, that's what you get. It's called prison nowadays. Soon as they freed us, they built those things . . . for us. Have a seat. I don't bite, but my dog will take a chunk outta ya ass if you make any sudden moves. Don't be rude, Pitts. Speak to Mr. Roulet."

The black pit bull barked twice, sat beside the desk, stared at me. His blue eyes were chilling.

"What would you like to drink?" she asked. "I only serve Hurricanes, categories one to five. Pick your poison."

Liquor and business did not mix. "I'll have a category 'no thank you.' I need to borrow five hundred thousand dollars," I said, then asked, "Can you have Pitts chill out?"

She laughed. Her belly jiggled. Pulling the lever on a daiquiri machine, she filled a bowl, added five shots of tequila, then placed it on the floor in front of Pitts. "He hasn't had his breakfast."

Pitts lapped until he moved the empty bowl several inches. His tongue hung from the side of his mouth. His paws slid on the linoleum until his stomach disappeared underneath him. His eyes closed. Open. Slowly closed. Didn't reopen. He snored.

Irene entered a vault, rolled out a black four-wheel suitcase large enough for me to pack clothes for a two-week vacation. She opened it, dumped the contents on her desk. "There you go. Five hundred thousand dollars. Line it up and count it out." She mixed another cocktail. I guess the number of shots dictated what category it was. She added six. That must've been a tornado.

I'd never seen that much money in cash. "Let's com-

plete the application first." I didn't want to get excited if
she was going to deny me.

"I don't do applications. Ralph recommended you.
You're good. In thirty days you pay me one million in
cash."

More of an incentive to win, but just like gambling and
my stocks, I'd walk away with nothing, except most of
my debt and my home would be clear. I counted the
money. Zipped up the bag. Headed straight to Ralph,
opened a new account, made a deposit.

As I left the bank, my cell rang.

"Hello, and, yes, I have your money. Process the full
amount to pay my account in full." I gave her my routing
and account numbers. Shit felt great.

Called Atlantis. "How're things going with Trymm?"

"I'm not sure if I can do this for two more weeks. He's
got a lot going on. A crazy stunned me," she lamented.

Couldn't be that bad. I had to win.

"Hey, if you quit now, you'll never know. Everybody
has somebody when you first meet them."

"Yeah, but with Trymm it's not somebody, it's how
many some*bodies*?" Atlantis said.

She had a point. "Don't let your work be in vain. Keep
the fake fiancé alive. At the end of the two weeks, tell
Trymm you're leaving your fiancé for him. Next time I
see him, I'm putting in a good word for you. You're beautiful. Hell, if he doesn't marry you, I will." I paused, giving her an opportunity to say something.

Atlantis was quiet.

"Look, Trymm is foolish, but he's no fool. I just got
off the phone with him. He's making moves in your direction. That nigga slow 'cause you got him nervous."

"Okay, I'll give him more time," she said. "What have I got to lose?"

"You're a smart woman. I'll check back with you in a few days."

Ending the call, my phone rang. I brought my car note current. I headed to The Crystal Room inside Le Pavillon, in search of my next victim.

Life was looking up for a brother.

CHAPTER 58

Elizabeth

Day 18

Cleaning out Einstein's bank account was eerie and too damn easy. He had no second layer of security, and the answers to each question were stored in his phone. The setup of a new computer wasn't problematic. Nefertiti forwarded his number to a temporary number she'd established, entered the code that was texted to her, then ended the forward.

In a matter of days, I had a million dollars banked in an offshore business account. Tomorrow I'd move from one offshore account to another, then close the original.

"Let's race," I told Nefertiti.

"Ten laps?" she asked, jumping into the pool at a private mansion.

"I need it." I'd rented an island in Fiji for the week.

Nefertiti yelled, "I can tell," then doggie-paddled to the side.

I dove into twelve feet, came up beside her. I kicked away my frustrations to stay afloat.

"Let's go." Nefertiti started swimming laterally.

Pushing off with my feet, I pulled the water with all my strength. Never had I not been in control of my career. I didn't need a getaway. I wanted to work. My teams were being led by a newcomer. I flipped, started lap two. Nefertiti was right behind me.

There wasn't a man I couldn't handle. This exploitation situation was unfathomable. I swam an extra two laps while Nefertiti finished her last. Lifting ourselves out of the deep end, we cocooned our bodies with plush white beach towels.

"Admit it. That was the easiest million you've ever made, Ms. Elizabeth Dawson." Nefertiti tossed her towel to the ground. "I know today is supposed to be R and R, but I couldn't sleep last night. I've got deets that are going to blow your mind."

I emphasized, "*We* ever made. Thanks to you."

Booting up her laptop, she turned it away from the sunlight. We put on our shades, sat at a table underneath a huge umbrella.

Nefertiti said, "You have to listen to this recording."

"Is this Blitz Einstein Roulet?"

"Yeah, what's up?"

"I have to inform you that this call may be recorded for—"

"What the fuck you calling me for? I paid you. In full!"

"Sir, you have not made any payments. If you don't make a payment by tomorrow, we're going to have to ask you to return the car, or we'll have to—"

"Bitch, touch my car and I'll kick your ass! I paid you! Check your system. And stop fucking harassing me!"

Nefertiti fast-forwarded to:

> *"Ralph, what's the balance in my new account?"*
> *"Zero."*
> *"What the fuck? I just deposited one million dollars last Thursday. Paid off three debts, but it can't be zero."*
> *"Blitz, I see where you transferred the million dollars to an offshore account."*
> *"A what? Nigga, you got jokes. You and Irene best not be playing games. Give me the balance in the 0069."*
> *"Sixty million, five hundred, eighty-seven and—"*
> *"Stop there. I'm on my way to your office to straighten this shit out."*
> *"It's karma with a capital k, man. You running game on these women with your boys. Y'all betting a million dollars on how many women you can fuck and ruin their lives on social."*
> *"I don't need you to be my conscience. Check that account, my brother. The million dollars is there. See you shortly."*

My lips curved so high, my cheeks hurt. "If he's got that much money, why is he playing games?" I questioned.

Nefertiti smiled, shut down her computer, picked it up. "Let's go chill for a moment. I have a plan."

Stepping onto the beach, I called out to our butlers, "We're ready."

Relaxing in the cabana, we watched the ocean waves splash upon the white sand. We were hand-fed tropical fruit from a golden platter.

"I can feed myself. Rub my legs and feet," Nefertiti told her guy. She leaned against a pillow, spread her legs, sucked her frozen piña colada out of a pineapple.

I patted myself on the back, told my soon-to-be lover, "Massage everything." Bracing myself on my elbows, I looked up at Nefertiti, "What's next?"

Nefertiti slid her sunglasses to the tip of her nose. "What do you think is next? We take *all* of it."

"Forget getting my job back. We're starting our own company."

I held my hand up. Nefertiti held her hand up. We slapped one another's palm.

Smiling, I said, "Let's do it!"

CHAPTER 59

Blitz

Day 23

"What the fuck you mean you don't know where my money is? You don't just misplace sixty-one million dollars, nigga!"

"You're right," Ralph said. "Just like I explained to your father, we're—"

"Nigga, you trying to get me killed! What the fuck you do that for?" I paced the short distance in Ralph's office. I swear if the ceiling-to-floor windows were wood, I'd beat Ralph's ass.

"Blitz, we're working on figuring out what happened. I need for you to calm down."

"Don't tell me to calm the fuck down!" I started jumping up and down.

Before I laid hands on Ralph, I stormed out of the bank. "Where the fuck you going with my car, nigga?"

I chased the tow truck six blocks before giving up. At least I was closer to my destination. I walked the rest of the way down Poydras Street to Drago's, trying to come up with a lie they'd believe. Even if one of them had questions, I decided it was best to say nothing. How was I going to explain to the crewe that the million dollars was gone?

All of it.

I sat at the oyster bar alone. Reserved three seats for my crewe. Had to calm down.

Got a text from my dad, **You know I'ma put my foot straight up your ass when I see you! If your mother and I are indicted, you're taking the fall.**

Politicians in New Orleans didn't do jail time. Dad was getting worked up over the wrong thing. We needed to get our money straight.

A call registered from an unidentified caller. I answered, "Hello," not giving a fuck at this point who it was.

"So you like playing games, Einstein?"

I sprang from my seat. "Who the fuck is this?" Looking around the room, I didn't notice anyone watching me.

The call ended. My cell rang again. I answered.

"Is this Blitz Einstein Roulet?"

I asked, "Did you just call me?"

She repeated her question. I repeated mine.

"No. Is this Blitz Einstein Roulet?"

I noticed Kohl approaching the bar. Said to whoever was on the other end, "All right, babe. I'll meet you later tonight at GW Fins. Bye," then ended the call.

"Fins? You spend way too much on these females," he said, sitting to my right.

I said, "You looking sharper than usual. Who you trying to impress? Your baby mama?" I laughed to annoy him.

"Where's your Rolex, bruh? Second time I've seen you without it in eight years."

With so much fucking happening, I hadn't thought about my watch recently. I rubbed my wrist. Lied, "Can't find it." Well, that was, in part, the truth.

"Sure you didn't pawn it? You might be in over your head, but this bet was your idea and I'm getting my money." Kohl smirked at me. "Never know, might have to smash one of your CEOs."

"So how's your count going?" I asked with a grin. "Ran out of strippers yet?"

Dallas approached us, turned the back of his chair to the wall. "What's up, dudes? Trymm coming?"

Kohl answered, "Yeah, said he'd be here shortly."

"One of those chicks probably have his dick tied in a knot," I said, then laughed.

Kohl stared at me, hard and long, then asked Dallas, "You still in love with whatever her name is?"

"I got some shit y'all will never believe unless I showed you," Dallas said, handing his cell to Kohl.

Kohl checked it out, handed the cell to me. I was quiet, handed it back to Kohl.

"How you feelin' about this, D?" Kohl patted Dallas hard on the back.

Dallas didn't respond. I understood.

"Nigga, where is your watch?" Dallas asked me.

Trymm walked up. Saved me from having to relive how those punks robbed me during daylight.

"Nig-ga, where you been?" Dallas asked Trymm.

Had to keep the focus off of me. "Ain't seen shit from you on social since Southern Belle. Guess old Clydesdale can't hang."

Trymm placed his iPad on the counter, stared at my wrist, answered, "Nigga, where is your—"

Dallas shook his head. "Don't ask."

Trymm sat at the counter next to me. "See y'all left me the seat with my back to the audience so I can't check out the females first," then added, "All I know is each of you betta show your face at my parents' anniversary party at Gallier Hall on the thirty-first. Six o'clock sharp."

Wasn't happening. That was report day. Had to make sure my shit was in order.

"One of y'all say something. Damn!" Trymm stopped our waiter. "Let us get four baker's dozen of them flame-broiled oysters on a half shell and a round of Hen."

"I'ma 'bout to trump all y'all. Let's do a count. Write down your numbers," Kohl said, handing each of us a napkin.

Trymm balled his up. Tossed it at me. "Hell no. All I want eight days from now is proof. Videos, confessions, social posts. All that." He tapped his iPad.

That nigga damn near guarded that tablet with his life.

Some random female dressed in denim short shorts, a man's fedora, and a fitted blouse thrust her cleavage in Trymm's face. She had big-ass nipples like Ramona's. Her hair was short, slicked at the back and sides. Lips shiny.

Dallas kept eating.

"I was at your yacht party. Remember me?" she asked him all sexy and shit, eyeing his iPad.

Is that right?

Trymm slid his iPad away from her.

Trymm looked at her. She eyed his tablet.

That iPad was the ticket to his downfall. I had a plan.

She moaned as she said, "I was hoping we could get together again without the other *ninety-nine* females that were all over your big banana boat."

Ninety the fuck what? Bitches?

Chick put a spotlight on Trymm. Started massaging his dick.

Dallas said, "Ditch that bitch!"

Trymm asked me, "Let's switch seats, homey, before I raise up outta here."

Next thing, she jabbed the flashlight into Trymm's dick. My brother yelled, "Fuck!" He grabbed his nuts, leaned over, holding his shit.

I wanted to laugh so badly, but that might've encouraged that crazy bitch to do it again. I started recording for entertainment later.

"My sister didn't suck your dick for you to degrade her on social media. Thought your lil yacht party was just for fun. Thanks to you, my sister's husband is divorcing her! She has to raise her son and daughter by herself! Had to pull them out of their school because kids wouldn't stop teasing them! You broke up her happy home! I should stun you again!" she said, reaching toward Trymm.

Wow. Black women are easy to get with. Hard to get rid of. Had me thinking if my shit was revenge.

The woman swiftly pointed the flashlight at Dallas.

Oh, bitch, you gon' die today. I moved the fuck out the way.

D grabbed her by the throat. Started choking the life out of her. Her mouth was open, but her ass couldn't say shit. She started turning red. She brought that shit on herself. She can't just go around stunning niggas.

"You don't look so good right now, brotha man," I joked at Trymm, then yelled out to our waiter, "Yo! Lay four more dozen oysters on us and another round of Hen on me. It's gon' take this nigga a minute to recuperate."

Trymm scanned the counter. Looked around the restaurant for the women. "Where the fuck is my iPad, homies? Where the fuck is my . . ."

"It's gon' take this nigga's dick a while to recuperate," I joked some more.

"Fuck you, Blitz. I'm still ahead of your ass," Trymm said, leaning on the counter.

I smiled. "Not for long, my brother. Not for long."

I texted, **Atlantis, take Trymm's iPad on the 30th and give it to me. I'll explain later.**

CHAPTER 60

Blitz

Day 30

Debbie was the true soldier.
As usual, I was the first to arrive. Had gotten off the bus two stops early.

Today my brother Dallas was tying a slipknot. I made my way to the back of the church. Pretended I didn't know I wasn't supposed to be there. Debbie met me in the dining hall, where food was being set up for after the ceremony.

"Here's your fifty dollars," I said, slipping it in her hand. I had to get cash off of my last surviving credit card. Was a matter of days before the bank canceled this one, too.

"No, you keep it. I really love Dallas, and I truly want to marry him," she said. "I'm not going to walk away from him at the altar."

Isn't like I'm turning down money. Shitz, where is the other half?

"Cool." I wasn't going to stand here persuading her otherwise. "I'ma go up front."

I took one look at Dallas and laughed. "Your eyes red as hell. You must've had a hell of a night."

Dallas straightened his collar. "Other than that, nigga, how I look?"

"Man, you really going through with this?" Kohl asked. "I know I said do it, but this ain't right, D. Let's just leave now."

"And walk away from the quarter of a mil you promised me if you win? Same goes for you, Blitz." Dallas's face was tight.

Mine too.

"Y'all suited like somebody died," Dallas said.

"If you follow through with your plan, you might be signing up for your funeral," Kohl joked.

When they found out the mil wasn't there, they might kill me. I was ready to get it all over with.

A lady came outside, announced, "Places, everyone."

I escorted some female I didn't know down the aisle. She went her way. I went mine. Stood near the front pew. D looked good.

The doors at the rear of the church opened. Debbie was pretty. She was a good pick for Dallas. Too bad this was all a game.

The pastor asked her, "Do you take this man . . ."

Debbie glanced at me, then gazed into Dallas's eyes. "I do" softly escaped her lips.

My brother slid that ring on her finger. Tears streamed down Debbie's cheeks. Wanted to tell her to lighten up.

The pastor asked my brother, "Do you take this woman . . ."

D looked at us, nodded his head toward the door. One by one, we stood in a single-file line.

As we followed Dallas, people gasped. Mumbled.

"Where's he going?"

"Is he coming back?"

"He can't be serious."

"This had better be some sort of joke."

The one thing nobody did was laugh.

Soon as we got outside, Kohl said, "That's fucked-up, D. Hope it was worth it."

"I'ma catch y'all later," I said.

Didn't want anyone to see me heading to the bus stop. I went inside this sports bar across the street to chill.

"Surprised to see you in here," the bartender said, pointing at the flat screen above.

Seeing my dad in handcuffs didn't bother me as much as seeing my mom.

THE CONCLUSION

The Crewe

Trymm

Life after the death of Kandy—capital *k*, small *y*—was the same for Trymm. He didn't make her commit suicide. Nothing could bring her back. But he realized he was right and wrong.

Black women easily fell in love, easily slept with strangers. They were easily brokenhearted. Just as they were easy, black women were equally, if not more passionate.

Losing the quarter of a million turned out to be a valuable lesson learned. What he couldn't learn was . . . how to love his wife. But following his father's advice, he'd heed and keep Francine first.

There would always be a pecking order. For now, until she decided to no longer be by his side, Atlantis would be in his life.

Dallas

Dallas discovered that young black women weren't easy. They were loving and trusting. At times Debbie

Carter had more strength than he. She was helping him,
one day at a time, cope with his PTSD.

Church had never been his thing, after his mother died.
Worshiping with Debbie, joining her church, and being
baptized gave him hope and purpose. Losing a father
whom he'd never known, Dallas vowed to always be
there for his wife and unborn child.

He still didn't give a damn about Uncle Sam. But Debbie had convinced him to collect his earned retirement
and disability.

Kohl

Big black gurls weren't easy. They were easygoing.
There was a difference.

Looking back on all that had happened, he knew relocating to Los Angeles was a fresh start, and a step up.
Kohl used his insurance settlement to negotiate an offer-
in-compromise with the feds. With the money he had left
over, he opened a cannabis club and hookah lounge adjacent to a New Orleans Creole Restaurant. The strip club
was no more.

He had lots of Ramona look-a-likes to choose from.
But there was only one William Bartholomew. Kohl set
up a travel account in William's name and promised his
son he could visit him in California anytime he wanted,
but under no circumstance was Kohl going back to the
NOLA.

Blitz

Blitz never figured out what happened to his accounts.

In a way that was a good thing. The crewe didn't
blame him, and the government couldn't charge him, his
dad, or his mom with money laundering, because they
never found the money.

His parents always had and still supported him. His mother repaid the voodoo woman. Where his mother got the million dollars from, she refused to say. Blitz lived in the same house. Purchased a new car. Paid his gambling debt. Successfully invested in new stocks.

What Blitz missed most was his crewe. They'd each gone separate ways. One day, maybe when they were closer to eighty years old, if they reunited, he'd tell them what really happened. For now, life went on. . . .

"Put whatever she's having on my tab."

Acknowledgments

I gotta do this like this bay-bay (dragging out the first *bay*), the way we say it in Nawlins. When you hear someone say it, this signifies the person feels strongly about what they are about to say. I am *fan*atical about my hometown, the Saints football team, and LeBron James!

For all the women speaking up and out about sexual misconduct, I support you. As a victim I understand why some females suffer in silence for up to decades. I encourage you to find resolution within yourself. Bad things happen to good girls and women.

All of my novels are empowering for females. I've published two nonfiction life-changing self-help books that females are raving about. If you read *Dicks Are Dumb: A Woman's Guide to Finding the Right Man* or *Never Let a Man Come First: A Female's Guide to Understanding Male Behavior,* you will understand why a lot of females suffer from what I call "baby doll love."

Shout-out to all my people at The Trolley Stop Café on St. Charles Avenue. Special thanks to my gurl Dana for holding it down and serving me way too much shit to eat!

My world revolves around family, friends, and fans. You are forever in my heart. Robert E. White, Shirelle Atkins, Maveita Richards, Victor E. Simmons Jr., Kysh Robinson Clemons, Hillary M. Denson, and all librarians—I appreciate your welcoming me into your branch to speak and read.

My career and continued success in the industry is made possible by my editor, Selena James, Steve Zacharius, Adam Zacharius, Lulu Martinez, Vida Engstrand, Claire Hill, Robin Cook, and everyone at Kensington Publishing Corporation.

Like mother, like son. Jesse Byrd Jr. has published several books for children. *Sunny Days, Werewolf in New Orleans,* and the award-winning (Paris and Los Angeles Book Festival) *King Penguin,* to name a few, are entertaining and educating the minds of our youngest readers. Visit Jesse at: www.JesseBCreative.com. I continue to pray all great things for Jesse and his beautiful wife, Emaan Abbass.

I have amazing siblings. Wayne Morrison, Andrea Morrison, Derrick Morrison, Regina Morrison, Margie Rickerson, and Debra Noel, I love you guys.

My true friend, Richard C. Montgomery, I love you, man!

To my gurlz: Vanessa Ibanitoru, Brenda Jackson, Cassandra Guy, Tina Robinson, Marion Whitaker, Marissa Monteilh, Carmen Polk, Kimbercy Marie Harris-Jones, Aje Huru, Yevonna Missy Johnson, Christal Jordan, Jessica Holter, Wendy Rogers-Curtis, and Numbiya Aziz.

Kendall Minter, no entertainment lawyer reps like you. Congratulations on the release of your book, *Understanding and Negotiating 360 Ancillary Rights Deals*.

What's life without social media, baby! Follow me on Facebook and Snapchat at TheRealMaryB, Twitter at HoneyBHonest, and Instagram at MaryHoneyBMorrison. Blessings to all of my McDonogh 35 Senior High fellow Roneagles. It was awesome seeing my class of 1982 at our thirty-fifth reunion.

Wishing each of my readers peace and prosperity in abundance. Visit me online at MaryMorrison.com. Sign up for my newsletter. Until we meet between the pages again, all praises to the Divine Power Who loves us unconditionally and gives us the power to choose whether we will love ourselves.

HEAD GAMES

Money. Love. Sex.
Spirits. Broken.
Rewind . . . Shattered.
Scratch. Spirits.
Hearts. Crushed.
Intentionally? Not. Yes.
Women. Invisible.
Pussy. Matters.
Bitch. Laugh. Cry. Trick.
Pussy. Matters. More.
Rape. Love. Women. Whores.
Matter. Not.
Got head?
Pussy. Matters.
Raw. Best.
Coming. Matters.
Not. Most.
Men. Win.
Head games.
Women.
Matter.
Not.
Really.

Boning is a sport handed from generations of men groping, grinding, *dick*respectful, desperate to come inside when it's cold, to come inside when it's hot, liquid frustration erupts, seeds splatter, fertilize, grow, reproduce more game, more girls, the hunt is best when the prey is new, the younger the better, the game is old, yet the game never gets old, players scout, fucking is a competition, not really ED, justify the lie, single, married, cheaters never take all, nor can they, no matter how much she gives, he never gives his all, walk away, the game, sex ad*dick*tion, real, they want to come, they have to come, they need to come, they live, molest, breathe, rape, die, to come, without forethought, she's a victim with no thought, whore, tramp, slut, thot, prostitute, trick, cunt, only after, his deposit, no return, consensual doesn't matter, absent her thinking, is he good, kind, my kind, what's left behind, is her *be*hind, to perform CPR on her mind, heart, soul, body, pussy, pussy, pussy, nobody gives a fuck, bitch man up, get ready for the next game, gamer, who will fan her flame, who will change her last name, whose to blame.

DON'T MISS

I Do Love You Still

From *New York Times* bestselling author Mary B. Morrison comes the seductive, no-holds-barred novel of a dazzling power couple who play their scandalous love-hate deceptions one game too far. . . .

Enjoy the following excerpt. . . .

CHAPTER 1

Xena

Silence gave sound to the voice inside my mind.
Rolling onto my side, I lay in bed facing the opened
window. Curtains flapped whipping a summer breeze that
brushed my naked body as though I was its canvas. I inhaled the warm air. I didn't want to be here.

Why was I living with one man knowing I was still in
love with my ex? Exhaling, I turned onto my back, bent
my knees, placed my feet flat on the mattress, then stared
into the darkness of the bedroom.

*Remember why you left him, Xena. I know. But I don't
want to be here.*

In the beginning, I was happy with my new guy. Dou-
bling back to a former boyfriend, I'd never done that.
After all the shit my ex had put me through, I should hate
him. I really wanted to, but . . . what had I proven by trying to hurt him the way he'd done me?

I touched my stomach. God knew my aching heart was
filled with love for my ex and repentance for what I'd
done. Couldn't stop thinking about it or missing him.
Doubted he'd take me back if I told him the truth of why
I'd left him.

4:50 a.m.

A familiar hand caressed my breast. I scooted, hips first, to the edge of the queen-sized mattress. Closing the gap between us, he hugged my waist, pulled me toward him. I resumed my previous position. Stared toward the ceiling fan that clicked each time it rotated.

Leaning in, he sucked my nipple. Didn't deny it felt good. My breaths became shallow wishing it was my ex.

"Not now," I said, facing him, trying to assume a fetal position to create space between him and my parts I knew he wanted to access.

Dragging me closer to the middle of the bed, he crawled on top of me, began licking my areolas. His hand massaged my B-cups, then he twisted my nipple with his fingertips. I didn't want to enjoy his touch right now, but my body could not deny the percolating energy circulating throughout my chakras.

Pop. Crackle. Pop. Noises emanated from the settling of his old colonial home, recently renovated on the inside.

He used his knee to spread my thighs, then penetrated me. Our morning ritual had begun. Squeak. Headboard. Squeak. Frame. His hips thrust back and forth. No side-to-side, figure-eight, or round and round clockwise followed by counterclockwise the way my last boyfriend used to do.

Our music was the chorus of a love ballad. I liked my current. I had done a good job of separating the sexual act from my feelings for him.

Closing my eyes, I squeezed my vaginal muscles super tight pretending he was my ex. Shallow breaths deepened into a soft "Haaa" as I exhaled into orgasm number one.

"That's my girl. Let it out," he said. Bracing himself on his forearms, he paused, then he sexed me in slower motion. "Give me another one."

The stimulation inside my pussy intensified. I released a bigger climax. For me. Not him.

"Don't hold back, baby. Give me all of my sweet juices," he moaned, shifting his mouth toward mine.

Quickly, I pivoted in the opposite direction as he kept stroking. In and out.

"Kiss me, baby." This time he slid his tongue from my cheek to my lips—trailing saliva—then forced it inside . . . lizard style.

Lust transitioned into frustration with each probe. He was never a good kisser. I cleared my mind. Focused on my task list for the day to calm myself.

Meditate. Go to the market. Meet my contract deadline for our client.

5:05 a.m.

His dick moved back and forth, all five inches in, then all the way out. Lightly he circled the tip of his penis at my opening, glided back in, pulled out. Entering me again, he poked my G-spot. Couldn't lie. Our sex was never wild, but he always made me wet.

Imagining he was my ex, I pulled my boyfriend's ass to me, hugged his shoulders, started groaning loud. "Ah, yes." I told him, "Go deeper inside me, baby." With my ex, I wouldn't have to ask.

"Um hmm. I love you so." Abruptly, his words ended mid-sentence, then he asked, "I'm not hurting you, am I?"

Nice of him to ask, but he didn't have the proper equipment to inflict vaginal pain. The lump in my abdomen hadn't gotten larger, but it'd been there for almost a year. Shaking my head in response to his question, the doctors said it was a fibroid tumor and that it didn't need to be removed. Nor would the lump prevent me from conceiving.

Escaping into a fantasy of one of the best love-making sessions with my ex, I visualized his long, girthy shaft snaking up the walls of my vagina. The opening of his penis moved about the depth of my pussy as though it were a searchlight looking for my soul. I'd pretend to hide my pleasure point, and he wouldn't stop fucking the shit out of me until he made me scream soprano . . . I missed him so much. Instantly my pussy became hot and my juices flowed like a waterfall for my current boyfriend. I tilted my pelvis up granting him total access to Niagara.

5:12 a.m.

"You're making me cum early," he said, then added, "you ready?" Delving to his max, inches shy of reaching my cul-de-sac, my new boyfriend froze.

Suddenly, his ass jerked backward. *Squeak.* He paused. Thrusting forward, he paused again. *Squeak.* One. Two. Back. Forth. His rhythm grew closer, becoming one continuous motion until he and the squeaking came to a stop. I felt his throbbing shaft, then he collapsed on top of me. His accelerated heartbeat pounded against my breasts.

5:16 a.m.

Rolling him onto his side of the bed, I pulled the spread up to my neck, stared toward the ceiling. Lying next to my current, not a day went by where I didn't miss my ex.

Was Memphis in a relationship? Had he forgotten about me? Did he crave spooning me the way I longed to cuddle with him? Trying to convince myself I'd made the right decision to break up with him, I told Adonis, "I love you, baby." My head understood what my man needed to hear. My heart knew the truth.

Lifting the plush yellow comforter away from my naked body, I scooted away from Adonis, sat on the edge of the bed, gazed over my shoulder.

I didn't choose him. On our first date at Paula Deen's Creek House, he'd told me he wasn't looking for a girlfriend; he wanted a wife. I wasn't in search of a husband. Desperately, I had to get out of my mom's house. Didn't want to move in with my best friend, Tina-Love. Her pussy had a revolving door. Men came and went. None of them stayed.

Adonis was considerate, generous, and in love with me. From day one I allowed things to be his way. Sighing, I pivoted in his direction, touched his face, traced the front of his neatly trimmed hairline. The dark hairs of his crown had started to thin. The softness of his beard against my fingertips flowed to a mustache that arched over supple red lips that greeted mine each day since we'd met a year ago.

Every day I told myself to stop reliving my past, each time I replayed the reel of my walking out of Memphis's house, into my mother's. In less than a week I was out of my parents' place and into Adonis's apartment building. Planting a kiss on Adonis's forehead as he snored deeper and louder, *Please, don't leave me, Z, I'll be back in Savannah twelve months tops,* echoed in my mind.

Aborting my ex's baby without telling him we were pregnant was wrong. I knew that.

CHAPTER 2

Memphis

"I know you have to leave, baby, but I wish you could stay with me a little longer," she professed, trailing kisses along my spine.

She was a sexy motherfucker. First time I saw her I knew straight up I was going to fuck the shit out her. Thin lips. Deep throat. Long, wavy blond hair. Ice-blue irises. Tall. Six-feet. Perfect size ten. Former high school volleyball hall of famer, she'd broken the record for the most number of game-winning spikes during her four years on the team.

Time was almost up for me here on the West Coast. All I wanted was to get back to the South and confront Xena regarding our unfinished business. I had to know why she broke it off. Tina-Love pretended Xena hadn't told her why.

Yeah, right.

I lay facedown across the massage table Natalie had bought me, fixated on my ex. I was nothing but good to her for five years. A brotha had recently turned legal, but the fact that Z was five years older and salivating ova kept my dick pointing north. An athlete like me could have my choice female. But I wasn't average in any department. Also, I wasn't perfect.

Telling Natalie the same thing Z had told me, I replied, "You'll be all right." Not certain about my future, not caring about hers. Natalie dug deeper into my quads. I felt her frustrations. She wouldn't understand, I had a lot riding on Z's love for me.

Olympic training camp was coming to an end. I didn't want to return to my hometown a failure in search of a nine-to-five, listening to fans reassure me I could beat Usain Bolt, having my IG followers DMing me not to give up. Sports flowed through the blood in my veins. I would become the world's champion; if Z hadn't abandoned me, I would've gotten an acceptance letter by now. I know I would've.

"I can't comprehend why she ended our relationship. I mean-I-I wasn't going to be gone forever, you feel me? Didn't want any other woman securing her spot. Gave her my all. But it's cool."

The hell it was. Blindsided, I hadn't sensed she was unhappy with my performance in or out of the sheets. A few hiccups here and there were the norm for guys, especially a track star like me. Z had issues, but I wasn't the one who'd fucked her up in the head.

Breaking the silence, I had to ask Natalie, "What do women want? I-I mean, her mother was the one who abused her. I'd never mistreat her. You. Any female. Most of y'all have man issues. Can't find, keep, or please one. That's not my fault."

Wanted to add, why females do everything for a man thinking that's going to make him love y'all, then when he steps to the next woman y'all feel betrayed when what really had happened was . . . you played yourself. But I wasn't that stupid.

Heard from our mutual friend Tina-Love, Z had found my replacement in less than thirty days. "I took her off the market first date. Something wifey about her that other women can't compete with. She's better than a Willie Wonka golden ticket. She's more like a gold medal, only one man can win, keep, and treasure until he dies. I thought I'd won her for life. I—"

Slap! "Shut upppp! Memphis!" Natalie screamed, commanding my attention. "I'm sick and tired of hearing about your precious Z! You don't call her name when I'm sucking your dick!"

Actually, I do.

Naked and assessible, I was not arguing with Natalie while I was facedown. Xena Trinity was in a unique category. Passion for me was in her voice, her eyes, her touch, her pussy when I tasted my baby. Penetrating her . . . damn. My dick hardened. She'd never disrespect me the way Natalie had done. Yelling out of control. Z would cry. I stared at the twenty-pound barbells on the black carpet of my living room, listening to sniffles. Teardrops plopped on my legs, trickled down to my shins.

"I told you when we started, this was temporary. Please don't cry." I didn't want to hear it.

"I thought you were over her. Now that you're leaving me you're bringing her up again. Are you planning on getting back with her?" Natalie's fingers firmly glided from my ankles up to my glutes. She squeezed my butt hard with both hands.

Verbally. Mentally. Spiritually. I'd never terminated things with Z. I couldn't, even if I wanted to. Circumstances were beyond my capability. Real love secured home plate. No matter how many pussies I hit, Z had my heart on lock. We had history. Z was forever my girl. All the other females were on first, second, third, the mound. I'd never told her, but Natalie was somewhere in outfield. Spoiled rich, privileged white female needed this middle-class black man's dick to feel good about herself.

If I never saw her again, that'd be okay.

"What are we?" she questioned. "What's our relation-ship status?"

You don't wait almost a year to solidify your place in a man's life.

Repeating the same motion, foot to cheek, Natalie had gotten better at releasing my tension, not hers. She'd also grown bitter over the year, wanting what I wasn't not agree-ing to: a commitment. I couldn't take a white woman home to my Jamaican mother. I was going to miss all the gener-ous things Natalie had done for me on a daily. Laundry. Cooking. Stroking my ego and sucking my dick at the same time.

Natalie was upgraded from her tryout spot. She was a free agent. If she traded me the way Z had done, I'd miss the perks. Not Natalie. I hadn't asked her for anything she didn't want to give me. Lifting my head, I readjusted the pillow, lowered my face into the donut-hole cushion. "What we have is and always will be special."

"Special? And what exactly is my place? Huh?" She stopped touching me.

Sitting up on the table, I placed my hand on her hip, cupped the nape of her neck, pulled her close. "Kiss me." I couldn't lie, she made me feel amazing. "Don't cry. We'll work this out when I get back," I lied.

Slowly, she shook her head, then said, "You're not coming back."

"I have to," I lied again. "My things are here."

I'd received an email that boxes were being delivered to my unit. Upon receipt, I was to pack up my personals, print and adhere the shipping labels. Someone would call me to arrange a pickup time and tracking information would be emailed to me.

"To get your clothes to Memphis. Really?" Gazing into my eyes, she continued, "I love you. What am I sup-posed to do without you?"

Natalie sounded like Z, except Z walked out on me.

"I've got to get ready for practice. I'll hit you up when I'm done."

Natalie wrapped her arms around my neck. Smashed her clit against my flaccid dick. "I've invested a lot of time in you. I want to go with you to Savannah."

That was not happening. I glanced around my furnished apartment. "Nah. You need to go on your mission trip to Havana. People in Cuba need you."

"And you don't?" she cried.

"That's not what I'm saying. I have to focus on qualifying for the Olympics. When you get back, we'll see where I am and take it from there."

Natalie was a twenty-three-years-young female who grew up in Beverly Hills. Didn't know what a W-2 with her Social Security number on it looked like. Post high school she traveled the world on missions to help people. Most women needed something or someone to care for. I'd become her stateside philanthropic recipient.

"You love me?" she asked, lowering her hands to my thighs.

One bedroom, bathroom, living, dining, and kitchen, I resided in 800 square feet. Natalie owned, free and clear, a two-bed, two-and-a-half-bath town house here in Chula Vista. Her parents didn't believe in her renting real estate. If I were the type of man to dog a female, I would've had her have me on payroll making weekly deposits into my bank account.

Puckering my lips tight, I shifted my mouth and eyes far to the left, then nodded, thinking . . . I loved her in an appreciative kind of way, for all she'd done. Yeah, that was it. "I do."

Natalie stepped back from the table, then demanded, "Say, it, Memphis."

I stood. "For real. I've got to get ready for practice in a few hours. Accompanying her to my door, I opened it. "We'll talk things over tonight. I promise."

Standing in the hallway, she said, "A radio producer contacted me. It was about you. He's trying to—"

Closing the door, I turned the lock, got my cell. Scrolling through photos of Z and me, I bit my bottom lip. Tears clouded my eyes, splattered on my screen. I wasn't a bad dude.

Why the fuck did she break my heart?

Connect with Us

Visit us online at
KensingtonBooks.com
to read more from your favorite authors, see books
by series, view reading group guides, and more.

Join us on social media

for sneak peeks, chances to win books and prize packs,
and to share your thoughts with other readers.

facebook.com/kensingtonpublishing
twitter.com/kensingtonbooks

Tell us what you think!

To share your thoughts, submit a review,
or sign up for our eNewsletters, please visit:
KensingtonBooks.com/TellUs.